LIFEWEAVER

DAN STATEN

With love and thanks to my wife for her help and support, as well as to several others who took the time to read and offer edits and feedback.

CONTENTS

Deor	VIII
Prologue	1
Part I	5
1. Under the Porch	6
2. The Darkness Within	18
3. Driven	28
4. Zealot	40
5. Hider	48
6. Reader	58
7. Harbinger of Death	70
8. The Hunt	78
9. Loneliness	85
10. Confrontation	94
11. Facing the Unknown	103
Interlude	111
Part II	122
12. Foiled	123
13. A Reason to Live	132
14. Tracker	142

15. Failure Is Not an Option — 149

16. The Smile of an Archos — 156

17. Prophetess — 165

18. Losing Sight of Land — 176

19. The Voice of an Archos — 182

20. Immortal — 188

21. Dark Heart — 198

22. Foolishness or Optimism — 209

23. Addict — 217

24. Maverick — 224

25. Legendary — 235

26. Secrets — 243

27. Slavery or Freedom — 255

28. Recruiting — 263

29. Reminder — 271

Interlude — 278

Part III — 285

30. Closely Guarded Secret — 286

31. Undeniable Finality — 293

32. Not Alone — 300

33. Skirmish — 311

34. No Backing Down — 317

35. Coward — 327

36. Free yet Prisoners — 336

37. Dissension — 345

38. Silvertongue — 353

39. Stolen   362

40. Living is at Stake   369

41. Counter   377

42. Gasping for Air   385

43. Escape   392

44. Regrets   400

45. Fear and Doubt   407

46. No Room for Miracles   415

Interlude   424

Part IV   436

47. The Vyeshen   437

48. Tales from the Past   444

49. Under the Mountains   453

50. Things in Common   457

51. Lesser Evil   463

52. To Save an Archos   470

53. Healing   476

Interlude   486

54. Liberation   498

55. The Unknown   510

Also by   516

About the Author   517

DEOR RIVER

1. AITROX'S CITADEL
2. JORDAN'S LAMP SHOP
3. SANCHE DISTRICT
4. PRATON DISTRICT
5. MOREL DISTRICT
6. OAK HOLLOW (SLUM)

7. MONDERO PARK
8. PILLAY'S ESTATE
9. OKO'S WAREHOUSE
10. KETU'S SHOP

PROLOGUE

T heru pulled the glowing metal from the forge and began molding the plate to fit a massive torso. Sparks exploded off the metal and the clanging of the hammer drowned out all other sounds. Theru felt his unprotected skin burning from the heat as he worked, but an external presence robbed him of the option to do anything about it. Theru's muscles ached from hours of work, and boredom set in even as his hands worked complex tasks beyond his understanding. A hot spark landed on his exposed arm, filling him with agony as it burned into his flesh, but the clanging of his hammer continued unabated, and no scream of pain left his mouth.

Theru felt the foreign presence in his mind driving him to work, but he had only seen an archos once. Its pale, grey skin and milky eyes sent a chill down his spine, and he was seized the moment he laid eyes on it. Eru hated the archos, almost as much as the vyeshen that drove them. The archos were, after all, slaves as well. The metal breast plate his hands fashioned would never fit on a human.

Something felt different about the archos that drove him today. She felt stronger, and more controlling. On some days a sudden flash of pain, like the burning spark that still chewed into the flesh of his arm, would have caused him to flinch and pull away before his controller's will could stop him. This archos pushed him unflinchingly on. Maybe Theru would be lucky, and she would push him to his death.

The breast plate hissed and steamed as Theru dipped it into the cold water. Once it cooled, his hands set about cleaning and polishing the finely crafted steel until he could see his worn out eyes and scruffy beard reflecting in it. His hands were almost done, but he hated the last step in this routine most of all. Theru's thoughts scarcely had time to settle on the pending task before he felt the powerful gusts of wind from one of the vyeshen masters' wings.

The final fitting of the decorative breast plate should have been a welcome relief from the grueling work and merciless heat of the forges, but Theru hated this moment most of all. Somehow, being driven to work felt like less of a violation of his agency than being restrained as the vyeshen approached to have the breast plate fitted. Every fiber in Theru's body longed to destroy the cruel beast as it approached, and it would be so vulnerable with its feathery torso exposed.

Theru saw no beauty in the massive creature's bright fiery feathers, and felt no soul in its large, aquiline eyes. He had seen too many of its kind feed on his friends and loved ones, plucking them up from the forges or fields and carrying them away in massive talons. The breastplate Theru's hands had forged today was for a particularly large vyeshen, but he still couldn't suppress his surprise at the creature's size as the vibrantly colored bird approached.

Theru's hatred for the thing filled his mind, even drowning out the lingering pain in his arm. More than anything he wished he could grab the hot poker from the forge and ram it through the monster's head. He felt the oppressive archos control at these times more keenly than at any other time. Suddenly, Theru felt the archos presence vanish in his mind, and he stumbled and fell as control of his exhausted body was unexpectedly returned to him. Why had the archos released him? Could it be that this vyeshen was looking to feed? Theru remained prostrate, not daring to look up at the murderous beast that loomed over him. Even if he dared, Theru could barely move from exhaustion.

Theru lay on the ground quivering with fear, expecting a cruel vyeshen beak to rip him open at any moment. Finally, he couldn't stand the suspense any longer, and he ventured a glance up at the massive, eagle-like beast. It stood there looking at him: still as a statue. The desire to destroy the monster surged within him, and he could hardly believe he wasn't actually seized. Most likely, he would die the moment he made a move for a weapon, but Theru wasn't about to let this fleeting taste of freedom go to waste.

Theru's exhaustion vanished in the rush of the moment. He quickly stood and ran over to the forge, willing himself through the heat to get to the tools. He grabbed the hammer and poker and turned back to the vyeshen slave master. To his surprise, the creature stood motionless, waiting for something. Theru didn't dare pause to wonder what was happening. He charged towards the creature, roaring a feral scream of fury and hatred as he swung the hammer into the bird's torso. He felt the satisfying crunch as the first blow crushed bones and dropped the monster to the ground, but he knew he hadn't killed it yet. Why hadn't the thing screamed out or protested in pain?

He swung the hot poker, feeling another satisfying crunch as wing bones and a few vertebrae broke with the blow. Still, the creature didn't resist, or even make a sound in protest. Then the truth struck Theru's mind. This vyeshen was seized by an archos! Suddenly, his feelings towards the creature changed. He couldn't bring himself to strike another blow. Not like this.

Kill it! Theru heard a powerful voice in his mind, and somehow he recognized it as the archos that had controlled him today. Theru looked down at the miserable creature, undoubtedly writhing inside from its injuries, but controlled so firmly it couldn't even tremble. He had done that to the creature. *Kill it!*, the archos voice insisted more firmly in his mind. *It's what you wanted, isn't it?*

Her statement took Theru back. It is what he had wanted, more than anything else in the world. He had wanted the freedom to do exactly what the archos was now giving him the chance to do. So why couldn't he strike the final blow? Theru looked down on the vyeshen, and suddenly he felt a kinship with the creature. This vyeshen now understood the terror of archos domination. Theru's tools clanged loudly as they fell from his hands. He couldn't do it.

Instantly, he felt the archos seize him, and he knew who rightfully deserved his hatred. Theru's hands hefted the hammer. With a quick blow to the vyeshen's skull, he knew that it was now dead.

I am Aitrox, and you are free! The archos voice rung through his mind as she released him from her control. Theru's first thought was to rejoice. His second was to quiver in fear at the thought of a new and terrible name: Aitrox.

PART I

CHAPTER I

UNDER THE PORCH

Am I evil? My father undoubtedly thought so, but I can hardly blame him. Even in the womb, I could influence others in subtle ways, but I was weak and vulnerable. If I had been any stronger, I would have been discovered while in the womb — discovered and destroyed. Expectant mothers would never knowingly bring an archos pregnancy to fruition. The time in the womb is the second most treacherous for an archos, second only to the vulnerable moments immediately following birth. Many archos avoid detection by their mothers, but they are not strong enough at birth to seize their father before he can destroy the newborn monster..

My mother, like all those unfortunate enough to give birth to an archos, didn't have a chance to survive. My unnaturally large head ensured that. I cannot blame my father, Telu, for the terror and hatred he felt when he saw me; nor can I feel surprised that he blamed me for his beloved Ama's death. My blank white eyes immediately told him what I was. I never saw the look on Telu's face, but I felt the hatred in his heart and saw myself for the first time through his eyes. I have few memories of my earliest years, but I can never forget my first vision of myself, or the undeniable intensity of my father's hatred for me. One thing was certain — in his eyes I was definitely evil.

"Thank you for your business," Jordan the lamp maker said, trying not to sound too desperate or eager.

"You make the best lamps in all of Deor," Andrew responded, his eyes shifting around uneasily. Jordan couldn't blame him. He just hoped his customer could keep his thoughts safely away from the unmentionable under his front porch.

"I will have your order of lamps delivered and installed in two days. Can I interest you in an extra barrel of oil at a discount price?" Jordan asked, almost reaching for the customer before stifling the gesture.

"No, thank you," Andrew said as he donned his top hat and buttoned his coat, his lip twitching nervously.

"Thanks again for your business. It has been slow since..."

"So it's true then?" Andrew's head jerked up, nearly toppling his hat.

"Rumors alone can ruin a business," Jordan said, wishing he could take back his careless words. Then again, if the rumors spread enough maybe the problem would go away. The fact that neither of them had been seized, even with perilously related thoughts, meant that this unmentionable may still be young enough to be vulnerable.

"A very unfortunate rumor," Andrew said cautiously.

"Yes, it has..." Jordan cursed himself for his repeated carelessness, but the mistake was made and Jordan's words were no longer his own. He had been seized and the terrible experience never got any easier. "...scared away virtually all my customers." The archos finished his sentence, but not without enough of a pause for Andrew to notice.

Jordan saw the terror surge in his customer's eyes, but could do nothing to calm him. He watched in aggravation as Andrew rushed out of his small shop, colliding with a display cabinet with a shattering crash; the broken glass cutting his hand. His top hat fell to the floor. Andrew scarcely noticed the cut, nor did he stop to pick up his hat in his hasty exit.

Jordan had expected being seized to feel less traumatic after the first time. Instead, the repeated experiences felt like fresh blows to an already broken limb. Jordan felt it in his mind, felt the intruder's awareness of his most personal and precious moments as well as his darkest secrets. Each time opened old wounds, and sullied his most personal memories. This archos knew of the affair he never could reveal to his late wife. This archos knew of that day he shared with his daughter fishing the Deor River as she confided her worries about her pending wedding. This archos knew the sacred moment of holding his only grandchild. This archos knew the last words his beloved wife had spoken for his ears only. The archos had held his grandchild, eavesdropped on his wife's final moments, sat on the boat with his daughter. His most intimate, personal and sacred moments felt sullied and betrayed anew. If anything, it grew worse each time.

He never would get used to the completely powerless feeling as another will used his body like a cheap tool. Jordan counted himself lucky: he hadn't been compelled to do anything terrible or cruel to himself or others, but had merely been used as a tool for his unwelcome ruler's basic survival needs. More developed archos had a terrible reputation for depravity and wickedness.

Jordan didn't consider himself a hateful person, but he could never find words for the animus he felt for the villain under his shop porch. There were times when his hatred almost drove him to grab a knife from the kitchen. However, he knew that the moment he picked up a knife, it would find itself in his own heart. You don't just stab an archos, not even a young and relatively vulnerable one. It could be killed, but it usually involved indirectly orchestrated calamities like arson. He could only hope that the demon under his porch would move on before someone tried to kill it. It had already cost him most of his customers. He said a silent prayer to Aitrox that it wouldn't cost him his home and shop.

The archos walked him out the front door of his shop and down the porch steps. He ducked his head under his porch; most likely the vile creature needed his eyes to guide itself out of its confined hiding spot. Jordan wanted to pull his head back, but could merely watch as the cruel creature came into view. He wore only a small loin cloth, leaving most of its grey, splotchy skin exposed. Thick, branching networks of red veins spread around its blank, white eyes. Jordan knew those eyes saw nothing, but still hated the feeling of them gazing at him. The creature could now use Jordan's sight to guide its movements. Jordan shuddered involuntarily at the sight of the black fingernails as it grabbed the wooden posts and pulled itself out of its den. At the same time, Jordan heard the clamor of two carriages colliding; but Jordan's curiosity could never hope to override the archos's control, and his eyes remained fixed on the archos.

Jordan knew the archos's purpose, though he couldn't understand why it didn't just oblige him to feed it himself. Maybe it knew just how bare his shelves were. By now, the vile creature had undoubtedly seized a few others and would use each pair of eyes and ears to guide its movements. Certainly, the passing victims would then spread rumors of an archos on this street, despite the risk of being seized again for thinking of the monster. The effects of the rumors could bankrupt him, lingering long after the unmentionable moved on.

Eru sat under the porch – his new home. He knew he couldn't stay for long, but he had finally grown strong enough to feel safe settling in one location for more than a day or two. For the time being, he saw, heard and felt nothing other than the chaotic swirl of minds hurrying by on the street outside. Each passing mind tempted him fiercely; taunting him with the promise of sight, sound, and touch. Only the greatest concentration prevented him from seizing the nearest person. Creases of strain and concentration showed on his large forehead as he fought to resist the hunger to seize a mind. He yearned for sensory input and knowledge, even as he despised the pain he inflicted and the hatred he felt from each person he seized.

It would be a mistake to consider Eru blind, or helpless, though he might have appeared so upon initial observation. His large, unwieldy skull housed a brain completely dedicated to an awareness of the minds around him. He felt someone new approach the shop, and sensed Jordan's anxiety to get a sale. When Eru was younger, he would have given the lamp maker more customers and huge profits. However, Eru didn't want to get Jordan killed, and even his few years had taught him the law of unintended consequences. If people believed the lamp maker had an archos making his money, he would likely end up dead when Eru moved on. Eru had already killed a florist that way – one more death on his young conscience.

Eru sensed hundreds of other minds flowing past the shop, their thoughts to occupied to pay the shop any attention. Occasionally, he felt the heat of thoughts straining to avoid rumors of an archos in the area. Even their indirect thoughts pulled at him, straining his resolve not to seize anyone. Every time he seized someone, his world was filled with senses he could never have on his own, and knowledge he could never obtain through his own study. At nine years of age, Eru already knew hundreds of professions, and many sciences. Through Jordan he had acquired the craft of lamp making and the master craftsman's lifetime of expertise in wicks and oils.

Seizing a mind always felt thrilling and empowering, yet terrible and vile. Eru's mind craved it while his heart loathed the pain he caused others – loathed the powerful reminder of his own wickedness. Holding back the impulse to seize a mind, even for a little while, took tremendous willpower. So long as people's thoughts didn't turn directly to him, it was bearable. The fewer people who knew the exact location of his den, the better. Fortunately, not many dared spread such rumors and risk his notice.

Most of the people in Deor believed the archos awareness bordered on omni-science. While the greatest of his race had networks and connections that could easily create that perception, few understood that a young archos like Eru didn't have that kind of reach. It was just as well for Eru. If people knew how vulnerable a Streetborn archos his age was, no Streetborns would survive to maturity. For all his power, he lacked the protection of Aitrox enjoyed by the archos born in her Sanctuaries.

Suddenly Jordan's careless thoughts hit Eru's mind with undeniable force. The awareness slammed Eru like a sledgehammer, shattering his resolve as in-stinct took over. The lamp maker had been doing so well. Relief, and a tinge of regret, accompanied the rush of new sensory information. Eru saw the terror on the customer's face – not an unusual experience for him. Part of him wanted to seize the man and kill him in the alley, protecting the secret of his new home. Eru stifled the thought, unwilling to kill for his convenience. Besides, the lamp maker needed the business, and neither Jordan nor the customer should be punished just because Eru failed to hide the moment he seized Jordan. Had Eru picked up Jordan's sentence without a pause, the customer probably wouldn't have known.

Eru knew his survival weighed heavily on Jordan's shoulders and wished he didn't have to be privy to his secrets and defining moments. Feeling the lamp maker's hatred for him added another vote on the running ballot Eru couldn't help but tally. Votes for Eru being evil? Thousands. Good? Zero.

Eru was determined to prove them all wrong, determined to redeem himself for his mother's death, determined that somehow he would change his father's mind. Eru wanted to show the world that he wasn't the monster his father believed him to be, but sometimes he doubted. Perhaps Eru was nothing more than a demonic abomination like his father believed. Eru had lost count of the people who had died under his influence. In his nine years' existence, he had ruined countless lives, leaving a slew of traumatized and ruined people in his wake. Eru had already learned that the heightened survival instinct of his kind often controlled him as unflinchingly as he controlled others.

Eru didn't feel an ache in his stomach indicating hunger, but his instincts told him he needed food. When he saw himself through Jordan's eyes, it gave him the spatial awareness to navigate the tight quarters under the porch. As he crawled out of his den, he seized two carriage drivers and deliberately caused an accident as a distraction to keep unwanted eyes from resting on him. Eru still needed a few more sets of eyes and ears today, but he preferred to choose them himself. Eru released both drivers, knowing neither would admit to having just been seized.

"By the High Queen! You're a fool!" one driver shouted.

"Your carriage is the one out of its lane!" the other snapped.

"Would you two grow up and get your carriages out of the way?" another snapped. A few carriages back in the log jam, a particularly fine carriage with gold trim and a driver in a suit made of the finest silk clanged his carriage's bell in *dignified* protest. Speaking to the drivers responsible would clearly be beneath the driver's station.

Spotting the nobleman's carriage, Eru knew he had found the one who would feed him today. He navigated the chaos easily, heading for the nobleman's carriage at the back of the line. He doubted the nobleman noted the streets his driver chose, making him a safe person to seize. Eru released the lamp maker with a mental sigh of relief on both their parts, as he willed the nobleman to open his carriage door. Eru climbed in.

Eru felt the fine silks and soft cottons on the man's perfumed skin along with his indignation and fear at Eru's nerve in seizing him. Taro enjoyed particular financial favor from Aitrox, and had considered himself above the dominion of a Streetborn archos. Such ostentatious pride and arrogance sickened Eru, reminding him why he disliked seizing noblemen, but also why he chose them. Feeling the loathing and hatred from them had less sting than from commoners. He felt no pity for the nobility, almost viewing the pain he caused them as justice for their pride and cruelty. At least this one knew enough about the archos not to let his thoughts wander to retaliation. Part of Eru almost wished he would.

"Rand," the nobleman, or rather Eru, called to his servant, "take me to the markets. I'm hungry."

"But milord, we are already late for your appointment," Rand objected.

"Do as I say!" Eru shouted, using the nobleman as his mouthpiece.

"Yes, milord," Rand said quietly.

Eru waited in the carriage as the driver continued to clang his bell as he waited for the log-jammed traffic to clear. Finally, the traffic started moving and Rand turned their carriage around en route to the market. Once there, he let Rand pick his food, knowing the driver would pick carefully to satisfy the discerning nobleman's taste. Eru carefully positioned the nobleman to block Rand's view of him as Rand handed his master the food. The nobleman seethed with fury as his hands fed Eru, like a lowly servant would. Eru couldn't taste the food but he relished the experience. Lacking any of the normal feelings of hunger or satisfaction, Eru's mind simply sensed when the body's needs had been met. He called to Rand one more time.

"Rand, turn into the next side street," Eru commanded.

"But, milord!" Rand objected again.

"Rand, do as I say. It would be a shame to send you back to the Sanche District." The nobleman's cruel threat flowed easily and yielded the expected obedience.

"Yes, milord," Rand said so quietly that Eru felt the emotional acquiescence more than he heard the words with the nobleman's ears. The carriage rocked slightly as the driver navigated the sharp turn into a tight alley. Eru stepped out of the carriage with anticipation, not just to be rid of the disgusting nobleman. The journey back to his den promised to be an adventure filled with new minds for the seizing. Part of him wished he didn't look forward to that experience as much as he did.

Aitrox lived as a goddess, and she ensured that everything around her bore witness to her splendor. Everything, from the thousands of statues that adorned her city, to the magnificent citadel she called home, testified of her majesty. Even the elaborate gown she wore displayed her grandeur for all to see. Her fiery dress seemed to have a life of its own, shimmering like a subdued flame on the verge of bursting into a wildfire. Innumerable variations of red and orange flickered and danced through the dress when she moved, often making the dress appear ablaze. The feathery gown fit her delicate body tightly. Feathers clung to the neck in a high collar. The unusual cut left her shoulders and back exposed, revealing her grey, splotchy skin. Long sleeves came to points near her hands, and the flowing train rippled down the steps of her throne. None but Aitrox knew the true origin of the gown. Indeed, she would kill any whose thoughts wandered to speculation on the topic. She wore it with pride: a trophy of her greatest triumph, when she slew the vyeshens' god, the Phoenix.

Dozens of servants attended her constantly, each under her unflinching control. Some fanned her body – not because she could feel the fanned air – but just because she enjoyed making them serve her. Others massaged her shoulders and back. She relished their revulsion as she forced them to caress and sooth her body. Others sampled from the platters of food around her – an unnecessary precaution – though she enjoyed their fear of the poisons for which they were supposedly screening. The last attempted poisoning had been centuries ago, but Aitrox sensed the threat before the would-be assassin even finished purchasing his ingredients. By now even the vague, indirect thoughts pertaining to her never escaped notice, especially if they had hostile implications.

Aitrox sat on her throne, her awareness touching on thousands of minds every moment in an unending scan of her city and the surrounding world. If she desired, she could sense the people on the far side of the world, though she couldn't seize over such great distances. Aitrox dominated the Deorean continent, a massive solitary island. Nothing escaped her notice, nor her reach here. Other powerful nations had tried to conquer her domain over the centuries; tried and failed. Still, her reach did not extend across the vast oceans with enough power to extend her empire, but no sailors had dared sail the waters near her shores in centuries. Still she watched the oceans with the bored inattentiveness of a seasoned guard at a quiet post.

Most of her focus remained centered on Deor and the surrounding regions. Constant vigilance bore a striking resemblance to tedium, but Aitrox knew she could never afford to underestimate the vyeshen. Even in defeat they always posed a danger, and she had reason to believe that they were actively and subtly working their schemes in her domain.

Aitrox took few threats seriously, knowing no human could harm her, but she knew to fear the vyeshen. She had, after all, killed their god, then used their race to create the building blocks of her power. She had lost track of the centuries of her rule, but she knew that time served the vyeshen better than it did her. If rumors hinted at vyeshen activity, Aitrox would find out the truth.

As she searched the city, she felt her mind pulled to several places simultaneously. Her people couldn't know how much it helped her when they invoked her name. At any given moment, she had keen insights throughout the city as people pulled her attention down on them. A particularly potent thought stuck out from the noise, not spoken or thought in passing, but directed with focused purpose on her. Aitrox would show whoever it was the dangers of such careless, arrogant thoughts. She recognized this one immediately and had to suppress a laugh. Rather than seize him, she felt it would be much more enjoyable to seize his carriage driver.

"Taro, Taro, Taro." She spoke through Rand, the nobleman's driver after she had him stop the carriage and step in to the cab.

"My liege, High Queen," Taro said, ignoring the irony as he bowed to his servant.

"You know not to call my attention without a good reason," Aitrox continued

"I'm s-s-sorry, my High Lady," Taro stammered.

"Tell me what could be *SO* important to merit troubling me?" Aitrox filled the words with sarcasm.

"You promised me that your archos wouldn't seize me!" Taro snapped, forgetting himself in his anger.

"So I did, and none have," the carriage driver replied.

"But, I don't understand..." Taro mumbled quietly, averting his gaze from his carriage driver's eyes.

"You mean you called my attention to complain because one of the Street-born took you? And you blamed me?" There could be no mistaking the dangerous edge Aitrox put into her words.

"My Lady, p-p-p-please, f-forgive me!" Taro said, his eyes darting around in fear as his perfumed skin tingled with a sense of his impending doom. Those were the last words the nobleman spoke as Aitrox seized him to carry out her punishment. She took her time with him, having had thousands of years to perfect the craft of torturing her victims. Breaking the glass window on Taro's carriage bloodied his hands and created the cruel shard that would be Aitrox's instrument. Aitrox reveled in her victim's terror as the blood began to trickle down his cheek and the slow, methodical process began. Aitrox even let herself experience some of Taro's pain just to feel alive. Hours later, one would have scarcely recognized Taro's mangled corpse, and the originally light carriage interior glistened a gruesome, wet crimson. Still, Aitrox's boredom, and her lust for terror and pain hadn't been sated. She let Rand live, reveling in the terrible trauma he would bear for the rest of his days. However, she arbitrarily picked a number, seventeen, and thus the next seventeen persons to discover the carnage of Taro's carriage suffered a similar fate.

The exchange with Taro did nothing to slow her search for news of the vyeshen, or distract her from the thousands of other minds she controlled. However, news of a new Streetborn occupied far more of her mind than anything else. She always enjoyed finding new Streetborn, gleaning amusement in the games she played with their hearts before breaking them and claiming another slave.

CHAPTER 2

THE DARKNESS WITHIN

I don't know if I will ever come to terms with the cost of my survival. I see how easy it would be to abandon any notions of right and wrong, to simply stop trying. Heaven knows my instincts certainly appeared to condemn me to an evil existence. In my younger years, my lack of control cost many people their lives. I can still remember each person who died under my compulsion. The staggering tally is more than a number, rather it is a tragic, intimate and personal *collection of failures. There have been many times in my life when I truly wondered if I was inherently and inescapably evil.*

"**H**urry up, boy!" a testy man said to the urchin polishing his boots. The rebuke fell on apparently deaf ears. "Sweet Aitrox!" the angry customer gasped as he followed the boy's eyes to Eru before being seized. Eru had already seized the boy, using his eyes to guide him through the dirty streets of the ghetto. Eru found children less painful to seize. Their young, innocent minds had fewer emotional wounds for him to bludgeon open, and fewer personal memories for him to sully. Children hated him less for the experience, and Eru knew he left a lighter taint on their hearts.

Eru used the boy briefly before moving on to another. He needed many eyes in order to guide him through the crowded streets, usually maintaining at least five people under his control. When the crowds thinned, he could get away with fewer, but today that was unlikely. He experienced a truly unique view of Deor, for he saw the city not just through others eyes, but through their lives. Each mind he seized offered a different feeling, almost like a unique mixture of flavors to experience. In addition to the various emotional perspectives, Eru had a vast depth of knowledge available to his powerful mind. In an instant, Eru spotted the slight limp in a passing horse's trot. He guessed the horse's shoe had been poorly fitted. Eru discerned the particular accent of a man buying bread, knowing him to be from a wealthy winery near the mountains to the west, but judging from his clothing, Eru surmised that the man sold and trafficked the wines without owning his own vineyard. Eru heard the rattle of another carriage, noting that the axle was cracked and it would soon need a major repair. He admired the pattern work etched with admirable skill on a carpenter's door, the design dating back to the old Duroke period. Deor came alive with everything Eru could take in, comprehending everything with the understanding of hundreds of master craftsmen, doctors, historians and scientists.

If Eru could have gotten past the vile feelings he felt from each person he seized, it would have been an exhilarating experience. Part of him would always crave seizing new minds, and learning about the world around him from as many vantages as possible – but it was like being forced to drink bile in order to sample the world's richest wine.

Eru knew he needed to avoid the crowded streets as much as possible, but some major thoroughfares were unavoidable. He had learned through painful experience not to underestimate Telu, his father. Telu would not rest until one of them was dead, and Eru knew he hadn't developed his senses enough to reliably sense Telu's intricate and indirect schemes.

Someday, Eru would feel more at liberty to pick any route he wished on his way home, but not today. The longer routes would take him through much more interesting parts of town, past academies, and past some of the finest master craftsmen in all of Deor. The thought of all that knowledge and expertise there for the seizing almost changed Eru's plans. No, today he needed to get back to his shelter quickly. Eru knew he still wasn't ready to risk such open movements even if the quick route back took him through the Sanche District.

Eru reined in his instincts in the Sanche District, only taking a few minds at a time; the less he saw, heard and smelled, the better. A pungent mix of mildew, sweat, sewage, and smoke smothered all thought momentarily. Through Eru's view of the Sanche district, he discerned the terrible emotional poverty that filled the district. Despair, hopelessness, and vice dominated and crushed the hearts of most here. The occasional bright soul stood out in the darkness, like a lone flower struggling to survive in a busy thoroughfare – so likely to be crushed at any moment. It was almost hard to believe such squalor could exist so close to the grandeur and opulence of the Pendro Quarter, one of the wealthier parts of the city. It felt like another world, yet even in the slums, some things remained constant.

Even in Sanche District dense spikes adorned rooftops, ledges and walls. Every structure in Deor seemed designed to be inhospitable to anything with wings – but the creatures had to end up somewhere. Pigeons choked the filthy streets here where no carriages would drive them away. Large piles of pigeon waste stacked against the grey, stained walls of the tiny homes. Many in the Sanche district served life sentences in the prison of poverty, making the barred windows oddly appropriate. Eru felt the hunger gnawing mercilessly in each person he seized, and sensed it almost as keenly in those he didn't seize. Everyone here felt spent, worn out, ruined.

A craven, beggar child called to him, too desperate or naïve to care what Eru was. Eru seized him without even realizing he had. Eru felt the misery of the poor boy's life, passing most days with hunger gnawing at him. He suffered the boy's sorrow of going home to find his father had drunk away the money to feed them that night. He felt the pain that forever lingered after his father's drunken beatings. He felt how the boy feared Eru, even more than his father, and how the boy hated the new unwelcome tormentor even more than his father's whiskey. Eru tallied that boy's negative vote with particular melancholy; one more vote against him. He would prove them all wrong someday.

Eru hurried through this part of town, anxious to get back to the relative comforts of his den. To anyone other than an archos, Eru's cramped, muggy nook would be anything but comfortable, but Eru couldn't wait to get out of the slums. In the Sanche District, few had anything to offer his hungry mind. He already knew all he could hope to learn about every profession practiced here – everything from polishing shoes to the oldest profession. In a way Eru felt a kinship with many, whose lives seemingly condemned them to evil from birth, but the thought that he too would be helpless to escape his fate terrified him. The man on the corner had desperately wanted to escape the hold of the slums, and rise above the life of crime and vice he had been born into. However, Eru knew of the blood the man had on his hands, and his ultimate surrender to the forces that held him down. Had he ever had a chance at a normal life? Not likely. In many ways, that man was everything Eru dreaded he would become: battered and broken until he was too tired and too weak to resist.

Here in the Sanche district, Eru felt far too comfortable with the darkness within him. The layers of subterfuge, deception, manipulation and control that existed here felt natural to him. Eru recognized the subtle hand gestures that marked his passage, and pitied those foolish enough to act on them. He felt several minds focusing on the intersection just ahead of him. Not long ago, such indirect thoughts would have escaped his attention, but his senses were growing more acute.

As he reached the intersection, their discipline broke and a flood of fifteen hostile minds activated Eru's survival mechanisms. Five attackers immediately lay bleeding, their knives plunged into their own rib cages. Eru fought against his reflexes, desperately trying to stop the doomed attempt on his life without spilling more blood. He knew that most who tried to kill him viewed their foolish attempts as a form of honorable suicide. Life in the slums had broken them, but they needed Eru's special kind of encouragement to end it all.

Eru didn't have the strength to seize all of the remaining ten at once, and three closed the distance to him before he could do anything about it. One larger man barreled into him. Eru toppled to the ground, unable to feel his grey skin slicing on a sharp rock, or the hard knock to his head that nearly rendered him unconscious. His assailant placed vice-like hands on Eru's throat. Eru couldn't feel the fingers digging into his neck, but his mind knew of the imminent danger and reacted in kind. Eru seized control of those immediately threatening him, fury and adrenaline driving his mind and adding terrible strength to his only real defense.

It all ended as quickly as it began, leaving fifteen bodies in the streets of the Sanche district. Eru seized a few terrified onlookers and used them to get him back on his feet. He saw the blood flowing from a deep gash on his arm. Fortunately he had seized several doctors in the past, and could easily treat his wounds. At least they didn't hurt. Once he returned to his den, the lamp maker's hands and eyes would attend to his needs.

Eru felt the terror of those he used to get him away from the scene of his latest crime – another fifteen dead at his hand.

"You should get that taken care of, Andrew," Telu said, gesturing to the crimson wrapping around Andrew's cut hand. Telu handed Andrew a hefty bag of coins in payment for information about the location of his target. Andrew knew better than to ask where Telu could come up with such sums of money. Rumor had it that Telu belonged to a particularly violent faction of the heretics.

"You will at least make sure that Jordan isn't hurt, won't you?" Andrew asked.

"I don't know what you are talking about," Telu said, giving Andrew a dangerous look. The more Andrew insinuated and implied what Telu planned, the more likely his plans would be picked up by his target. He hadn't told Andrew anything, but people only paid to know where a Streetborn archos lived for one reason.

"You will make sure Jordan isn't harmed," Andrew persisted stubbornly.

"Shut your mouth!" Telu snapped, reaching for a dagger at his side.

"Promise me," Andrew said, his eyes moving nervously as he saw Telu's threatening gesture.

"I'll do what I can," Telu replied, hoping to stop Andrew's thoughts before they spoiled his carefully laid plans.

"What does that mean?" Andrew asked.

"It means you should think about other things," Telu said, grinding his teeth.

"Jordan has already lost so much. He's desperate for business. It would be easy to –" Andrew's words cut short as Telu plunged a dagger into the man's chest. Telu had warned him. Such lack of discipline would spoil all of Telu's carefully laid plans. For a brief moment, Telu felt pity for Andrew who stared at him with shocked, uncomprehending eyes before collapsing in the alley.

"I will do what I can," Telu said again – deciding despite his better judgment to honor the cause Andrew had given his life for.

"I'm sorry, Ama," Telu said quietly – words he had muttered hundreds of times over the years. Telu knew he had become something his late wife could never condone, even if it was all for her. He had already lost his soul in his quest to ensure that no mother would suffer Ama's cruel fate. His life, and the lives of others, didn't matter when weighed against the greater good he fought for.

Telu could hardly contain his thoughts or quell his anticipation. Had Andrew just blown everything? If these plans failed, the blood of those who died tomorrow would be on Andrew's hands.

"I need four large barrels of your best lamp oil," Telu said as he stepped into a mercantile.

"I only have two in stock, sir," the shopkeeper responded.

"That will do," Telu said. "Have them delivered to 370 Hanu Drive by tonight." Telu dropped a heavy bag of coins on the counter and turned to leave.

"Sir, don't you want your change?" the shopkeeper called after him.

"Consider it payment for your discretion," Telu said as he stepped out of the door. The shopkeeper smiled, confused at the generous overpayment.

Telu bought another two barrels of lamp oil from a different merchant, a new carriage from another, and a barrel of gunpowder from a third. Last of all he visited a driver service to hire a carriage for a special delivery tomorrow evening. They of course could never know he was hiring a man to die for Telu's cause. For Andrew's sake, he forged a letter to Jordan telling him to be at the Aior Estate at seven thirty tomorrow evening. The prospect of replacing all the lamps and lanterns in such a large estate would get him to leave his shop. Telu arrived back at his apartment and got to work. He opened his toolbox, grabbed a pair of tweezers, and set about putting the finishing touches on the timing mechanism. An hour or so later, he finished. Winding it up, he tested the countdown. The rhythmic ticking sound was almost impossible to hear, until the final ominous click. Telu suppressed a smile and fought back his anticipation. At seven-forty tomorrow night, his wife Ama would be avenged.

Oko staked out the archos citadel alone, as he did virtually everything in life. He had come here to kill an archos, and knew nobody else could be trusted with that knowledge. Oko knew that other Hiders existed, but few had managed to stay alive as long as he. Secrecy, and above all things, isolation kept him alive.

He laughed at the irony of finding isolation and stealth amidst the throngs who came to worship. The crowds would protect him, keeping any hostile eyes from recognizing that someone could be seen but not sensed. Oko had cased this congregation for weeks, looking to get a count of the Aegendi this archos controlled.

"Praise the High Queen!" a worshiper exclaimed, as an invisible force lifted him above the amazed onlookers. *The Wizard's handiwork,* Oko thought to himself.

The citadel's hall had been built like a spectacular stage for the miracles and spectacles of the archos. Massive statues of archos figures lined the main auditorium, all bowing their heads to the largest statue, Aitrox herself. On all sides, large stained glass windows filled the room with a myriad of colors to bewilder onlookers. Just in front of the statue of Aitrox, an elevated stage allowed the gathering crowds to watch the spectacles as they unfolded.

"Praise Aitrox, the great being whose will we all fulfill," a man called.

"Glory to Aitrox," another voice called.

Oko moved through the crowds cautiously. He knew that his fake mustache, darkened hair, and walking cane successfully hid his real identity. People would be likely to remember the man who struck down an archos in broad daylight and left unharmed. He didn't want them remembering any features that could lead back to him. It had been so long since he had killed an archos, and never had he tried something this brazen. Oko had tired of taking out Streetborns, but he wondered if he had chosen a target beyond his ability today. Hopefully, his ambition wouldn't be his undoing. Perhaps that was why most Hiders died young.

Oko waited for the levitated worshiper to settle back to the stage before drawing in closer. He limped deliberately, using his cane to further the illusion. Like Oko, his cane had a secret the archos couldn't know about. If the worshiping session followed routine, his moment would come soon.

"Come," a woman's voice called. "All those who seek the blessings of Aitrox, come pay homage."

The crowd pressed in to the archos standing on the stage, with people kneeling at the feet of Oko's target. Many wept and plead for blessings for sick loved ones. Oko limped up with the throng to kneel.

"Bless me, Aitrox, for I have sinned," Oko said with a cynical smile as he pressed the button on his cane. A quick metallic sound accompanied the unsheathing of the hidden blade. In a single fluid motion, he raised the weapon and plunged the blade into the archos's chest. The splash of red stained the stage, his outer vest, and the clothes of other worshipers around him. He had done it. Using a hidden knife, he severed a hand as his trophy, leaving the cane jutting from his victim as a morbid token of his triumph.

Terrified screams mixed with muffled exclamations of surprise and morbid pleasure. Apparently, not all who came to worship did so out of love for their god. Oko quickly stood and jumped from the stage, turning towards the nearest stained glass window. He expected the crowds to part in confused terror, but the opposite happened. He saw the gaze of thirty onlookers all following him with a unity that could only mean one thing. Oko should have known to expect another archos would be here. With at least thirty people under its sway, this would be a tough escape.

Oko pulled another dagger from a concealed sheath, readying for a fight. He hadn't expected to need it. The unified throng moved in pursuit, and he cut a man down. Before the man even hit the ground, a new person stepped in to fill the gap. Then, things turned for the worse. Oko ran his blade through another pursuer but the person didn't even flinch. The wound closed so quickly the blood only trickled a few inches before drying up. This archos had an Immortal. He caught a flicker of motion out of the corner of his eye, and ducked just in time to dodge the heavy rock that passed where his head had been. The projectile smashed through one of the stained glass windows with a crash. The citadel grew brighter as undiffused light poured in.

"Great, an Immortal and a Wizard both!" Oko grunted to himself, as he scampered up a statue and onto a decorative ledge. The ledge removed him from the press of the crowds and gave him a straight path for the window. He moved with the grace and agility of a man whose life had been dedicated to the martial arts. Even on the narrow ledge, he easily avoided additional projectiles as he rushed towards the broken window and dove out. Oko dropped the ten feet to the hard street below. He tucked and rolled as he landed, but the cobblestone still left him with several painful bruises and a few scrapes. Not far behind him, the Immortal followed, taking the fall with far greater ease. Another heavy piece of stone collided with the street just to his right, exploding on impact; the shattered debris stinging his hands and face.

The Immortal jumped on Oko, but Oko ducked and twisted out of his grasp just in time. He quickly swung his dagger, nearly chopping the Immortal's foot off and buying him some time to escape. Oko stumbled to his feet, just ducking the next projectile to come from the direction of the citadel. The heads of several passing pedestrians lifted and turned towards him. Oko smiled cynically, knowing he may have overdone it this time.

Help me! His mind pleaded, though he had no idea to whom or what he prayed. He turned and ran into the crowds. He couldn't explain why the same people who had been seized only moments ago now went about their usual business, but he wouldn't complain about the mysterious halt to the pursuit. As soon as he felt he had run a safe distance from the citadel, Oko cast aside his mustache, his outer shirt, and vest – down to his last layer of disguises. He changed his walk, shedding the limp and walking more like the university student his clothing suggested him to be. He pulled out a small booklet, pretending to read it absentmindedly as he walked. In a matter of seconds, nobody who had seen him at the citadel could have recognized him.

Oko would never know about the presence that lurked, watching his exploits from the shadows of a nearby alley. Once the Hider disappeared into the crowds, a large creature took flight, gaining altitude quickly and flying west with great speed.

CHAPTER 3

DRIVEN

I will always marvel at the impact my mother had on me. I clung to the memory of her love for me, her unborn child. She didn't know yet that I would be an archos, and she had lofty dreams for me. I felt her terror and surprise when I seized her just before birth, but despite such a terrible twist of fate she died with hope for her archos child. I will always cherish my memory of her, and always regret every failure that betrays her hopes and validates my father's feelings for me.

Jordan's eyes thoroughly inspected Eru's injuries, removing his shirt and trousers. Eru had to be thorough, depending completely on Jordan's eyes to compensate for his absolute lack of feeling. Several rough scrapes and bruises marred Eru's splotchy grey skin. Blood flowed from the gash on Eru's arm. That cut required urgent attention. Eru guided the lamp maker as Jordan's hands stitched the cut on Eru's arm. His bleeding had to be addressed, but the growing fogginess in his mind worried him. He must have hit his head very hard.

Eru struggled to maintain hold over the two watchers he kept outside – just in case. He took great care to keep his location secret, and doubted anybody had dared follow him after such a slaughter. On top of that, Eru knew he would likely sense any people coming for vengeance, but extreme caution had saved his life before. Usually, he could easily control four or five watchers in the surrounding blocks, but right now he could barely maintain two.

Seven forty-five tomorrow.

Jordan dropped the thread and needle. Eru's concentration broke as he recognized his awareness picking up something important. Seven forty-five – Eru assumed it to be a time – but was it morning or evening? Could it be something else – an address or an invoice number perhaps? Not long ago Eru would not have even picked up such an innocuous and vague thought, but his senses still hadn't developed enough to glean specifics.

Ama will be avenged. Eru recognized the thought and the zealous hunger behind it: Father. Eru knew his father better than perhaps any other – knew his murderous hatred and zeal. Eru had survived his first two months by seizing Telu. Telu's hands had cared for Eru, while his heart grieved for the loss of his beloved wife. In those early days, grief kept them both alive. Ama's death had crushed Telu, breaking his will and leaving him numb and unfeeling. It was only after Eru had left his father behind that Telu's slow recovery began. Most Streetborn archos kill their fathers, but Eru couldn't betray the memory of his mother. Sometimes Eru wondered though: would Ama have wished for Telu to continue living as a terrorist who committed atrocities in her name? Yet, every time Eru had an opportunity to kill Telu, the memory of Ama's love and kindness held him back. He couldn't help but feel the painful irony that the memory of the same person could inspire such opposite behaviors from father and son; Eru desperately resisting his murderous nature while his father seemed to embrace death and revenge.

Knowing his father had put another plan in motion didn't make it any easier to pin down the specifics. Eru's mind felt foggy, unable to focus, almost blind. Even the minds near him felt nebulous and blurry. It reminded him of the time he saw the world through the cataracts of an old aristocrat. Eru realized that his head must have hit the ground harder than he thought. He knew the perils of head trauma, especially with his own inability to feel the usual symptoms.

Eru shifted the lamp maker's priority away from the scrapes. A black eye, along with swelling and scrapes on his cheek, gave him a beaten, ragged look. He had no pupils that could constrict, and no way of seeing if his non-descript eyes crossed or wandered. Other than the large bump on the back of his head, he didn't know if he could find any visual signs of trauma. A closer inspection however gave him cause for serious concern. A small discharge of clear liquid oozed from his ears.

Eru focused Jordan on immobilizing his head, but it proved trickier than he had expected due to his foggy mind and unwieldy skull. His ears continued to exude a clear liquid, but Eru knew it was better outside than in. Diagnosing an injury of this type would be simple if Eru could feel the usual symptoms. Doctors had studied human brains and physiology, but no doctor had ever been foolish enough to study an archos brain. The unknown could prove his undoing.

Eru felt the control of his eyes on the street suddenly blank out, and knew himself to be in mortal danger. Desperation drove him to attempt a treatment that comprised one doctor's darkest memories, even though he had saved the child. Drilling a hole in a child's skull left a lasting impression on the doctor Eru had seized. However, Eru saw a better alternative. Jordan washed one of his thin screwdrivers with alcohol before placing it in Eru's ear and pressing firmly.

Eru knew it would destroy his ear drum, if he ever had one, but he kept the lamp maker working the tool inward. Crimson blood mixed with the viscous discharge. Eru guessed he had to penetrate a bit further.

The slow trickle from his ear turned into a gentle flow of clear fluid with streaks of crimson. Eru had the lamp maker wash his instrument again before going to work in the other ear. He knew he took terrible risks, but he had no doubt he would die if he didn't do anything. Soon he had a steady flow of fluid from both ears, but felt no immediate improvement with his thoughts. Only rest and time would tell if his emergency treatment had worked. Eru struggled to get back to his den, and in the end made Jordan carry him. He felt his hold on the lamp maker weakening. A poignant mix of emotions filled Eru, as he contemplated death. Would he be reunited with his mother Ama? Would she welcome him? Would he be free from the hatred, violence and despair of his kind? Eru almost welcomed death as he thought on those questions. What would be his legacy? Had he lived up to his mother's dreams for him? Had he done a single thing to make the world better? He knew the answers. His legacy would be no different than any other archos. Death had been his calling card, left behind him without fail. Disappointment and despair filled his heart, but he felt Ama's hope overshadowing his shame. He wasn't ready to die.

Jordan tucked Eru into the far corner of his den before Eru released him. He couldn't have held the man for much longer. Seconds later, Eru's world went completely dark. The whole city of Deor could have been shouting his name, and vowing to kill him, and Eru wouldn't have felt a thing.

Jordan felt the vile archos release him and he scrambled out from under the porch as quickly as he could. Cobwebs grabbed at him, and sent chills down his spine. He could still feel the fleshy squishing sensation as he drove his screw driver into the archos's ear. Entering his shop, he saw the bloody puddles on his floor. Jordan grumbled to himself as he fetched some rags to clean up the mess. The gruesome experience had left him feeling sick to his stomach. Part of him resented the archos more for the experience – for letting him get so close to killing the wretch, daring him to just push a bit harder. Jordan had felt so painfully close to freedom, yet helpless to claim it. He could almost imagine himself just pushing harder than his seized hands had permitted, leaving the archos dead. He could have been free. Jordan quickly quelled the thoughts.

Now that the archos had released him, Jordan felt the turmoil over a potential opportunity at freedom. Seeing the monster in such feeble condition gave him hope that he could get his life back after all. The archos deserved death! Surely the vile creature had killed many people to survive as long as it had, and it had ruined many lives before it found its way to his shop. Jordan should do the world a service by killing him while he had a chance. Yet who was he kidding? Jordan knew he was no murderer.

Fortunately for Eru, a letter carrier arrived at that moment, distracting Jordan from the realization that he hadn't been seized and killed for his thoughts. When Jordan finished reading the letter, he forgot everything about the unmentionable under his porch. He had work to do in order to take advantage of such a great opportunity.

The doctors Eru had seized didn't know the workings of the archos brain, and its incredible capacity for survival. Even in the womb, the archos mind drives the body's development to allow surviving birth after only twenty-eight weeks; any longer and their heads would be too large to survive birth. An archos mind develops incredible dominion over the body and creates an impressive regenerative capacity. If an archos survives child birth, its mind has passed a crucial threshold. The archos brain was wired to respond to threats of any nature. The same driving force that made an archos kill in response to danger also drove the body to rapidly heal dangerous wounds. In the severest cases, such as Eru's, his mind dedicated itself wholly to survival and repair – a necessary risk that left him completely blind and vulnerable. It was the first time Eru had experienced unconsciousness.

Sleep now brought Eru needed recovery and the first ever dream for an archos. Eru had only vague memories of the time in the womb, but his dreams took him back into the mind of his mother, Ama.

"Our child," Ama laughed as she spoke. "I can hardly believe my own words. I thought it would never happen after so many years." She took Telu's hand and smiled affectionately at him. Telu touched Ama's stomach with pride in his eyes.

"Oh, Telu, do you think I will be a good mother?"

"Of course. You'll be the best mother Deor has ever seen," Telu said excitedly.

"I hope so," Ama answered quietly.

"You have the best heart in all the world – a great gift to pass on to our child," Telu said as he squeezed her hand.

"How can we raise a child in this world? Will she be happy? Can she hope for a better life?" she asked.

"What makes you think it's a girl? I am kind of hoping for a son," Telu teased.

"Okay then, do you think he'll be able to find a better life? Will he make a difference?" she persisted.

"Of course he, or she," Telu smiled, "will dethrone the unmentionable queen herself. With you as the mother, it's as sure as sunshine." Eru felt Ama's hope, as she imagined herself holding her newborn child.

Eru woke with no way of knowing about the tears flowing from his eyes. He felt the excitement of the lamp maker as he worked to prepare a few of his best lamps for presentation in a few hours. Hundreds of minds flowed past his den, but for the first time in his life, he felt no hunger to seize any of the passersby.

Seven forty-five. The thought hit his mind like a sledge-hammer. He quickly seized the lamp maker, needing to know how much time he had left. The hands on the clock indicated five-thirty in the afternoon. Had he been out that long? At least his father hadn't planned a morning attack or he wouldn't be thinking at all now. Still, he had very little time to find Telu's latest scheme. He felt the lamp maker's dismay at Eru's timing. It didn't take any effort to discover Jordan's excitement over the letter from a nobleman, the good break he was long overdue.

Eru released him, knowing that the letter should at least save the man's life. He seized the next person to pass in front of the shop, seeing no point in hiding his den anymore. Eru knew Telu well enough to know that his plan might level the entire block. Escaping with just over two hours would be easy. Saving all the innocent people from dying because of him would be anything but easy.

Eru climbed out of his den, seizing two others to help him in his efforts to search out Telu's plan. To his consternation, the fogginess in his mind kept him from seizing more people. He needed every vantage point he could gain, but could barely hold on to three people. He hadn't been so weak in years, and never at such a terrible time. Eru divided his limited resources. He had to get himself away, but his main attention went into finding clues or signs of Telu's plans. If he couldn't seize more people simultaneously, he could try something else. Eru's awareness moved through hundreds of people, jumping around like a flighty bird. He knew not to expect deliberate, hostile thought. Telu would not be so careless. Instead, Eru searched for people whose tasks would take them near the lamp maker's shop.

Eru continued the search as time moved inexorably towards the moment of the attack. He hid safely in a pile of garbage against an alley wall several blocks away from the shop, but his awareness roved desperately in search of his father's handiwork. Having found a relatively safe hiding spot, he released his guide so he could seize other minds for searching. With thousands of people leaving their jobs, he found hundreds whose paths would put them near his den around the critical time. Pedestrians likely posed no threat. He suspected that Telu would need a carriage or wagon to fulfill his murderous ambition. Most likely a driver rode in blissful ignorance, on his way to his death. Eru moved through possible candidates with frustration and mourning. If they weren't part of Telu's plan, they would be casualties.

He seized someone with a sight line to one of the city's clock towers to check; seven-forty. At least the lamp maker had left his shop already.

Eru knew he had run out of time, so he quickly turned his focus back to the street in front of his den. Immediately he spotted a wagon that had come to a stop in front of the shop.

"Jordan's Lamps and Lanterns," the driver said to himself as he opened the final envelop Telu had provided. He had opened the letter just minutes ago, keeping the final destination out of his thoughts and thus eluding Eru's detection. Eru had underestimated Telu's cunning.

A moment later, a loud snapping sound caused several passersby to jump in surprise. Telu had prepared a time device to lock the wagon's wheels. There would be no moving the wagon now. Eru seized the driver immediately and put him to work searching the wagon. The driver realized his fate in that instant, and it broke Eru's heart. His wife and newborn daughter would wait in vain for his return. He would never hold his daughter again. Eru felt the future the driver would miss out on, and the poverty that would await his wife. She would lose her husband and a steady income, condemning her to a life of begging or whoring. Eru had to save the man.

Seeing the barrels of lamp oil, he realized his own foolishness at choosing a lamp maker's shop for his den. He may as well have chosen a pyro-technician's shop. He felt his muddled awareness like a man coming out of a drunken stupor. Why did it have to happen now? He could only control three! Telu's handiwork couldn't be undone by just three people. Eru had failed again. No, he could not fail!

He drove the three he controlled with fierce intensity, feeling muscles pull in their backs as they tried to move the heavy barrels of oil off the wagon. One man's knee buckled, sending a jolt of unexpected pain into Eru's awareness. Eru released him, and grabbed the next unfortunate person to walk by the wagon. The first barrel tilted and fell to the street with a grating crash. Oil flowed from it, coating the street, the wheels of passing carriages, and the shoes of any person unfortunate enough to step in the viscous liquid. Eru clenched his jaw in frustration as the flammable liquid spread, soaking everything it touched with its ominous sheen.

The anticipated, yet unmistakable and unwanted odor wafted to the noses of those Eru controlled: gunpowder. Telu meant business, and his business was death. Eru's attention settled on the barrel from which the scent emanated. The driver rushed to the barrel as desperate to stop the bomb as the mind controlling him.

Eru hefted at the barrel with two sets of strong arms, but it didn't budge. The muscles in their backs gave out first, with a barrel that weighed far more than it should have. Telu had filled the bottom half with lead. The wagon had been structurally reinforced for the load – a testament to Telu's planning and determination. One thing was certain: three people could never have moved that barrel. The groans and grunts of their exertion halted, replaced by the quieter sound of their panting and a subtle sound he hadn't noticed before. *Tick, tick, tick, tick...* silence. Eru had failed.

Seven forty-five. Eru felt his father mark the time, sensing his anticipation. Wherever he was, he was watching, concealed.

A brilliant flash, a tremendous boom and a wave of heat ended Eru's control over the three at the carriage. He felt the terror and panic of hundreds of people in the near vicinity. Nothing discernible remained of Jordan's shop. Fragments of the wagon lay strewn throughout the block; a single spoke of a wheel protruding from a dead victim's body. Fire burned on the cobblestone street where oil from the first barrel had spread. The broken wheel of a toppled carriage spun wildly on its axle as the cab burned. One occupant managed to climb out, a terrible fiery form that ran only a few feet before collapsing. Others never made it out of the cab.

The spilled oil spread death down the street as flame followed its tracks to more victims. The flames engulfed carriage wheels, pedestrians' legs, and horses' hooves indiscriminately, converting people to fiery demons, and horses to terrible images from legends. Their screams didn't last long before the fires consumed them, and their tortured bodies fell to the street.

Neighboring shops and homes shuddered and collapsed in delayed response, crushing the fortunate instantly, and imprisoning the unfortunate for the short time they had left to live. Their cries for help went unheard in the maelstrom of panic outside.

A tortured horse whinnied in agony from its wounds, drowning out the screams of the passengers in its wagon. People mindlessly ran, stricken with panic and thinking only to get away from the terror. Eru seized a bystander and rushed back into the chaos to search for survivors, but as the full scope of the disaster hit him, it was too much for him to bear. All of this came because of him.

Eru pulled his awareness away from the terrible scene, desperately wanting to escape from the site of his failure. He wanted to get as far from his old den as possible. He soon controlled a carriage and had the driver take him anywhere, so long as it took him away from this hellish scene.

He's gone. Ama, you can rest in peace. Telu obviously believed Eru dead or he wouldn't have let his thoughts turn so directly to him. He stepped out from the alley he had carefully chosen to keep him close to Jordan's shop, yet safe from the blast. The dancing flames and collapsed buildings brought a smile to his lips. He had done it. His son was finally dead.

In Eru's weakened state, he couldn't resist his instincts, and he seized his father for the first time in almost nine years. Through his father's eyes he saw the carnage and mayhem with terrible intensity. Eru smelled the charred flesh and burning homes so intensely vividly that he nearly choked. Telu's eyes seemed to pick out the details and nuances with unrivaled clarity. Through Telu's eyes he counted every singed hair, blister, cut and burn on a wailing survivor instantly: one thousand two hundred thirty-three singed hairs, three hundred thirty thousand seven hundred seventy-nine visible follicles burned hairless, twenty blisters of sundry sizes, ten cuts and one continuous burn. Eru knew the count to be accurate.

Never in his life had Eru felt more justified to kill than now. He controlled the fate of this mass murderer. Telu deserved a fate more painful and cruel than anything Eru could give him. His father had blood on his hands, and Eru could call him to accountability right now, and ensure that something like this never happened again.

Telu's hand moved to one of his many concealed daggers. His uncanny hearing registered the grating sound of the blade coming from its sheath. Eru would make Telu's death slow. The agonizing deaths of Telu's victims demanded that justice. The knife moved slowly, cutting a long painful gash up Telu's forearm. Eru's knowledge guided the blade to inflict pain but not lethal damage. Eru willingly participated in the pain – a small penance for his failure and existence.

The memory of fifteen dead men in the streets of the Sanche District, men he had killed just yesterday, gave him pause. How many had died at his hand? Who was he to exact justice when he had taken or destroyed uncounted lives? Didn't Telu act out of his own sense of justice? Yet these reservations didn't slow the progress of the knife as it took another pass up Telu's arm.

Ama's voice of protestation clamored desperately in Eru's heart. How would she feel if her child murdered her husband? Eru released his father. The knife fell to the pavement as Telu clutched his arm and skulked furiously away from the scene of his crime. Telu knew he had failed again. Next time it would be perfect.

Aitrox had a lot to think about, even while twenty slaves served her needs and thirty of her subordinate archos held worship services under her control. She couldn't remember the last time something had surprised her. Archos had always proved predictable before, but this Streetborn caught her off guard and made life interesting. He possessed something she hadn't believed any archos could preserve: a sense of compassion. That would be a fun thing for her to toy with.

The new Streetborn hadn't been the only surprise, making this the most exciting week in centuries. She never would have guessed a Hider would try to kill one of her archos in the middle of worship, or that he would succeed and live to tell about it. Somehow, the Hider had managed to break her hold on her pursuers – yet another impossibility. At least it broke the monotony of immortality. She hated Hiders, but their existence made her wonder. All the other Aegendi unlocked amazing potential under archos control, perhaps her greatest triumph. The Hiders represented the culmination of her enemies' subtle manipulations, but they should still be like other Aegendi. What would happen if she could seize a Hider? Would that power amplify under archos control? She almost felt giddy with excitement for a new challenge. Just detecting a Hider is almost impossible, and her past attempts to seize one had failed. If the Hiders exhibited the same tendency as the other Aegendi, then even her powerful mind could scarcely imagine the possibilities.

CHAPTER 4

ZEALOT

Our very existence polarized people. My father, and the group of heretics he belonged to represent one extreme. On the other end of the spectrum you found zealots. Most in the congregations attended out of fear, or a false belief that worship reduced their chances of being seized. Some, however, worshiped the archos with zeal equal to my father's. In both the heretics' and the zealots' minds the archos enjoyed a deified status. The only difference was their choice to

worship or destroy their deity. I almost accepted the view
of myself as deity, as most archos do. Life would certainly
have been easier if I had.

Tears streamed from Eru's blank eyes and down his grey splotchy cheeks. He pushed the driver of his carriage with the fury and anger that burned within him. The carriage rocked gently with the fast travel. The passenger-side wheels of the carriage lifted off the road slightly as he swerved around a slower coach. He smiled at the angry curses and unique hand gestures of the driver he passed, and the people he sent diving out of his way.

Eru didn't care about life anymore. He hated everything, hated the guilt he felt for failing hundreds of people back at Jordan's shop. Life hated Eru, and right now he returned the sentiment. Sowing death was his only true talent, that or failing whatever he set out to do. He saw a murky puddle in a low spot on the street and swerved the carriage towards it. Muddy grime splashed onto the pedestrians on the sidewalk, and all over his driver. A particularly well dressed woman screamed her displeasure over her ruined gown. Her escort grabbed a rock and hurled it at the carriage, his suit coat and finery hardly any better off. The rock hit the wall of the carriage with a thump that made Eru chortle. At least someone shared some of his fury.

In better circumstances, he would have noticed the gradual return of his mental capacities. In his current state of mind, the unfortunate timing would have only added to his frustration. He felt the world around him with clarity again, sensing he had traveled far enough to have outrun the word of Telu's latest attempt at his life. The people went about their business, oblivious to the carnage a few miles away. His directionless flight from the disaster took him to the heart of Deor. The Grand citadel, more a palatial complex than a single building, climbed into the sky on the other side of the Deor River. Towering spires jutted into the heavens with sharp violent points. Cruel spikes crowned the top of the outer walls. Even the massive statues of Aitrox bore sinister spiked crowns, for reasons Eru could never guess. Only two bridges granted access to the island citadel: one on the east, and one on the west.

Eru sensed a large congregation in a smaller citadel as his carriage charged past. He feared the congregations for what they could reveal about his people. The only other time he had neared a worship meeting, he sensed the overwhelming fear coming from the people inside, and refused to believe anything worthy of adoration could inspire such feelings. This time as he rushed past, Eru had to know. He had to see what could draw people to these congregations. He suspected that many came by archos compulsion, but didn't believe that could possibly explain the tremendous numbers of worshipers. Maybe he would find something in the citadels that could end his hatred of himself and his people.

His carriage nearly swerved out of control with the abrupt halt he compelled the driver to make. He knew better than to enter the citadel himself, but he wanted to have a few eyes and ears inside. He climbed out of the carriage and then released the driver and his irritated passenger. The driver grimaced in disgust as he tried to scrub the mud off his vest.

Eru watched the worship service from eight different views, surprised at the variety he found in the attitudes of those he controlled. Four of them showed the fear he had expected, a fear now escalated to furious terror at the betrayal of their hopes. They had been seized in the past and believed that attendance at worship would protect them from repeat occurrences. Three of the others he controlled had come due to a strange curiosity, but the last one completely took him off guard.

Ado, the first zealot Eru had ever encountered, rejoiced at being seized. He worshiped the archos much like a hostage could grow to love his captor. He lacked none of the fear at being seized, but in his warped eyes he had been granted communion with the will of Aitrox. Eru had hoped to find love for the archos in a devoted worshiper. Perhaps Ado loved Eru in his own way.

Eru watched a group of people walk an injured man up to a statue of Aitrox, his arm badly mangled and bleeding from some sort of terrible accident. He saw the unmistakable pain in the man's eyes, wondering what he could possibly hope to gain by worship. Had Eru not seen it through eight pairs of eyes, he wouldn't have believed the miraculous healing. In a matter of moments, the man's arm returned to its perfect, whole state.

"Praise Aitrox!" the healed man exclaimed. "Blessed be the name of Aitrox forever for healing me!"

The furor in the congregation exploded with excitement, and left Eru confused. He sensed the wonder in the crowd, and couldn't figure out what this could possibly mean.

"Accept Aitrox and be one with her will, and you too can be blessed," a large man's booming voice declared from the stage.

"The archos are agents of her will. Praise the archos!" another voice called.

Eru looked up to the stage at the archos who led the congregation. She wore a small tiara of iron, demonstrating her high favor before Aitrox. She raised her hand, and Eru watched in bewilderment as five or six people in the crowd lifted off the ground with her motions. Cries of adulation and amazement filled the citadel as the worshipers flew through the air.

"Aitrox has smiled on this congregation!" the sonorous voice on stage proclaimed. Eru felt a strange desire to please the deep voice that called to the congregation. He noticed how the man's words stoked the flames of devotion in the crowds and incited a multitude of spontaneous exclamations of devotion.

Eru released and seized people rapidly, jumping through the crowd. Were these miracles real? If so, could Eru perform them? Could the archos really possess such power? Eru understood engineering and construction enough to conceive rigs with wires and mirrors to create such miracles and illusions, but nothing that could have worked from so many different vantage points. As if in response to his thoughts, he watched as the flying worshipers crossed paths in ways that couldn't have happened with cords. How did the archos tap into such powers? Everything Eru had learned from seized professors, scientists and engineers told him such things should have been impossible. He seized others near the healed man, scrutinizing his arm and looking for any indication of fraud. Injuries could be easily faked, but the lingering blood on the man's torn shirt looked and smelled convincing. He had sensed the pain and fear in the man's heart, both almost impossible to fake.

Eru released his people in the citadel and withdrew, shaken to his core. All his life he had fought against who he was, determined not to be the evil his father saw. Had his father been the one in the wrong? Did the archos enjoy some form of divine mandate as the worship services taught? Perhaps those who refused to accept archos divinity would see them as evil, but why would one who served a goddess care what they thought? Eru had refused to believe the accounts of miracles, assuming even memories of others to be clever fabrications of the archos. He had always believed the congregations and citadels to be an evil scheme for Aitrox to dominate and control masses far larger than she could ever reach through compulsion alone.

Eru maintained his hold on Ado, the one who dreaded yet worshiped him. Was it right for one to fear his gods in this way? As the worshipers dispersed with the ending of the service, Eru led Ado out to the alleyway where Eru remained concealed. Only when he saw himself through Ado's eyes could Eru safely move from his hiding place. Eru felt the surprise and the strange sense of elation from the worshiper when Ado first saw him. Ado felt honored that Eru had chosen him, privileged to be one who could help a young god grow into greatness. Eru found comfort in the implications of this man's worship. A deity didn't have to question his right to take a life. In this man's eyes, the fifteen whom Eru had killed just the day before only further exalted him. In this man's eyes, Eru couldn't have failed at Jordan's shop. Even those deaths demonstrated the will of deity. Eru released the man and smiled as Ado knelt uncompelled before him and kissed his feet.

"Oh, blessed archos!" he said quietly as he groveled at Eru's feet.

"My name is Eru." Eru spoke through an onlooker he seized.

"Praise Eru!" the man said. Eru had never heard another speak his name, finding it impossible not to seize the man who called his attention so explicitly. Eru could get used to the strange pleasure Ado took in becoming one with a god.

Aitrox almost felt disappointment at the Streetborn's latest decisions. She had been watching him with a Reader to get insights into his thoughts and emotions. If he came into line so easily, perhaps she simply hadn't given him enough time to mature and become an archos like all her other underlings. She sighed in disappointment at the thought. Bringing him in line was supposed to be fun.

Even the schemes of the greater archos within her citadel left her bored. Oso, a mid-level archos in her citadel, had ambitions to overthrow her, but posed no threat. Only her original enemies, the vyeshen, even had remote potential to challenge her. She feared the unknown the vyeshen represented, but almost longed for them to make a move. Constantly scouring the city for evidence of their influence bored her to no end.

At least Aitrox could enjoy watching some of Oso's schemes unfold, though she had seen similar schemes hundreds of times. Murder and violence among her subordinate archos always had a flare for the dramatic, but she found she needed to find ways to make even that more interesting. Oso believed that he could rival Aitrox after claiming the Aegendi from Leo, the Grand Archos second only to herself. Oso had spent years secretly marshaling Aegendi, or at least he thought it had all been secret. He had avoided Leo's notice only because Aitrox had kept him distracted and frequently seized. She was bored of Leo, and ready for a new Grand Archos to try and supplant her.

Leo didn't have a chance against the force Oso had marshaled. Any moment now and Oso would play his hand. Leo had grown too complacent, confident that Aitrox would never let an inferior archos supplant him. Aitrox could hardly wait for the feelings of shock and betrayal Leo would feel before he died. She seized one of Leo's servants and watched Leo's pending doom with a bored smile on her face. At least the servant she had seized would give her a good view of the fight.

Leo sensed Oso's lethal intent, but lacked the power to seize his foe. It hardly mattered. Oso would learn the foolishness of challenging the Grand Archos who had Aitrox's protection. Leo had felt the power of Aitrox, leaving even him feeling like a toddler commanded by a domineering mother. She would never let Oso defeat him. Leo sensed Oso outside his chamber, ready to come and kill him, or die trying.

Leo stood and willed two of his Brutes to hold the chamber door closed. Two Brutes could rip the doors off their hinges, or make them virtually impassable. Oso should have at least challenged him in a less defensible position. He seized his Prophet staring at the door, anxious to see if Oso had some tricks up his sleeve. He saw the doors explode off the hinges, tossing his Brutes like dolls. The Prophet's foresight gave him just enough warning to will his Wizards to push back against the door and avert the crisis. He hadn't expected Oso to have enough Wizards to send the heavy, Brute-enforced doors flying. Where was Aitrox's help?

With his Wizards pushing back on the door, and his Brutes offering rein-forcement, Leo could still survive this encounter. Perhaps that was why Aitrox hadn't intervened yet. She had more important things to do when she could trust in his capabilities to carry the day. Leo smiled at the implicit vote of confidence from Aitrox.

The windows exploded chaotically as three people swung into his chamber from above. Leo quickly had a Wizard divert his effort momentarily from the door to push shards of glass through the assailants, almost laughing at Oso's stupidity. A large shard impaled one man, but he barely noticed it jutting out of his ribs. All three attackers pulled large chunks of glass from their bodies and dropped the grizzly crimson daggers nonchalantly. Three Immortals! Where was Aitrox? Leo realized now that she had forsaken him. He named her openly in his thoughts, and she ignored such an affront to her senses. She had to know of Oso's plans, and that could mean only one thing.

The three Immortals charged, but he easily held all three Immortals at bay with the foresight and agility of his Prophet. He had given his Prophet an iron blade with Aitrox's leave, and the Prophet made good use of it. With the foresight the Prophet granted, Leo could use all his servants with the lethal agility and balance of a predator. One Immortal paused to hold her severed foot in place long enough for it to reattach. The Prophet easily held the other two at bay in the meantime. Leo had been wise to keep his Prophet secret from his underlings. Without it, the three Immortals would have been his end.

The heavy doors to his chamber suddenly burst open, as Leo brought his Brutes into the more urgent battle with Leo's Immortals. Leo's Brutes and Wizards hadn't anticipated the sudden change, and the door exploded outward. A barrage of copper balls showered into his chamber, but Leo's Wizards stopped them before they could strike any of his Aegendi. A few struck the three Immortals, bursting through their ribs and heads with gruesome showers of red. The Immortals barely noticed the wounds, as the holes closed almost instantly.

A man and woman jumped into the chamber through the windows, moving with the balance and grace of Prophets. How had Oso hidden two Prophets from him? Leo knew his end had come. Oso had bested him and Aitrox had betrayed him. He would at least deprive Oso of the benefit of having his Aegendi. Leo willed each of his Aegendi to plunge blades into their chests, but Oso's two Prophets gave him the foresight to foil even that. Oso's Wizards locked the hands of the Prophet and two Wizards, leaving the two Brutes and one Wizard to die. Leo let himself feel the pain of his dying Aegendi. Somehow, feeling their pain made his own death more real.

CHAPTER 5

HIDER

Part of me enjoyed the short years with zealots serving my needs. I look back on this time in my life with mixed feelings. My zealots allowed me to grow my power by serving and protecting me even when I hadn't seized them. In that way, this time laid a foundation I would desperately need. For a short time, I enjoyed respite from self-doubt and loathing, but claiming the role of a young deity felt terribly wrong in the deepest part of my heart. Increasingly, I found that I loathed my zealots, and that brought up a question I never could answer to my satisfaction. Shouldn't a god love those who worship him?

Eru effortlessly controlled twenty minds throughout the city. Being able to extend his will for miles allowed him to settle into a villa without worrying about being discovered. Eru had gotten used to the feeling he was being watched, believing it to be a natural consequence of his developing awareness. He felt hatred emanating from most minds he controlled. Even the five zealots in his dominion both loved and hated being seized in a cruelly masochistic way.

Eru kept Ado by his side, having the zealot massage his neck and apply ointment to his grey skin. Eru couldn't feel the cramps in his neck from supporting his larger skull, but he believed the massages improved his capacity to control. Ado took great honor being the one Eru had chosen as his personal attendant. Whenever Eru released the man, Ado praised him, profusely begging for Eru to seize him again. Eru had learned to resist the pull of his spoken name, but not easily. Usually he didn't bother fighting it, having no reason to do so.

Eru had taken a small villa in the Praton District, a well-to-do neighborhood, for himself. Located in front of a beautiful park on a quiet street lined with maples, the place was an ideal home for Eru. Fall in particular was a spectacular season on this street as the green turned to vibrant hues of gold and red.

Eru loved the location, as much for its beauty as for the nature of the environment itself. Unlike the slums, the people here lived free from the constant nagging of hunger or the stress of paying the next rent payment. Unlike the truly wealthy in Deor, the people here seemed to understand money, letting it serve them rather than enslave them. Families frequented the park, and Eru relished the pleasure and happiness he sensed from parents and children at play every day. As children romped in the piling leaves, Eru too got to feel something of what it would be like to be a child.

Eru would have paid five times what the landlord charged for his place, prizing it as perhaps the most beautiful place in the world. Of course, he had no shortage of access to funds, though he preferred not to simply steal the money. Practicing the trades and skills he knew from those he seized at least provided something to keep his mind busy, and a means to help others in his own way. Right now, one of his zealots worked in a clinic, easily convincing the busy staff he was a doctor from out of town. Eru's knowledge served the clinic well, and it brought in good money. A younger man he controlled picked up work assisting a master blacksmith after Eru arranged for the blacksmith's apprentice to miss work for a few days. Eru smiled at the smith's effusive praise over the masterful work Eru crafted through the youth he controlled.

"You sure you never worked a smith before, Jeo?" the blacksmith said gruffly to the boy.

"Never, but my father sold anvils," the youth answered, as Eru chuckled at his joke and the nonplussed look from the smith.

"By the High Queen, that didn't make any sense. Your father sold anvils." The smith shook his head. Eru sensed the discomfort in the blacksmith, feeling his thoughts touch on concerns about drawing Aitrox's attention with his loose tongue.

Eru particularly enjoyed working the forges. He left all the senses unfiltered from the youth, relishing the heat, the noise, the smells and even the rattling vibration of the hammer as it reverberated up his arm. He loved the forges, but didn't work them simply for pleasure. If anybody knew why Aitrox controlled the supply of iron so aggressively, Eru knew it would be the blacksmiths.

Eru kept the money earned by his zealots, but always left half the pay earned by others he seized. They invariably felt ill-served by the archos who put them to work and stole half their earnings - never mind the fact that many he seized started the day begging. If they could just get past being seized, they had an opportunity to learn a trade and get out of the gutters. The nearest slum to his villa, Oak Hollows, felt identical to the Sanche district in all the ways that mattered. After a week or two working a person, some showed promise to continue in their vocation without Eru's intervention.

In most cases, he didn't bother with a second day. Most in the slums lived under control of a different kind of monster, every bit as dominating over their minds and bodies. People rarely fell so low without the help of alcohol or opiates. Others born in the mire often succumbed to the same monster, learning by example, or just seeking escape. Short of controlling such people for months on end, Eru knew he could do nothing to stop them from finding refuge in their addictions after the trauma of being seized. Did their earnings for the day of work only exacerbate the problem? Eru had to hope otherwise, or he would have stopped trying altogether.

Eru worked every day, a munificent benefactor to those he seized, despite the frustrations at his own inability to help people out of their destructive cycles of addiction. He had taken at least one person out of the slums in his year of trying. In the same timeframe, uncounted numbers fell short, leaving Eru increasingly frustrated. Shouldn't a god have more power to benefit his underlings? So long as those he seized hated him, the majority would reject his generosity simply out of ignorance. They would never understand his magnanimous intent.

When the day wound to a close and the blacksmith paid Jeo, Eru let him go with the full purse. He felt generous today, having found the day working the forge particularly invigorating. The boy showed promise for Eru's next success. It had been a long time since Eru had found someone to teach for a second day. He released Jeo with high hopes, before turning his attention to a less pleasant task back at the forge.

Eru would have loathed scouring a mind a year ago, but he had left the naïve days of his youth behind. Scouring amplified the trauma of being seized as Eru probed deep into every recess of the blacksmith's mind. He peeled away old suppressed memories, discovering the details of a forgotten childhood nightmare. He dug through every conversation the smith ever had. Eru experienced every moment of the smith's life, able to recall it all perfectly for his own uses afterwards. Scouring a mind often left the victim incapacitated for hours, but Eru had a question he wanted answered. This smith had knowledge that touched on the black market for iron, but whoever oversaw the smuggling operations knew to take extreme precautions against incursions just like this one. This smith had even worked iron before, but he never saw the face of the person who delivered it to his forge.

By the time he finished scouring the blacksmith, the lamplighters had lit the streetlamps to fight off the darkness. Eru had brought his zealots back to the villa with his usual reflexive precautions. Telu was still out there, and Eru sometimes wondered if his father could identify any of his zealots. As a precaution he brought them all home through very round-about ways. He even checked one into an inn for the night before having him sneak out of his room. Eru knew his zealots needed to sleep, and looked forward to another night without holding anyone under his control. He released Ado from his control so Ado could sleep.

"Praaiise Errru," Ado said with a slur in his voice. He spoke with that slur more frequently, now. Perhaps Eru needed to let him get more sleep at night.

Eru sat in his villa with his ten faithful zealots sleeping peacefully around him. He felt the hunger to seize others, but knew he could easily resist that urge all night. Eru couldn't stop thinking about the boy, Jeo. The boy had so much promise, he just couldn't stop hoping that he could bring this boy out of the ghetto. Before he realized it, he had let his awareness wander to find Jeo back in his shanty. He seized Jeo's sister to get an update.

Tears ran down Jeo's cheeks as he hid his face in shame. Eru had seen that shame in many he seized, never quite able to understand it.

"Give me the money, Jeo," his father, Boro, said gruffly. Jeo handed the bag of coins over silently. Boro whistled as he counted the coins. "You did well!"

"I told you, I didn't do anything," Jeo said, his voice muffled as he buried his face, sitting in a fetal position.

"Hey, good fortune like this doesn't come our way very often." Boro smiled.

"What's so good about it?" Jeo said, casting an angry glance at his father.

"Hey, son, I am sorry about what happened to you. Come on, I'll cheer you up." Boro offered him his hand and pulled him to his feet. "It's time to make a man out of you," Boro said as he pulled out a bottle of cheap whiskey.

Eru tried to seize Boro and stop him before he could do the damage, but realized his senses felt nothing where Boro should have been. How could that be possible? Why now of all times? Eru watched in consternation as Jeo took his first sip of whiskey.

"That's a good boy," Boro said as he ran a hand through his son's hair. Jeo smiled and finished his shot glass.

Eru pushed with all his might to seize Boro, but felt not even the slightest awareness of the man's mind. Unable to watch the man drink away his new hope, Eru released his eyes in the shanty and returned to his usual nightly void. Why couldn't he help even a young boy like Jeo?

Aitrox could hardly believe this stroke of luck. She had been growing bored of her Streetborn, finding his altruistic slant on the archos power rather mundane and quaint. Still, she kept a Reader close enough to check up on him regularly, and it had just paid a big dividend. Had this Streetborn just succeeded in finding a Hider? She hadn't guessed that watching the unusual little Streetborn could have been so worthwhile. The best part about it was that this drunk had no idea who, or what, he was. Had he known, he would have severed all connections to family for theirs and his sake. He still loved his family, giving Aitrox the perfect opportunity. She could hardly wait for the Streetborn to go away, but she knew this had to be one of her deepest secrets. Finally, she seized the boy and made her move.

"Boro," Aitrox said through Jeo. Somehow it never mattered who she spoke through, there could be no doubting the authority behind her voice. Boro dropped his bottle of whiskey with a start.

"Who are you?" Boro asked with a nervous slur in his voice.

"The High Queen," she said, knowing he would believe.

"Aitrox!" he exclaimed, fear filling his countenance.

"Boro, open your mind to me," she commanded.

"What?" he said in confusion.

"Open your mind to me," she persisted. Jeo slapped his father across the cheek.

"Impossible! You can't seize me!"

"You are trying my patience." Just to show him she meant business, Aitrox smashed Jeo's head into the corner of the table. He fell to the floor in a gruesome heap with a lethal wound to his forehead.

"Jeo!" Boro screamed, terror burning in his eyes. "Please, no!" he wailed as he collapsed over his son's dead body.

"Boro!" His daughter spoke, her young voice carrying the same authority and presence. "Your daughter will be next."

"Ok, ok please! Let her live. I'll do anything!" Boro knelt before his daughter, his eyes red with grief and his cheeks soaked with tears.

"Open your mind to me," Aitrox commanded again.

"I don't know how!" he exclaimed.

"One," Aitrox said ominously as Boro's daughter pressed a fork to her neck in warning.

"How?" he begged.

"Two," she continued. Just before she said three, she sensed Boro's presence and seized it immediately. Once she seized him, she killed the daughter, the only witness to her discovery. This had to be one of her closest kept secrets.

"Good morning," Aymis said with her usual smile as she popped her head into the baker's shop.

"Aymis, it's far too early for you to be so bright-eyed," the baker said in return.

"Hey, my friend," she winked with her salutation, "your day's already half over. Doesn't that make it about noon for you?" she laughed.

"Don't remind me," he said with a groaning yawn as he stretched his arms above and behind him.

"The rolls smell delicious this morning!" Aymis took a deep breath and exhaled with a smile on her face.

"Yeah, they do," the baker said, but Aymis heard something more. *I'm so tired of the smell of flour and yeast, you have no idea.*

"How could you get tired of that smell?" Aymis asked.

"I never said that..." the baker said defensively. "How did you..."

"I don't know what you mean," Aymis stammered. "I'll have my usual order please," she said, pretending to inspect some pastries she couldn't afford.

"There you go, two loaves fresh out of the oven," the baker said with a yawn.

"Thank you, my friend," Aymis said with her usual smile. "Have a good afternoon!" Aymis laughed at her joke as she stepped out of his bakery. She made her way through the empty streets, smiling kindly at the lamplighter who snuffed out the streetlamp as the morning light slowly grew.

Why's she so happy? Aymis heard the thought in her mind, sensing the lamplighter's sour disposition over the chilly morning. Her smile quickly vanished, and she hurried back to her small flat. Was she going insane? How did she hear these voices? Could she really be hearing people's thoughts?

She slipped into her flat as quietly as the squeaky door allowed, hoping not to disturb her mother, Janis. Janis worked a night shift as a maid in a nobleman's home. She had expected the job to be easy, but her master had a nasty habit of leaving big messes in the dining room, kitchen or ballroom for his night staff to have cleaned by morning. Aymis's job felt easy by comparison, though her hands often ached after a long day working in a tile factory.

She quickly swept the dust from the cracked ceiling off the counter, and unwrapped one of the fresh loaves of bread. Taking another deep whiff of the aroma, she honestly couldn't understand how the baker could ever get tired of that smell. She pulled a chunk of bread from the loaf and ate her breakfast with a content smile on her face. She saw the crack in the ceiling, felt the ache in her hands from the long days in the factory, and shared her mother's worries about paying next month's rent, but none of that mattered right now. She savored the fresh bread with a swig of goat's milk, grateful for what she had. So many people were lucky to have anything to eat, much less fresh baked bread for breakfast. She woke early every morning to let her mother take their only bed when she finished her shift, but she counted them both lucky to have jobs and a mattress to sleep on.

Aymis cringed at the squeaky front door as she stepped into the hall and headed down the stairs. She wrapped her old, worn scarf around her neck to fight off the brisk morning air. Fallen leaves blew in the breeze, and clouds glowed with similar orange hues with the sunrise. She shivered with the chill as she rubbed her arms to keep warm. Aymis looked forward to the heat of the factory on a chilly day like this. She signed the factory roll card as she started her day.

"Good morning, Elle," Aymis greeted the secretary who watched the log book.

"Good morning," Elle replied. *What is her name again?*

"It's Aymis," she offered without realizing she had done it again.

"Excuse me?" Elle asked, a bewildered look on her face.

"My name," Aymis offered with a smile. "It's Aymis."

"Of course," Elle said.

"Have a good day, Elle," Aymis said as she stepped onto the factory floor to work.

"You, too," Elle said with a forced smile. *That was strange.*

Aymis struggled with the tedious work on the factory floor that morning. In theory, the confused thoughts that filled her mind shouldn't have affected her productivity with such a repetitive task. However, a single question raced through her mind, constantly distracting her from anything else. *What is happening to me?*

Telu knew he took terrible risks by watching the villa, if his suspicions proved correct. Sources told him of a regular group of four men and one woman who appeared to live in the villa. He had one followed for a few weeks just to be sure. The same person worked in a medical clinic for a few days before moving to a blacksmith's forge, and even to a shoe maker's shop once. He saw the indicators he looked for, and could only hope his observations had escaped notice.

If he lost the trail again, the closing window of opportunity would be forever lost. For all he knew, Eru had already matured and grown too aware for any plans to have a chance at succeeding. He couldn't afford to fail like he had with the lamp maker. Failure now would mean he could only hope to succeed by finding a Hider; possibly more difficult than his current goal. Only a Reader had any chance of recognizing a Hider, if anybody did. Failure now meant he may die with his ambition unfulfilled, so he resolved to pull out all the stops. This time it would be flawless.

CHAPTER 6

READER

I struggled to understand why I despised my own zealots. Once I recognized the cause, it felt so obvious. I loathed the pretext of piety which they used to mask their desire to avoid accountability. Rather than live their life and accept the consequences, they had their archos live it for them. Why should I be charged with living their lives when I hardly knew how to live my own? I couldn't have known the effect my prolonged domination over the zealots would have, but I *do not hold myself fully responsible for destroying them. For fleeing the weight of consequence, they brought the heaviest, most terrible consequence on themselves.*

That night may have been the longest in Eru's life. His jaw clenched in anger and frustration: anger at a world that naturally pulled everyone in it down, a sort of personal gravity; frustration at the consistency of his failures. Perhaps going against the grain of his nature could only leave splinters and marred wood after all.

He wanted to do something to make the world a better place, a place where people could thrive and find happiness, a place where archos could do something other than traumatize and ruin lives. Eru tried to fight his way out of his self-pity. The constant fearing for Jeo's welfare filled his mind and slowed the passage of time. Eru desperately wanted to check up on the boy, yet he couldn't bear to find the youth a ruined drunk. Had he brought that on the boy?

Eru almost wished he could sleep, like the zealots around him. He let his mind touch Ado's sleeping consciousness, surprised at how little he sensed. Usually a sleeping mind, while relatively inactive, still worked over the happenings of the day. Ado's mind felt... empty. Ado didn't even dream.

Eru's powerful archos mind wandered, even while Jeo dominated his primary thoughts and concerns. Nighttime was always a surreal and unusual experience as Eru's senses touched on the dreams of the sleeping. Tonight as the minutes dragged on, Eru felt himself trapped in a dark nightmare, unable to escape. Eru remembered the first nightmares he had ever sensed. Dark creatures haunted Ama's sleep with dreams so vivid, she could scarcely differentiate them from waking. Things lurked in the shadows, furtive and stealthy, watching her. She tried to tell Telu of the dreadful winged creature, watching her like a gargoyle, but never could bring herself to do so. Eru remembered her dreams of trips into the alleys near her home, irresistibly compelled to seek the being she knew watched her. The aquiline creatures clung to the alley walls, with hook-like claws on their unusual wings. Their piercing gaze sent chills down her spine, and left Eru grateful not to dream.

Trea, one of the zealots, stirred as the first hints of the morning light filled the room. Even without another's senses to verify, the regularity of Trea's morning routine told him sunrise wasn't far off. Trea sat up, and with her waking mind came the stronger pull to seize her. Eru felt that hunger, like a person wanting food. He always prolonged his fast, though his zealots' waking minds stirred his appetite like the aroma of fresh bread stirs a starving beggar. After a long night in the void, the first zealot to turn their thoughts to him, or speak his name, would be an impossible force to resist.

"Praiiiissse Errruuu," Ado groaned, sounding as drunk as Eru feared Jeo was. Eru seized him, sensing the relief in Ado's mind even as Eru revisited his most painful memory.

"Catch me, uncle Ado!" Jana exclaimed gleefully as she readied to jump from a tree branch that was level with Ado's shoulders.

"Wait your turn, dear," He said as he turned to help Lena, Jana's more cautious twin sister, down from a different tree. Jana jumped anyway. Desperately, Ado tried to help both his nieces, his mind working so quickly that only in recollection could he recognize how it processed the choices and the consequences instantly. He simply didn't have the agility nor did he have enough hands to keep both girls from getting hurt. Catching Lena in a one armed hug against his ribs, he reached for Jana with his other hand. He caught hold of her arm, but his grasp only worsened Jana's fall by pulling her awkwardly forward. She landed terribly, knees striking the ground first and her body snapping like a whip and smashing her face into the grass. "Jana!" Ado exclaimed as he hurriedly set Lena down and turned the girl over. From the looks of things, she probably had a broken nose, and Ado worried about a gash on the knee that struck the ground first. "Jana, I am so sorry! Tell me where it hurts," Ado said kindly.

"My nose," she said almost unintelligibly, due to her tears, the bleeding nose itself and her banged up lip.

"Here, hold this to your nose," Ado pulled out a handkerchief from his vest and gave it to her. Nothing happened. "Jana, please take..." Jana's terrified exclamation cut Ado off.

"I can't move my hand!" she exclaimed, a flash of panic in her eyes.

"Lena, hold the handkerchief to your sister's nose," Ado said firmly. Lena obeyed immediately, despite being terribly squeamish about blood. Surely Jana was just a bit shocked from the fall. Ado pulled out a spare handkerchief, something he always knew came in handy on the days he watched his nieces, and readied to clean Jana's cut knee. "Jana, this is going to sting some," he said before touching the cloth gently to the wound. Jana didn't even flinch. That was the moment when Ado knew his beautiful niece would never be the same.

Ado's brother, Joro, never forgave him for what happened to his daughter. Try as he could, Ado never could convince Joro how impossible the situation had been. Ado never forgave himself either. Choice and consequence had cursed his niece, and Ado despised the unfairness of it all. Even though being seized revisited that terrible memory with his niece, at least it brought him relief from ever having to make such an impossible choice again. The archos gods were the ones who should decide people's fates, not him.

Ado seemed particularly lethargic this morning. Eru loved mornings, hardly able to understand how so many people struggled with them. He felt the differences in the minds of those he seized, but Eru found even foggy, waking minds refreshing after the long nights. Not too long ago, Eru had lacked the endurance to last the whole night without seizing someone in their sleep. Seizing people in their sleep served an archos poorly. They could compel them to wakefulness, but could do nothing about their lethargic minds and bodies. Leaving them asleep invariably filled their nights with terrible nightmares. Eru preferred remaining in the void, alone with the only sense he possessed. Now, through Ado, he relished the sunlight streaming through the blinds in his villa.

He walked Ado to the window, and pushed the blinds aside. Eru felt the chill of the morning creeping through the windows. Outside, the fiery red leaves of a maple tree still clung to the branches, while dried leaves from other trees swirled in the breeze. Eru seized a pedestrian, momentarily interrupting his walk to work so he could enjoy the sound of the blowing leaves, and the touch of the cool autumn air on his cheeks. The passerby breathed in deeply, and Eru felt the cool air fill his lungs invigoratingly. He released the worker, sensing the man's confusion, and relief, that he had been released so quickly.

The pleasure of feeling the world come alive around him couldn't take his thoughts away from his fear for Jeo. He didn't know what he would find when he let his awareness search for the boy. He searched for Jeo in his shanty, surprised not to find him there. Had he passed out somewhere in the slums? Eru tried to find the younger sister, but she couldn't be found either. What had happened? Eru had to get eyes in the home immediately to find out. He seized a neighbor and ran to investigate.

Eru had experienced his share of death, but that didn't lessen the horror of the gruesome scene he saw. Jeo and his sister lay dead. Eru recognized the grizzly handiwork of another archos here, but why? Why Jeo? Had he brought that fate on them? He would never know the details, but he didn't doubt that Jeo would be alive had Eru left him alone.

Eru pulled his awareness back, like a turtle pulling into its shell. He maintained his hold on his zealots. As the day advanced and the sun rose higher in the sky, Eru sank deeper into darkness and depression. His zealots reflected his dark feelings, skulking around the villa with morose expressions on their faces. Eru had Ado massage his neck, and Trea prepared dinner, as the long miserable day of hiding in the villa looked ready to lead to an equally long, miserable night.

Remembering the unusual slur in Ado's speech, he released him to sleep several hours earlier than normal. To his surprise, Ado said nothing when released. Confused by the break from the normal routine, he turned several eyes onto Ado to investigate.

Ado's eyes lolled in their sockets, his irises barely visible. His tongue sat lazily on the lip of his open mouth, and drool ran down his chin and dripped onto his chest. He made quiet moaning sounds, much like a deaf child might do without realizing others could hear him.

"Ado," Trea spoke for Eru. She reached out and tapped his shoulder, but he showed no indication he even knew others were in the room. Eru felt for

Ado with his mind, and found only a shell of the man remained. He seized him, and felt the difference immediately. He could use this shell perfectly, giving Ado a false semblance of life, but inside, Ado was a shell, his only emotion a faint sorrow for what he had become. Eru released Ado, recoiling both physically and mentally.

"K... kiiiiiillll..... m...mmmeeeee," Ado groaned softly. Eru felt something snap in Ado's mind, knowing those would be his last words. Only sorrow and regret remained in Ado's soul. Eru seized what remained of him, again finding his body functioned perfectly under Eru's control. Eru had a lifeless puppet, a shell of a man just begging to be filled by his archos mind. Eru walked Ado into the kitchen to fetch a knife before walking into the bathroom to fulfill Ado's last wish.

Telu made the final arrangements with two separate property management firms. Alone, their particular treatments to the water tanks of a few particular villas would be harmless. Overlapped in such close proximity, however...

It took him a day or two to forge the paperwork necessary to masquerade as the property owners for each of the villas. The maintenance companies wouldn't have given him the time of day without them, nor would the collections firm. However, Telu had played his role well, telling them that his tenants worked night shifts, and instructing them to chain the doors shut with a collection note left on the doors.

Last of all, Telu walked over to his counter, where a spread of unfinished letters, banners and signs lay scattered about. One wouldn't have expected such an innocuous thing like writing to be the most hazardous part of his plan. Pieces of paper covered most of the written words, lest Telu mistakenly read the message himself. He deliberately left partial words to finish, leaving only the last letter he had written visible to give him context. His head ached with concentration as he worked out the remaining letters without letting himself form the desired sentence. He finished one sign by adding the letters 'il'. On another letter he added the 'ru' at the end before folding the letter and sealing it in an envelope. One by one, he finished the banners, letters and signs. Telu smiled and sighed in relief. He had done it, and lived. He had accomplished something only a Hider would have dared, and he couldn't even tell anyone about it.

Aymis tried to focus on her work at the factory, but couldn't keep her thoughts off the strange things that had happened. During her short break for food, she decided to put a new theory to the test. She pulled opened her small personal locker and grabbed the chunk of bread from the bakery. The bread still carried the aroma she loved, and, at least in her mind, it felt slightly warm to the touch. She smiled, and took a moment to enjoy her food before turning her thoughts to her theory.

Aymis tried to watch Jeron inconspicuously, but apparently he noticed.

Why is she staring at me? Jeron gave her a quick glance before looking away.

She was right, but how? Aymis couldn't believe what she had discovered. She could hardly focus on work for the rest of the day. Repeatedly, she stopped her work to look around the factory floor to try the trick on her coworkers. It hardly mattered that work in the tile factory seemed to suppress anything but the most tiresome, bored thoughts.

"Aymis," her supervisor said with a gruff voice as he walked up to her.

"Yes, Deru," Aymis replied.

"Are you okay?" Deru asked.

"I'm a little distracted today. It's just a small personal matter," Aymis said apologetically.

"You realize that you are at least an hour off pace to meet your quota today." *She's usually one of my most productive workers.*

"I know. I'm sorry. I will make it up," Aymis said, trying not to smile at his unspoken compliment.

"I won't stay here after hours so you can meet your quota," Deru replied. *Does she think I don't have a family to go home to?*

"I am sorry, I wouldn't presume to impose on your busy schedule," Aymis replied. "Can I make up the difference by exceeding quota for a few days?"

"I don't know," Deru began, "I can't have the quality of your tiles suffer."

"They won't. Please, I can't afford to miss pay a single day. I won't be so off task tomorrow. I promise." Aymis struggled to fight back the desperation in her voice. If she missed quota even one day, she could come up short for next month's rent.

"I will be keeping an eye on your work until you make up the difference. If it were anybody else..." Deru turned and walked away, leaving the statement hanging. *Like she will actually make up her quota.*

Aymis' face flushed red, and she clenched her hand in a fist. "You calling me a liar?" She snapped, before she could stop herself.

"Excuse me?" Deru said, turning around. *By the High Queen, she's in rare form today.* "What is your problem today?"

"Whatever it is, it isn't your blasted business!" she said, again shocked at her own words.

"That's it. Get out now! Don't bother coming back tomorrow either," Deru said, his cheeks crimson, and his hands shaking.

"Please, I'm sorry. Please sir!" Aymis begged, tears streaming down her cheeks.

"I will have Elle pay you for the tiles you made today, even though you are far below quota," Deru said, as his anger simmered down. *Oh Aymis, I wish I could let this pass, but I cannot set that kind of precedent for the other workers. I'm sorry.*

Aymis stared blankly at her boss, hardly believing what had just happened. She wiped the tears from her eyes, and tried to stifle the sniffling. Only then did she realize that every pair of eyes in the factory settled squarely on her. She looked around the factory, wishing she could hide under a rock in a dark cave. A barrage of thoughts assailed her as she laid eyes on the crowds around her.

What's got her so riled up?

Stupid girl.

Looks like we'll be seeing her on the corner begging or worse.

Humph, I always wondered why Deru hired women.

Tears filled her eyes, and she pushed through the crowd, looking down at the floor in shame. *How could I have been so stupid?* Deru had treated her with more patience and kindness than she could ever have hoped for from a factory supervisor. She knew she shouldn't hold him accountable for the stray thoughts that had set her off. The High Queen knows, she had plenty of thoughts she would prefer others not hear. Even so, she heard the thoughts as if he had spoken them, and the words felt like a slap in the face. By the time she realized what had happened, it was too late.

She stopped to sign out, averting her gaze from Elle as much as possible.

"Thank you," Aymis said as she accepted the small bag of coins for her last day's work. Even in firing her, Deru had been generous. He didn't have to pay her anything if she didn't meet her quota.

"Good luck, Aymis," Elle said. *She was the only one who bothered to remember my name. Morning sign in will be more drab now.*

"You too, Elle," Aymis said, looking up and giving her a farewell smile. She stepped out of the factory and back into the busy streets of Deor. What was she going to do now? She had to find another job, or put both herself and her mother on the streets. She couldn't allow that to happen. She knew that finding another job would be difficult, but part of her couldn't help but feel excitement as her mind imagined her in a new job that paid at least double her old salary. Janis, her mother, always teased her for her unconquerable optimism. Even now as she walked back to her small flat, worry and fear surrendered to the joy of a rare opportunity for her.

She hadn't been outside the factory during the day for years, and she couldn't help but enjoy some of the sights and sounds as she walked back to her small flat. She had forgotten how many carriages filled the streets, and how much she loved horses. Their beautiful shining coats and flowing manes brought a smile to her face despite her current predicament. She saw a small crowd gathered around a street corner. A few people clapped, and others smiled and gasped at whatever they had gathered to see.

A man had a small hand-painted sign asking for money in exchange for his magic tricks. In his small top hat, she spotted enough coins to have paid several days of her salary. Aymis watched intently, hoping to discover his secret to earning such good money.

"Do another trick for me," a well-dressed gentleman said.

"That'll be five coppers," the performer responded.

"Very well, but for that much, you will use my top hat instead of one of your rigged props."

"Oh, ho, ho! I like a challenge," the performer said with a smile and a flourish of his coat. The gentleman took off his hat and set it on the ground in front of the performer.

I have never managed with something this heavy, the performer thought.

Aymis gasped in surprise as the top hat lifted off the ground, wobbling and shaking. The performer ground his teeth, and squinted his eyes in concentration. With the hat a few inches off the ground he grunted a command to the gentleman.

"Feel free to check for strings, quickly!"

The woman who held the gentleman's elbow prodded him, "Hurry, Aro!"

Aro knelt down to inspect the floating hat. He passed his hand under and above the hat. Still kneeling, he looked up at his lady, a shocked look and a smile on his face. "I don't believe it."

"By the High Queen! That's wonderful," she said with a smile.

"That will be five coppers," the performer said with a sigh as he let the hat settle back on the ground.

"Well worth it," Aro said as he dropped his coins into the man's hat.

"And here are five coppers on my part as well," the woman said as she dropped more coins in his hat with a clinking sound.

Aymis could hardly believe anything she had just seen. Just as amazing as the man's trick was the money he made sharing it. Maybe she could do something similar. The ten coppers he had just earned would be a full day's pay back at the factory. She could easily earn that much, if not more.

Aymis left the crowd and made her way to a carpentry shop, suppressing the urge to run. She couldn't afford to buy anything significant, but hoped she could get a scrap piece of wood for a good price.

"What can I do for you?" the carpenter asked as she entered the shop. *Poor wretch, probably wants a job.*

"I would like to buy one of your scraps of wood, please," Aymis said with an eager smile.

"What are you going to use it for?" he asked.

"I just need to make a small sign," Aymis said.

"Will this do?" he asked, showing her a piece that far exceeded her expectations.

"Well, how much do you want for it?" she asked.

"One copper," the carpenter replied.

"I'll tell you what," Aymis began, "if I can tell you what you are thinking, I get the piece for free. If I'm wrong, I'll pay two coppers for it."

"All right," he said with a smile. "What am I thinking right now?"

"'This sure beats dealing with another unqualified job applicant'," Aymis said confidently.

"Well, I'll be!" he said grinning. "Here you go."

"Thank you, sir," Aymis said, taking the wood and leaving the shop before he could change his mind. Aymis smiled like a kid in a candy store and a full purse of coins. This was going to work. Having managed to get the wood for free, she had the money now to take care of the rest of her needs.

An hour later, she sat on a street corner with a small deck of tarot cards and a sign that she believed read "psychic readings, one copper." She didn't know how to read, but she could hear the calligrapher's thoughts repeating those words as he painted the letters for her.

Aymis had no idea what the Tarot cards meant, or even how they were supposed to be used. It hardly mattered for her purposes. Once she convinced her customers she possessed psychic powers, she could use the cards however she wanted and they would believe. Of course, being able to read their thoughts made the first part of her job simple enough. Part of her felt guilty for lying to these people about their future employment, the faithfulness of their lover, or the various other requests people made. She justified it all by considering her routine an entertaining performance, like the man who lifted the top hat. Business had gone well enough to more than make up for her missed quota at the tile factory.

Clink, a copper coin sounded in her open bag of coins.

"Let me guess, you'll start by telling me what I am thinking," a man said as he sat down next to her on the curb and looked her in the eyes. "So, tell me, what am I thinking right now?"

"'This is a sure-fire way to get seized and enslaved,'" Aymis said, before the meaning of the words sunk in.

Aymis's eyes bulged with fear. "Who are you?"

CHAPTER 7

HARBINGER OF DEATH

Ado's fate shook me to the core, the final nail in the coffin of Eru the benevolent god. It seemed that accepting the notion of archos supremacy could only lead me to become the same malevolent force as all the other archos, a fate I refused to accept. For a year, I found shelter from the world that hated me in the notion of archos divinity. More importantly, my time as a benevolent deity, albeit a failed one, gave me purpose to drive away the self-loathing. Ado's *death destroyed my house of straws, leaving me completely exposed to the world's hostility, and my own self-image.*

"Leave me!" Eru shouted via his zealot named Trea. Eru refused to seize any others, wanting them to leave of their own volition.

"We would never leave you, Eru!" Choro, the youngest of the zealots exclaimed.

"Don't you see what happened to Ado? Worshiping an archos destroyed him!" Eru exclaimed.

"It didn't destroy him, he found communion with the will of the archos," Choro objected.

"No. There was nothing but regret and sorrow left. The archos will bring you a fate worse than death," Eru rejoined.

"Trea! How can you say these things?" Choro objected. "How can you blaspheme the archos so openly?"

Eru wanted to scream at them all, but realized that words couldn't change their minds. In desperation he tried seizing Choro, hoping that a new voice may have greater impact.

"Go, and never return! I am a harbinger of death!" Choro shouted at the rest of the zealots.

"No!" Trea objected as soon as Eru released her. "Eru is just trying our devotion! It is all a test. Ado passed and found harmony with the archos!"

"Praise Eru! We will not forsake you!" all the zealots exclaimed.

"Please!" Eru begged, using Trea and Choro in unison. "This is not some twisted notion of a trial of your faith! Worshiping the archos will destroy you! Take your lives back." Eru saw the fervor that burned in their eyes, but felt the fear buried beneath their devotion. If Eru spoke the truth, then Trea had forsaken her budding family for a lie. If Eru spoke the truth then Choro had left a lucrative career and a fiancé who loved him for nothing. If he spoke the truth, then responsibility weighed heavily on their shoulders, for each of them had chosen to embrace and worship the archos. Eru had never felt so helplessly incapable of influencing others.

"Gaaahh!" Eru exclaimed. He wasn't used to feeling so powerless and impotent. He could make them do anything he wished, but his power of compulsion could never touch what a person chose to believe.

Finally, in complete exasperation, Eru seized each of his zealots and took them into different parts of the city. Closing their eyes, he spun them around until the combined dizziness of all ten nearly made Eru topple over in his villa. Next, Eru seized escorts to take each of his zealots and walk them another mile or two into the city before opening their eyes and releasing them. He made sure to avoid any dangerous parts of the city, knowing they would be lost late into the night.

Eru knew they would find their way back to the villa by morning, despite his best efforts to get them lost in the city. He seized a pedestrian walking home from a day's work in a nearby textile mill, and used the worker to guide himself away from his home. Eru longed for one more day to enjoy the park, and the advancing fall season. For the first time in his life, he left more than a den or hiding place; he left a home.

Eru grabbed a thicker coat to hold out the autumn chill, and left his villa for the last time. His breath, and that of his guide, billowed in misty swirls that glowed in the lamp light. Flakes of snow drifted lazily in the still night air. Eru felt the sting of cold on his guide's ears, reminding him to wrap his scarf high enough to cover his own ears. The evening streets of Deor buzzed with activity as people made their way home from a long day's work. Having just abandoned his home, Eru's mind had no reason to pick up on the man who walked up to the door of his old villa and chained it securely shut.

The letter carrier rapped on the door with the metallic knocker, making an echoing 'clunk.' A maid opened the door a sliver to keep out the evening chill.

"What is it?" she asked.

"I have a letter for your master," the letter carrier said.

"Well, he's not here right now. Come back tomorrow," the maid said as she pushed the door closed.

"Wait, please," the courier said as he stuck his foot in the gap. "I won't get paid unless someone reads this letter tonight. Please, it's urgent. If you just read the letter, you can send him word immediately."

"This had better be urgent." The maid took the letter and broke the seal. She could barely read, but the letter's simple contents didn't challenge her literacy. "I will kill the archos Eru," she read out loud.

I will kill the archos Eru. The sudden thought hit Eru's awareness like a runaway carriage charging into a busy intersection. Before he realized what had happened, a young maid lay dying in shock and terror six blocks away. The courier, unfortunate enough to hear the maid, lay draped over the blunt points of the porch rails like a funeral shroud hanging for others to see. *Father!*

Eru knew Telu's depraved work when he saw it, though he had to marvel at the cleverness of a scheme like this. Rather than try in vain to hide his efforts, he would use misinformation and noise to mask the real threat.

I will kill the archos Eru. Eru seized a carriage driver who was unfortunate enough to be following a carriage that suddenly unfurled the banner off its back. Again, the sudden blow left him unable to stop his natural reflexes. The driver threw himself over the front of his carriage, bouncing his passengers violently as the wheels passed over him. His carriage toppled and slid to a grating halt on the cobblestone street.

I will kill the archos Eru. Eru seized the pedestrian who first glimpsed the unveiled sign on a busy street corner. Eventually, the thought repeated itself in hundreds of minds. Telu had chosen his moment with malicious wisdom. Eru desperately tried not to harm those unfortunate enough to read the signs, and in some cases he succeeded. However, the thoughts kept coming, relentlessly smashing into his mind like the storm surge of a hurricane. With every new set of eyes that read the sign, his strength to fight it diminished.

I will kill the archos Eru. A new sign caught the attention of several people on a different street corner. *I will kill the archos Eru;* two more banners, one on a carriage, one hanging beneath a shop window. *I will kill the archos Eru;* another letter delivered by a courier. *I will kill the archos Eru;* another sign. *I will kill the archos Eru;* another letter.

Hundreds of people read the message as the signs spread throughout the city in a rough circle surrounding his villa. The assault on his awareness overwhelmed him, and Eru watched in horror as his instincts took over. Eru seized one person after another, killing or maiming them in whatever way presented itself. Eru felt the terror in each soul he seized as he compelled them to do such terrible things to themselves. Never before had anyone dared engage in such a frontal assault on an archos's senses, but few heretics ever fought the archos with a zeal to match Telu.

In Eru's overwhelmed condition he felt nothing of the happenings at his old villa. Telu had targeted his villa specifically, but the toxic fumes spread to the neighboring homes. Eru's neighbor burst out his front door, a cloth wrapped around his face, carrying his daughter. Close behind, stumbled the mother, gasping and choking as she carried their youngest. They barely escaped. The neighbors on the other side hadn't been so lucky.

It felt like an eternity before Eru could seize people and destroy each of the terrible signs. Six simple words wrought death and misery. Nothing Eru could do would ever console the wives, children, brothers and fathers who lost loved ones today. Finally, the last banner fell from its carriage and the carnage came to an end. Eru surveyed the chaos in the blocks around him, mortified at the destruction his power had wrought over such a large area in such a short time. The terror of Jordan's shop paled in comparison.

Eru felt the fear that filled the city around him, knowing that his name had become synonymous with death. He had to put an end to this madness, knowing that could only come with another death. He just didn't know whose death that would be, his or his father's.

"Who are you?" Aymis repeated, still trembling slightly at the shock of her latest customer's thoughts.

"Someone who can help you," the man said evasively. *Please listen to me. I would rather not kill you.*

"Help me, or..." Aymis couldn't finish the sentence.

"You are a powerful Reader. I should have been more careful," the mysterious man said more to himself.

"Reader, what are you talking about?" Aymis asked, choking back a fear-inspired sob. "Are there others like me?"

"Oh yes, girl, there are. The Aegendi are our enemies' most critical secret," the man said as he pulled out a pocket watch. *Any time now.*

"Aegendi? I don't understand," Aymis said, gaining some composure as confusion overpowered fear.

"There are people who can do unusual things. Most never realize they are Aegendi until they are seized. Our enemies' power amplifies the gifts."

"Our enemies? You mean the archos?" Aymis asked.

"Never say that word again!" the man snapped angrily. *You're lucky I don't kill you right now.*

"Sorry, sorry, please just don't..." again Aymis couldn't bring herself to fully acknowledge the man's threatening thoughts.

"If you don't learn discipline quickly, you will wish I *had* killed you," he said, looking at her closely.

"So, what kinds of gifts do others have?" Aymis asked, anxious to get him thinking about something other than killing her.

"Most Aegendi are hardly different from others without being seized. Most Readers, for example, only get impressions or hunches they can easily ignore. You are obviously a powerful Reader if you can read my thoughts."

"How do you know I haven't been seized?" Aymis asked.

"I don't know, but if I believed you had been seized you wouldn't be alive right now." The man said the words so casually it sent a chill down Aymis's spine.

"Are you an Aegendi?" she asked, unnerved by how frequently the man's thoughts rested on killing her, and anxious to divert those thoughts again.

"I heard your breathing quicken when I thought about killing you, and I know how many coins you have in your bag with a quick glance. They call my kind a Hawkeye. Being seized is a terrible experience for one like me," he said in response. Aymis sensed enough just in his body language not to press for details.

"So, why do the... um, our enemies, seek after Aegendi?" Aymis asked.

"Haven't you guessed it yet?" he asked condescendingly. "The Aegendi are the key to the miracles at any congregation, and the tool our enemies use to control the entire city, despite their relatively small numbers. If an Aegendi is seized, the archos never lets him or her go."

Aymis wanted to ask why this man had been let go, but remembered the distinct impression not to press for those details. "So why are you helping me?" Aymis asked, knowing already that the man didn't care if she lived or died.

"Because we want you to help us," he said, looking her squarely in the eyes.

"You mean, help the heretics," Aymis said, taking an educated guess. The man smiled in response. "I guess I don't have much of a choice, do I?" she finished as she guessed the intent behind the smile.

"You learn quickly," he replied. *Looks like I won't have to kill her after all.*

"What will happen to my mother?" she asked.

"She must never know about you being an Aegendi. You must guard that secret with more than your life. If she knows you are part of the heretics, or that you are an Aegendi, she is counted amongst our enemies," the man said as he looked at his pocket watch again. *It should be done by now.*

"Why do you keep looking at your watch? What should be done now?" Aymis asked. She saw a flash of anger in the man's eyes that he quickly suppressed.

"It's a personal matter that is none of your concern," he said. *Vengeance.*

Aymis heard the thought, feeling the lethal intent behind it. In that one moment, she knew she had fallen in with a very dangerous man. Her heart skipped a beat, and she resolved to protect her mother in the only way she could now. She could never knowingly bring a man like this into her mother's world, which meant she could never see her mother again. Her mother would likely end up on the streets without both of their incomes, but that fate had been determined when she got fired that morning.

"My name is Aymis," she said, realizing the two had never been properly introduced. Maybe he would find it harder to kill her if he knew her name.

"It's a pleasure to meet you," the man said in response.

"Well, if I am going to put my life in your hands, and leave my mother, at least give me your name," Aymis said bitterly.

"You don't miss much," he replied.

"Well, I *am* a Reader," Aymis said as she wiped a tear from her cheek.

"So you are. My name is Telu," he said as he offered his hand and helped her to her feet.

CHAPTER 8

THE HUNT

I do not consider myself a fool to have longed for father's forgiveness and love, just a naïve child. Telu had long ago sold his soul to the religion of hatred and vengeance. Like my zealots, he had invested far too much in that decision to change his course. In my younger years, I couldn't see that. My father's first terrible impressions of me loomed over me like heavy clouds, darkening my outlook on everything. Some would say the deaths from Telu's schemes didn't fall

*on my shoulders. I knew differently. I clung to my idealism
selfishly, refusing to save uncounted lives by taking one.
I could have prevented all of the deaths Telu caused. The
horrific last moments of all of those victims haunt me to this
day.*

How did I go so wrong? Eru worked over the question, trying to find what moment set him on such a destructive path. He had been too careless about his location, believing himself to have grown strong enough that even Telu's cunning couldn't escape his notice. How had Telu tracked him down? Eru hadn't left his villa for months, and rarely if ever seized anyone in close proximity to his old den. Back in the lamp maker's shop, Eru had felt the lingering fear in the minds of people passing the shop. He felt none of that around the villa. His neighbors probably would have been shocked to know an archos lived next door to them. Had they known, perhaps they could have avoided their terrible fate.

Eru moved through people in the thinning crowds of the city, using all the vantage points to guide him further and further from his latest calamity. Eru hitched a ride on a few carriages in his wanderings, seizing the passengers but leaving the drivers oblivious to his presence. He let them take him wherever they intended to drive, not caring where he ended up. The passengers experienced a terrible trip, but at least they arrived undelayed. The last sights of those he had just killed: horse hooves trampling him, pavement rushing to meet him, or the glistening lamps blurring through swirling waters haunted him. For a year he had hoped that he could rise above the destruction of his kind. For a year he had pulled against the tension in a bow's string, foolishly. It all came crashing back on him now.

Now he knew how wrong it had been to accept the adoration of the zealots. He missed the comfort of usurping the title of deity. Lacking that justification for his nature stripped him of defense from the loathing of those he controlled. With his grown awareness, he felt the hatred of the world around him like a naked man under the blistering desert sun. He saw the error of that decision clearly after the fact, but it didn't explain how he could have let this latest disaster happen. If anything, his timely decision to abandon those notions saved his life, and in turn resulted in hundreds of deaths.

Why did he let Telu try? That question sunk deep into Eru's mind, bringing the moment of his failure into full focus. He had made a lot of mistakes in his young life, but none perhaps as weighty as letting his father live. A dead father could never come to love him, but Eru knew now that the living one never would either. He had been selfish, valuing his own longing for acceptance from his father higher than the lives he knew Telu would take in the future. Eru understood Telu like no other could. He had felt Telu's unyielding hatred for him on several occasions, but none more terrible or frightening than when Eru seized him after the attack on Jordan's shop. Eru understood enough to know that more deaths would come if he left Telu alive. Still, he let the man live.

Eru could never bring back the people who died at his command. They died due to his weakness. First, a year ago he had lacked the strength to do what should have been done, and now on this terrible night he lacked the strength to resist his instincts. Eru had to get stronger. He had to find the strength and the courage to do what must be done. He had to find and kill his father. His father would be a tough quarry to track down, but Eru knew that failure would mean more innocent deaths. Failure was not an option. The hunt was on.

Telu didn't trust her. Aymis could tell that even without reading his thoughts. He refused to let her out of his sight, even insisting that she share the small dank room he had rented in a hostel. She didn't doubt that he would even insist she change clothing under his watchful eye, if she had clothing to change into. Telu didn't trust her, but he also didn't know her. Just because he would have killed someone who tried to hold him hostage didn't mean Aymis could ever do that.

Aymis couldn't help but worry for her mother. Soon Janis would be evicted from their shoddy apartment. Alone Janis could probably pay for a spot in a hostel, not unlike the place Aymis now found herself in. Compared to this place, her old worn down apartment felt luxurious. The room smelled of mildew, and Aymis suspected the bed sheets hadn't been washed in ages. Telu at least had paid extra for a room. Most people in the hostels slept in cramped quarters surrounded by other bunks. Aymis lay on the rough wooden floor, holding still to keep from getting any splinters. Telu lay in his bed, lecturing her unendingly about their *enemies.*

Aymis focused her efforts on understanding the man who had saved her from a life of imprisonment under the dominion of her enemies. Did she really believe them to be her enemies? She had no reason not to believe Telu. To believe otherwise would likely mean dying in their service. Even so, she couldn't bring herself to believe the world to be as terrible and cruel as Telu painted it. Life was cruel, she couldn't dispute that. She had just been forced to abandon her mother, but even that cruel stroke saved her from captivity. Ultimately they would have been separated no matter which way the winds carried her. Life was definitely cruel, but fate had touches of kindness as well. Couldn't Telu's enemies be the same? She studied Telu, hoping to understand why he felt so strongly.

"You must never read one, or you will be seized immediately," Telu said. "Are you listening?"

"Sorry," Aymis said as the inattentive glaze on her eyes vanished.

"Stay out of my mind," Telu growled. "There's nothing for you there."

"I am sorry," Aymis said quietly.

"Just because a burglar can enter someone's home doesn't mean he should, or that he is welcome."

"I said I am sorry," Aymis responded, not wishing to be lectured.

"Just – don't do it again," Telu said with a cold gaze. Aymis recognized the threat in his eyes.

"So, don't read one of our enemies," she said, anxious to get back on his lessons.

"Right. Your ability is a tremendous asset to us, but it puts you at risk as well," Telu continued, resuming his instruction.

"Why is that?"

"You have the ability to see the thoughts of others. Unlike the rest of us, you can know if someone has been seized. The heretics have always been a scattered and broken organization. Any time we organize enough to do anything worthwhile, they compromise us and kill the leadership. If you sense that someone in our group has been seized, you must kill them." Telu looked her in the eyes as if to measure her for the task.

"Can't I just signal others?" Aymis asked nervously.

"And what signal or sign could you keep hidden from them? They will know anything you tell the person that has been seized," Telu responded. *Foolish girl, won't last long with those morals.*

"Well, it hardly matters then. The moment an ally is seized, they will know I am an Aegendi and seize me too," Aymis replied. "If I haven't been seized, then we haven't been compromised."

"Humph," Telu grunted.

"Besides, you're the only heretic I have met. When will I meet the others?" Aymis asked.

"Like I said, we are scattered and disorganized. I have funding from a nobleman who is sympathetic to our cause, though he also funds a large congregation and is officially loyal to them."

"Well, if you are really worried about being compromised, then I will have a secret signal only you know. If I meet any others, they will get their own unique signal. Your sign will be different from anyone else. That way I can warn others without risking discovery," Aymis replied.

"Humph, I suppose that could work," Telu grunted. *She's smarter than I expected. Of course she is right about one thing. If we are compromised she will be the first to be taken and the rest of us will be dead. I may have to kill her yet.*

"Why..." Aymis stammered. *Blazes, this man thinks killing people will solve all his problems.* "Why are you so afraid of me?" she finished her question.

"I usually kill Readers. Letting one into my operations is a terrible risk. If you are seized, the minds of all around you are left wide open. They can scour all the minds in a room instantly. All of our secrets and plans could be compromised in one moment."

"So why didn't you kill me?" Aymis asked.

"I haven't killed you yet," Telu paused ominously, "because you are powerful enough to be helpful." *And I have enough blood on my hands already.*

"I see," Aymis said somberly. "I hope everything works out."

"So do I," Telu responded. "Get some rest. Tomorrow we move to another hostel." Telu turned the lamp down and rolled on his side to sleep. Aymis couldn't help but search out this strange, dangerous man's mind despite his warning. *The burglar who gets in and out undetected offends nobody.*

Maybe it worked this time. I am still alive, that's a good sign... I guess. Who am I kidding? I cannot go to her in failure. I will know tomorrow if I can return to her. If not, we begin the hunt for a Hider. Aymis realized instinctively that she must never let Telu find a Hider, whatever it was. She would only survive as long as he found her useful.

Sleep eluded her as her mind raced through the momentous day's events. In one day she had discovered she could read minds, got fired because of it, then been kidnapped by a murderous heretic bent on revenge. She knew she should be terrified for her own safety, but through it all, her mother's well-being concerned her the most.

Oko picked up the soiled banner from the muddy puddle. He had a good idea what he would read based on the carnage that unfolded here a few hours ago. Oko felt a strange thrill, knowing he could read what he would find without risk.

"I will kill the archos Eru," he whispered to himself with a smile. Whoever made this banner either had courage or a death wish. Oko searched the surrounding blocks for this Streetborn. Killing Streetborn no longer satisfied him, but it did mean one less archos in the world, and one more grey hand to trade as bounty. They provided their own challenges, being as elusive as a cricket in the night, but once he found them it felt like killing a toddler. Of course, several of the Streetborn Oko had killed were scarcely older than three. Eru, whoever he was, had obviously grown to be a crafty Streetborn. Whoever hunted him also showed a terrible flare of cunning and a ruthless disregard for life. Oko knew how dangerous it must have been for the creator of this sign. Judging by the number of deaths on the surrounding blocks, this had been one of many such signs; all presumably to distract the target from some more subtle threat. Oko assumed that the real threat had missed its mark. Otherwise far fewer people would have died. Perhaps this Streetborn had developed enough power that only a Hider could kill him now. The thought made Oko smile. He had a new quarry, one that may be worthy of his talents.

Oko ripped the banner up, knowing it could kill the street sweeper, if he happened to be literate. The destruction and death fit inside a roughly drawn circle centered on a particular street. Right at that center point Oko found a locked up villa. He broke in through the windows to see who had emerged the victor in the clash between the heretic and archos. Unfortunately, one family had died, but the middle villa remained empty, with no archos body to be found. Oko knew this could only mean one thing. The hunt was on.

CHAPTER 9

LONELINESS

Ever since my birth, I lived under my father's constant influence. He controlled everything I did. He dominated every aspect of my life, right down to my emotional state. I hunted him to make sure that no more people die from his schemes, but also because I desperately needed to escape his shadow. It was a big step for me to let go of my longing for acceptance from my father. It should have felt liberating, but it left me feeling lost and confused as I floundered in search of something to live for.

Finding Telu proved harder than Eru had hoped. His father moved around like a vagabond, changing names almost as frequently as he changed location. Eru would lose the trail for days before recognizing his father's face in someone's recollection. Telu had spent years learning how to escape Eru's perception, and his mastery showed. Eru continued the search, hoping for a stroke of random luck. In a city the size of Deor, someone as crafty as Telu could hide indefinitely, even from an archos.

Eru felt the cold of the early winter storm through those he controlled. Snowflakes swirled in the wind, piling up against buildings and walls. People wrapped up tightly as they hurried home from work. Eru wrapped up enough that even his unusually large head escaped most people's notice under all the hoods, hats and scarves. Eru loved winter, and the relative anonymity the cold weather provided him. He could walk the streets without feeling the fear and loathing of those who noticed him. People could easily have recognized him as an archos if they cared to take the time. Most however hurried to their destination, more concerned with escaping the cold than observing other shivering passersby.

Eru didn't feel the temperature, which was both a blessing and a hazard. Snowstorms gave him the freedom to wander the city and search far and wide for his father, but carelessness could cost him. He wrapped up excessively to prevent the kind of problems most would feel long before they were a serious threat. Eru stayed out in the storm, scanning the hostels and apartments around him. Weather like this meant he could easily work through large hostels, boarding houses, and apartments packed with people fleeing the chill. His father's trail had gone as cold as the weather, but that wouldn't stop Eru from enjoying the frigid winter night.

The light from the street lanterns lit up the swirling flakes in spectacular patterns. Eru loved watching the billowing patterns of breath from each person he controlled. The sound of snow under their feet registered through all their ears.

Eru felt the winter air filling the lungs of his observers, and cold's invigorating bite on the tips of their noses. Eru loved winter.

Eru watched a group of children playing in the snow on Hillside Park. Children squealed their pleasure as they rode toboggans down the hill. Others trekked back up the slope enthusiastically, breathing heavily with the effort. Snowballs flew across an improvised battlefield. Eru sensed their pleasure, taking in as much as he could about the kind of childhood he would never know. All around him, people hurried past, few bothering to stop and even smile at the children's revelry. Eru watched their play with several pairs of eyes, momentarily forgetting himself and wandering too close to their play.

Eru felt the sudden focus of one of the boys, who mistakenly took him for a late comer to their fun. Before Eru realized what had happened, he seized the boy, instantly turning the boy's play into a nightmare. Eru wished the boy's playful thought could have escaped his notice. He wanted to join in the battle, knowing he would lose embarrassingly, but have fun in the process. Eru released the boy immediately, wishing he could do more to lessen the trauma of the moment.

"Hey, that's an archos!" the boy shouted angrily. "Get him!"

"No!" Eru gasped through multiple mouths. The boy didn't know any better, his angry response the likely reaction from a kid his age. Eru felt the angry attention of multiple minds turn on him, and desperately fought to restrain his protective reflexes.

Eru subdued them instantly, sensing the trauma the children would remember for the rest of their lives. One by one, though with blinding speed, Eru seized each of the children and threw them to the ground. He broke one boy's leg by having him jump off his fast moving sled at a bad moment. He felt the flash of pain in another boy, as he made him fall in such a way that he broke his arm. One boy's head hit a tree trunk. That one collapsed in the snow unconscious, crimson staining the snow from a gaping wound on his scalp. The rest of the children escaped relatively unscathed thanks to the deep snow softening their fall. At least Eru hadn't killed any of them. The children that hadn't been seriously injured scattered like sheep fleeing a wolf, leaving Eru alone with the moody crowds of adults.

Eru immediately seized someone near the unconscious boy. John was the boy's name. Eru looked at the boy with the care and concern of a father, knowing him far better than his own father did. John hadn't seen his father in years, but his mother had always done a good job caring for him. He lived a few doors down from the park, and his mother would certainly be frantic with worry. It bothered John how much she doted over him. Eru had the man carry John home, even while he seized two more men to guide the other two hurt children to their homes.

"Who is it?" John's mother Marry called. Eru recognized her voice instantly.

"I am a doctor. Please let me in, your son is hurt," Eru said.

"Oh, by the archos, no!" she exclaimed as she swung the door open and saw her son's bloody face. "What happened?" Marry quickly herded the man into her home and closed the door to keep out the cold.

"My guess is that he was seized," Eru answered. He knew better than to let Marry know that the 'doctor' was under control of the same archos who had hurt her son. He needed her as calm as possible.

"Cursed vile creatures!" She hissed under her breath. "Praise Aitrox that you happened to be on hand to help him." Eru couldn't help but notice the strange contradictions in her words. Like many people in Deor, phrases like 'Praise Aitrox' rolled off her tongue with little if any thought to their meaning.

As Eru led the other two boys to their homes, similar exchanges unfolded as their parents expressed concern for their child and gratitude for their good fortune that a doctor happened to be on hand to help. For the next hour Eru's search for Telu slowed as he focused most of his attention on making sure that he managed all three 'doctors' well enough that nobody would suspect his involvement. Perhaps a day or two later when they compared their stories, they would realize what happened.

Eru stifled the hurt and frustration at his own carelessness. At almost eleven years old, Eru was about the same age as the children, but his mind had already experienced hundreds of lives. Eru felt like a lonely old gaffer at times like this.

Friendship was never the privilege of his kind, but Eru had a tendency to long for the unattainable.

Eru sighed in tired exasperation, sending cold wispy clouds from his mouth. His search for Telu would be slower while he helped the boys, but it was the least he could do. He left the abandoned park, with the sleds and toys sitting as sad reminders of the small disaster. Eru turned his focus to the next boarding home. Immediately he picked up Telu's distinct impression left behind in the minds of the landlord and a neighbor. Few people left such a distinct emotional imprint on those they met as Telu. He exuded animosity, making others uncomfortable instantly and grateful that he wasn't the kind to strike up further conversation. Apparently, Telu had checked into the boarding home that very morning.

"You did this?" Aymis said in shock as Telu unlocked the doors to the chained up villa.

"Our enemies show no mercy to us. If we aren't willing to fight with the same brutality, we will never defeat them," Telu answered, not a note of apology in his voice.

"But if you knew one of them lived in this villa, why did you have to kill the innocent neighbors?"

"Everything has to be done indirectly to avoid their notice. If any people I hire even suspect they have been hired to act against one of them..."

"But this is wrong!" Aymis shouted. "How could you?" She wiped tears from her eyes, and fought back the rage that burned inside her. For the first time in her life, she truly hated someone.

"Don't!" Telu snapped back, barely subduing a quick flash of rage. "Don't tell me what is right and wrong!" he growled quietly. *You have no idea the evil I am fighting to destroy.*

Aymis wanted to shout at the man, to tell him he had become every bit as evil as his enemy. Instead, she bit her tongue, fearing for her own safety. "There's nobody here," Aymis said quietly, after a cursory glance around the villa, hoping to move Telu's focus back to relative stability.

"I failed again," Telu said quietly.

"Please, let's leave. This place makes me nervous," Aymis said. Telu's chin lifted and his eyes rested on her. She heard no thoughts in particular, but suspected that Telu had learned the art of keeping his intentions just beneath conscious thought. She saw enough in his eyes to know to be afraid.

"Looks like we are going to start searching for a Hider," he said.

"A Hider?" she asked, trying to conceal her fear.

"Hiders are invisible to our enemies, very rare, and almost impossible to find."

"So, how are we going to find one?" she asked.

"You mean, how are *you* going to find one?" Telu corrected her pointedly. "Only Readers can find them. If you can't read someone, then there is a good chance they are a Hider."

"You mean I am going to have to try to read every person in Deor until I find someone whose mind I can't read? That's ridiculous!"

"Of course it is," Telu snapped. *I thought you were smarter than that.* "The Hiders who haven't been killed are usually trying to kill our enemies. Plus, they also find safety in numbers where they cannot be singled out."

"And that means?" Aymis asked.

"It means we have worship services to attend," Telu replied. "Remember, do not read one of our enemies! Try not to stand out. Give praise when the crowds do, and do not look at them."

Aymis didn't bother to mark the days that blurred together with daily attendance to the congregations. She and Telu moved through congregations quickly, usually casing one out for a day or two to see if they could find any Hiders. Telu changed his name with every congregation they visited, insisting on the necessity of his precaution. She offered to do the same, but he actually laughed at the suggestion. She had never heard him laugh before, and found the experience... insulting.

Aymis learned much about the archos at the congregations, searching for any signs of kindness or goodness in them. She paid close attention to the worshipers, particularly interested in those who had been seized. What she felt struck fear and sorrow into her heart. They all reminded her of Telu to some degree or another. Having never been seized herself, she found the insight into the experience terrifying. Could beings who willingly inflicted that on others be anything but evil?

Aymis watched the Aegendi in each congregation with particular consternation. She felt the pain of their imprisonment, and their guilt for perpetuating the archos lie. She saw in their minds the fate that awaited her if an archos seized her. Part of her almost wanted to thank Telu for saving her from that fate. Of course, she sometimes wondered which would be worse, being an archos slave or Telu's terrified attendant.

Winter advanced, and still she saw no clues or hints of a Hider. With the growing cold, her thoughts often wandered to her mother. What had become of her? She hoped that Janis had found a way to make things work. Maybe Telu would let her go once she found a Hider, and she could find her mother. But she knew enough about Telu to know better than seriously entertain such hopes. She grew so tired of going to the citadels, she almost wished she could find a Hider just to stop going. She knew that her life would end the moment Telu felt he didn't need her, but sometimes that felt a pleasant alternative to the daily worship. The citadels made her skin crawl and left her feeling dirty.

Aymis loosened her scarf and brushed the snow from her shoulders as she entered yet another citadel with a tired sigh. She shivered, but not from the cold, as her gaze wandered to one of the many large statues of Aitrox.

"Praise Aitrox and seek communion with her!" a booming voice called from the stage in the front.

"Praise Aitrox," Aymis said dispassionately with others in the crowd.

"Behold the benevolence of your goddess!" the voice called with a sweeping gesture towards one of the statues. Aymis focused on a severely wounded man. *Just seize me now so I can get this over with!* She felt the pain in his thoughts, and his exhausted boredom at this terrible routine. He lost track of all the times he had been beaten to near-death before his archos seized him, unlocking his gift and providing the crowd with a miracle. Telu said they were called Immortals, perhaps the most unfortunate of all the Aegendi. The archos made particularly cruel but effective use of them.

"Praise Aitrox," Aymis said through gritted teeth, in unison with the crowd.

"Excuse me," a man with a walking cane said as he bumped into her. Aymis focused her gaze on him, but felt like her eyes had played a trick on her. She saw the man, but sensed nothing from him. Part of her felt it to be a trick of her imagination, but she knew that her long search had come to an end.

She watched the Hider cautiously throughout the remainder of the meeting, admiring his craftiness. Always he stuck with the crowds, where she almost lost him against all the others who she could sense. He used the crowds like a hunting lion uses the grasses, moving with masked, lethal intent. Had he not bumped into her, calling her attention to him at such close proximity, she never would have found him. She saw in his gait a confidence that few possessed, knowing that he enjoyed the truly rare gift to be free with his thoughts.

Aymis felt the satisfaction at achieving something few could claim to have done. She, a lowly Reader, had found a Hider. She had no doubt that the archos running this congregation had several pairs of eyes looking out for Hiders, but they obviously had failed. She couldn't help but smile slightly at that thought.

"Glory to Aitrox," Aymis said reflexively in unison with the crowd, as the archos dismissed them for the evening. Aymis wrapped her scarf tight against the cold. Outside, the snow swirled furiously and the wind howled. She looked out into the cold, grateful for the thicker coat Telu had bought her.

"Well, did you get what you came for?" Telu asked his usual question to end worship. Surrounded by hundreds of worshipers, he couldn't be more direct.

"Not yet," Aymis replied.

Aitrox sighed in boredom. Even with the looming attack from Oso, she had nothing to worry about, and even less to interest her. She wondered how much longer Oso would wait before making his doomed attempt. She baited him on, never seizing him despite his blatantly threatening thoughts. She felt his confidence grow. He actually believed that she couldn't seize him! The thought made her laugh. Even if an archos managed to become so strong, none could marshal enough Aegendi to be a threat to her. Oso had mustered an impressive collection, but Aitrox had secrets far more powerful than her unrivaled army of Aegendi.

Aitrox sighed again. *Why do they even bother trying?*

CHAPTER 10

CONFRONTATION

Ado excluded, I had never deliberately killed someone with my power. True, my instincts had taken over uncounted times, but I never wished death on any I controlled. I knew what had to be done with my father, but doubted I had it in me. The memories of drowning in the Deor River, or being crushed by carriage wheels, kept me focused. I reminded myself that similar things would happen to more innocent people again until one of us died.

E ru sat on a park bench and rested his head on his hands. Without his zealots to serve him, he found he had to rest the muscles in his neck more often to keep his awareness sharp. He couldn't feel the soreness in his muscles like he could feel in people he controlled. Instead he felt it indirectly through the dulling of his senses. He had released everyone, letting himself focus completely on the awareness of others around him.

The winds picked up their intensity, swirling and howling around Eru. He sat in the snow storm, oblivious to the furious wind, or the small drifts of snow piling up against his legs on the bench. He let his awareness move through the thinning evening crowds as the night grew older. The aftermath of his latest incident with the sledding children dominated the emotional landscape that evening. He felt mothers consoling distraught children, trying to use the moment to teach them about the dangers of the archos. He felt the uneasy tension settling in on the area as rumors of his 'attack' on the children spread. A few blocks away, a congregation finished worship, and a new surge of minds braced themselves to venture through the cold. There he was. Eru readied himself to seize his father, but in the moment of truth his determination wavered.

"You seemed to pay closer attention at worship today," Telu said as they distanced themselves from the scattering worshipers, each en route to their homes.

"Did I?" Aymis asked, bundling up tighter against the cold, also hoping to hide her face from Telu's inquisitive gaze. "It was just another congregation."

"Was it? I saw your eyes following someone in the crowd," Telu persisted.

"Oh, that? I thought I recognized an old friend. Turned out to be nothing," Aymis said, trying to sound casual about it. She looked anxiously ahead to the boarding home and the escape from this terrible weather.

"Are you sure you don't have something to tell me?" Telu persisted, stopping them both in their tracks. Aymis heard the threat in his voice, and knew he suspected her lies.

"Of course. Why would I lie to you?" she asked in response, deciding that admitting her lie could prove more dangerous.

"I don't know, but I can think of a good reason for you to tell me the truth!" he growled as he pulled out a knife and stepped towards her.

"Pulling a knife on me won't change the truth," Aymis said with a nervous wobble in her voice.

"Just because I can't read minds, doesn't mean I can't see your lies," Telu said angrily.

"Please, Telu, this is crazy!" Aymis said, choking down a fearful sob.

"Crazy? Crazy! You have more tells than a bad gambler. I could have spotted your lie even if I weren't a Hawkeye." *You forgot about that didn't you?* Telu laughed coldly. "I'm going to give you one more chance to come clean before you start losing fingers."

"Okay! Please, just calm down," Aymis begged. "I thought I spotted a Hider, but I was wrong. I followed someone through the crowd until I realized he was not a Hider at all." Aymis hoped she could hide the lie in her partial truth.

"There, was that so hard?" Telu said, calm civility returning to his voice.

"I'm sorry I lied to you. I just felt stupid for the mistake," Aymis began.

"So you are sure you managed to get a read on her then?" Telu asked. "You sure she wasn't a Hider?"

"Positive."

"You lying tramp!" Telu screamed as he grabbed her with terrible strength and wrenched her hand out of her coat pocket. *You'll lose more than your fingers by the time I'm through with you.*

"No!" Aymis screamed, but her wails of terror and protest fell on deaf ears.

Eru felt after Telu's mind, foolishly hoping he had abandoned his quest to kill him. Telu had attended a worship service, though Eru could hardly imagine why. Maybe, Telu had had a change of heart about the archos. He knew better than to believe his father capable of such a change, but wishful thinking often ignores reality.

He felt Telu's sense of distrust and suspicion grow as he interrogated someone near him. Eru immediately sensed the undying fervor that burned in his
father's mind. Telu had mastered fanning the flames of his hatred while keeping
the source just on the verge of conscious thought. Immediately, Eru knew his
father hadn't changed. He should seize him now and end their struggle.

Fear grew in the mind of the girl Telu interrogated. Eru sensed her dilemma,
knowing she feared for her life no matter how the conversation ended. Without
ears to hear, Eru didn't know specifics of the exchange, only feelings and scattered thoughts. He felt her terror and determination growing. Whatever she had
chosen to hide from his father must be important if she would stake her life on
it. Eru felt the situation escalating and knew he would have to intervene soon.
Why couldn't he just seize his father and be done with it?

"Let her go!" a man called from the distance as he rushed to Aymis' aid.

"Stay out of this!" Telu shouted at the stranger.

"Father, let her go," the stranger said sternly.

"What…" Telu asked as he pulled Aymis closer, moving the knife towards her
neck.

"Telu, don't make me kill you," the stranger persisted. Aymis gasped upon
hearing Telu's actual name. He hadn't used it for weeks, and none in this part
of town should have known it. Hearing his name apparently caught Telu off
guard as well.

"No, no, no!" Telu shouted. "You can't be…"

Aymis turned her attention to the stranger, and recognized the signs of
someone under archos control, though something felt different. Hatred and
anger still filled the stranger's mind, but she felt something different in the seized
man. Why would an archos care about the fate of a young woman? Did this
archos know she was an Aegendi? If so, why hadn't she already been seized?
Why didn't the archos just kill Telu?

"Father-" the man began, but Telu didn't let him finish the sentence.

"Don't call me that! Never call me that!" he shouted furiously.

"I'm not the monster you believe me to be," the stranger said, fighting back grief in his voice.

"You killed her!" Telu roared. "You killed her!" he repeated, choking back his sorrow.

"I couldn't stop that. There's so much about me you don't understand."

"No! I understand enough. You're an archos!" Telu raised his knife to Aymis' throat as anger swelled in his heart. He had no reason to kill Aymis now except for the burning hunger for someone to die for what his son had done.

"Let her go. No more innocent people have to die," the stranger said as he stepped forward.

"Stay back!" Telu snapped as he backed up with his hostage.

"Telu, I don't want to seize you. Don't make me," Eru implored.

"Please, Telu," Aymis sobbed.

"No more innocent people have to die. Stop hunting me, and this can all end peacefully. It's what Ama would have wanted," Eru said.

"How dare you defile her name?" Telu hissed. "How dare you presume to know what she wanted?"

"I know her better than anyone. For months I felt the beauty of her heart, and the love she had for both of us. She hoped for so much more from both of us." Eru's spokesman wiped a tear from his eyes as he spoke.

"N-no..." Telu stammered. Aymis felt the doubt lingering in his thoughts. "Ama demands vengeance for the child you stole from us. For the future we should have had together."

"She would want you to be happy," Eru said. "Nobody else has to die."

"This can only end one way," Telu hissed.

"Let her go," Eru commanded angrily. "Don't make me do it."

"Don't you get it? Don't you see why I do this?" Telu said, finally thrusting Aymis to the snowy street and stepping towards the stranger in defiance. "You gave me no choice when you left me alive! You should have killed me. You should have sent me to be with her!"

"I have enough blood on my hands already," Eru responded.

"Not yet," Telu said quietly. "I WILL KILL YOU, ERU!" he shouted.

"No!" the stranger's voice gasped, but it was too late. Eru couldn't resist Telu's ploy. As Telu finished his sentence, Eru seized Telu and plunged his knife into his ribs, through his winter clothes. Eru released him as soon as his instincts allowed, hoping to give his father his last breaths of life without his presence intruding.

"I will..." Telu coughed and sputtered as his eyes rolled backwards, "kill you, Eru." Telu's hands pulled the blade from his chest in a grisly splash of red before plunging it again into his own ribs. Telu's body went limp and the last hate-filled spark flickered from his eyes. The swirling snow continued to fall, changing from white to deep red in a gruesome stain on the ground.

Aitrox almost looked forward to Oso making his move. She already knew every detail in his plans, and even had to smile at his schemes. He had worked it all out so very well in his mind. Supremely confident in his collection of Aegendi, and falsely assuming Aitrox incapable of seizing him, his victory felt guaranteed. She recognized his logic, finding pleasure in his false conclusions. She would enjoy this confrontation immensely. She sensed Oso's determination as he moved his Aegendi into position outside her holy sanctuary. He had planned everything, believing he knew exactly what to expect. Aitrox would enjoy completely disproving that notion.

Oso's Wizards knocked the doors out of their frames, sending bits of rock scattering where the hinges broke from the stone. The doors shot through the chamber, bearing down on Aitrox with terrible speed. Aitrox sensed Oso's confusion at the lack of resistance and smiled. He actually believed he had achieved surprise. At the last second, her Wizards easily deflected the doors. They flew to both sides, careening through the crowds of servants like massive meat grinders. Ahead of the Wizards, a group of Immortals entered the chamber.

Oso had expected the Immortals to serve as vital shields to stop whatever traps or hazards Aitrox could have up her sleeve. They entered her chamber without incident, followed closely by the Wizards. Each Wizard carried a solid iron spear, the trick up his sleeve. Three Prophets rushed into the Holy sanctuary, guarded by Immortals and Brutes. The Prophets rushed towards Aitrox's Wizards, unleashing a barrage of throwing daggers to keep her Wizards distracted from the real threat.

Once the Prophets saw her Wizards react to their assault, Oso knew he had the window of opportunity with his own Wizards. Their spears shot straight for Aitrox so fast, only his Hawkeyes could track them. Oso could hardly believe it when he saw the spears impale her. They collided with her body in gruesome glory and Oso knew his ascension to godhood was at hand.

Two of Aitrox's Brutes came to her aid, extricating her from the throne. They snapped the spears just behind Aitrox, leaving them lodged in the throne. The grizzly iron spikes remained impaling the throne, covered in Aitrox's blood. Then, to Oso's consternation and surprise, Aitrox smiled! She stepped forward as if unmolested by the numerous iron rods still skewering her. The jagged, crimson shards of the spears jutted from Aitrox's back. One looked to have passed straight through her heart.

Aitrox enjoyed sensing Oso's premature elation, then seeing it crushed by shock and disbelief. She walked towards him, ignoring the knives and darts Oso's Prophets now turned her way. She didn't even bother using her Wizards to deflect them. One by one, the blades dug into her body, splattering blood on the polished stone floor. Oso's Brutes turned their attention to her, waving their clubs menacingly, but she paid them no mind. She removed the spears, then the daggers, looking as unconcerned as a person enjoying a pleasant spring day. One Brute's club smashed into her body, crumpling her rib cage like a house of cards and sending her hurtling back to her destroyed throne, yet she stood again as if nothing had happened.

How could this be happening? Oso watched in disbelief as Aitrox pulled the spears from her body. Iron was supposed to be her weakness. Oso had gone to tremendous effort, even for an archos, to acquire enough iron to make those weapons. Why else would she forbid possession of the metal? How could Aitrox be both an archos and an Immortal? He had had no warning, no rumors, but the possibility should have crossed his mind. She had, after all, lived for centuries longer than any other archos. He still could hardly believe it as he watched her devastating wounds heal themselves, noting that even her spectacular feathered gown restored itself to perfect order. In a matter of moments, she looked as if nothing had ever happened, with not even a stain on her incomprehensibly beautiful dress.

Oso realized that he had rushed into his death, but he should have known Aitrox would never be so merciful. She seized him effortlessly. Oso sensed how easily she overpowered him and recognized the full extent of his folly. She had played with him like a cat with a mouse. Eventually the cat kills its prey, and Oso took some measure of hope in that thought.

As if in response to his hope, Aitrox showed him the fate that awaited him. Aitrox commanded Oso to seize a servant in a side chamber of her holy sanctuary. What he saw through those eyes conveyed the fate worse than death that she had prepared for him. Seven other archos lay comatose in that room. Their heads lolled lazily on thin necks, and drool ran down their wrinkled naked bodies. Oso had seen similar signs in people he had broken, knowing from experience their cruel existence. He had never thought an archos could be broken in a similar way. Eventually old age offered merciful escape to the broken, but these archos looked wrinkled and aged centuries beyond the grave. On closer inspection, he noticed how each one had a single fiery feather tied to his wrist.

Aitrox sat back on her throne, already immaculately cleaned and repaired by her army of seized servants, basking in Oso's terror. She had grown accustomed to the misery of her broken archos, their voices part of the ever constant background noise in her awareness. Adding Oso to the mix brought the whole chorus alive in her mind. It would only become more beautiful to her after he broke. With one archos dealt with, Aitrox decided to give the Streetborn she had neglected some maternal guidance. She hadn't had this much fun with the archos in centuries.

CHAPTER II

FACING THE UNKNOWN

Only an archos can truly understand what it is to control someone during his final breaths of life. All the other times I seized Telu, I felt only his hatred for me. It blinded me to the fundamental motive that drove his zealous effort to kill me. He never expected to succeed. In the end, he got what he wanted, but lacked the courage to do for himself.

E ru had never controlled someone in the moment of death before Telu. Reflexively, his mind released people fractions of a second before passing, a detail Eru appreciated. Telu, however, died with one thing on his mind, killing

Eru. Something about witnessing death in such an immediate, personal way, made Eru shudder. Death, the ultimate mystery, wasn't meant to be observed that way.

Eru hoped to see evidence of something beyond death. Aitrox's congregations preached that death returned a soul to communion with her greater will. Only the zealots embraced that doctrine as their own, but most people Eru seized believed something awaited them beyond the grave. The idea gave Eru some comfort that perhaps a second act followed this tragic life and all things could be made right.

Telu had shared one deeper driving desire – the desire to be with Ama again. Eru looked for her, hoping to feel her waiting to welcome his father home. Maybe Ama refused to welcome the man Telu had become. If so, how would she receive Eru? Suddenly the thought of a second act beyond the grave didn't feel so comforting. Eru felt for anything that could indicate what happened to Telu's being when he died, but found no answers.

Eru left the scene of his father's death. He felt the loss more profoundly than he expected. He felt no love for Telu, and certainly wouldn't miss his persistent efforts to kill him, but he felt the profound loss of his dream to find redemption. All his life, that motivated him. What did he have left? Could he find the motivation to continue fighting against his powerful drive to kill? Then again, maybe he could finally escape a life of violence and murder. With Telu gone, maybe he could settle on a more permanent residence. No more innocent people had to die.

Around him the snow storm intensified and the temperatures plummeted. Winter storms could be dangerous for an archos. Eru felt the cold's merciless gnawing at the ears and arms of a homeless man a few blocks away. He felt a growing awareness of the storm in the minds of those in the homes closer to him, as they added coal to their heaters or wood to their fire. Eru knew that hypothermia could settle in with little warning, and that his own layers could be damp and cold already. He had to get out of the storm. Eru seized an unfortunate man, interrupting an argument with his wife.

"Don't you walk away from me, Ketu!" Ena, the angry wife, called after the man as Eru had him walk to the front door. "I'm talking to you!" she persisted.

Ketu opened the door, and Eru stepped in from the cold. He sensed the confusion and anger in Ena's mind quashed by terror as Eru pulled back his hood and unwrapped his scarf. Snow fell from his shoulders in soggy clumps. Soon a puddle of water surrounded Eru's boots on the tile floor. Eru felt Ena's dread, fury and indignation at having her home invaded so unceremoniously. After all, Eru hadn't even knocked.

Suddenly, Eru sensed a similarly uninvited presence unbidden in his mind, a power that left him feeling like a newborn babe. Aitrox's awareness smashed through his emotional sanctuaries deep into the most sacred, profound parts of his heart. He felt Aitrox, a secret twin in the womb, intruding on his first awareness of his mother. Aitrox shared Eru's first view of himself through Telu's hate-filled eyes. Aitrox watched, passing deserved judgment on Eru as he failed at the lamp maker's shop and again near his villa. How had Eru become so cavalier about inflicting this kind of experience on others?

Aitrox wielded Eru's mind with irresistible force. Eru had never understood why those he seized blamed themselves for anything he made them do. Eru had always wondered why being seized left others feeling ashamed and violated. Only now as he felt the terrible cruel yoke of an archos for himself did he begin to understand. Eru could intellectually absolve himself of responsibility for whatever Aitrox would make him do, but the terror and hatred in Ena's heart rested solely on Eru. Aitrox's mastery of Eru left no room for him to resist, yet Eru felt terribly violated and guilty as she wielded his seizing power like she would any other person's hands.

Aitrox's cruelty, or was it Eru's, worked it's terrible, demonic violence on Ena and her family. Ena grabbed the brass poker from the rack of fireplace accessories wielding it with deadly proficiency under Eru's power. Ketu never stood a chance, even though he died unseized. Eru desperately wished he could have seized the man to give him a chance to fight back. Instead he felt his capacity so deliberately and effectively used for cruelty and death.

Eru couldn't have imagined the terror to feel his faculties so terribly misused by another will. *Please, no!* Eru screamed in his mind as Ena ran up the stairs into the children's rooms. Eru heard the terrified screams of the children, and felt the incomprehensible agony in Ena's heart. He tried to block out Ena's senses and limit the haunting visions and sensations, but Aitrox's control forbade even that. Eru felt the jolt of each blow through Ena's hands, and heard the terrified screams of her children through her ears. The fear in their minds paled in comparison to the terrible sorrow and dread that clamored in Ena's heart. Eru's mind released Ena, leaving her with the cruelest of fates. Eru heard Ena's terrible cries of agony and despair through the ears of her neighbor, his next victim.

Please let this end! Eru exclaimed in his heart, but the horror had only just begun. Aitrox continued to use him, making Eru walk the neighbor into the kitchen to find a butter knife. *No! No!* he wailed in his mind, but Aitrox seemed to mock him, as she had him seize yet another family across the street.

The heavy storm clouds lingered from last night's blizzard. The sunrise filled the morning sky with spectacular crimsons and purples. Eru stood outside a small shanty, several blocks away from Ena's villa. A single mother and her three children lay dead inside. The tearful trail of murder passed through every home on the way to the pitiful shack that marked the end of the killing spree. Eru felt completely numb, his capacity to feel pummeled out of him. Aitrox had driven him hard through the night, cutting families down like a gardener trimming an overgrown lawn.

Finally, Aitrox released him, leaving him alone with his trauma and misery. He leaned back against the shack's doorframe and sunk to the ground. Burying his head in his knees, the sobs flowed as freely as the blood from his latest victims. Telu's death should have marked the end of the violence and slaughter on his account. Why did Eru believe that things would be any different now? How could murdering his father put an end to future murders at his hand?

Eru tried to tell himself that these deaths didn't fall on his shoulders, but found little consolation. He had been the instrument of death. The fact that he could do nothing to stop it only left him feeling powerless and violated. He had been made into exactly what he dreaded. Eru had been right about one thing: the killing would only stop when either he or Telu died. He had just been wrong about which one it had to be. He seized the next person unfortunate enough to pass on the street, ready to follow Telu and his mother into the unknown.

"Are you okay?" the man under the archos control asked. Aymis focused on the man, and realized he had been released.

"I think so," Aymis replied. She had never seen a person die before. She felt her mind reeling from the shock. She doubted she would ever forget the gruesome scene that unfolded in the street on this terrible night. Telu's body sat covered in snow, a splash of crimson adding color to the monochromatic scene. She knew the world had been relieved of a dangerous killer, but that didn't stop her stomach from churning at the sight.

"Let's get you inside," the man said as he offered her a hand up. "My name is Jono."

"Thanks, Jono." Aymis took his hand and pulled herself up from the snow.

"I hate those things!" Jono said with a shudder.

"Yeah," Aymis said quietly, grateful Jono couldn't read her thoughts. Jono would never be able to see past the trauma of being seized to recognize the unusual behavior the archos exhibited through him. Everything Aymis had ever heard corroborated Telu's claims of archos being cold-blooded killers who care nothing for the feelings of others. Yet Jono voiced concerns that flew in the face of everything she had heard of the archos. She sensed in Jono the same hatred that had dragged Telu down to his grave. Fortunately, like most, Jono's hatred would probably never push him to the same extremes as Telu.

"The storm is bad enough outside; you can stay the night here," Jono offered kindly as he opened the door to his flat. Aymis stepped in quickly to escape the cold.

"Thank you," Aymis said as she unbuttoned her coat and hung it on the rack by the door. She warmed her hands by the wood-burning stove, rubbing them together and breathing on them to speed the process.

"Dear, please bring a blanket into the front room," Jono called.

"What happened?" a woman asked, as she brought a blanket to Aymis.

"We had a run-in with one of *them*," Jono said, putting an unmistakable twist to the word 'them.'

"By the High Queen, I hate those things," his wife said in response.

"My name is Aymis," Aymis said, trying to get them talking about something other than hating the archos.

"Oh, I'll be seized, where are my manners? I'm Ela," she said, offering Aymis her hand. *She's a cute one. Maybe Tono would court her.*

"Thank you so much for your kindness," Aymis replied, her cheeks flushing red over Ela's unspoken match making.

"I'm sure you've had a terrible ordeal. We don't have much, but please make yourself comfortable," Ela replied warmly. *Oh, Tono likes the shy girls.*

"I'm not shy, I'm just sort of shocked, that's all," Aymis responded before catching herself.

"Of course not, dear," Ela responded, a confused look on her face. "Nobody said you were."

"We don't have a spare bed. You'll probably be most comfortable on the floor near the stove," Jono said apologetically.

"I am sure I will be fine, thank you," Aymis replied.

"I will let my son, Tono, know someone is out here. He leaves early for his job in the bakery. Hopefully he won't wake you up when he leaves," Jono said as he stepped out of the room.

Aymis took the blanket and tried to get comfortable on the floor by the stove. Sleep came fitfully due to the hard floor and the terrible evening's events still fresh on her mind. The image of Telu's dead body lying in the snow haunted her sporadic dreams. Her mind kept working over the details of Jono's compelled conversation with Telu. Telu's relationship to an archos explained his hatred for them, but shed no light on the archos' words.

"Nobody else has to die." Jono's voice, speaking another's words, echoed in her head. *"I don't want to seize you."* Who had ever heard of an archos that didn't want to seize an enemy? Why hadn't the archos seized her? Could Telu be wrong about the archos? Could this one be different? *"Let her go."* Had this archos actually chosen to protect her? It had saved her life, risking a traumatic confrontation with Telu for her sake. She could hardly believe this discovery. She had to find Telu's son, and find out more.

Despite Tono's considerable efforts to slip out for work quietly, the clatter he made in the kitchen followed by the squeaking door snapped Aymis completely from the pretense of sleep. Sunrise was an hour or two away, but she didn't want to wait any longer to start searching for Telu's son.

Oko examined the dead body that lay in the street, brushing the snow off the corpse's face. Oko thought he recognized him from the congregation. Oko had seen him leaving with the young woman who wouldn't stop watching him. As a Hider, Oko had learned to pay particular attention to anybody who paid attention to him.

Footprints in the snow led from the street to a small complex of flats. Oko had no way of knowing which door the footprints led to, but he could wait until the girl from the congregation came out. He huddled under the eaves in a corner by the porch that kept him mostly sheltered from the swirling wind. It would be a long, cold wait, but Oko had weathered worse nights. Oko knew that the archos could have killed the girl as well, or taken her into its permanent service, but he had no other chance to track down these dangerously inquisitive people.

Oko started awake with a gust of wind, cursing himself for such an amateur lapse. Judging from the growing morning light, he had missed a few hours. As the sky grew lighter, with spectacular color, Oko donned a pair of spectacles and a feathered cap. He didn't have enough time to do more to change his appearance, but hopefully it would be enough to keep any people here from identifying him. The first person he saw leave the building looked like he hadn't slept all night. Oko couldn't be sure, but he could take an educated guess at the cause of the man's insomnia.

"Good morning," Oko said, tipping his hat to the man.

"Morning," Jono said with a yawn.

"Rough night?" Oko asked.

"You could say that," Jono replied evasively.

"Yes, being seized can be..."

"Who said anything about being seized?" Jono snapped. Oko smiled, knowing he had guessed correctly. "Why do you care anyway?"

"Information. What did you do under the archos' control?" Oko asked.

"I just spoke," Jono replied.

"Who with?" Oko asked.

"The archos' father. We argued," Jono answered, keeping his answers as short as possible to avoid thinking about the painful events of the night before.

"Don't say it if you know it, just tell me yes or no. Do you know its name?" Oko knew the terrible risk he took with such a question. Thinking the name or speaking it produced the same effect. Still, he had to know if he had found his quarry.

Jono nodded in response.

"Does the archos' name start with an E?" Oko asked.

Jono nodded in reply. "Thank you," he said as he tipped his feathered cap and left. Oko knew he almost had this Streetborn now.

Interlude
First Contact

J ante soared through the open sky, grateful to leave the rest of the vyeshen behind. The eyries high in the mountains held no interest for him, and Jante already knew the threads of every living thing within twenty leagues of the mountains. How could the others be content? How could they *not* long to explore and discover new threads? Jante had tried in vain to stir up interest in the myriad of new species he had discovered beyond the familiar foothills.

Only Shanje humored his talk, if you could call it that. Vyeshen communication involved no words, just pure conveyance of thoughts, images and feelings. Shanje was one of the few who expressed a remote interest in expanding knowledge of the threads of life, yet he too had advised caution. What more could the vyeshen need? They had, after all, attained perfection; their bodies having become a glorious homage to their god, Phoenix. Disease, sickness and aging no longer threatened them, having been rooted out of their threads millennia ago. To some of his kind, Jante's hunger to learn more smelled of malcontent and ingratitude.

Jante's spectacular plumage shimmered in the sunlight, an intoxicating rainbow of yellows, oranges and reds. In the bright light of spring, he practically appeared ablaze as he soared further and further afield. As he flew his mind felt the threads of all life below him, and he comprehended the order of the entire spectrum of life. The glorious harmony always thrilled Jante. Not long ago he had discovered a new grazing creature – one that appeared to threaten this perfect balance. Its appetite seemed too voracious for the grasses and trees to support it, and it reproduced too quickly.

His initial impulse had been to correct the grazer's threads. Changing an entire species would be hard, requiring the cooperation of all the vyeshen. Jante's explorations had taught him to trust that nature had already provided the balance. It hadn't taken Jante long to discover the complimentary threads of life, woven together to create predators he had never seen before. Nature had once again created its own perfect balance.

Jante's latest explorations took him to the seemingly infinite expanse of water several weeks flight from the eyries of his race. The adaptations he found in the aquatic creatures fascinated him. Such salty water should have been toxic, but life flourished beneath these waves.

Jante's vibrant plumage reflected off the waves below, as he glided low and let his mind soak up the threads of thousands of new life forms. Even what had initially appeared to be rock turned out to be a massive living structure. It extended unendingly into the horizon in both directions, running parallel to the shore. The awareness of this bewilderingly vast collection of new threads, new life, and new harmonies to discover almost completely overshadowed his senses of sight and hearing. He barely noticed the strange, incongruous structure in time to swerve before colliding with it.

Jante had never seen anything like it before, and its very nature baffled and eluded his mind. It had far too much order to be natural, but nothing about it had even a shred of life. If his eyes served him correctly, the hideous thing was composed of dead trees. Who could do such a thing, and why? What purpose could trees serve when dead beyond providing branches for a vyeshen nest?

Most of the structure was now submerged under the water, and nature in her perfect adaptability had already been making life flourish in its ruin. Schools of fish took shelter from the currents, and hid from larger predators in the belly of the thing. A once magnificent, straight tree poked up from the structure at an odd angle, standing naked and void of bark. It had no natural branches, but something had added an artificial branch of sorts – far too straight and orderly to have grown that way. Jante couldn't even begin to guess at the purpose for the odd structure, but the artificial branch would offer him a perfect perch to land on.

Jante landed carefully, knowing that the structure had been in the water for some time, and had already begun to decompose. It creaked ominously under his weight, and the whole structure rocked gently with the waves. As the tide rose – another concept completely unknown to Jante – the waves smashed into the structure with greater intensity. Crack! The base of the dead tree snapped suddenly as a particularly large wave rolled over the structure. Jante started in surprise but took flight without incident. The uncounted time studying had brought him no closer to understanding what he had found.

Then, he felt it. A new set of threads approached the shore from the thickly wooded forest bordering the beach. Shanje knew immediately that the creature these threads described had been responsible for the inharmonious, deathly structure that decayed on the shore here. He had never felt threads so complex, excluding those of his own kind. Above all, he had never perceived a creature with intelligence as brazenly dissonant with the harmony of nature. Long before the creature emerged from the woods, Jante distanced himself as a precaution.

Jante's powerful eyes focused on the new creature far below him. It walked on two legs. It covered some of its own hide with the dead hide of other animals, and carried other strange, dead objects. Jante sensed its attention rest on him as it looked up, but he felt no cause for concern. There was surely nothing the creature could do to him at such a distance.

Pain. It happened so fast, Jante barely had any time to react. Fortunately, he picked up enough of the creature's thoughts to attempt to dodge. Unfortunately, the sharp projectile flew with terrible speed and still pierced Jante's right wing. Every flap of his wings filled his mind with agony unlike any he had felt in centuries, but he knew that landing anywhere nearby would put him at the mercy of this new creature. The world wobbled and spun erratically as Jante struggled to steady his flight, and he knew it would be for naught. Before long he plummeted to the forest canopy, still perilously close to the creature that had shot him out of the sky. He could feel its thoughts – the thoughts of a predator honing in on its new quarry.

Shimmering red and orange feathers lazily drifted to the forest floor far below Jante. A portion of Jante's torso had been shredded painfully by the forest canopy as he crashed into the trees. Despite the intense pain, none of Jante's wounds posed a serious threat. Jante had long ago modified his own threads to improve his natural healing, and he had always been one of the greatest with the threads of life. Unfortunately, his hunter had no intentions of letting him live long enough to heal.

Jante saw into the hunter's mind, finding the creature's way of thinking as unfamiliar and disconcerting as the decaying structure others of his race had constructed. The hunter's threads of life showed a myriad of adaptations Jante had never conceived of. Their minds were powerfully suited to molding the inanimate and dead to suit their needs. Jante saw how the hunter's body, too, had been crafted with an almost perfect focus on this purpose. Insidiously dexterous front paws remained free at almost all times to be put to uses beyond Jante's ken.

In some ways, the creature seemed almost comical to Jante. Stripped of its tools and devices, a single wolf would make quick work of him. Yet, equipped as he was, Jante wouldn't have dared confront him directly even if he were not wounded. The hunter seemed so agonizingly slow, clumsy even, but Jante could comprehend enough of its mind to know that its tricks and contraptions more than compensated. Even the hunter's hide was so fragile and soft, but the thick carcass of a dead beast protected it remarkably well. Mutilated remnants of dead trees further empowered this hunter by converting weak paws into dangerously sharp and long weapons. How had a species that thrived and grew so powerful through death ever come into being?

The strange predator crept furtively through the forest, peering up into the treetops in search of its quarry. Unfortunately for Jante, the vyeshen had never felt any need for camouflage, and he knew his vibrant feathers made him an easy mark for his stalker. Jante started nervously as he saw his hunter crouch and pick up one of his feathers. Just seeing the creature touch his sacred plumes left Jante feeling violated and dirty. The creature put one of its paws up to shield its eyes from the light filtering in through the canopy and looked up, straight at Jante. Jante felt it the moment their eyes met and knew he had been spotted.

Jante desperately longed to take flight, but his pierced wing had become completely useless to him for the pain. Just breathing hurt terribly with the gashes that ran down his torso from his entry into the forest. It had been a miracle that he had managed to grasp a tree branch as high as he had, and thus avoid tumbling to the hard forest floor.

Jante watched as the hunter grabbed a feathered shaft and fitted it into a device made of dead tree and animal sinews. The tip of the shaft in particular caught Jante's eye. Jante had never seen such a material. He immediately could tell that it had never had life, yet no stone or rock in Jante's experience ever glistened in the light or held an edge so keen. Few animals had claws so sharp or strong, and only the vyeshen feathers shone so beautifully in the sunlight. The shaft's beautiful tip held Jante transfixed by its splendor, intoxicating and beguiling his mind. It almost seemed a beautiful way to die – pierced by this spectacular object.

Then the shaft took flight and struck Jante's already wounded wing, passing through it and lodging deep into the tree trunk. Pain surged through Jante's body, snapping him from the trance. Jante turned his rage, fury and fear onto the hunter, barraging him with the full intensity of his feelings, the vyeshen equivalent of screaming at another. The onslaught caught the creature completely off guard, terrifying and bewildering him as a flood of painful, alarming and furious images and feelings overwhelmed him.

It was the first time Jante had heard the vocalizations of this species, as it screamed strange, panicked sounds. Jante perceived the intelligence and structure in what the hunter screamed, knowing it to be far more than the dumb, meaningless sounds many animals made under duress. Yet, it wasn't through hearing that Jante understood the meaning behind the hunters terrified screams. The creature's frantic proclamations trailed off in the distance, "Fire devil! Demon! Monster!"

Jante passed the night in terrible pain, trapped high in the tree. None of those wicked creatures returned. Jante suspected that they might come for him in the morning. Their senses didn't suite them well for night hunting, a fact Jante felt grateful for. At least he had an idea how to drive them off if they were to return. They were easily frightened when alone, but Jante had sensed a very strong social component to the hunter's life threads. He did not want to risk encountering a pack of the hunters in the morning. Fortunately, if Jante judged his injuries correctly, he should be strong enough to attempt a short flight by sunrise. Few other vyeshen could recover from injuries even half as quickly.

As the first touches of morning light illuminated the tree tops, Jante felt the pack of hunters drawing near. It was all he could do to fight through the pain and take to an awkward flight from the trees. Below him he sensed at least a hundred of those vile creatures converging on the tree where he had been trapped. His wounded wing screamed in protest with every beat, but Jante knew he had to push on. There could be no mistaking the lethal intent, nor the determination in the minds of his prey.

Jante pushed on for several agonizing hours, long after he had last felt any hint of the hunter's life threads. Finally, he set himself down gently in a tall tree. Exhaustion nearly overwhelmed him. Under better circumstances, he could have trusted himself to pass the night high in the treetops, but Jante knew he would likely topple right out of the tree. So, despite the risk, he settled to the forest floor and found the best hiding place an exhausted, wounded, massive, and vibrantly colored bird could find. The bushes hardly concealed him, but there was nothing more he could do.

The ordeal of his close encounter with this new species left him shaken and terrified. He had never seen a creature with advanced enough life threads to pose any threat to the vyeshen. He had never imagined any creature could thrive on such disharmony with nature, as these did. Jante had always found that nature had a balancing answer for any seemingly disruptive species he discovered. This time, he knew that there could be no balancing this species disruptions. He needed to rally the rest of his kind. Maybe with the combined efforts of all the vyeshen, they could bring this errant species in line.

The vyeshen had never attempted altering an entire species – excluding their own kind – before. Jante didn't know if it could be done. After the pain and terror of Jante's first encounter, he almost hoped they would fail, and thus be justified in simply wiping the vermin out. As Jante drifted to sleep, his thoughts wandered to more pleasant things– the memory of that beautiful, glistening material that had so easily pierced his wing. The desire to see that again, to learn of its origins, and maybe even take some back to the other vyeshen almost made him return. Perhaps those creatures had left the shaft lodged in the tree where he passed the night before. Only the realization that he had no way to extract the shaft and retrieve the tip changed his mind.

Jante could hardly believe what his eyes were showing him. His understanding of their threads of life had told him to expect such numbers, but it was one thing to understand something, and another entirely to see it. He had also known to expect their disruptive influence on the balance of nature, but again that left him unprepared for the reality he, and twenty other vyeshen that accompanied him, now saw.

Jante had been the first to find a small cluster of the creatures. They had built their nests by the land they had altered to grow their food. Huge pieces of the forest had been destroyed, replaced by plants the vermin cultivated for their own purposes. Despite Jante's past experience, the startlingly different way these creatures thought surprised him anew. Couldn't these creatures see how unharmonious their actions were? Didn't they see that as their numbers swelled, everything else around them fell farther and farther out of balance? Didn't they care?

Finding the larger herds proved easy from there. All they had to do was follow the scar the creatures had carved through the land connecting the first settlement to others. Occasionally they spotted a poor, enslaved beast pulling contraptions loaded with food along these scars. Following these interconnecting paths eventually led the expedition of vyeshen to the sight they now beheld from high above.

The size of this particular herd defied anything he could have anticipated, and the sheer havoc the sprawling collection of their dwellings and nests wreaked on nature infuriated him. So much of nature's life had been pushed away by the vermin. The cacophony of noises rose even to Jante's ears as he looked down on the swarming vermin – so small they looked like insects from this height. The smells of burning wood, bodily waste, and other refuse also reached Jante's finely tuned beak. He had not expected to find them in such intensely concentrated clusters.

'*There are too many of them,*' Shanje sent, conveying the thought far more powerfully than any words could do. Jante knew he was right.

'*We should not have waited,*' Jante replied, his communication carrying with it all of the arguments he had made with the vyeshen council for uncounted years. The council had dismissed his early warnings about the species' prolific nature, and their impressive adaptability. In their experience, few species had the capacity to spread far beyond the niche nature had carved out for them. Try as he did, Jante had not been able to convince them that these creatures were different. Besides, the council argued, even if the creatures spread to our foothills, they pose no threat to us. Now that the creatures had spread into the lands known to the vyeshen council, they finally had sent out this exploratory expedition. *'Do you still think these vermin are not a threat to us?'* Jante asked.

Jenu, another member of the expedition, joined in the discussion. His thoughts rested on the smaller clusters of the creatures out among the fields where they grew their food. Perhaps if they shaped their threads, the changes would gradually spread into the larger population. *'We could start with the smaller packs and let the changes slowly assimilate into the herds.'*

Jante wished that Jenu's idea could work. Unfortunately, these creatures spread so quickly that the only hope for meaningful change resided in making changes directly to the large herds. *'No, we must change the large herds or our modified threads will be overwhelmed and lost in the larger whole.'*

Shanje disagreed with Jante's plan. Few vyeshen possessed Jante's skill with the threads of life. Changing a creature's threads required delicacy, caution and skill. Doing so while remaining unknown to the targeted organism was a task beyond most vyeshen. The human nests were so tightly packed together that a vyeshen would have no hiding place to work from either. *'Attempting that would destroy us.'*

Jante recognized the wisdom in Shanje's reply. Why hadn't the council listened to his warnings all those years ago? Why hadn't he returned to check on this disease to give his people warning of its spreading? In the back of Jante's mind, he knew the answer to both of those questions. Even now as he watched the chaotic swarms of vermin bustling far below him, he hungered for another glimpse of that strange adapted stone. He felt a similar, though far weaker hunger in the minds of all the others.

Jante could not hide the intoxicating allure that held him spellbound on that first sighting as he recounted his ordeal with the council all those years ago. The council felt the power that even Jante's memory had on their minds, and wisely feared what it could do to their kind. Just the memory of Jante's initial account now swayed the feelings of each of his companions. The council had chosen to ignore these creatures in the hopes that such an alluring and tempting substance would never again reach the minds of a vyeshen. Deep in Jante's heart, it was the sway of that glistening, lifeless matter that scared him the most. Now, the vermin had brought their enticing materials right to the borders of vyeshen land. One thing was for certain – the vyeshen were going to change.

Change – it was at the very heart of the vyeshen power – the essence of their gift from Phoenix. Yet, despite their ability to change the very threads of life around them, his kind dreaded change. The vyeshen had adopted the role as custodians of natural balance, protectors of the status quo. Now this new species forced them to adapt, something the vyeshen hadn't done in uncounted centuries.

Shanje agreed with him completely. In fact, he felt the beginnings of a new idea. As the idea formed in his mind, it took hold in Jante's, Jenu's and the others as well. Jante's first encounter had shown that this new species had a mind open to vyeshen touch. If they couldn't change the species, perhaps they could create a new subspecies to control them. Such a task would be far easier, and far safer.

By now the vyeshen expedition had already left the massive cluster of nests they had been watching. It was as if their wings had already started taking them where their discussion was slower to arrive. It didn't take long for them to be looking down on a much smaller group of the species' nests. Perhaps a few hundred of the vermin lived in this smaller outpost. Some still worked at killing the trees to make room to grow more of their food. Then Jante's eyes caught the glimmer he had been hungering for all this time. Before he could stop himself, he dove lower for a better look.

A muscular male of the species had a very large piece of the shimmering material attached to the end of a wooden shaft. His muscles rippled as he swung it in powerful sideways arcs into the wedge shaped gash he inflicted on a tree. The tree teetered and shook with each blow. The wanton destruction of life, and the brazen disruption of nature's order hardly registered in Jante's mind. Not even Phoenix's feathers shone in the light with such splendor. Not even Phoenix's talons had the strength of this magnificent substance. Even if the vyeshen were to discover how to find and create such substances, Jante knew that neither their minds nor their bodies were suited to the task.

The rest of the vyeshen expedition had also spotted the man felling the tree. Heedless of their safety, the entire group dove from lofty heights for a closer look. As the tree the man worked creaked and groaned in its death, the metal's alluring call burned itself powerfully in the hearts of their entire group. The yearning overpowered Jenu completely, and he dove down – talons reaching, grasping – for the intoxicating substance. The male who wielded it lunged to the side just in time.

Jenu's heedless, crazed dive had not been that of a calculated hunter. Having missed his mark, the massive bird floundered and collided with the ground. It all happened so fast. Before Jenu could recover and take to the sky, the sharp, keen tool smashed into Jenu's torso, crushing his wing and wedging itself deep in his chest. Jenu was dead.

Losing sight of the glistening tool's head as it buried itself deep in Jenu's ribs broke the hold it had on Jante and the others. Terror and horror struck their hearts at the first vyeshen death in uncounted centuries. Jante shrieked in rage as he dove for Jenu's murderer. This time the creature failed to dodge, and Jante's powerful talons clasped him around the torso. The creature screamed in terror as Jante's sharp beak and powerful claws took out their rage on him.

Shouts drifted on the breeze towards Jante and the others as the creatures swarmed to protect their own. *Let them come!* Jante thought. They would pay for the terror of this day. The vyeshen attacked their pray with reckless abandon, as fully entranced by their rage as they had been by their lust for metal. The dissonant shrieks of the vyeshen mingled with terrified screams from the other creatures as they battled. The vermin fell in larger numbers before the vyeshen, but the deadly projectiles brought many more of Jante's friends to their deaths. Ultimately, the vermin's numbers won out and only Shanje and Jante managed to escape, each with several wounds.

PART II

CHAPTER 12

FOILED

Choice. I learned how precious it was when Aitrox seized me. In those terrible moments I gained a sense of empathy for those I had traumatized. I never would have guessed that losing the gift of choice would leave me feeling so violated and wronged. One may feel they have no choice, if they had to obey or die, but that isn't entirely true. It is one thing to have your choices unjustly influenced by wicked people presenting terrible consequences. It is another thing entirely *to be robbed of the freedom to choose. I would have rather died than let Aitrox use me as she did, but she robbed me of even that escape.*

Once I experienced the trauma of having my choice taken completely from me, I understood why people would always despise the archos. It was wrong of me to steal such a precious, fundamental part of humanity from others, even for a short time. It didn't matter that I did so in order to survive, or that my very nature pushed me to continue doing so. At the very least, I knew I was wrong to have become so nonchalant about inflicting that misery on others. I knew there was something terribly wrong with the very nature of my kind.

'E*ru. His name is Eru.'*

Eru recognized the feeling of Jono's mind thinking his name, but Eru managed to resist the pull to seize him. Eru perceived enough to know that someone was asking questions that his awareness should have easily picked up on, someone who made Jono very uneasy. Something or someone other than Telu hunted him. Eru sensed a different mind seeking him out, tugging at his reflexes to seize her, but she held no malice or violence in her heart.

After the terrors of the night, Eru felt he might welcome the hunter that escaped his awareness. Perhaps such a being could kill him and thus avert untold future tragedies.. Eru felt an unusual kinship with his father. Telu had longed to die, but lacked the resolve to kill himself. Telu had hunted Eru, hoping to find vengeance, but expecting to find escape. Now Eru let this new hunter pursue him, hoping to have his own wish granted. In that way at least, he and his father were not so very different after all.

Eru teetered down the busy street like a blind drunk. Trying to walk without seizing anyone was dangerous, and served little purpose. For all Eru knew, he could be walking in a circle, getting nowhere. Still, he refused to seize another, but longed to get as far away as possible from his latest disaster. Despite the nobility of his intentions, he found it impossible to avoid drawing people's attention. In his heavy winter garb, nobody knew him as an archos, and his meandering, wobbly movement automatically led people to unkind conclusions, bringing critical gazes his way. In his traumatized state, Eru lacked the strength to resist seizing the person behind such unfriendly gazes.

Eru meandered through the city streets, not caring where he went, so long as it took him away. As much as possible, he stayed in the void, releasing those he seized immediately. Having nobody seized, he had no way of knowing that he had tripped over a dip in the street. He toppled into an icy puddle at the edge of the street, but he didn't hear the splash of his fall. The cold icy puddle soaked his thick winter clothing, but he felt nothing of the chill.

Eru felt his mind growing sluggish, and mistakenly attributed it to a need for rest. Then something kicked into action deep in Eru's mind. Before he knew what happened, Eru seized a passing carriage driver and the man leapt from his driver's seat to come to his aid. The carriage swerved as the reins pulled to the side, before the driver let go of them. The horse's hooves narrowly missed crushing Eru's skull, a fact Eru regretted. Eru watched in consternation as the horses and wagon plowed into a group of pedestrians, the carriage toppling on top of a few people. He heard the screams of pain, shock and fear through the driver's ears, an all too familiar sound. More people hurt because of him.

Eru tried to release the driver, a man named Thomas, but couldn't. Eru recognized the feeling: his survival instincts had taken over. Thomas lifted him out of the puddle – *how long had I been in the puddle like that?* Eru asked himself, but realized he had no way of knowing. The man he had seized pulled the cold wet clothes from Eru's body. Thomas unbuttoned his jacket and pulled

Eru into his chest. Eru felt the terrible cold touch of his skin against the man's torso, but that paled in comparison to the way Eru had ruined Thomas's life.

Thomas's meager income as a carriage driver barely supported his family, but he wouldn't keep the job now. The carriage owner was a cold, hard man who wouldn't care that an archos had seized the driver. Eru recognized the unfair guilt Thomas felt for the people his carriage had just harmed in the crash. Thomas hated him, and rightfully so. It didn't take long for Eru's body to warm enough for the danger to pass. Eru released Thomas. Thomas quickly buttoned his coat back up and ran to the crash site, now surrounded by curious onlookers.

Eru allowed himself to seize a few people to get out of the situation, seeking somewhere warm and quiet where he could rest and hopefully find new clothing. He felt the awareness of his hunger, and entered the inn on the corner for food.

"Welcome to Traveler's Sanctuary," the innkeeper said with his back to the door as he worked with the cook on breakfast for his guests.

Eru seized the innkeeper and his cook. Their fear, anger and violation stung like salt on a fresh wound. Eru felt the man's loathing, and hostility just barely under control. Nothing would please the innkeeper more than seeing Eru die. At the moment, Eru shared the same feelings, and no longer wished to wait for his mysterious hunter to find him.

Eru had the innkeeper pick up a knife from an uncleared table and approach. Eru watched expectantly from the innkeeper's eyes. Eru raised the knife to strike him down, feeling the man's excitement, sharing it with him. In a moment it would all be over.

Eru looked down at the blade protruding from the innkeeper's rib cage, sharing the man's shock and pain. He should have known such a thing would happen. The moment the innkeeper's thoughts acknowledged his own hateful desires Eru's instincts kicked in. Why would it have been any different just because Eru wished to die? Using another to kill him could never work. Eru had just killed another innocent man.

Undeterred by his failure, Eru brought the cook into the dining area. He felt the new surge of fear and grief in the cook as he saw his boss bleeding to death on the floor. Eru used the cook's eyes to guide himself over to another table. Eru grabbed another knife with his own senseless hands and positioned it to plunge it into his ribs.

Eru's instincts kicked in again and the cook knocked the knife out of his hands. Eru hadn't even noticed how his faculties brought the cook over to him. He recognized the involuntary intervention of his instincts. He had hoped suicide would be easier for someone who couldn't feel pain. Instead his frustration only heightened as he felt every effort foiled by his own nature.

Eru had the cook hand him the knife again before releasing him. Perhaps with nobody under his control he could take matters into his own hands. He did his best to stab himself, finding the task surprisingly difficult with no way to feel or see if he succeeded. His basic awareness of his body in space helped him guide his hand through several violent stabbing motions. By now, he expected to be bleeding so profusely that he only had a few minutes left. He stayed in the void awaiting his death like a child waiting for his father to return from work. Would Ama welcome him? It no longer mattered. Even if nothing awaited him, if life were a one-act play, he finally felt at peace. He had done it.

Time passed, and Eru realized something had to be wrong. He seized the cook, who was working in vain to stop his boss's bleeding. To Eru and the cook's consternation, Eru remained noticeably un-bloodstained. The knife sat on the floor at his feet. When had he dropped it? Without someone under his control, he couldn't have heard the clang as it hit the floor, or even noticed the lack of the knife's weight in his hand.

Eru left the inn, fuming over his failures. Why couldn't he, the sower of death, bring in his own personal harvest? People died at his hand in more ways than he cared to imagine, yet nothing he did to himself succeeded. Vivid recollections of carriage wheels crushing his hosts, or cold swirling waters consuming him filled his mind. That was it: the Deor River. Fortunately for Eru, a bridge crossed the river only a few blocks away. Eru commandeered a carriage and rushed for the bridge. He watched the busy morning travelers as he passed them, chafing at every slow carriage that delayed his purpose. Arriving at the bridge, he stopped the carriage and released the driver. Using only one pair of eyes to guide him, he stepped up to the edge. Eru climbed over the balustrade before releasing the eyes that watched and stepped off the edge. He had done it.

Suddenly the water rushed up to meet several other pairs of eyes as Eru's reflexes took over. Eru felt the biting cold water shock their lungs and lock their muscles. Even his domineering will couldn't overcome the power of the cold on their bodies. A few sunk immediately. Eru unwittingly seized new would-be rescuers to replace those whom the cold water overcame. Eru's heart screamed in protest, but his reflexes controlled him as unflinchingly as if he were seized. In the end, this suicide attempt nearly succeeded, but he found a strong enough swimmer to rescue him just in time.

The swimmer who saved him brought him to shore where another person under Eru's control pulled him to safety. The exhausted, hypothermic man collapsed on the shore, abandoned by Eru's faculties to die. The next hours were an indistinguishable blur, as his mind drove people to attend to his needs. He felt the warmth of the tub of water as someone checked it before putting his chilled body in. He tasted the wholesome, warm soup through someone else's mouth before he was fed. In the background he sensed the loathing of people under his dominion, but even now he lacked the capacity to let himself die.

As the day passed and twilight drew nearer, Eru felt clarity return to his thoughts along with a renewed determination not to fail again. Apparently killing himself in the presence of others was nearly impossible. The river still seemed his best bet, but he couldn't allow himself to try with others near him. He tried not to count the lives that mistake had taken. No more people should die on his account.

Eru felt the grief, shock and fear around him, recognizing the familiar harvest brought to those unfortunate enough to reap what he had sown. Eru felt the loss in the home he now controlled. The woman who fed him soup had lost her husband to the river, and now found herself compelled to save the one responsible. Families had lost bread-winners, fathers, and husbands just outside this home. He had fled the lamp maker's shop, the villa, and the shanty from this morning to escape this atmosphere. Outside the window, Eru's eyes saw the busy evening traffic crossing the bridge where he had drowned so many innocent people. Even those who had no connection to the victims felt the weight of grief as they passed.

Eru used the crowds to guide him back to the bridge where he sat on a bench and waited for the evening crowds to dissipate. In a few hours the streets would be empty and nobody would have to die trying to save him.

Aymis wished she had the enhanced abilities Telu said she would experience under archos influence. Being privy to only the immediate thoughts in a person's mind didn't lend itself to finding an archos when one has been conditioned not to think about them. She didn't even know which way to go. Telu's son could have been a mile away or more when he intervened on her behalf.

Aymis smiled, teeth chattering teeth with the morning chill. Despite the impossibility of her current task, and the trauma of last night, she knew she had plenty to smile about. The archos she wanted to find had saved her life, and given her back her freedom. Telu may not have been an enslaving archos, but he had dominated her life all the same. She breathed in the bitter cold morning air, savoring her freedom. The tip of her nose stung, and the cold bit into her ears like a hungry rat.

She rubbed her ears and wrapped the same old scarf, a gift from her mother, tighter, refusing to let the cold win. Even the terrifying events of last night, and her reason for being out here this morning gave her hope. Likely, she was a fool to seek out any archos, but she had to know if this one was different. The possibility of unending captivity under an archos hung over her like a threatening storm, casting a gloomy shadow on her future. Any possibility of a benevolent archos felt like a ray of hope against the dark prospects for her future.

An archos did this! Aymis heard the thought in a man who scurried from a nearby home. She recognized the terror and shock in his thoughts and saw them etched clearly in his face. What in all of Deor had happened?

Aymis ran to investigate, feeling her pulse throbbing in her eyes with terrible anticipation. The vision of Telu's bleeding corpse flashed in her memory, giving her pause. The implications of more archos murders so near, and soon after Telu's death, cast a shadow on her hopes. She didn't know if she could bear to find out. Yet she had to know the truth.

Had she known the atrocities she would see, she would have run screaming rather than enter the villa. The walls in the humble family room looked as though it had been painted a reddish brown. She recognized the shape of a mother, clasping her children in a vain effort to protect them. Aymis's stomach knotted up in revulsion. Had she eaten anything for breakfast, or dinner last night, she would have left it at the grisly scene.

Aymis ran like a child fleeing a pack of wolves. How could anyone inflict such atrocities on another person? Certainly nobody with even a glimmer of goodness could possibly condone such barbarous acts. Telu had been right about the archos. Anything that did such evils must be destroyed. Telu's misguided zeal aside, she felt a newfound respect for his courage in taking on the impossible. Aymis fell to a bench, ignoring the snow she sat on, and the chill that it drove into her core. Tears flowed like a river, and she cried with no concern for the uproar she made.

Aymis's cries added to the mournful choir that grew with new mourners from almost every home on the street. How could an archos be so eager to seize and kill? How could the same archos that had been so desperate not to harm Telu, have done this?

"You killed her!" She remembered Telu's angry accusation levied against his son. She echoed his vitriolic accusations, passing condemnation for the deaths of men, women and children all up and down the street.

"I couldn't stop that. There's so much about me you don't understand." She recalled Jono's voice speaking the rebuttal. How could she hope to understand such barbarity? Had the archos claimed to be powerless to prevent death? She

knew the truth behind Telu's death, but how might it have appeared to one who arrived moments after? Aymis knew better than to believe that family had pushed an archos as Telu had, but what didn't she know?

"I don't want to seize you. Don't make me." Jono's voice echoed in her mind. The same archos who voiced those desires wouldn't have willingly seized and murdered entire families. Could this have been the work of another archos? Jono's words restored the smallest sliver of hope. Aymis dried the tears from her and resumed her search.

Oko had never seen a Streetborn with such an incredible propensity for murder. Even Oko's hardened sensibilities towards death couldn't prepare him for the trail of destruction he found. This kind of senseless violence gave Oko purpose, and justified his means. Oko killed, but always with purpose, and discretion. This archos murdered for recreation, leaving a wake of terror and trauma behind. By the time he finished investigating the last shanty on the tour of death, the evening rush filled the streets. The lengthy, gruesome tour left his head spinning and his resolve hardening. The archos responsible for this must not escape his judgment. Oko remembered the brazen courage another had demonstrated in hunting this monster. He reiterated the words written by that man's foolhardy hand: I will kill the archos Eru.

CHAPTER 13

A REASON TO LIVE

I didn't want to die, but I couldn't bear the thought of more people dying because of me. So I sat, waiting; waiting until I could feel the city around me asleep: waiting for my time to die. I felt people's minds, and longed for what they had — a normal life. Had Aymis never found me, I wouldn't have realized the extraordinary life I could live.

E ru sensed every one that passed him, grateful that none suspected the one who had killed so many had returned to the scene of the crime. Eru's heartstrings played painful songs as he felt the stories of the regular lives they enjoyed. He felt a father's happy anticipation of his daughter's excited embrace welcoming him home. Another young man's mind stewed over fretful concerns about the woman he courted. Did she love him? Someone else fumed over frustrations with an obnoxious coworker in his mercantile firm. None of them knew how precious their lives, with all the simple joys and headaches, truly were.

Eru knew the majesty and cruelty of the world like only an archos could. He held the memories and experiences of uncounted lives all stored in his powerful archos mind. He knew the joy of loving and being loved, though it would always be vicariously. Eru knew to appreciate the small beauties of sight, sound, touch and taste. Deprivation engendered appreciation. Deprived of his own senses, he could never stop marveling at the world around him. Deprived of love, he knew the precious gift when he felt it in the lives of virtually all he had seized. Even as he sat there in the void, Eru perceived the beauty of the world he was about to bid farewell to.

Eru felt the lives moving around him, with a renewed sense of awe for each one, worth more than all the iron in Deor. As the crowds thinned, Eru's resolve hardened. His existence could only threaten and destroy the beautiful lives of others. His world grew bleak and drab as the streets of Deor emptied. With the streets empty, he seized someone in a home several hundred yards away. He had never tried to guide himself with a single pair of eyes so far away, but he wouldn't let himself act with anyone close enough to get to the river before he died.

Eru moved awkwardly with such a distant perspective to guide him. He climbed over the balustrade one last time, finding his depth perception particularly challenged with such a limited, distant view. He readied himself to release the one watching him and the fence simultaneously, when he caught unwelcomed motion. Someone's long shadow cut a dark silhouette through the cold misty streets. The light from multiple street lamps cast long shadows, each originating at the feet of a young lady. Eru sensed her coming, and realized his pursuer had found him.

Eru wanted to let go of the balustrade, but couldn't risk her being seized and dying to save him. If she had come to kill him, it hardly mattered, but something felt different about her. Eru sensed something he had never expected from someone seeking an archos – hope. It was all Eru could do to keep from seizing her the moment she saw him, and realized she had found her quarry.

'Please no!' He felt her exclaim in her mind as she realized his intentions. Eru recognized her as the one Telu had held hostage last night. *'Eru please stop!'*

Eru seized her, unable to hold back when she used his name. He felt the usual pain he inflicted from seizing her, but felt something shockingly different about her. Through her he saw into the minds of people in all the homes around him laid bare. She magnified his innate senses with an intensity he had never thought possible. More shocking than her unexpected effect on him was her lack of hatred for him. He felt her desperate hopes to find an archos that didn't destroy. He regretted that he couldn't fulfill her wish. Fear filled her with her first ever experience under archos dominion, and her terror that she may never be released. Was it foolishness for her to seek him out? Had she done the right thing?

Part of Eru's heart dreaded the answer to her doubting questions. Eru could see into her innocent and optimistic heart. The hardships in her life had done nothing to dim the light in her soul, despite everything Telu had put her through. Eru had seized more people than even his powerful mind could count, and never had he felt someone as remarkable as she. A heart so resilient, good and strong didn't deserve to be touched by his ability. Eru didn't belong in her company, but he couldn't bring himself to let her go. For the first time ever, he felt a heart that didn't loath him.

Eru felt her presence in his mind, a disturbingly similar experience to having Aitrox intrude on his most sacred, painful moments. *No!* She shouldn't have to see the monster he was. One as gentle, and unsullied as she shouldn't see the darkness that filled Eru's life. She should be spared the sight of the uncounted deaths at his hands. Then Eru realized the true reason why his soul trembled at the thought of her seeing all of his secrets. She would certainly add her vote to the unanimous tally against him, and he couldn't bear that thought.

Aymis perceived the terrible massacre of last night with horror and sorrow. She became the secret twin in Ama's womb and Eru sensed in her a kindred spirit to his late mother. No moment in Eru's short life escaped her beholding and Eru despaired. He couldn't hide anything from her penetrating perception, and so he knew she, too, would condemn him. Eru waited in terror for the moment when he would feel Aymis's heart darken with loathing for him.

Aymis felt the fear and pain at being seized, and almost despaired. Only her ability to do what most could not, and see into the heart of the archos who controlled her, kept hope alive. What she saw in Telu's son rewarded her hopes more than she could have imagined. Telu had warned her that reading an archos would mean she would die in subjection to its power. Yet she immediately knew that Eru would never enslave her as Telu had warned. She felt the intrusive touch of Eru's powerful mind digging deep into her most cherished memories and understood perfectly why everyone loathed and dreaded the archos. Yet she felt the amplification of her reading ability most keenly as her own senses reached to the furthest recesses of Eru's soul.

As she came to know her captor as deeply and intimately as Eru now knew her, the invasiveness of being seized faded until it felt more like a bonding experience. She felt like she had known Eru since the day of her birth, as if she had practically raised him from his infancy at the same time. Her heart marveled to find a soul like Eru's, so determined to defeat the evil inside him, and so tragically tortured over his failures. Her heart wept as she felt Eru's longing for acceptance, for a single voice to speak through the clamor of condemning shrieks and console him. She would have smiled if possible as she perceived all the ways Eru tried to help people, and shared his sorrow for every time his efforts ended in pain and failure.

Aymis felt love for Eru, surprised in her mind at how quickly it came – yet in her heart it didn't feel fast at all. She knew every second of Eru's life. In many ways, she felt closer to him than even her mother, for not even Janis knew her heart like Eru did now. Only a few seconds had ticked by on the large citadel clock down the street, but a lifetime had passed in their minds.

Eru felt her love for him. It warmed his heart like the rays of the summer sun breaking into the long winter. The light filled his soul, overwhelming his awareness of the world around him. He felt the way a rat must feel, sticking its head out from the sewers into the morning sun and fresh air. Eru would forever treasure that first moment when he met Aymis.

Aymis walked over to Eru, feeling him control her limbs like a benevolent puppeteer. She helped him climb back to safety, feeling relief when she saw him no longer teetering on the edge of death. Aymis could not have saved him, but his instinctive power would have compelled her to try. Even uncompelled, she probably would have jumped in after him, knowing she couldn't let an archos as rare and precious as Eru die without trying to save him.

Eru released her once she had guided him back to the safety of the street bench. For the first time in his life he wanted to live. He craved the light of her being as he had never craved any before, but he couldn't betray her trust or her... friendship.

In the brief but potent moment when their souls touched and truly comprehended each other, Eru knew he had found someone he could trust unconditionally. More importantly, he realized that she could read his thoughts as he could hers, allowing them to communicate freely. Just that simple gift – the gift of guilt-free communication made Eru want to shout for joy.

"Heeeaaahhh," he unwittingly vocalized with a smile. Eru didn't hear the sounds, and had never even realized he could vocalize anything himself. Aymis heard it, and laughed warmly. Eru sensed the joy she shared with him over this sublime encounter.

'It's a pleasure to meet you, too.' Eru didn't have to see her to know she smiled with her thought.

'You have no idea,' Eru blurted, realizing that only Aymis could have any idea how singular and precious this moment was to him. *'Actually, you do.'*

'I am so glad I found you, my friend,' Aymis replied.

'Friend? Are you sure?' Eru asked, as fear filled his soul. Someone like him shouldn't have friends. They would end up dead.

'I know why you are afraid, but don't be,' Aymis answered. *'You are not a terrible monster.'*

'But, I have killed so many, and I will certainly kill again,' Eru answered. He knew that there was little point to their conversation. Aymis already knew his

fears, regrets and insecurities as well as he did. Eru subsequently knew how she would respond, but for some reason he needed it to come from her.

'Not with me helping you. I know your heart, Eru.'

'But, I don't know the first thing about being a friend,' Eru objected. How could he let anything start with her? It couldn't possibly end well, and it would only hurt worse to lose her later rather than cut ties right away.

'Don't fool yourself, Eru. You have seen examples of loving fathers, loyal friends, and devoted siblings in the lives of people you have seized,' Aymis answered.

'But...' Eru stammered in his mind. *'I don't want to lose you.'*

'You won't. No matter what,' Aymis replied. *'I will always be your friend.'*

'I'd tell you to pinch me to make sure I am not dreaming, except it wouldn't do me much good,' Eru said, surrendering to his happiness.

'I hadn't expected you to be funny,' Aymis responded.

'Not funny, just giddy. How is this possible?' Eru asked.

'I told you, I am a Reader,' Aymis responded.

'Reader? So I am guessing that means you can read thoughts,' Eru thought.

'Yes, Readers are one type of Aegendi. You felt what happened when you seized me. Like all kinds of Aegendi, my gift becomes something far greater under archos control.'

'So, there are other kinds of Aegendi? That explains the miracles at the citadels,' Eru replied.

'Your father taught me about some of them. Most Aegendi don't even know they have a gift. Only the really powerful ones can do anything unusual without archos help.'

'Like you, you were reading thoughts without meaning to,' Eru added, recollecting some of Aymis's memories.

'I guess that means I am strong,' Amis replied shyly. *'I saw a man levitate a top hat without being seized. He probably made a very powerful Wizard under archos control.'*

'Has he been seized then?' Eru asked.

'I can only assume so. He set up a street show for coin. I doubt he escaped detection. Your father saved me from a similar fate,' Aymis thought with a shiver.

Their conversation stirred Eru's recollection of Aymis's feelings for Telu, and everything his father had forced her to do.

'*So, my father was looking for someone immune to the archos?*' Eru asked. His powerful mind quickly filled in gaps from a moment in his past that haunted him. Suddenly he understood why he couldn't save the boy, Jeo. '*That means that Jeo's father was...*'

'*A Hider,*' Aymis finished. '*The High Queen, and those she controls devote almost all their energy to hunting and killing them.*'

'*That explains a lot,*' Eru thought to himself. His powerful archos mind recalled the details from that fateful day clearly. He recalled a feeling of being watched that he had dismissed at the time as part of his growing awareness. That feeling went away the morning he found Jeo's family dead. '*I was being watched, and had unknowingly discovered a Hider. I did bring death to Jeo's family then.*'

'*Stop doing that to yourself!*' Aymis snapped angrily in her mind. '*Stop blaming yourself for things you couldn't have known or controlled! How could you have known that would happen? How could you have known Boro was a Hider? Their deaths fall on other shoulders, not yours. You need to forgive yourself, and allow yourself to be happy.*'

'*I think a Hider may be hunting me,*' Eru said, ready to change the subject. '*This morning. I felt Jono's thoughts focus on me. Someone was asking about me, but I could only feel Jono's thoughts about me.*'

'*Oh, please no!*' Aymis thought, her lips quivering with fear and grief.

'*What?*' Eru asked, feeling her fear spilling into his heart.

'*Remember what I was trying to hide from Telu? I had found a Hider in the congregation. He must have followed us,*' Aymis responded, panic in her thoughts.

'*Why would he do that?*' Eru asked.

'*According to Telu, the Hiders that stay alive protect their secret violently if they have to. I must have been too obvious when I watched him in the congregation. He's coming for me now. I have to go.*'

'*Don't leave me!*' Eru exclaimed, feeling fear like never before.

'Don't you see? This Hider wants me dead. If he finds you, an archos, he will kill us both! I have to hide from him, to protect you,' Aymis practically shouted in her mind.

'I won't let that happen!' Eru said with conviction.

'How will you stop him? He's a Hider. You can't do anything!' Aymis responded impulsively.

'I eluded Father for years. I know how to stay hidden. Besides, I may not be able to seize him, but I can still keep him from you if I know he is coming.' Eru clenched his jaw in determination.

'I can't let you risk your life for me. I can't let you kill to protect me,' Aymis answered.

'Before you showed up, I wanted to die. If I lose you...' Eru couldn't finish the thought.

'Eru, don't...'

'No!' Eru tried to stop her, but it was too late. At the thought of his name, Eru unavoidably seized her, releasing her almost as quickly. *'I'm sorry!'*

'Don't apologize for it, my friend,' Aymis answered assuringly. *'What was I saying?'*

'You were about to try and talk me out of protecting you. Save your breath, or your brain power,' Eru replied.

'Friend,' Aymis said, feeling satisfied with the substitute for his name. She felt his pleasure at her choice. *'This isn't a joking matter!'*

'I have never been more serious,' Eru responded sincerely. *'If a Hider is hunting you, then I will do everything in my power to protect you. However, I think the Hider was looking for me, not you.'*

'But,' Aymis began to object, before realizing she could never change Eru's mind.

'Ok, Friend. You win,' Aymis responded as she helped Eru stand. In a strange, indescribable way, Eru had just enough information from Aymis to allow her to lead him like she would a blind child. She guided both of them to a nearby hostel, where she used the last of Telu's coins to pay for what remained of the night for both of them. Her legs ached from the long day searching for her new

friend, and the experiences with their first encounter left her mentally drained. She left Eru bundled up, knowing it better to conceal his archos attributes with a Hider on their trail. She unbuttoned her coat, and let it fall to the floor before collapsing to her bunk. Despite the thought of a murderous Hider hunting her, she found sleep immediately.

Eru lay on his bunk, feeling the awareness of all the amazing minds around him. Even in sleep, he basked in Aymis's presence. She had given him a reason to live. If this Hider tried to hurt Aymis, Eru would kill him without regret.

Aitrox marveled at yet another first inspired by this unusual Streetborn. The ability to watch an archos without them sensing her presence had proved to be an invaluable asset. Boro likely had a few more months before he broke and his gift diminished slightly. Unlike all the other Aegendi, Hiders could not be seized again once released. Of course, his gift proved unusually useful with this Streetborn. Watching him with complete anonymity had just given her a new first: jealousy.

Not since she took the Phoenix's greatest asset had anybody possessed something she coveted. This Streetborn however had earned something no archos had ever won. The young Reader, Aymis, actually loved him. But, Aitrox cared nothing for the love of her subjects. Did a landlord care if the rats in his basement loved him? The very notion of loving someone, of giving him or her that kind of dominion over you, was foolishness. She had no need for anyone to love her, having sufficient power without. Still, the novelty of the experience intrigued her, even as it vexed her to know she couldn't just seize the Streetborn and take Aymis's love away from him.

There was another reason not to seize the Streetborn just yet. Apparently, a Hider would be paying Eru a visit soon. The Streetborn had an uncanny knack for stumbling across Hiders. Aitrox doubted she would find the leverage she needed over this Hider. It almost felt a tragic waste to kill them now that she knew how to put them to such good use, but she knew she couldn't afford to let any others discover that secret.

CHAPTER 14

TRACKER

Meeting Aymis gave me the first semblance of a real life.
For a time, I was content to merely bask in her presence
and revel in the novelty of acceptance. I felt I had earned
a period of respite. The world around me however, had no
intentions of giving me a sabbatical from sorrow.

'**G**ood morning!' Eru beamed, but Aymis didn't hear his greeting. He
would have to get used to the fact that she could only hear his thoughts
if she turned her attention to him. He felt a pang of jealousy for all those who
could call her attention to them. Perhaps if he seized her...no, he could never

do that for such a selfish reason. Eru felt her groggy mind wake, and sensed her thoughts turning to breakfast.

Eru seized someone just outside the hostel and went about securing their breakfast. By the time they stepped out of the hostel into the cold morning, someone waited for them with steaming bread and hot cider.

'Friend, you shouldn't steal,' Aymis chastised him. Eru felt the sting of her disapproval more than he had expected. His entire life had been full of nothing but disapproval from others, but he never had reason to care like now.

'We needed breakfast,' Eru replied as he ate the soft doughy bread. He never would have the pleasure of tasting food for himself, but he enjoyed the smell he picked up from his underlings.

'I won't eat it,' Aymis thought.

'Is this all that different than when you claimed to be a psychic? I have to eat to live. So do you,' Eru rejoined. Eru felt her mind yearning to eat the bread and drink the cider. *'What does not eating achieve? It won't give anything back, but you just go hungry.'*

'Well, I am really hungry,' Aymis conceded. *'And it is really cold this morning.'* Eru felt her pleasure and satisfaction as she sipped the cider and swallowed her first bite of bread.

'Look, Aymis. I don't like taking from others any more than you do. I just don't know if there is a better alternative. If I seize someone and have them work to earn us money, I am stealing their time and hurting them at the same time. You know I have tried to help others by teaching them trades in return, but you also know how well that turned out.'

'I know. We'll figure something out,' Aymis answered.

'Not while we have a Hider on our trail we won't. My only priority right now is protecting you,' Eru thought.

'I almost forgot about that. You're right, Eru,' Aymis responded. Eru seized her before he could stop himself, feeling like he just slapped his only friend across the face.

'I am so sorry!' Eru exclaimed in his mind as he released her.

'Please, don't apologize, my friend,' Aymis responded. *'I will learn to be more careful. Thank you.'*

'For what?' Eru asked, slightly confused.

'For caring enough to respect me. I never would have thought an archos would show any consideration for me,' she answered.

'Of course.' Eru's pale grey cheeks flushed red over his first thank you.

Eru focused on evading his new pursuer. The next few days would be crucial. If the Hider lost their trail, perhaps they could avoid him indefinitely. Until then, Eru would take no chances. He kept as low a profile as possible, seizing people briefly. He couldn't allow any of the eyes he used to recognize Aymis as his companion. Often he had her walk on the other side of the street or follow a considerable distance behind. He fell back to his old stealthy habits easily, augmented this time by a new purpose. He would gladly live this way the rest of his life to protect Aymis.

'It's him! Eru!' Aymis called, deliberately bringing Eru's focus on her. Eru seized her, and didn't let go. He saw into a pair of eyes, disturbingly empty compared to all the minds laid open around him. He saw murder in the man's impenetrable gaze. The eyes released her gaze, scanning the crowded street for another. Eru seized every person he could manage and circled Aymis protectively. To his surprise, however, his opponent ignored them completely. The Hider wasn't after Aymis after all. That could only mean one thing.

Aymis' magnified awareness filled Eru's mind with the thoughts of every person on the street but the one who mattered most. Eru ducked through the crowds, knowing who his opponent sought. Suddenly, the street exploded with trauma and fear that he recognized all too well. The person nearest the would-be assassin tackled him, and several others jumped onto the pile. Eru felt their terror as Aitrox's hostile will filled the street.

Oko slept in the same home that the archos had used after his massacre at the bridge. He couldn't pretend to understand the insanity of this archos, but it only added to his reasons to find and kill him. An insane archos was like a bull in a china shop; it had to be put down quickly.

He couldn't have gone far that night, but Oko knew better than to hunt an archos at night. On the empty streets, he would stand out. He twirled his walking stick in frustrated anticipation as he paced the room. He arrived just an hour after the archos released a pair of eyes in this home. Oko managed to learn enough to suspect that the Reader from the sanctuary had been pressed into his service. Poor girl. She meant him no harm, but any Aegendi who knew his face, even while disguised was too great a risk to leave alive.

Oko left early the next morning, hoping to pick up the trail quickly. He regretted not having any time to put together a sufficient disguise to ensure the Reader couldn't recognize him, but he couldn't pass on a hot trail. Once he got close, he could pick up on the cues left behind by those the archos seized to travel. He hadn't hunted a Streetborn for years, but he still could pick up on the subtle patterns of disorder and panic as easily as a tracker could identify a wolf's tracks.

Oko moved through the crowds of morning commuters like a lion on the prowl. He followed the signs of his quarry like a scent on the wind, seething with anticipation. He hadn't killed an archos in a long time, especially not one as murderous as this Streetborn. As the morning advanced, and the sun finally climbed high enough to dispel the shadows at street level, he knew he had nearly closed the gap. Then his eyes unexpectedly met with the eyes of the archos's Reader, and he saw the flash of recognition.

"Well, I'll be seized!" he cursed under his breath as he saw a crowd of uncannily unified people surround and protect her. Oko smiled at the ruse, knowing the crafty ways of a Streetborn well enough not to fall for the diversion. He continued to search the crowded streets for the Streetborn, expecting to find him stealthily slinking into the shadows. His breath billowed with the cold winter air.

Oko scanned the crowds of people bundled up against the winter chill. Unfortunately, their apparel worked against him, by hiding all the obvious archos traits. Before he could find his prey, the man next to him jumped onto his back. Oko grabbed the arm that wrapped around his neck, but another shoulder barreled into his stomach, knocking him to the ground. He felt the weight of another person piling on top of him and heard the cracking of the man's ribs beneath him. How could a Streetborn seize so many?

Oko unsheathed his knives and slashed the stomach of the man on top of him. Blood soaked him, as he slashed the next person on the pile. As the bodies on top of him went limp, another jumped on, but Oko just managed to get out before being trapped under the weight. Around him, uncounted pairs of eyes followed him with lethal intent –far too strong for a Streetborn.

Eru watched in terror as the body count piled up. Who was doing this and why? How had another archos found this Hider without Eru noticing its presence or influence? Eru had seized a few people who knew how to fight, but never anyone who moved with the same lethality as this Hider. He wielded a long knife in one hand, and a converted walking stick in the other, ducking and dodging people while cutting his way through the crowd.

'Make it stop, please!' Eru heard Aymis's pleadings. With her under his control, they both perceived all terror and pain that filled the crowds. Eru had a life time to get used to those feelings, but Aymis had never seen this kind of terror and brutality. Eru released her, but kept several people around her for protection. He saw the intended path for this Hider's escape, and had to make a decision.

'I'll kill him myself,' Eru thought.

'No, please!' Aymis begged.

Aymis's plea for mercy resonated in Eru's soul, and he knew he couldn't deny her. Were the Hider still an immediate threat, perhaps he would have done differently, but not likely. Aymis and her wellbeing meant everything to him now, and she wanted him to help the Hider. He seized a few people in Oko's path and did the best he could to clear the way. Hopefully, he could orchestrate the Hider's escape before he changed his mind about it.

Oko felt the chill of his wet clothes cutting to his bones. He ignored the crimson color, just grateful that none of the blood was his own. His walking stick slashed another attacker down, as he moved closer to his escape through the alleys. Ahead of him, four people tackled and restrained others in front of him, inexplicably clearing the path for his escape. Oko knew better than to question the unusual turn of events, and decided it best to escape with his life while he could.

Oko ran through the alleys, cutting down every unfortunate beggar and panhandler who stepped up to block his path. He rounded a corner and jumped into a vile pile of trash. Rather than try to outdistance the archos range, he would just stay hidden long enough for his prey to move on.

Oko uttered a stream of curses and invectives directed at Aitrox over his failure. Any other person would have been killed for such harsh, blasphemous words. Oko on the other hand had perfected the art of defaming her, having had plenty of opportunity for practice. He had been too careless, knowing his quarry had a Reader.

The fetid stench of the garbage filled his nostrils and invoked his gag reflex. He welcomed the warmth of the refuse and the cover it provided from potentially hostile eyes. He waited for his clothes to dry before risking exposure to the cold. By the time he climbed from the disgusting pile, he felt so sick to his stomach and dizzy he could barely walk. At least it served as a new form of disguise. He had gone from a wealthy trader or accountant to a drunkard transient, smelling and looking the part with his grossly stained clothing. Even the ghastly blood stains looked more like dark mud now.

Oko added the final touches to his improvised disguise, adding a swagger to his walk and a slur to his voice. He used his walking cane as another prop, waving it at any who looked at him as he warbled anything from a hostile threat to a plea for money. His pocket-watch read three-thirty in the afternoon by the time he exited the alleys several blocks from that morning's confrontation.

He had scarcely taken three steps onto the street before he saw about twenty pairs of eyes focused on him with unnatural unity. He realized then that he had fallen into something far bigger, and more dangerous than hunting a single Streetborn, but he probably wouldn't survive to figure out what it was.

CHAPTER 15

FAILURE IS NOT AN OPTION

When the Hider came after Aymis, I knew I had to protect her. When I saw the toll the experience exacted on her, I realized the that my life was not even remotely conducive to companionship. The thought of losing her nearly broke me, but the thought of destroying her... I couldn't let that happen. I would kill for her. I would die for her. I would return to the hell of life alone for her. It seemed my time in the sun wasn't meant to be.

E ru felt fear in his heart, unlike anything before. He had known what it meant to fear for his safety, and even the safety of others, but this was different. Never had he feared for someone he loved, and never for a tragedy as abstract and yet painful as the one he now felt looming. Eru sensed the trauma Aymis struggled with, harrowing her heart like a virgin field whose unsullied earth had never been broken by the farmer's cruel tools.

What would happen to Aymis's innocence and unwavering optimism now? He feared losing her to the realities of his cruel world and harsh existence. A person with such a pure heart as hers was never meant to be part of his world, yet he couldn't bring himself to contemplate life without her. They had only shared a day together, but she knew him like nobody else.

'Aymis,' Eru called, but her mind was focused elsewhere. He felt her pain more profoundly then his own sorrow. *'Aymis, please.'* She didn't respond. Eru saw her with multiple pairs of eyes. She sat on the sidewalk weeping, the moist air frosting on her cheeks. Nothing Eru had seen with thousands of eyes and hundreds of memories pained him so profoundly. Eru walked over to her, oblivious to the frantic clamor of panic on the street. He parted the sea of confusion until he stood next to her.

Eru removed the glove from his hand and reached to touch her with his sickly grey hands and sinister dark fingernails. He felt the shock and revulsion from all those around him when they saw the archos in their midst, no doubt the cause of this bloodshed. Their loathing washed over him like a toxic wave.

'Oh, Aymis, I am so sorry,' Eru exclaimed.

'Don't!' Aymis snapped, filling Eru with fear and doubt.

Had he lost her? 'But, Aymis, please!' he began.

'No, Eru! Go away!' she thought, cold accusing eyes resting on him. He seized her with the use of his name, reeling from the wave of hurt and accusation that flowed from her. He perceived the conclusions she had drawn, and immediately understood. Understanding however didn't diminish the pain of her accusa-

tions. She believed he had driven people to the slaughter just to protect her. How could he have willingly seized people, knowing the Hider would just cut them down? How could he have let so many people die to protect her? He felt each accusatory question in her mind, and each one nearly broke his heart. She could not, would not accept their blood on her hands. Just having to witness their deaths, and sense the immeasurable trauma through her gift would leave her forever scarred.

Fortunately for both of them, seizing Aymis opened his mind to her and provided both sides of the story. Only then could Aymis see that Eru hadn't seized anyone to attack the Hider. Only when she saw how he used people to facilitate their enemy's escape did the accusation and hurt melt from her eyes.

'Aymis, I am so sorry,' Eru apologized as he released her.

'No, Eru! I should have known that was not you. It was not your fault,' Aymis responded.

'I know, but I am sorry you had to see this,' Eru thought sympathetically.

'I am not strong like you, Friend,' Aymis responded as she sniffled and wiped a tear from her cheek.

'You don't want to be like me. What you may call strength, I call numbness. Never become jaded like I have.'

'But, I never want to feel like this again!' Aymis gulped a sob and looked away from him as she responded.

'I hope you never have reason to,' Eru responded, squeezing her shoulder gently like a protective father. She loved him like a mother or sister, and had several years on him. However, at this time, he felt responsible for her protection from the cruel world that had left him jaded forever.

'Can we please get out of here?' Aymis asked. Together they got up and left the latest scene Eru would forever long to forget, knowing it to be indelibly printed in Aymis's mind. The first time is always the hardest to forget. Hopefully Aymis would never know what it is to have a lifetime of such memories.

'Are you going to be all right?' Eru asked, but got no response. Aymis had withdrawn again, and it didn't take Eru long to realize she wished for some privacy.

Eru guided them through the city, hoping to get as much distance as possible between the two of them and his new foe. A Hider would be a far more dangerous opponent than Telu in some ways, but Eru felt a sense of relief for other reasons. His new nemesis didn't have to resort to catastrophic assaults that left neighborhoods devastated. If he could lose the trail, people wouldn't have to die on account of their duel. Most likely, Aitrox had killed the Hider already.

Eru wanted to peek into Aymis's thoughts, hoping she was holding up. More than that, his thoughts wandered to her like a father's turning to a newly adopted daughter. He would do anything to protect her and keep her happy. Unfortunately, the notion of happiness and safety didn't feel compatible with Eru's life.

He felt two painful and terrifying resolutions building simultaneously. Aitrox had to be dethroned. The entire archos establishment had to be defeated. He knew the impossibility of the task, but he could give his life for the cause. He couldn't, however, drag those he cared for to their deaths on such a fool's errand. Happiness and safety were not his lot in life, a more painful realization after his short time in the light. Archos were creatures of darkness, and it was time for him to return to that domain.

Aymis struggled to keep the terrible memories of that morning from replaying in her waking vision. She saw the Hider cut an innocent person down, splashing blood in a ghastly spray. She felt that person's fear at being seized by a wicked and hostile presence. She could scarcely keep the images out of her waking vision. The thought of sleep, and the dreams to accompany it, made her shudder.

She could hardly believe the monumental, terrible and wonderful changes that had come into her life. Having witnessed the unbelievable violence the archos were capable of, she could understand Telu's zeal. She also understood Eru's determination to end the violence, even at the cost of his own life, but, like his father, Eru had misplaced the focus of his efforts.

Both Telu and his son recognized the same terrible wrong that plagued the world. Having been thrust so suddenly into the middle of it, Aymis wondered how she had ever let herself accept the archos domination as a fact of life.

Insulation and impotence had numbed her to the glaring evil that marred the world like a ghastly scar. Up until today, her life's circumstances had insulated her from the full brunt of archos cruelty, making it easy to ignore it. She had always felt powerless, impotent against such an inescapable force as the archos, making it natural and easy to accept the terrible blight they left on the hearts of every citizen in Deor. Aymis felt it when Telu took her to worship. She saw the ominously beautiful statues of the goddess she had always lived under and felt her oppressive handiwork in everything around her. Everything about the city of Deor, and indeed the entire empire, existed as a reflection of Aitrox's will. Every death, every calamity, it all fell on her shoulders and left her hands stained with the blood of millions. It had to stop –but how? Aymis recognized the folly and truth behind her determination. How could she possibly hope to stop a goddess? Likely, she had already fallen under Aitrox's scrutiny. The heretics' centuries of failure and obscurity proved the futility of her goal. Alone, she could possibly hope to stay away from archos attention, Eru excluded, but with every recruit to her cause the risk of exposure multiplied.

Who was she kidding? Why set out on an impossible task that would invariably add to the cycle of violence and death? Could she doom others to unbearable deaths at the hands of the archos? If she chose this path, she knew the terrible deaths from the last few days wouldn't be the last. Perhaps it was best to accept the state of the world. No! Violence, trauma and terror would continue with or without her involvement, and that couldn't be accepted. She wanted to run from the darker world she had so recently discovered, but knew she couldn't abandon Eru. Without her, he would never escape the world she had just stumbled upon. She couldn't turn her back on him any more than she could ignore someone who fell among thieves.

How could she hope to defeat the archos? What hope did she have? Eru. As preposterous as it would appear to those who couldn't read his heart, she knew that an archos like him probably was born once every few millennia. She had to help him find a way to get others to see him as she did, but how? She could vouch for him, but who would believe her? It didn't matter what she did, people would interpret Eru's deeds as the work of an evil archos. That realization alone frustrated her to no end.

'*Eru,*' she thought, deliberately calling his attention down on her. She felt the moment of seizure like a slap in the face, but one she had expected.

'*How are you holding up?*' Eru inquired anxiously.

'*I could be better. I need to talk to you about something. You may think I am crazy though,*' Aymis answered.

'*What's on your mind?*' Eru asked, realizing he could easily find out, but enjoying the fact that he didn't have to.

'*I want to overthrow the system,*' Aymis replied, doing her best to discipline her thoughts, knowing it would be a critical habit to develop. It would take years to master it as Telu had, if she were fortunate enough to last that long.

'*I don't think you are crazy,*' Eru answered. Aymis sighed in relief. '*It has to be done, but not by you.*'

'*Well, who then?*' Aymis asked.

'*Me.*'

'*But you need help,*' Aymis responded.

'*No! This is no task for someone like you,*' Eru said protectively. '*Horrors like this morning will be unavoidable. I don't want that for you.*'

'*You need me,*' Aymis said. '*You can't do this alone.*'

'*I'll likely fail no matter who helps me. I don't want your broken soul on my conscience,*' Eru responded.

'*You're doing it again,*' Aymis retorted. She often found it hard to bite her tongue, holding back thoughts and retorts that came to mind, much less keeping them from coming to mind at all.

'*What am I doing again?*' Eru asked, frustrated.

'*You're torturing yourself. You are not to blame for any path I choose,*' Aymis chided.

'*This is not the world I want for you. The light in your heart was never meant for the darkness where I am going,*' Eru said, sounding like an old father despite the fact Aymis had at least four years on him.

'*You cannot choose the world for me. This is the world I have. How could I possibly pretend things are different? I cannot ignore it, and I cannot leave you to face it without a light, my light, to help you.*' Aymis stopped in her tracks and stared intently at Eru, hands on her hips. She saw into those strange featureless eyes and the reality of the situation sunk in. Here she was staring into the eyes of an archos and trying to convince him to let her embark on a suicide mission with him. Only a few weeks ago she would have laughed at such a preposterous idea.

Aymis felt the turmoil in Eru's heart. She saw how he longed to protect her, saw the notion of self-sacrificing and suffering he felt loath to abandon. She felt how firmly rooted the belief sat in his heart that happiness could never be his. Part of him almost feared to bring the wrath of the fates on him for overstepping his bounds and enjoying even this brief time of joy.

'*Friend,*' Aymis thought affectionately, '*you cannot hope to destroy an establishment based on sorrow and terror with more of the same. You cannot give hope and joy to others while denying it to yourself. Please, don't do this to yourself. Don't do this to me.*'

'*Aymis, I can't,*' Eru began. Aymis saw the quiver in Eru's lip. '*I can't let you help me.*'

'*Yes, you can,*' Aymis responded. '*Whatever you say, I will be by your side. Short of seizing me and driving me away or killing me, and I don't think you could do either of those things.*'

'*Aymis...*' Eru tried to protest again.

'*Friend, you deserve this.*' Aymis touched his cheek, knowing he couldn't feel the touch but unable to withhold the gesture.

'*Well, I guess failure is not an option then. Thanks, Aymis,*' Eru responded.

CHAPTER 16

THE SMILE OF AN ARCHOS

I will always question my motives for accepting Aymis's help. Was I being selfish? I told myself that I let her help me because I couldn't succeed without her, but could I succeed at all? I knew that I couldn't cast aside her help if I had any hope to succeed, but I cannot deny that my selfish desire to have her with me influenced that decision. Regardless of my motives, when she convinced me not to drive her away, it was the happiest moment in all my life.

E ru and Aymis wandered aimlessly through the streets of Deor. It felt oddly contradictory to start out such a momentous decision by meandering without direction or purpose. They both wanted to do something monumental to start their cause. Instead they roamed the streets like leaves blown by the cold winter wind. A random, seemingly purposeless path actually had a deliberate need driving it. If the Hider had survived Aitrox's attempt to kill him, they hoped to leave him no trail to follow.

Eru had no idea how to go about a goal as ambitious as defeating Aitrox. Unlike Aymis, Eru had felt the power he now deliberately opposed. Eru didn't doubt Aitrox already knew his intentions, and left him alive only because she saw no threat. Aymis would never understand that, which was probably for the best. Understanding would possibly crush her precious optimism, and Eru could not allow that. Even now, he felt her hope warming his heart. How could someone so full of light and hope not chafe at everything Eru represented? He knew he should send her away, but no amount of logical rationale could overturn the decision now.

Eru's mind worked over the new goal, quickly identifying several impossible necessities. Without some means to protect others from archos power, anything he and Aymis built would only serve as their guillotine. Without the means to defeat Aitrox – a being many thousand times his superior – any path they followed only led them to their grave.

Eru thought over everything he knew about his opponents, a task his powerful mind could do rather quickly. How could he hope to defeat the High Queen? What did she fear? Iron. Perhaps she didn't fear the metal, but she forbade the ownership of it under penalty of death. Only those in Aitrox's favor could openly possess the metal, but why? He knew he could only find out by acquiring some and studying its effects. Was iron poison to an archos? Was it her great weakness?

By late afternoon, he had taken to using carriages to relieve Aymis's aching feet, and hopefully create large gaps in any trail a Hider would try to follow. They bounced around the city, like a fly in a bottle, well into the evening. About the time the street lamps flickered to life, Eru found an unexpected surprise.

He stopped the carriage and the two of them got out, much to the relief of the original passenger.

"Thank you, and sorry for the inconvenience," Aymis said as she stepped down. She chose to ignore the passenger's angry reply as the carriage rolled away.

'Friend,' she called to Eru, letting her attention settle on him like a hand tapping his shoulder, *'where are we going to sleep tonight?'*

'This home looks as good as any,' Eru replied. Aymis looked up at the beautiful home.

'Are you serious? They would just as soon spit on us as let us in,' Aymis responded.

'I wasn't planning on asking,' Eru responded.

'But—' Aymis objected.

'Look, Aymis, we could spend all night asking and get nothing but frostbite and sleep deprivation for the effort. More importantly, every home you would ask leaves a larger footprint for our Hider friend to recognize,' Eru responded.

'Eru!' Aymis exclaimed. To her surprise, he didn't seize her this time, but she felt the concentration and effort the restraint required.

'All right, go ahead and knock, but don't tell me I didn't warn you,' Eru replied, trying to hide his excitement for the surprise he had worked out.

'What are you up to?' Aymis asked.

'Nothing,' Eru lied. *'Go ahead, knock.'*

'Thank you, friend,' Aymis replied as she climbed up the marble steps. Snow sat on the shoulders of a beautiful sculpted woman who held her hands out in welcome. Behind her, vines crawled up the porch pillars, looking like dead serpents in the winter. She grabbed the knocker, feeling the cold of the metal through her knit gloves. Aymis lifted the door's knocker and tentatively tapped, surprised by the loud hollow clunking sound. Maybe Eru had been right about this. Maybe it was foolish to try asking. Aymis hoped nobody was home, but the warm light streaming from the window betrayed that hope. The door creaked open just a crack to hold out the cold.

"*What do you want?*" a woman's voice called. Aymis thought she recognized the voice but couldn't be sure.

"Pardon me, ma'am," Aymis began tentatively.

"Aymis?" the woman's voice asked in shock. Recognition filled Aymis's mind.

"Mother!" Aymis exclaimed.

"Well, I'll be seized! I thought you were dead!" she squealed giddily, as she swung the door open. "Come in, come in!" Aymis and Eru stepped into the spectacular home, and the carriage outside rolled away.

"H-how..." Aymis stammered as she gave Eru a knowing look. *'Thank you, Friend,'* she thought to him.

"Praise the archos! I thought you were dead," Janis repeated as she wiped tears from her cheeks. New wrinkles adorned her sunken eyes, and a new bolt of grey shot through Janis's dark hair. Aymis saw into her mother's mind, sensing the sleepless days and tormented nights she had endured. The new wrinkles and grey hair added a sense of strength to her, like someone who had been smashed against a stone and survived.

"I am so sorry," Aymis said. "I wanted to find you and make sure you were okay." Janis hugged her, and kissed her cold cheek as her answer.

"Who is the boy? Is he a friend?" she asked, looking at Eru for the first time. Eru remained wrapped up enough to hide the obvious signs of his archos nature.

"Mother, you may want to sit down. Promise me you will remain calm," Aymis said, putting a hand on Janis' shoulder. She sensed the jolt of uncertainty in her mother's mind with her warning. "Everything is ok, better than ok. Please," Aymis pleaded. Janis looked into her eyes and calmed down as she sat on the chair that cost more than Janis would earn in a lifetime.

"What's going on?" Janis asked, a note of uncertainty in her voice.

"This is my friend. He saved my life, and he is the one you should thank for my finding you," she said.

"You will never know what an incredible gift you have given me," Janis replied, the uncertainty in her eyes diminishing slightly.

"Actually, he probably knows more than you guess." Aymis paused, trying to work up the courage to finish. "He's an archos."

"What? No!" Janis exclaimed as she stood in a panic, backing up and knocking over her chair. She bumped a table against the wall, causing a vase to wobble and fall. Janis's hand snapped the vase from the air without even looking for it. In a different set of circumstances, Aymis would have paused to admire her reflexes. However, it escaped her notice.

"Mother, listen to me!" Aymis begged, tears filling her eyes.

Eru's smile vanished as he sensed the pain his presence now caused both Aymis and Janis. Did he think it could have gone any different? He should have remained outside to give them some time together first. What was he thinking? He felt Janis's terror rising like a deadly tide, dispelling the unbridled joy of only moments before. He felt the pain in Aymis's heart as her mother spurned her.

"You're not my daughter!" Janis growled before turning to Eru. "You killed her!"

"No! Mother!" Aymis grabbed her shoulders and shook her violently. "I am not seized!"

"Prove it!" Janis snapped.

"I can't. You know that," Aymis said with more frustration than she had intended.

'Aymis!' Eru called, but she didn't hear him. *'Aymis, it is obvious. Would I have had you knock? Would I have bothered to bring you to your mother? Please!'* Eru felt his thoughts shout at her, but she lacked the archos capacity to focus on multiple things.

"Mother, he's not like the others. Why hasn't he seized you? Why would he care to reunite us?" Aymis tried to explain.

"I don't know," Janis stammered.

"Would an archos knock? Don't you see? He is as blind as a bat right now. He isn't controlling anyone," Aymis continued anxiously.

"But, why?" Janis asked, as tears welled in her eyes. "Why did he take you away from me?"

"He didn't. I already told you, he saved my life. Someone very dangerous had taken me from you," Aymis answered. "I have so much to tell you. Where can we sit down to talk?"

"Janis! What's all this racket about?" an angry voice called from the other room.

"I'm sorry master," Janis said apologetically.

"Why aren't you cleaning the kitchen?" he said as he stepped into the entry-way. "Who are these people?"

Eru sensed the man's condescending and hostile feelings towards Janis. He hadn't known Janis for long, but she was Aymis's mother. Her master looked on her with scarcely more regard than a cockroach. Eru immediately knew what to do about this. He seized the man, almost enjoying the experience.

"I am so sorry my dear Janis. Please forgive my unkind words," her master said. "I'll take care of the kitchen tonight. As a matter of fact, I think my servants all deserve some paid time off." Before Eru guided Penro into the kitchen to begin working, he searched out the other servants in his estate, sending each home with a confused but happy look on their faces.

"Well, I'll be seized," Janis gasped. "I'm fired."

"Maybe, but it's worth it," Aymis said with a grin as she watched her mother's boss step into the kitchen. "Let's enjoy your last night on the job together."

"I was ready for a change anyway," Janis said with a hesitant smile. A loud clamor of crashing pots, pans and broken dishes came from the kitchen.

'Oops!' Eru thought sarcastically. Aymis heard him this time and laughed.

'You meant to do that!' she answered.

'He shouldn't treat Janis so poorly. I intend to make sure he fires her,' Eru thought with a smile.

'You really shouldn't,' Aymis responded, unable to keep from chuckling.

'It's the least I could do,' Eru joked back.

"What's so funny?" Janis asked.

"My friend here is just giving your master a taste of his own medicine," Aymis responded.

"Master Penro will be in a foul mood when it's over," Janis said, unable to stop from laughing. "He can hear me even though he is seized right?" Aymis nodded. "This will be fun." Janis smiled as she walked into the kitchen.

Eru watched her with a growing smile as she walked up to her master. He sensed Penro's anger to see his servant approach him so brazenly, seized or not. Of course, he assumed everyone in his house was seized. Eru realized he could save her job, but Janis already felt liberated by the hope of a change.

"Master Penro, consider this my notice. You don't deserve the pleasure of firing me," Janis said boldly. She walked out of the kitchen, beaming like the first spring sunrise.

"Are you going to manage without your job?" Aymis asked apologetically.

"Right now I don't care," Janis said. "I don't want to let that spoil the best night of my life."

"Fair enough," Aymis laughed.

"We have some catching up to do," Janis said as she led them into the receiving room. Aymis sat down on the couch, not worrying about how her dirty clothes likely left the couch in need of a cleaning. If she guessed correctly, Master Penro would take care of it before all was said and done.

"So, where to start," Aymis began. Eru sat on the couch, feeling happier than he had ever felt in his life. Janis sat down on the other side of a fine carved coffee table. Eru recognized the subtle expression of her discomfort, her mind wanting something in between them. Even her overwhelming desire to be close to Aymis couldn't immediately overpower years of fear and distrust. Yet, as the shock of being confronted with an archos faded, Janis grew more comfortable. Before too long, she had moved onto the couch next to Aymis, obliging Eru to move to a different chair.

He reveled in the immeasurable joy that radiated from Aymis and Janis together. He had done this. An archos could bring happiness into the world after all. No matter what happened, he knew he would never forget this day.

Oko cut a few would-be attackers down before ducking back into the alleys. Usually crowds served a Hider well, but with his cover blown they meant almost certain death. Even in the alleys, people poured from shanties and hiding spots, forcing him to cut down each person Aitrox threw in his way. The stench of alcohol, sweat, and grime overwhelmed him as a transient tackled him with more strength and coordination than he should have possessed. Oko slammed into the alley wall. Bright splotches flashed in his vision and his knife fell from his hand. He felt his head spinning from the impact, but he kept his wits about him enough to grab another knife from his boot. He pulled it upward, opening the attacker from his stomach to his sternum.

He stumbled through the alley, determined to keep moving. His life depended on it. A Streetborn couldn't have this kind of reach or capacity. No Streetborn he had observed could seize more than twenty, but he had faced many times that during their first encounter. He couldn't imagine why one of the higher ranking archos would care for a Streetborn, but it was the only explanation.

Oko peaked out from the alley, hoping against his better judgment that he had lost this persistent and capable foe. A massive brick shattered against the wall just above his head with a jarring crash. Oko reflexively ducked and protectively shielded his face. A Streetborn with a Wizard! Impossible! He retreated into the alley, knowing he had been trapped. Another brick shattered, hitting the wall with enough force to leave a crater. Oko threw himself to the ground as another projectile curved into the alley and flew just over his head. He hated Wizards. With no better options, he crawled into another pile of garbage and hoped he could remain concealed.

Further down the alley, the same projectile that barely missed Oko crushed the chest of a seized pursuer, dropping him to the ground instantly. Another pursuer filled the vacancy immediately as a crowd tore through the alley in search of their prey. Oko heard them rummaging through piles of garbage and tearing down some unfortunate beggar's improvised hut. He heard them drawing closer and realized he only had a few moments left. He didn't want to die, but he had always known the archos would get him eventually. He at least had made a good run, killing more archos than any Hider he had heard of. It had only been a matter of time before he crossed the wrong archos, but who'd have thought hunting a Streetborn would have led to his demise?

A strong pair of hands grabbed the scruff of his now ruined vest and pulled him to his feet. He never did get used to the uncanny wrongness of multiple eyes staring at him so uniformly. Now he never would. The eerily uniform mob surrounded him. One of them had picked up one of Oko's knives and raised it to strike. Oko appreciated the irony of being killed by his own blade, the same blade that had killed several archos.

The knife fell to the ground with a clang, just barely missing Oko's foot. The surprise in the man's eyes couldn't compare to the shock in Oko's. Suddenly, the unsettling unity in the crowd vanished, replaced by disparate manifestations of confusion and shock. They looked around the alley, disoriented and bewildered as they dispersed like leaves in the breeze.

"Well, I'll be seized!" Oko gasped as he fell back against the wall, letting himself slide down to the ground. His eyes remained open, hardly even blinking, but his mind scarcely registered anything he saw. He leaned his head backward and let his eyes wander up to the sky, a small channel of white cutting through the dark silhouette of the buildings. In his flustered state of mind, he didn't notice the mysterious shape clinging to the wall high above him.

Dark wings clung to the smooth wall, leaving the aquiline creature looking more like a cancerous growth on the building. The mysterious creature remained still as stone, watching Oko with its eyes, but seeing him far better through other senses beyond Oko's ken.

CHAPTER 17

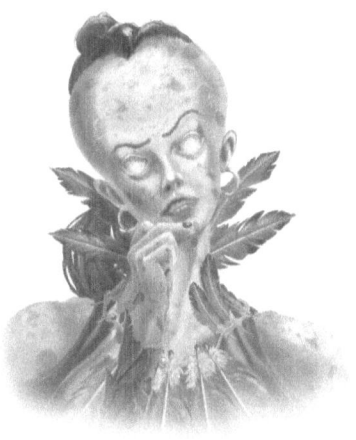

PROPHETESS

Reuniting Aymis with her mother, and finding another person who overcame prejudice, made it feel like anything was possible. Had someone suggested it, I would have rushed off to overthrow Aitrox right then. I discovered how joy can be an inexhaustible resource, multiplying when it is shared rather than diminishing. Unfortunately, terror and sorrow are no different in that regard. I couldn't see it then, my perspective distorted by rose colored spectacles, but times like these would be few and far between on the dark road ahead.

"I t's all so hard to believe," Janis said quietly as Aymis's tale unfolded. The two of them passed the night hours talking. Janis hardly noticed when her shift should have ended. Eru had Penro greet the day shift servants as they arrived, giving each of them a few days of paid time off.

"Now, mother. Are you calling me a liar?" Aymis asked with a smile as she teasingly emphasized the question that got her fired at the tile factory and set everything in motion. Fortunately, Janis recognized her joke for what it was.

"Well, you do have shifty eyes," Janis teased in reply.

"Excuse me, my lady," Lord Penro said as he finally emerged from the kitchen. The sight of the ostentatious noble wearing cleaning gloves, an apron, and a belt holding different brushes and dusters elicited uncontrollable laughter from both women.

"Friend! You are having too much fun with this," Aymis said aloud through her laughter.

"Please, it's nothing. Cleaning is such a satisfying experience. Keeps me rooted," Penro said.

"I could get used to this," Janis smiled. "So what are your plans now?"

"I don't know what my friend has in mind next. Defeating the rulers feels like we are setting out to move a mountain with nothing but a spade. Where do you start?" Aymis said. Penro got to work on the couch, causing her to find another seat.

"The first thing we should do," Penro interjected, "is spread the word that there is a kind archos in the city."

"Who will believe that?" Janis asked.

"Well, right now, two people. A week from now maybe three or four," Penro's voice said.

"They don't have to believe it, yet," Aymis began thoughtfully. "All we need is for the story to circulate. Almost like we are trying to create a legend or myth."

"Well, it would certainly make a popular story among the slums and poor districts: an archos who inflicts the rich with servitude at the hands of the poor." A flicker of excitement flashed in Janis's eyes.

"The thing is that we can't have seized people spreading the stories. One person claiming that he was seized when he told the story, and all credibility is lost," Penro said.

"Good point," Aymis agreed.

"I can spread the stories," Janis said thoughtfully.

"Mother, no," Aymis objected. "I don't want you involved in this."

"And how do you think I feel about your involvement? I am your mother for Aitrox's sake!"

"Mom!" Aymis snapped. "Do not say that!" Penro scrubbed the couch so vigorously it shook the end tables with each push of his brush.

"Right, sorry." Janis' hand reached out her hand and caught the lamp that fell from the end table behind her. "Child, if I didn't know how headstrong you were, I would tie you up to keep you from doing anything foolish."

"I am not a child anymore, mother," Aymis said defensively.

"Aymis, you aren't even old enough to be a proper lady. Besides, you will always be my child. I remember being your age and feeling much like you do. My parents were sure that your father was nothing but trouble, but they knew they couldn't stop me either. They were wrong about your father though."

"I thought..." Aymis began.

"My parents believed that your father would bring me nothing but sorrow. They were mostly right, but I did get you through all the hell he put me through."

"What are you getting at?" Aymis asked.

"Well, I know I can't stop you from doing what you want. Like my parents, I am afraid for you. You don't know what you are getting yourself into," Janis said with a particularly motherly tone in her voice.

"I know enough to want to keep you from being pulled in," Aymis said, returning to the initial subject of their argument.

"And I know enough to want to help," Janis responded.

"Mother, please, no," Aymis implored.

"Aymis, all I will be doing is telling people a true story."

"A dangerous, true story," Penro interjected.

"Exactly, you could get seized by telling that kind of story," Aymis continued.

"Only if I am careless. Besides, nobody else can tell the story. You need me," Janis responded.

"No. I will do it," Aymis said, looking her mother squarely in the eyes.

"And what will happen when you are linked to your friend here?" Janis said, gesturing towards Eru with a nod. "Everyone will assume you were seized when you told the stories."

"She's right," Penro said.

"No, she's not! All I need to do is start the story. Before long, nobody will know who started the story, nor will they care."

"Aymis," Penro said. "You insisted that I let you help despite my objections. You know we need all the help we can get."

"But– " Aymis began.

"You won't change my mind, Aymis. You will have to tie me up and throw me into a cellar," Janis interrupted.

"Just be careful," Aymis relented as she looked back to Janis.

"Where do you think you got your stubborn streak?" Janis smiled. "I know I can't stop you from this insanity, but I won't be able to sleep at night if I don't help out somehow."

"I don't know, mother. What will happen if people learn you're connected to us?"

"I won't let that happen," Janis said.

"But that means..." Aymis stammered, tears welling in her eyes.

"I know, but at least I know you are still alive. Yesterday I thought you were dead," Janis said through tears of her own.

"But where will you go? What will you do without your job here?" Aymis asked.

"Honestly, quitting my job here is one of the best things to happen to me in years," Janis said, putting on an almost convincing front.

"But, if you came with us, I would know you are ok," Aymis insisted.

"I am too old for dangerous ventures. I would only get in the way. This is the best way for me to help," Janis responded, still maintaining her strong façade.

"I suppose you are right," Aymis said despondently.

"All this talk of farewells and good byes; let's not worry about that for now. Stay for a day or two as my guest. I insist." Penro bowed with a royal flourish.

'What are you doing?' Aymis thought, turning and glaring at Eru.

'You obviously could use some more time with your mother before a permanent farewell. We can safely stay here for a couple of days. I would rather not have to witness more teary farewells before they are called for.'

'But the Hider?' Aymis asked.

'Is most likely dead at the hands of Aitrox. If not, he should take a while to pick up our trail,' Eru replied.

'Thank you,' Aymis thought, knowing Eru felt the love and affection in her heart.

'Enjoy this time while you can,' Eru responded. Penro looked up from the couch, just in time to catch the first rays of the morning sun.

"I love mornings," Penro said with a smile almost as bright as the sun streaming in through the windows. "You two must be tired. Please, make yourselves at home, though you really ought to bathe before going to sleep."

"Oh, this is going to be fun!" Janis said with a giddy smile, looking almost as young as Aymis for a moment.

"I don't understand. It's just a bath," Aymis replied.

"Just wait until you see the washroom," Janis said with a playful wink. Aymis followed Janis up the stairs and into the most opulent washroom she had ever seen.

"Well, I'll be seized," she gasped. "This is amazing!"

"This is the guest wash room. Penro's niece visits for two weeks on the year. She is the only one who ever uses it," Janis explained.

"What about you?" Aymis asked.

"Oh, don't worry, Penro's master washroom is just as extravagant," Janis said with a smile. "You don't even have to heat the water. He has pressurized pipes with water heated by the furnace that he keeps running all winter." Janis turned a knob and started as water immediately began pouring in.

"Adjust the temperature with these knobs," Janis instructed. Before long, steaming water poured into the tub.

"No wonder you were so excited. This is unbelievable!" Aymis said, sounding like a child in a candy store.

"The soap is on that dish," Janis said pointing, "and you have extra perfumes and soaps just for your hair on the shelf right there."

"Thanks, mother," Aymis said with an enormous smile, as she gave her a look to indicate she wanted some privacy to disrobe. Janis stepped out of the washroom as the water continued to flow into the tub. Aymis admired the mirror, another thing she had only heard of until now. She looked so different from the girl she would occasionally see reflected back at her from shop window panes not long ago. Soon the steam from the bath fogged up the mirror enough to end her musings and call her attention back to bathing. She climbed into the hot water slowly, taking time to get used to the heat. It felt wonderful.

She sat immersed in the tub with suds and foam spilling over the sides. Every muscle in her body relaxed, and she breathed the moist, clean air with pleasure. She had never seen such a beautiful washroom, much less bathed in one. Her mother had always understated the wealth of her boss. Seeing everything she lived without, Aymis understood why her mother never said anything. That wouldn't stop her from enjoying it while she could. Aymis smelled as beautiful as a flower garden by the time she was done. She doubted her hair had ever been this clean in her life.

Aymis wrapped up in the thick, soft towel and dried off before donning a robe and indulging in some sleep in what she believed to be the softest feather bed in all of Deor. She slept soundly for several hours. She stretched her arms high above her in a satisfied yawn as she climbed out of bed. Aymis smelled her beautifully perfumed skin, and felt so keenly aware of her cleanliness that the sight of her old clothes sent a shiver down her spine.

She threw the filthy rags into the garbage bin. Aymis walked into the closet, a room larger than the flat she and her mother had shared. Each outfit she saw must have been worth at least six months of her wages. She wondered if she would find anything she could possibly feel comfortable wearing.

"Aymis? You awake?" Janis asked quietly as she tapped on the door.

"Yes, mother," Aymis replied.

"Are you decent?" she asked.

"Just a second!" Aymis called as she adjusted the robe she had slept in.

"I see you discovered her wardrobe," Janis said with a playful wink. "Let's see how you look in one of those lovely gowns."

"I don't know, mother," Aymis objected timidly.

"Nonsense! You are my princess and I insist. Besides, it will be fun."

"Oh, all right," Aymis said, though she couldn't bring herself to sound as reluctant as she wanted to appear. "If you twist my arm." She smiled, giving up any pretense of dislike for the notion.

The clothes she chose fit her well considering she stood a few inches shorter than Penro's niece, and had considerably less meat on her bones. Despite her smaller frame, she felt about ready to pass out for lack of air as her mother tightened her bodice for the first time.

"You look amazing," Janis said with a smile. "It will make a wonderful part of my story: The archos who made a street urchin into a princess."

"So, I am a street urchin then?" Aymis teased in reply.

"Just for the purpose of the story that is," Janis laughed.

"Let's try another gown," Aymis said, sounding like the giddy teenager she was.

"I think you would look stunning in red," Janis said as she pulled out another gown.

"Red is my favorite color," Aymis said with a sparkle in her eye.

Aymis wished time could stop flowing, that their joyful reunion would never end. She loathed the thought of leaving Janis, but knew she couldn't let her mother come with them. Not that life in the slums would be safe or pleasant for her mother but at least it wasn't a death sentence. Aymis did her best to catalog every memory, hoping never to forget this precious last day. She still wished that Janis would not get involved in their plans, but at least it meant that her mother wouldn't be in as much danger as she and Eru. She couldn't let her mother come with her.

A vague worry loomed in the back of Aymis's mind, refusing to come into focus as she worked to remove one gown and let her mother help her into the next. The weight of all the fabric felt oddly comfortable yet oppressive at the same time. It held her firmly, caressing her with its soft smooth texture. She couldn't guess how someone could ever learn to dance wearing so much clothing. Still, seeing herself in the mirror, looking like someone out of a story, made her smile. She put on a matching pair of shoes, admiring them in all their strange, uncomfortable beauty.

"How does anyone walk in these?" Aymis said through her laughter as she wobbled around in the high heels. She took a few steps, teetering like a drunkard and almost falling before Janis caught her. Seeing her mother's sure hand and quick reflexes brought her nebulous concern out of the shadows. Telu had said something about people who had uncanny reflexes. He also surmised that being Aegendi often ran in the family.

"It's not that hard," Janis said, laughing at her daughter's awkward steps.

"Oh, like you could do any better?" Aymis teased.

"Is that a challenge?" Janis asked, walking over to select another pair of shoes and putting them on. She walked in the shoes with decidedly more grace than Aymis had managed.

"When did you learn to walk in shoes like those?" Aymis asked incredulously.

"Sometimes when Penro entertains guests, his servants have to dress formally," she answered. "He is at least *good* enough to loan us our outfits." Janis walked around the room with ease, her hips swaying gracefully with each step. She made it look like the unnatural shoes were what a lady was meant to wear. "You see, it really isn't that hard. Just imagine you are walking on tip-toes to sneak off to work without waking me up."

"I thought that..."

"Of course, I heard you leave every morning, but I didn't want you to feel badly. It was sweet that you were so considerate, and fun to watch you thinking you were stealthy and clever," Janis said almost apologetically.

"Well, I'll be seized," Aymis said in surprise, throwing a hair pin at her mother, hoping she would drop it. Instead, Janis caught it effortlessly. Aymis tried in vain to suppress the dismay she felt at her observation.

"What's wrong?" Janis asked, creases of concern showing her age.

"It's nothing," Aymis lied.

"You are a terrible liar," Janis persisted.

"I think you are an Aegendi," Aymis answered.

"Me? That's absurd," Janis said dubiously.

"Telu said he thought it may run in the family."

"But, I can't hear thoughts like you can," Janis said confusedly.

"I think you have a different gift. Telu called people with your gift Prophets."

"And what could I do if I were a Prophetess?" Janis asked.

"Just forget I said anything," Aymis said curtly.

"Aymis, answer your mother's question," Janis said sternly.

"No," Aymis said as she turned away.

"Would you rather I ask our friend?" Janis asked threateningly.

"No, please don't!" Aymis implored, whipping around to look pleadingly to her mother.

"Then tell me what this gift you think I have does."

"Prophets usually just seem to have uncanny reflexes. When they are seized, they can see things before they happen. Telu said that a Prophet can make an archos almost invincible," Aymis explained.

"You think this just because I caught the hair pin you just threw at me?" Janis asked.

"Not just that. When Penro knocked the lamp over this morning, you caught it without even realizing you did. Last night, you caught a vase exactly the same way," Aymis said, trying to build her case.

"But, you never noticed anything before now," Janis objected.

"Telu told me that most people's gifts are subtle enough that you don't think much of them if you aren't looking. I never knew to keep an eye out for things like that. I am sure that I just missed the signs."

"I don't know, that seems a bit shaky to me," Janis answered doubtfully.

"You just have to make sure you are not seized," Aymis said.

"Wait a second. If I am a Prophetess, then I can help you," Janis said excitedly.

"No!" Aymis snapped.

"What? I thought that it was good news."

"If you are a Prophetess, you would be used as a tool for killing. Eru and I are going to have archos and Aegendi blood on our hands before this is over. I don't want that for you," Aymis objected.

"I appreciate you trying to protect me, but I want to help!" Janis answered.

"It's not just that," Aymis said quietly.

"Well, what is it then?" Janis asked.

"Even with my friend, and his good heart, being seized is terrible. I can bear it because I see the pain he feels seizing others. I don't want you to hate my friend. He has suffered enough."

"I survived the worst your father could do to me. I am sure I can handle it," Janis said confidently.

"No, that is exactly why you can't encourage our friend to seize you. It would force you to revisit all of that, and it would be terribly intense and real in your mind. It pains him to do that to others, but it is just part of being seized."

"But, I won't let that change my feelings about Eru," Janis said reassuringly.

"You can't say that. Please, we need you to be sincere when you talk about a kind archos. We need that story more than anything else right now. There may come a time in the future when we need your gift, but we won't be fighting anyone for some time. If you want to help us, please pretend we never had this conversation." Aymis looked at her mother with the pleading eyes that had gotten her out of trouble so many times.

"When you are ready to fight, I want to use my gift to protect you. Promise me, you will let me do that," Janis said, clenching her jaw and putting her hands on her hips.

"I promise," Aymis replied.

Aitrox couldn't believe this Hider had escaped yet again. She lacked solid proof, but she suspected her old enemies, the vyeshen, had something to do with it. She had defeated them so soundly, even conquering their god, but she knew better than to underestimate a race with their power. Change is a dangerous thing. Rumors she continued to pick up implied that a few vyeshen may be infiltrating the city. In the past they were easy to feel and just as easy to seize, but that was centuries ago. At times now she thought she sensed one in the city, but it felt ephemeral and almost slippery. The thought of her enemies' possible adaptation actually made her feel fear.

She had almost forgotten how fear felt, and its intriguing effect on her mind. She felt her awareness sharpen in response to a perceived threat. How long had it been since that had last happened? She could almost locate these vyeshen, now that she thought about it more intently. She felt them like fleeting wisps of smoke refusing to be contained or confined. She should have sensed their threatening thoughts like a spider feels the touch on its web, but as long as they kept their actions small and indirect she couldn't pin them down.

Even as she devoted most of her mind and her thoughts to her old enemies, she still worked over the issue with the Streetborn. She wanted to laugh at his quest, knowing she could squish him like an ant. Still, she felt a strange amusement in his little game. She would enjoy watching him try, and even learn some from his cleverness before she destroyed him. Perhaps she could put his quest to good use.

He may be just what she needed. Give him enough success, and maybe he will draw the vyeshen out of hiding. Aitrox hadn't seized and broken a vyeshen in a long time. Aitrox smiled in expectation of the satisfaction of breaking another vyeshen, almost like the old days of the emancipation.

She sat on her throne, being massaged by five servants and fanned by ten more. Maintaining the status quo was safe, but also boring. She hadn't felt this alive with anticipation, and dare she say it, uncertainty in a long time. She felt the shiver her smile drove into the hearts of her servants, and laughed.

CHAPTER 18

LOSING SIGHT OF LAND

Leaving Penro's estate was harder than any of us would have expected. My heart yearned to just stay there and give Janis and Aymis that story book ending. We all knew that couldn't be, and felt the need not to linger. Staying too long would only embitter our parting. Alas, knowing that all good things must end doesn't make it any easier when the time comes.

E ru normally found tasks like cleaning terribly mundane, but the unusual circumstances changed his outlook. He effortlessly sensed Janis's amusement: it bubbled in her heart like a confectioner's pot. He could hardly blame her for finding the reversal so gratifying. If anything, Penro deserved a few years of serving his servants, a small compensation for the way he had always treated them. Eru could get used to giving nobility their just desserts. He mused about doing similar things to add more weight to their story of a benevolent archos. A few soup kitchens funded by a nobleman's purse could add momentum to their cause.

He almost enjoyed the hatred he sensed in Penro as he slaved in the kitchen and then scrubbed the couch. Coming from some people, loathing was a compliment. Unfortunately, he could only drive the nobleman so hard. His soft hands blistered quickly. The soreness in Penro's back nagged at Eru, combined with the ache in his left knee. Eru had worked him hard, even for one accustomed to hours of labor. Once Penro finished restoring the sofa to immaculate condition, Eru walked him into a servant's room and had him sleep.

With Penro asleep, Eru returned to the void. Sometimes he almost preferred the way his mind perceived the world in feelings and thoughts without another's senses and thoughts getting in the way. His awareness ranged far into the city, picking up on all sorts of scenes from everyday life. Eru basked in the peace of young husband as he snuggled close to his pregnant wife and felt their baby's kicking. He relished the satisfaction of a master carpenter as he put down his tools for the night and contemplated the armoire that neared completion. He focused on a child's pleasure over the story his nanny read to him about a kind-hearted spirit that lived in the trees and helped people who got lost in the forest. In a few months, he may just catch similar moments with a new story about a kind archos who helped the poor. Of all the emotions Eru sensed, Aymis' happiness shone through the strongest. Eru only wished he could give Aymis more time with her mother. Their brief moment in the sun would soon end, replaced by a long, dark night. Eru felt time's inexorable forward march, plodding with heavy foreboding steps towards their farewell.

They spent the night in Penro's estate because Eru knew Aymis needed the rest. She hadn't really slept the first night as she and Janis caught up on the months apart. A few hours of fitful sleep in the day hardly made up for it. She fell asleep for the night a few hours before her regular retiring hour. Janis however hadn't diverted from her regular schedule by much. Eru sensed her sitting at Aymis's side watching her sleep soundly, sharing a mutual peace among the two of them.

After a few hours, Janis stood from where she sat and turned her thoughts to Eru. He felt her thoughts focusing on him, and knew she wanted to talk. He had already gotten used to the luxury of direct communication that he and Aymis enjoyed. He seized Penro, pulling him from his sleep after only a few hours. Penro's bitter mood, upon waking and realizing that he hadn't been dreaming, almost soured Eru's temperament. He brought him into the room, and had him light a lamp for them to see by.

"I never did thank you," Janis said, looking at Eru as she spoke.

"If I could, I would give you years of days like this. You deserve it," Eru voiced through Penro.

"Aymis asked me not to tell you something," Janis said quietly.

"Then don't tell me," Eru said firmly.

"I think you should know," Janis insisted.

"I trust Aymis. When she's ready, she can tell me," Eru stated confidently.

"You really are amazing. I thought all of your kind were evil, controlling monsters," Janis said thoughtfully.

"Well, I am controlling, and have wondered if I am an evil monster on many occasions. Penro here probably would consider me all those things still," Eru said through Penro. Janis paused, taken slightly off guard to hear Penro's voice speaking about himself in that way.

"Aymis believes I am an Aegendi," Janis blurted out.

"Well, I see where she learned to speak her mind," Eru replied with a slight edge of frustration in Penro's voice.

"She didn't want me to tell you because she is trying to protect me," Janis continued.

"What gift does she think you have?" Eru asked. He sensed Janis's hesitation, a small sliver of doubt still gnawing at her heart. "Better yet, don't tell me. I don't want the temptation."

"If she is right, then you need my help!" Janis said. "I am grateful to you for respecting her wishes, but I want to protect my daughter. I want to use my gift to keep her safe."

"If you understood how precious Aymis's trust is to me, you wouldn't ask me to betray it. All of the iron in the world couldn't pay me to. Had she not found me when she did, I would have either died or ended up like all the others of my kind," Eru replied. Eru's sincerity came through clearly in Penro's voice.

"Can't you at least seize me so I can know if she is right?" Janis asked. The craving to seize her gnawed voraciously at Eru's resolve. Curiosity fueled his appetite. Seizing Aymis had opened a whole new world to him. What would Janis's gift do for him? She wanted him to do it. She offered herself to his mind willingly.

"No. Please don't make me do it!" Penro's voice sounded desperate, almost afraid.

"You really are unbelievable, like something from a story or legend," Janis said thoughtfully.

Eru said nothing in reply, being forced to exert all his strength not to seize Janis. It didn't help to have Janis's thoughts so directly focused on him. He didn't dare say anything through Penro. If Janis didn't change her thoughts soon, Eru feared he would be unable to stop himself. One thing held him back from the edge and provided him with self-control – the thought of Aymis's pain and disappointment if he failed.

"Perhaps. I'll let you get some rest," Janis said as she nodded to Penro and made her departure. Eru sighed as the pressure eased in his mind with Janis's thoughts wandering to other things. Eru watched Janis leave through Penro's eyes. Penro knew to restrain violent urges towards Eru, directing all of his rage at the woman he held responsible. People often ended up dead in Eru's wake, but he couldn't let that happen to Janis. Part of Eru thought to just kill the noble and be done with him. No, Eru knew that he couldn't kill Penro in cold blood. Aymis needed him to be better than that. If they were to have any chance defeating Aitrox, he had to be better.

"If you try anything to hurt her," Eru spoke to Penro, a man talking to himself. "Don't think I can't protect my friends as I do myself." Eru let that threat hang in Penro's mind. Eru's fears eased as his warning sunk deep into Penro's cowardly heart.

"I love you, mother," Aymis said with teary eyes as they embraced and bade farewell. The cold frosty touch of her tears chilled her cheeks. They stood on the street corner a block away from Penro's estate. Eru longed to go back, though he didn't miss Penro's growing anger. Had they stayed much longer, Penro's anger might have become a threat to his life.

"We'll see each other again soon," Janis said, though the doubt in her eyes belied her words.

"You be careful," Aymis responded, sounding more like the mother sending off a child.

"My job is easy. You take care," Janis said as she wiped a tear off Aymis's cheek and brushed aside the hair that fell over her face.

"Where will you go?" Aymis asked.

"I will figure something out," Janis replied. "I won't miss that place."

"I don't know, that bath was pretty amazing," Aymis smiled through her tears.

"Oh, Aymis," Janis said with a tearful laugh, "I will miss you."

"Yeah, I will miss you, too," Aymis answered with tears of her own. They stood, hugging for several minutes before releasing each other. A carriage stopped and Aymis climbed in, followed almost immediately by Eru. Eru had hoped to ease the pain of farewell with a clean separation. The grief in their hearts felt like anything but a clean separation. He felt more like a butcher than a surgeon right now.

The bustling chaos of the city grew in Eru's mind as the carriage carried them back into the frenetic heart of Deor, the domain of the goddess he sought to destroy. Her hostile influence loomed like a dark sun, casting its evil unlight onto the world. Eru let his thoughts return to the precious memories he had just left behind. It wouldn't be the last time Eru would find himself wishing to be back at Penro's estate, enjoying the light of a mother and daughter who had just been reunited.

Aymis watched her mother, standing on the corner and waving her handkerchief. The wagon jostled with each bump in the cobblestone street, and the horse's hooves clopped with an almost hollow sound in the cold morning. The carriage felt like a small ship embarking on an impossible voyage into the unknown. She had set about to destroy a goddess. She watched her mother disappear in the distance, feeling like a young sailor losing sight of land for the first time.

CHAPTER 19

THE VOICE OF AN ARCHOS

Trust is one of the greater gifts in life, harder to earn and easier to lose than love. I didn't understand that at first, and the thought that Aymis would hide anything from me hurt. Being an archos, it is easy to forget how different relationships are for people. I had only had a friend for a few days, and I had no way to understand what it meant to earn someone's trust. That may have been the most important lesson I learned from Aymis.

E ru relayed them through several carriages to obscure their trail. He doubted the Hider had survived Aitrox's wrath. Aitrox could crush even a Hider with ease, reminding Eru of the impossibility of his goal. For now, Aitrox seemed not to mind his ambition, but he knew she had to be aware of it. He felt naked and exposed, jealous of the true freedom only a Hider could know. He felt the world's hostility towards him like sandpaper on raw skin, but something else bothered him even more. Eru felt the pain in Aymis's heart, regretting it more than hundreds of deaths.

'How are you doing?' He reached his mind out to her, hoping she would hear.

'I have been better,' Aymis answered.

'I am sorry,' Eru consoled.

'I just didn't think it would be this hard. In some ways it was easier before,' Aymis answered.

'If there is anything I can do...' Eru offered.

'Friend, I appreciate it. Thank you so much for what you did.' Aymis wiped a few tears with a handkerchief from Penro's estate. Her new clothes and clean hair had worked a remarkable transformation in her, so that an old friend would hardly recognize her. She kept her old scarf as a memento from her mother. Its worn, faded colors contrasted against her refined, new outfit.

'I just hate seeing you like this,' Eru said.

'I will be fine. I just need some time to myself,' Aymis replied.

Eru took the hint and gave her the space he could – as he continued their sporadic and random travels through the morning. He sensed her grief so strong tears flowed unnoticed down his own cheeks. Had he done the right thing to bring them together? Aymis's pain had been a dull ache in the back of her heart. Now the raw, immediate sorrow of separation seemed an unfair price for her to pay.

Something else bothered Eru, growing in his mind. It started like a small pebble in one's shoe, a mere nuisance that grows until it cannot be ignored. Aymis didn't trust him. She had tried to keep her mother's gift a secret from him. How could she question his unwavering concern for her wellbeing? It hurt him terribly that she didn't trust him, that she tried to hide something from him. The quiver in Eru's lip, and the furrow of concern in his forehead didn't escape Aymis's notice.

'Friend, what's wrong?' she asked.

'Why didn't you tell me you thought your mother was an Aegendi?' Eru asked, trying to hold back any accusatory tone.

'She spoke to you didn't she?' Aymis asked. *'I should have known she would.'*

'Yes. She told me that you think she is Aegendi,' Eru answered. *'Why did you try to hide that from me?'*

'Eru,' Aymis noticed the touch on her mind as Eru just managed to refrain from seizing her, *'you are the best friend I could ever hope for.'*

'Then why did you hide that from me?' Eru asked, a tragically sorrowful expression on his face.

'I didn't mean to hurt you. I have only known you a few days,' Aymis explained.

'But, I know you have seen into the deepest reaches of my soul. If you can't trust me, then how can I hope for others to?' Eru asked.

'I do trust you,' Aymis answered. *'I trust you with my life! How can you ask more than that?'* Aymis answered with a question of her own.

'Then why did you hide that from me?' Eru asked again, ignoring her question.

'Because I don't trust you with my mother's life,' Aymis answered. The bluntness of her answer felt like a slap to Eru's face. Aymis waited for a response but none came. Eru sat in the carriage, his head bobbing with the rocking motion, and his blank eyes wandering without purpose.

'Friend...' Aymis called. Nothing. *'Friend, please...'* she asked again. *'Eru,'* His head popped up and his awareness focused on her without seizing her. He was getting much better about that. *'Let me explain... I know that our goal will cost a lot of lives. I know your pain for the deaths you believe lie on your hands. If I had told you about my mother's gift, I would have made her a weapon in our hands. I couldn't do that to her. I don't want her to go through the same guilt you have experienced,'* Aymis explained.

'You didn't trust me not to do that to her?' Eru asked.

'It wasn't my place to share my mother's secret with you. I didn't know what would happen. We may find her gift useful in the future, but not yet.'

'You are right,' Eru answered, *'but it still hurts.'*

'Please, don't torture yourself over it. I was protecting my mother from the life of an Aegendi,' Aymis answered.

'She asked me to seize her,' Eru stated.

'But, you didn't,' Aymis replied.

'No, I knew you wouldn't want that for her.'

'Thank you for earning my trust,' Aymis thought affectionately. Eru hadn't imagined anything Aymis could say could mean so much to him as those words. He shuddered at the thought of how things might have gone had he seized Janis. Had he seized her, he would have lost this moment with Aymis. Most of Eru's thoughts reveled in this moment, even while his mind continued to work through their overarching goals.

'That does bring up a related concern. Even if we achieve the impossible, it will mean little if we don't give the people hope. If people can't trust me, then I will be nothing more than a usurper of power in their minds.' Eru said.

'We need to find something to separate you from the rest of the archos,' Aymis answered.

'We need to give some truth to the stories Janis will be starting,' Eru answered.

'True, but as long as people have to be seized in order for you to interact and communicate people won't trust you. It's hard to claim benevolence while you hold others at knife point,' Aymis answered.

'You know that's not what it is like,' Eru said defensively.

'I do because I am a Reader. Do you think mother didn't notice a contradiction with your kindness to her expressed through cruelty to Penro?' Aymis asked.

'I see what you mean,' Eru responded.

'What if you learned how to talk?' Aymis asked.

'What good would it do me? I won't even know if I am saying things right.'

'I knew a deaf man who could talk,' Aymis countered.

'Yes, but he probably went deaf after learning to talk,' Eru objected.

'That doesn't matter. You know how to make other people's muscles work so they can talk. Why is it much different?' Aymis asked excitedly.

'Well, first of all, I can't even feel the vibration in my throat. I don't even know if I have a voice,' Eru answered, thinking he had made his case.

'You have a voice. I have heard it. You can tell when your arm is moving. Isn't it the same with your jaw and your tongue? Couldn't you practice an awareness of when you are tightening your, um what is it?'

'My vocal cords?' Eru helped out.

'Yeah, what you said. Couldn't you practice working the muscles there?' Aymis asked.

'I hadn't really thought about it. You have seen how I walk. I will never have the coordination of someone who can operate with his own sense of touch to work with. My voice will be similarly awkward, if I can do it,' Eru answered pensively.

'You already can listen to other's thoughts. Once you figure out how to talk you won't have to seize people just to communicate!' Aymis exclaimed. A flicker of excitement flashed in her eyes as they settled on Eru.

'I guess you're right,' Eru responded with a smile of his own.

'That's perfect! Imagine the stir it will make when an archos speaks with his own voice!' Aymis beamed.

'Yes, that will definitely surprise a lot of people,' Eru mused.

'It's more than that. Nobody will believe an archos claiming he doesn't want to seize people with the voice of someone he has seized.'

'I see where you are going with this,' Eru said. *'Let's give it a try.'* Eru took a deep breath and thought about the muscles in his throat as he exhaled.

"Hmmmmmmmmmmmmmmmuuuuuuaaaaaaaaah," Eru hummed with a warbling pitch in his voice that he didn't hear. Aymis struggled to suppress a laugh.

'Well, we won't be making any plans for a singing career,' Aymis teased.

'I feel ridiculous enough without you teasing me,' Eru answered.

'Sorry, it just surprised me, that's all,' Aymis apologized. *'Remember to open your mouth. Let's just try to create a stable pitch for now.'*

"Huuuuuuuuuoooooouuuuuuaaaaaaaaaaaah," Eru moaned with less fluctuation.

'Well, I'll be seized,' Aymis said.

'That much better?' Eru asked expectantly.

'Oh, well, it was better. I just forget how young you are. I don't think your voice has even changed yet,' Aymis said with a chuckle.

'You mean, I sound like a little child?' Eru said, understanding perfectly. He had seized enough doctors to understand puberty, but he had never stopped to wonder if the concept applied to an archos.

'I think it's cute,' Aymis confirmed his question with a chuckle.

'Great, my squeaky child voice will really inspire people,' Eru thought sarcastically.

'Don't be so hard on yourself. It is a good thing,' Aymis answered.

'That's easy for you to say. You aren't the one who has to feel self-conscious about it,' Eru replied.

'I am serious. People will be a lot quicker to trust you if you have a child's voice,' Aymis said.

'Quicker to trust me or to patronize me?' Eru countered.

'You need to look for the good in things more,' Aymis lectured. *'Go ahead and give it another try.'*

"Huuuuuuuuh," Eru's voice held steadier, though it still wouldn't win any prizes for musical beauty.

"Much better!" Aymis both said and thought. "Let's keep working on it."

"Uuuuuuuuuuuuuuuuuuuuuuuuuuuuuh," Eru said, sounding steadier and less breathy than before.

"Good," Aymis said proudly. "You'll be speaking in no time."

CHAPTER 20

IMMORTAL

*I still had much to learn about trust and keeping secrets.
I mistakenly believed that trust meant no secrets. I didn't
understand that there are many motives for keeping secrets.
Secrets can be terribly dangerous. Aymis was right though.
Had I known what she planned, I wouldn't have let her do
it.*

"Are you tired?" Eru asked. His powerful archos mind quickly made the connections between making others speak, and speaking for himself.

Eru knew he wouldn't be winning any awards for dictation or oration, but that didn't matter.

"I think I would like to call it a night," Aymis said aloud, feeling her pride over his first successful words. She knew she did not have to speak, but it felt so good and natural to talk with her friend. "We should find shelter before the storm gets worse," she finished. Snowflakes fluttered and swirled in patterns around the streetlamps, visible only where the light illuminated them. Even in their carriage, Aymis saw her breath in the bitter cold night. She looked out to the street, watching a small flow of people brave the cold. Where were they going?

"Let's stop here," Eru said.

"Good idea," Aymis replied. Aymis focused on the people crazy enough to go out in the cold, hoping to pick out their intention. She felt the strange mix of fear, anticipation and obligation that could only mean one thing: Congregation.

Their carriage came to an abrupt stop, and Aymis helped Eru get down from the carriage. In the cold winter night, Eru's pale skin and dark fingernails took on a particularly spectral appearance. They walked up to a small town home, a notable improvement over Aymis's original living conditions, but it felt like the depths of poverty compared to Penro's estate. They came to the door and Aymis knocked.

"What do you want?" a wary voice asked through a crack in the open door.

"Please, miss, we are cold and need a place to shelter for the night," Aymis said quietly.

"Ugh, beggars," the woman at the door said.

"Not beggars," Eru said with his high, innocent sounding voice as he removed his hood and revealed his unmistakably archos features.

"Well, I'll be seized!" the woman gasped.

"Actually, I would rather avoid doing that." Eru responded. Aymis could hardly believe how quickly Eru's talking developed. He would likely always sound odd, but she could even pick up some emotional inflection now.

"Please, my friend doesn't want to seize anyone, but we have to get out of the cold," Aymis said.

"But aren't... aren't you..." the woman stammered, "aren't you seized?"

"No ma'am," Aymis answered.

"This is some sort of trick," she said doubtfully.

"May we come in?" Eru asked.

"No, go away!" The woman answered fearfully. Eru felt her fear and un-certainty. Either they were a pair of scheming beggars, or worse yet, an archos really stood at her door. Even without seizing others, Eru still provoked fear effortlessly. Eru had hoped it would be easier to dispel people's doubts. He seized the woman and opened the door. Aymis and Eru stepped in, closing the door behind them quickly.

"Please, don't make me seize you again," Eru said himself as he released the woman.

"By the unknown gods!" the woman gasped when Eru released her.

"We will sleep by your wood burning stove, and we won't bother you," Aymis said apologetically. "He is not the monster that the rest of them are."

"I will keep the children in their rooms tonight," the woman said.

"That is probably wise," Eru said, feeling her fear like a hot coal on his skin.

"Eru," Aymis said, deliberately dropping the name and trusting Eru not to seize her, "I am going to go for a walk."

"Eru?" the woman asked before she could stop herself. The fast repetition of his name came like two dizzying blows. Eru barely managed not to seize her in response. The intense concentration required not to seize either of them distracted Eru from the oddity of Aymis's departure during the storm.

"That is my name, but please don't use it casually. You have no idea how hard it is not so seize someone who uses my name."

"Well, I don't know what game you are playing here," the woman said, just managing to suppress the irritation in her voice. Eru, however, noted it like he had been shouted at.

"I need a place to sleep," Eru responded calmly despite her hostility.

"But why here?" she asked. "Leave us alone, please!"

"Your neighbor to the south has his first job interview in months tomorrow morning. One door to the north, the husband is recovering from a broken leg. Would you rather I stay with either of them?"

"But..." she began to object.

"Your family presented the best opportunity while causing the least inconvenience possible. Inns are far too public and visible considering my enemies." Eru noted her initial thoughts of fondness for his enemies. "Trust me, my enemies are your enemies. Kara, isn't it obvious that I am fighting against everything my kind represent?" Eru asked, picking this moment to first use her name.

"Well... now that I think about it... you're not like the others. I have been seized before," she said.

"I am sorry you had to experience it again tonight," Eru replied.

"You are only a child. How old are you?" she asked.

"I haven't counted exactly, but I am somewhere around eleven years old," Eru said.

"You don't know your age?" she inquired incredulously, curiosity starting to win over her fear.

"My birthday is a day I would rather forget. It is one of the darkest days of my life and not a moment worth commemoration," Eru said.

"How can you hear me talk without seizing someone? How can you talk yourself? How can you exist at all? Your kind has always been..." Kara trailed off.

"Evil, yes, you can say it," Eru assured her. Kara sat down on a chair in her kitchen and gestured for Eru to do the same. He just stood there, his blank white eyes wandering around the home like two children lost in different parts of the same forest.

"You can sit down if you would like," Kara said when Eru didn't respond to her gesture.

"Without seizing you, I don't know where any of the chairs are, and I would rather stand than find out," Eru replied.

"Well, let me bring you a chair then," Kara said as she picked one up and walked it over to him, anxious not to be seized again, but almost as anxious to have Eru sitting. The sight of an archos seemed more intimidating with him standing in the entryway, a dark unbidden guest. At least with him sitting, he appeared less threatening. "You can sit down now."

"Thank you," Eru said as he sat in the chair. He felt his awareness free up a bit as his muscles relaxed, the only indicator he would ever have that he was sitting.

"So, can you hear then? You already break all the rules. Is that how you and I are talking?" Kara asked.

"No. I can sense your thoughts when you speak them, and I have learned to talk. You probably have noticed how unusual I sound," Eru answered.

"You sound fine," Kara assured him. "I-I mean," she stammered, afraid Eru would know she was patronizing him, "it sounds a bit awkward and broken, but for someone who can't hear his words you are doing great."

"Thanks," Eru said, trying to sound modest but having no idea how well he pulled it off.

"So tell me, what brings you here?" Kara asked.

Eru noted the tense, nervous fascination making her heart beat faster and her hands twitch. Kara's heart felt a morbid, alluring sense of danger and curiosity. Her rational mind told her to run as if the hounds were chasing her, but a strange intrigue and sense of adventure kept her there. Eru also suspected that she wouldn't feel safe for her children with Eru left unsupervised in her home.

"That is a long story," Eru said evasively. He didn't exactly feel like recounting his whole life story to her. Kara's curiosity left him feeling more like some strange exhibit for people to gawk at. "Let's just say that Aymis and I are starting on a long, impossible task. We happened to be here and we needed to get out of the cold."

"Except she seemed awfully anxious to get back out there didn't she?" Kara reminded him.

"She has been through a lot, and she needed a moment or two to herself," Eru replied, though her question reminded him of her absence, leaving him feeling more alone and exposed. She had been gone for longer than he expected. He thought about reaching for her, just to find where she was, but decided he owed her some privacy. Even if she would never know, he didn't want to betray her friendship. Still, a part of his mind began to worry for Aymis and wonder when she would be back.

"It sounds like an amazing story," Kara persisted. Eru wanted to tell her to mind her own business, but he recognized an opportunity to plant another seed. He knew better than to expect every place they stayed to have someone as morbidly fascinated by his presence.

"Well," Eru began crafting the story. He only bothered with the truth where it suited him. Instead, he worked in a few more moments and stories like the one Janis would soon recount. The truth didn't always make for good rumor and legend. All the while as he talked, a growing portion of his mind fussed and fretted over a different matter: Where in all of Deor was Aymis?

Aymis rubbed her hands together as she held them to her mouth to warm them. Her misty breath seeped through her fingers like a bunch of small serpents rising to the black heavens above. The blank dark of a winter snowstorm left the sky looking like a gloomy, heavy blanket. Big snowflakes fell casually to the ground. Aymis remembered as a child trying to catch such large snowflakes on her tongue. She smiled as she tilted her head back and stuck out her tongue just for the fun of it. A rather large flake landed on her tongue, nearly covering it with the cold dryness that immediately turned to a wet refreshing touch.

The bite of the cold on her ears, and the chill of the air in her sinuses reminded her that she had best get going before the cold got the better of her. She hadn't come outside just to catch snowflakes on her tongue. Still, Aymis made sure to enjoy the calm, quiet beauty of the evening snow storm. Even the cold's unfriendly gnawing at her ears and nose could be forgiven for the sake of times like this. Somehow the world felt in a deeper silence when it snowed. Even the sound of the snow packing under her steps felt quiet, almost reverent. Aymis loved the sounds of a summer night, the crickets and other small sounds of life, but silence this deep and pristine brought its own pleasure and beauty with it.

She followed the small trickle of people towards a citadel she could now see at the end of the block. Its warm light spilled into the streets, almost spoiling the magic of the cold winter night. Seeing a place bound to be full of noise and spectacle felt wrong on a serene night like this. Aymis almost turned back, knowing Eru would not have approved of her plan. The fact that he hadn't seized her to stop her meant he probably had respected her wishes for privacy. She could learn a thing or two from him about that. Even in two days with Janis, Aymis had indulged in her gift to snoop on her mother's thoughts on a few occasions. Both times, she felt so bad she had to confess, and both times Janis acted justifiably indignant.

Had Aymis's purpose for leaving Eru been for a simple evening of introspection, she would have turned around and returned to the peaceful enchantment of the night snowstorm. She had a different objective. She had expected an archos to know so much more about his own kind, and about the Aegendi. How could they possibly hope to defeat the ruling archos armed with as little information as they had? She knew Eru would have forbidden her to come, but Aymis would rather not require Eru to seize someone to do the snooping she could do on her own.

She heard a voice calling out praises to Aitrox, faint in the distance. Seeing the warm light of the citadel now heightened her awareness of the bitter cold and she quickened her steps. Finally, she stepped into the citadel and the warm air engulfed her. A shiver ran through her body, as every inch of her exposed skin declared just how cold it had been. She unwrapped her old, dirty scarf and held it in her hands as she stepped into the crowd, unsure what she hoped to learn tonight.

"You have glorified the archos by coming tonight!" a spokesman shouted from the stand. Next to him, a surprisingly young archos stood. He wore grey robes, and an iron rod hung from his necklace. Aymis guessed he could only be a few years older than Eru. What if Eru started a congregation? She dismissed the question immediately, knowing Eru would reject the notion.

"Glory to the High Queen!"

"Praise Aitrox!" Several other exclamations filled the building. Aymis looked around, sensing the hostile glare of the statues. Before, those statues had unnerved her, but now she felt like her enemy stared at her with those eyes. Now that she wanted to kill Aitrox, she almost ran like a scared puppy from the statues. How could she ever hope to do anything? How could she not try after everything she knew Aitrox was capable of?

'No! Please, no!' Aymis heard the screaming thoughts of a woman, injured and battered so badly she couldn't speak. Aymis focused on the woman, and immediately recognized her terrible plight. She was an Immortal. Her jaw looked broken, and terrible gashes ran up her cheek. Deep purple filled an eye socket. The eyeball looked like a gruesomely popped balloon. Aymis almost threw up at the sight, much less the notion of this woman enduring such injuries on a regular basis. No wonder the poor woman just wanted to let it all end. For her, being seized would end the pain, but only prolong the terror.

"What happened?" the congregation's spokesman asked.

"She fell in front of a carriage and was trampled by the horses and nearly crushed by the wheels," a man answered, choking back tears. "Please, you have to save her!"

"As Aitrox wills it," the spokesperson responded.

Aymis watched as the archos lifted his hand and the battered woman floated through the air over the crowd. Many gasped in awe, but Aymis fought back the urge to scream. *'This is all a lie! Don't you see? Don't you see how wrong this is?'* Fortunately for her, she had learned a few things about the value of holding her tongue. Calling attention to herself here could mean a quick death, or a life enslaved by someone terrible and cruel.

The woman came to a stop in front of the archos, who touched her with his evil, grey hand. Aymis felt the chill of hatred fill the battered woman's heart and Aymis shed a tear for her ordeal.

"Behold, the power of Aitrox for those who obey her will!" the man on the stage shouted with a dramatic flourish. Just as Aymis knew would happen, the woman's injuries healed instantly, leaving only another layer of thick scars on her heart.

The citadel filled with hundreds of sundry exclamations of praise, worship and adoration at the spectacle, and many fell to their knees. Aymis hadn't expected the sudden action, and quickly found herself standing alone like a tall tree in a field of grass. The eyes of the spokesperson met hers, and something dark and terrible touched her mind.

A young woman stood alone on the street corner looking slightly out of sorts. In the cold winter weather, her clothes couldn't accentuate her figure to make her an object for unsavory eyes to stare at, but she would be decidedly homely in any attire. Her shoulders lacked the feminine grace, and her hips didn't quite curve enough to be beautiful. She kept her face down and shielded herself from the wind with an extravagant fan. A few curious onlookers wondered what a woman of means was doing all alone on the corner. Next to her on the street post, a small red line had been left, but it escaped the notice of anyone who didn't know to look for it. Casting a few furtive glances around, she ducked into an alley, a most improper and unlikely place for a lady.

"That's a creative disguise," someone said to her in the dark with a laugh. She said nothing in return.

"What, no kind words from the madam?" another hidden face asked mockingly. She shot the man a deadly look.

"Sorry. Your business is your own, and you have every right to protect your identity. That is if you are who you claim to be," the first said.

Silently she handed him a small bag, and he grabbed it with trembling hands. He nervously looked into the bag before pulling his face from it gagging and coughing. A single shriveled finger, with leathery tendons and a visibly exposed knuckle would elicit such a response from most people. Despite its age, there would be no mistaking the fact it was an archos finger. The grey skin looked almost like leather, but the black fingernail had that unmistakably sinister shape.

"She's a Hider all right," the man coughed. The other silently handed the lady an envelope and the two of them left like their lives depended on it. Oko watched them run, knowing they had good reason. Oko had killed messengers in the past when they lingered long enough to make him uncomfortable. Oko despised this disguise more than any of his others, but it did produce the best results. He opened the letter they handed him and read anxiously.

'Five pounds of iron will be in an unmarked box under a bench in front of 123 Villefront Way at 5:00 am on January 3rd. Deliver four pounds to the blacksmith at 231 Andrews Blvd and keep one pound as payment.'

Oko smiled a rather un-ladylike smile when he saw how richly this job paid. It was a good thing, too. That was his last archos finger. Without another kill, he could not prove himself to be a Hider, meaning he couldn't pick up another job.

CHAPTER 21

Dark Heart

I was used to threats to my own life, and even the terrible consequences my self-preservation instincts wrought. I could not countenance threats to another person I loved. I knew in the back of my mind that, as an archos, I drew death and destruction to me like flies to a carcass, but I clung to the hope that I could protect Aymis. Little did I know the light Aymis would shed on my own nature, and even the hidden secrets of my people.

Aymis felt the archos's touch on her mind, much like the times when Eru just managed not to seize her. Her heart skipped more than a few beats, as she waited for the enslavement that she would never escape. She had hoped the archos would not notice her tonight, having attended enough congregations with Telu to feel a false sense of security. Now, she found herself squarely in the focus of an archos who lived up to the evil reputation of his kind in every way.

Aymis's heart resumed its beating shortly after, and she breathed again, as the terrible moment never came. She felt him pushing, trying to get in but something held him out. Knowing better than to question her good fortune, she turned and ran from the citadel. In her panicked state she didn't care about the stares of all the confused onlookers, nor did she notice a few pairs of eyes that followed her with an unnatural unison.

Aymis ran down the steps into the snowy night. The large pleasant flakes had changed to thousands of small specks that blew in the howling wind. The wind pulled at her angrily, its hostile icy fingers trying to stop her escape. She stepped onto the walkway and the icy ground betrayed her, sending her toppling to the hard, cold street.

A jarring flash of pain filled Aymis's mind and she thought she heard a quiet snapping sound as her arm wedged awkwardly against the street with her fall. She screamed in agony and panic, but knew she couldn't let it slow her retreat. Aymis still sensed the archos pushing on her mind, hitting the mysterious barrier with a sort of telepathic battering ram. She felt his enmity and hatred for her and his hunger for her gift. How he knew she was Aegendi would be a question for another time.

Aymis struggled to her feet, fighting through the pain in her arm. Then a merciless hand grabbed her broken arm, sending a disorienting surge of pain through her. With another agonizing scream, she punched the person square in the face, but his grip didn't relent. In desperation she thrust her knee into his groin, and fled when he keeled over and released her.

Aymis did her best to run despite the dizzying pain from her arm, and the treacherously slippery walkways. By this hour, the streets were mostly empty, except for the occasional carriage. She looked over her shoulder, and breathed a sigh of relief to see no more pursuers. In the distance, the man who had grabbed her still bent over in pain.

Aymis slowed to a fast walk, taking awkward, cautious steps on the slippery path. A terrible chill crept over her body, augmented by the sweat from her panicked run. Her teeth clattered so loudly she feared she would wake the neighborhood up, and every shiver that ran down her body only made her arm hurt that much worse. She wrapped her scarf tighter, and tried to hurry, but dizziness and exhaustion nearly overwhelmed her with each step.

The world around her began to spin, reminding her of the games she used to play as a child, seeing how dizzy she could get before falling over. She managed a few more steps before falling to the snow, her ears ringing so loud she didn't even hear her body plop to the ground.

'Help, Eru!' Why hadn't she thought of that before? *'Help, Eru!'* she exclaimed.

"So, I had this nobleman scrubbing his own couch," Eru said with a rather unusual sounding laugh.

"Well, I'll be seized," Kara exclaimed with laughter of her own.

"Not unless you want to scrub your couch," Eru joked in reply.

"I never would have guessed an archos could have a sense of humor," Kara said. As the night drew on, Eru had noticed Kara's tension fading. Fear still lingered in her thoughts, but by now she had grown accustomed to the figurative spider on her arm. As she relaxed, so did Eru, as demonstrated by his odd, dry sense of humor.

"Hey, archos are people too – well, sort of. I like to think I am a person anyway," Eru replied more seriously.

"So, what happened to the nobleman?" Kara asked, anxious to return to the story.

"Well, I wa..." Eru stopped mid-word.

'Help, Eru!' He heard it in his mind, but couldn't quite locate her. Aymis was in danger. *'Help, Eru!'* The second time brought his awareness to her, and he seized her right away. He sensed her relief with his presence, and would have wanted to catalog that unusual moment as something to cherish were it not for the pain and fear that overpowered it. Eru knew she had a badly broken right arm, and her body was already showing signs of shock. Eru felt the chill throughout her body and the clammy moisture of her sweaty clothing, wicking heat away from her like a candle in reverse. What had happened?

He saved that question for later, knowing he had to act now or he could lose her. Eru filtered out most of her senses, even dimming the hearing from her ringing ears. He forced her to stand, blocking as much of her pain from his awareness as he could. Still, he grimaced in discomfort at the jolts of pain each step sparked in her arm.

"What's wrong?" Kara asked, a note of alarm in her voice. Eru heard nothing of her words or her thoughts. "Eru!" she called, but Eru didn't even notice her call.

Tears welled in Eru's eyes, for the torturous ordeal he pushed Aymis through. This was exactly the kind of thing he never wanted to do to her, but he had to get her back to safety and away from the cold. One miserable step at a time, Eru brought her the two remaining blocks back to Kara's home.

Knock, knock, the door sounded. Eru hoped Kara would hear and answer on her own. Aymis stood shivering terribly on the doorstep as the wind howled and whipped around her. Knock, knock, the door sounded louder this time.

"Answer it!" Eru remembered to say, hissing the command like a sinister serpent.

"Yes, sorry!" Kara yelped as she jumped from her seat and ran to the door. A cold

gust of wind rushed into the room as Aymis nearly toppled in the last few steps.

"By the high queen! What happened to you?" Kara said, her face almost as ashen as Aymis's. Eru released Aymis, now that he had her back in safety. Aymis's sobs of terror, pain and fear filled the small room. Eru couldn't hear them with his ears, but the notes they played on his heartstrings had just as powerful an effect.

"What happened, Aymis?" Eru said, knowing she lacked the clarity to focus enough to hear his thoughts. Her quiet, terrible cries continued unabated.

"She's hurt!" Kara said in alarm.

"I know!" Eru answered, again not caring how his angry hiss would affect Kara. Kara guided Aymis gently over to sit by the wood burning stove, and threw another log in.

"Kara, I am going to seize you so I can treat her injuries," Eru said, not bothering to ask, seizing her before she could vocalize her protest.

Eru got to work immediately, removing Aymis's coat. Sweat from Aymis's ordeal left her clothes cold and damp. Aymis protested faintly with pain as Kara's hands gently removed the damp clothes. Kara ran into her bedroom, grabbing a sweater before ripping the blankets away from her sleeping husband, Olo.

"By the High Queen! What are you doing, woman?" he shouted after her, but Eru ignored his protests. Before long Kara's angry husband stepped out of his room in a groggy but furious huff. Eru seized him immediately and put him to work. Putting the new, dry clothing on required a gentle touch, but Eru's skilled mind guided Kara's and Olo's hands. He spread the quilt on the tile floor before having Aymis lay down. Elevating her feet, he placed a pillow under her head and wrapped her tightly in the blanket. Then he turned all the vents from the stove to channel the warm air her way. Slowly her shivering subsided and Eru turned his attention to her broken arm.

A dark splotch on her forearm a few inches above the wrist covered the ghastly spectrum of purples, reds and yellows. The doctors in Eru's repertoire of past victims had seen few breaks this severe, but he knew how to treat it. Kara ran to the cabinet, hoping to find something to dull Aymis's pain. Finding a bottle of cheap whiskey, he had her return and force it down Aymis's throat. Aymis coughed and sputtered a bit with the burning alcohol on her throat, but soon she had swallowed enough to make even an alcoholic woozy. Eru found two sticks in the pile of wood for the stove and got ready to do the worst part.

"Bite down on this," Kara's voice said as she put a stick up to Aymis's mouth. She obeyed silently. "I am sorry, but this is going to hurt."

Olo straddled her legs at the knees to help keep Aymis from struggling while Kara's hands worked her broken arm to set the bone. The stick in Aymis's mouth cracked and splintered as her teeth sunk into it. Her gasps of pain came out muffled but still with enough volume to wake Kara's daughter.

"Mommy, what's wrong?" the young girl's voice called.

"Go back to bed, sweetheart," Eru said through Kara, hoping to sound enough like her to convince the daughter to obey.

"Anna, go to bed now!" Eru commanded through Olo. Anna obeyed with a fearful yelp before ducking back behind her door as she closed it.

It felt like an eternity before Eru had the bone properly set and he used the other stick as a splint. Olo's stockings worked nicely to tie the splint in place. With the bone set, and the whiskey working its magic, Aymis's body relaxed and she slipped into a shallow sleep. Eru put Kara to work making a chicken broth for Aymis. When she woke, she would need food and warmth to help get her back to a semblance of full strength. Only when the broth simmered on the stove did Eru release Kara and Olo.

"I am sorry I had to seize you," Eru said.

"Sorry? You invade our home, seize my wife and I, and you have the audacity to say you are sorry, like that will make it all better?" Olo replied angrily.

"Honey," Kara began, trying to calm him down.

"Don't you *honey* me Kara! I want this monster out of our house!"

"Olo, please be careful. You have no idea how hard it is not to seize you when you are so angry at me. Please..." Eru trailed off. Kara recognized the sincerity in Eru's pleading, and in his desire not to harm her husband.

"Olo, control yourself. Please! Even our visitor can't hold back if you don't calm down." Kara said with an edge of fear in her voice. Whatever Eru's intentions, if he killed her husband, she would never forgive him. Eru sensed the flash of fear in Kara's heart as she contemplated raising their daughter alone. That thought gave Eru strength, likely saving Olo's life. After a few more angry huffs, Olo calmed down.

"He talks?" Olo asked, an edge of irritation still evident in his voice.

"Among other things," Eru said with a smile.

"Don't do that again please," Kara asked, and Olo nodded his affirmation.

"I will do my best to avoid it," Eru answered.

"What in blazes is going on?" Olo inquired, looking like someone who believed this all to be a strange nightmare.

"Eru, here, is different than other archos," Kara explained.

"Please, be more careful with my name," Eru said with strain in his voice, still weary from resisting the pressure of Olo's anger.

"What should I call you then?" Kara asked.

"Aymis calls me 'Friend'," Eru answered.

"How about... 'Visitor'?" Kara said with a pause.

"Suit yourself," Eru consented, not revealing the disappointment in his voice. He could hardly blame her for the slight, but he still felt it. At least she didn't choose usurper, intruder or enemy.

"So, visitor, what are you doing here?" Olo asked.

"We hoped to just shelter from the cold without bothering anyone, but things rarely are that simple for us," Eru replied.

"Well... um," Olo tried to begin before his courage failed him. Eru however, heard the unspoken thoughts and replied accordingly.

"I know you would like us to leave, and I can't blame you," Eru said.

"Olo, would you really send the poor girl out into this storm in her condition? Besides, they will have to sleep somewhere. Would you force our visitor to impose on one of our neighbors?"

"I suppose not," Olo answered begrudgingly.

"I am sorry for imposing so forcefully," Eru replied.

"At least you haven't forced us to scrub our couch," Kara said with a chuckle. Eru smiled at the reference.

"Well, I would go back to bed except you have stolen my blankets," Olo said testily.

"We can all share Anna's blankets," Kara said.

"Not like I have much choice," Olo grumbled as they left Eru alone with Aymis.

Eru sat next to Aymis, feeling her sleeping mind wander. He wanted her to wake up so he could find out what happened, but that would have to wait. For the time being, he just watched her like a protective father.

'*I will kill the Streetborn.*' Eru sensed the hostile thought from an unfamiliar source. At the same moment the window burst into a thousand shards as something heavy shot through it, smashing through the opposite wall, continuing through the master bedroom's outer wall and out the other side of the town home. Another crash followed immediately, and a heavy projectile just missed Eru's head.

Eru's awareness found the hostile will almost immediately, and he seized the threat before realizing he had just seized an archos. Eru had seized dark hearts before, but nothing could compare to the evil he felt here. No wonder the archos had such a vile, wicked reputation. This archos, named Tero, had only lived a few years longer than Eru, but he sowed death like a greedy farmer. Eru saw every moment of Tero's life, starting with the wicked trauma inflicted on his mother, who had the misfortune of discovering she was an Immortal the moment her newborn seized her in child birth. For fifteen years, Tero had exploited her, torturing her for every worship service.

With the control of the archos, Eru felt his own capacities expand. Eru felt the Wizard that had nearly killed him moments ago. A thrilling rush of power filled him as his mind comprehended the power of this Aegendi. Tero's Aegendi were now his. Despite his age advantage, Tero's capabilities didn't measure up to Eru's. Eru's years of discipline had developed a mental strength far beyond his years. Ironically, despising his power appeared to increase it. In that regard, Eru supposed he surpassed all the archos, but he was instantly reminded of the impossibly strong power he had felt when Aitrox had seized him, and his confidence vanished.

Eru didn't waste any time on Tero, putting him down with a few Wizard-propelled projectiles. Tero had remained behind in his citadel, but that didn't hinder Eru in any significant way. The archos fell dead in the citadel before the shocked eyes of his own congregation. Eru watched in satisfaction with several eyes of his own. Chaos erupted in the citadel as screams and commotion filled the building. People crammed through the double-doors frantically, pushing and clawing to get away.

After several chaotic minutes the building emptied, leaving only those under Eru's control. Eru inspected Tero's corpse out of a morbid satisfaction to see the monster lying in his gore. He reached down with a pair of hands to claim the necklace holding the small rod of iron. The usually nondescript metal dripped archos blood, making it beautiful in a gruesome way. Eru felt the iron rod with a rush of anticipation; certainly iron held some great secret. This tiny rod was worth a small fortune, despite the fact that the metal existed in abundance in the mountains. Just possessing iron instantly put a man on Aitrox's list of enemies, or trusted vassals.

Eru released everyone in the citadel except the man who stood with crimson-stained hands holding the iron. They scattered like sheep before a pack of wolves. The Immortal, Tero's mother, just stood there with an unreadable look on her face.

"Supe," Eru's man said, having learned her name when he seized Tero, "you are free to go." She stared back at him blankly. "Please, go." Eru wanted her to go, knowing the terror she had endured every day for almost two decades. Supe didn't speak, and Eru found it difficult to discern the thoughts in her shattered mind. Still, he tried as best he could to speak to her.

Eru felt her eyes focusing on her son's corpse, though her mind couldn't grasp the possibility of a world without that monster's constant cruelty.

"He can't hurt you anymore."

Confusion swirled in her mind, mixed with disbelief that any archos would not simply pick up right where her son had left off.

"The hell you have been forced to live is the very thing I want to stop," Eru said.

Supe's confusion and disbelief only grew stronger. '*You don't stop the archos. It's not possible,*' her scattered feelings and thoughts seemed to say.

"I will end the tyranny of the archos, or more likely die trying," Eru said.

Supe's mind filled with uncertainty about her life, and where she could go now. Eru sensed something unexpected in her heart, reminding him of an alcoholic's craving for something destructively addicting. She wanted him to seize her, craved the feeling of her gift quickening and invigorating her body.

"You are free," Eru told her, determined not to feed her destructive craving. The man he spoke with turned from her and began the walk to bring the iron rod to Kara's place. The cold wind and swirling snow struck him with a fierce blast before Eru could filter out the sensation. With the heavily falling snow, Eru blazed a new set of tracks. Not far behind, Supe added her own set of footprints, skulking cautiously in the distance but never letting Eru's man out of her sight.

"I'm telling you, an archos had my master scrubbing the dishes and cleaning the couch!" Janis said enthusiastically.

"You be careful miss," the man standing next to her on the street said as he did his best to warm his hands from the faint heat given off by the lamp. The look of hunger chiseled into his lean cheeks looked like an ominous forecast for the future ahead of Janis. "Such stories are dangerous to tell."

"I am not afraid. Even if my friend were to seize me, he's not the usual monster," Janis responded.

"By Aitrox you're not too bright," the man said caustically. Janis would have objected, but the hostile will that had just seized her couldn't have cared less what the transient thought. Janis felt the archos's sense of triumph at the stroke of luck as he saw the world through her eyes. She saw the world in what should have been an indiscernible chaos of shadows and ghosts, but it all made sense to her through her gift. The present caught up to the ghosts of moments before, even as new shadows and ghosts continually forecast the immediate future. Her heart sunk in despair, as she comprehended the terrible murderous weapon she would become under her new master's power.

As if in response to her tragic realization, she felt her hands move against her will as they grabbed the man, easily thwarting his attempts to dodge, and snapped his neck with an expertise that wasn't her own. She was indeed a Prophetess, the most terrible discovery of her life.

CHAPTER 22

FOOLISHNESS OR OPTIMISM

Through Aymis's misadventure I learned several important secrets of my kind. First, that an Aegendi becomes sealed to her archos master, a bond that can only be broken by seizing or killing the archos. This explained why many archos held frequent congregations in a desperate search for every Aegendi they could find. Second I learned that I could seize another archos. That should have been obvious from the time Aitrox seized me, and by the unflinching grip she maintained *on the city. Still, Aitrox always seemed like something more than an archos. The rules didn't apply to her. Lastly, I learned how my strength grew with every moment in the void. At my young age I already had an advantage over many of the archos. Thus Aymis's recklessness gave me several keys to defeating Aitrox. Bringing her down would be like toppling a wall one brick at a time.*

"By the unknown gods!" Olo exclaimed in anger as he burst from Anna's room with the commotion. "What is happening?" Eru kept most of his focus on the citadel where he currently had a pair of eyes and hands searching his fallen foe. He released the Wizard, who stood just outside, confused and unmoving.

"Please, tell the man outside that he is free," Eru said to Olo.

"What are you talking about?" Olo asked angrily.

"Tell the man outside that his archos master is dead, and he is free now," Eru persisted firmly.

"Um... okay," Olo said, looking slightly bewildered.

"What happened?" Kara asked, peeking out of Anna's room in shock at the mess.

"Get back in Anna's room!" Olo snapped. Eru couldn't blame him, since Olo had no way of knowing what had happened, or if they were out of danger.

"It's okay, you are safe now," Eru responded.

"Like blood and ashes we are safe!" Olo protested. "We have an archos in our home."

"Olo, please take my message to the man outside," Eru said with an irritated edge to his voice.

"Well, seize me! I am going," Olo grumbled as he grabbed his heavy coat and wrapped it around his robe, stepping into the dark night and swirling snow in his slippers. Outside, a man stood shivering violently in clothing scarcely suited for such weather. Olo felt the snow's moisture seep in through his wool slippers, chilling his feet and reminding him that his own attire was hardly any better.

"What are you doing out here?" Olo asked testily. "Did you see what happened to my house?"

"I did that to your house," the man said through chattering teeth.

"You're joking, right?" Olo said through his own violent shivers.

"Well, my archos did it through me."

"So, would it make any sense to you if I told you that you are free?" Olo asked as he started to put things together in his mind.

"Free?" the man asked in surprise. "You... you're not seized?"

"Thank the archos, no!" Olo exclaimed. "Look, I am freezing. If you need to get out of the cold, you can come inside. Not that it's much better in there." Olo turned and scurried back to his home, followed closely by the stranger. He pushed in, anxious to get out of the howling wind. The broken window let the wind and snow in, barely providing any improvement.

"Kara, close the stove's vents in here, and in our room. We will have to all crowd into the Anna's room for the rest of the night," Olo said as he stepped in. Kara hurried to oblige.

"Please, Olo and Ako, can you carry Aymis carefully?" Eru said, calling the Wizard by his name.

"It's her," Ako gasped. "And her archos!" He turned to run out the door.

"Easy! Easy!" Olo grabbed him before he could get away.

"Ako, if I wanted to seize you, I would have already," Eru said reassuringly. "Aymis needs to get out of the cold, please!" Eru's words fell on deaf ears as Ako's fist smashed Olo's nose and he bolted for the door. Reluctantly, Eru seized the desperate Wizard. Olo staggered backwards, raising his hands to his nose in time for the first gush of scarlet blood to stain his hands as it spilled down his robe.

"Olo! Are you okay?" Kara exclaimed as she ran to his side. Eru grumbled in frustration over the absolute chaos he had brought into this home; so much for a quiet night of not seizing or disturbing anyone.

"My nose is broken! Do you think I am okay?" Olo said, blinking with dazed eyes as he steadied himself. Kara guided him into Anna's room before coming back out to help move Aymis. She stirred Aymis awake with a gentle shake of her left shoulder. Aymis groaned and followed Kara's lead, so foggy with sleep Eru knew she wouldn't remember this at all.

As the chaos slowly subsided, Eru had a moment to contemplate the Wizard he now had seized. He sensed his gift with a rush of excitement and longed to use it. He could understand why other archos would keep such people as their slaves, but Eru knew he couldn't do that. Eru perceived the hatred and terror in Ako's mind and knew he would never willingly join their cause. Years under the yoke of such a cruel archos had indelibly imprinted a hatred and loathing for all archos in his soul. Eru could hardly blame him.

Eru hadn't wanted to seize the poor man, but Eru knew that the Wizard wouldn't survive the cold night, wet, exhausted and disoriented as he was. He hated doing it, but knew he had to either seize the man or let him die. Now that Eru had seized the Wizard, only an exceedingly powerful archos could enslave him, and that was some comfort to him.

Outside, Eru saw the home standing dark with snow swirling in through the broken window. The bearer of his iron had just arrived. Eru walked the man in through the door to bring the iron to him. Kara gasped seeing the man standing at the door with blood stained hands and clothes. She quickly ducked back into Anna's room. Eru should have thought about that a bit, but there wasn't much he could do about it now. He walked the man in and handed the iron bar over to Eru. Using the man's eyes as his guide, Eru walked into Anna's room to join the others. As the door closed, he released the deliverer, leaving him dazed and confused but free.

Eru felt Anna's confusion and fear, knowing her to be crying. Seeing her father stagger into her room with blood gushing from his nose had been scary, but having an archos in her bedroom was too much. "Mommy!" Anna screamed, burying her head in her mother's shoulder.

"It's okay sweetie, everything is okay," Kara said, but Eru felt the lie in her words. There was nothing okay about putting a young girl through such a terrifying night.

"Someone else is coming," Eru said, sensing Supe's approach.

"No!" Kara protested. "No more of your visitors!"

"I am not controlling her," Eru said defensively.

"I don't care! My daughter has been through enough." Kara said over Anna's terrified sobs. "If another person knocks on that door..." she said threateningly.

"That won't be a problem," Eru said.

"What are you talking about?" Kara asked.

"She climbed through the window," Eru responded.

"What? Get rid of her! What is she doing here?" Kara asked as her head turned towards the sounds of unwelcomed footsteps on the other side of the door.

"She's looking for me," Eru answered. "It's not what you think. She is harmless and confused." The hinges of the door into the parent's room squealed as the footsteps grew fainter. Eru felt Kara's anger at the intrusion into her own room. Only her confused, terrified daughter held her back from rushing to drive away the intruder.

The steps grew louder as they stopped outside their room. Anna's fearful sobs intensified, and Olo stepped to block the door, but dizziness forced him to sit back down. The door opened slowly and a cold rush of air blew in. A blank faced woman stood in the door, indifferent to the shard of glass from the window jutting from her stomach. Kara noticed it, gasping as she saw the blood that ran down the woman's leg and left a gruesome path of crimson to mark her footsteps.

Eru immediately turned more attention to Supe. He felt the urge to seize her and feel her gift working, a temptation he had avoided so far by almost ignoring her. He realized now that she would probably bleed to death if he didn't seize her and let her gift work.

"By the..." Kara gasped but couldn't even finish her exclamation as she watched the stranger pull the large glass dagger from her stomach with a gruesome, moist sound. Her wound closed immediately and life filled the stranger's eyes.

Eru walked Supe into the room and had her sit on the ground next to him. As he released her, he understood why she had come.

"My head," Aymis moaned as the sound of Olo closing the door woke her. Olo had left at sunrise to notify his employer of the night's events and get a few days off to repair his home. Everyone else remained huddled in the small bedroom waiting for Olo to return.

"I have been given three days off, unpaid of course, but at least I still have a job," Olo said bitterly.

"Not so loud!" Aymis whispered, raising her hands to her ears. "Aaaaah!" She gasped at the pain in her splinted arm when she moved it.

'Hold still!' Eru thought, hoping Aymis would hear. When no reply came, he spoke. "Take it easy," he tried to say softly, having no real idea how loud his voice was.

"I thought it all was a nightmare," she said as she covered her eyes with a part of the blanket.

"It was. Just one we had to live through," Eru responded.

"You are talking so loud," Aymis protested.

"He is actually speaking very softly, dear," Kara said. Her regular volume sounded like shouting in Aymis's sensitive ears. She cringed in response. "Sorry," Kara whispered.

"What happened?" Eru asked, grateful to hear he had been talking softly.

"I went to a Congregation," Aymis said with a guilty look on her face, though the blanket hid it from Kara. Eru on the other hand, didn't need eyes to feel her guilty conscience.

"Oh, Aymis! What were you thinking?" Eru asked in disbelief. He wanted to yell at her, to berate her for her foolish and reckless behavior. However, everything she had gone through as a result felt like punishment enough.

"I wanted information," Aymis said shakily. Eru could feel her struggle to fight the pain in her arm and head. She had never drunk alcohol before and the heavy dose of whiskey didn't agree with her very well. Her pale face looked almost green. She turned her head to the side and vomited. Kara and Anna both gagged in response to the foul smell.

"You should have told me," Eru rebuked.

"You wouldn't have let me go," Aymis protested.

"True, but what did you hope to achieve?"

"We can't beat them if we don't know anything about them," Aymis answered defensively.

"So, that's what this is all about?" Olo said with a nasal, angry voice.

"It is not what you think," Eru replied, feeling defensive.

"Oh, yes it is! You are actually trying to beat the archos! You are one, for Aitrox's sake!"

"Don't say that name!" Eru snapped.

"The archos rule is wrong," Aymis answered.

"It may be, but a hopeless struggle to change things is worse!" Olo growled, his voice sounding hollow and pinched from his badly broken nose.

"We have to try," Eru protested.

"Why? The only thing you will do by fighting them is make people miserable before you die! Our home is ruined, and poor Anna has been terrified, and for what?"

"Don't blame my friend. This is all my fault," Aymis said, blinking and putting her good hand to the side of her head in discomfort.

"No! You are both fools! Why wage a war that will only agitate the archos and make things worse?" Olo asked, refusing to relinquish his point.

"You may call it foolishness, but I call it optimism," Eru retorted, though he struggled to feel much of it right now.

"You're impossible!" Olo said in a huff as he stepped out of the bedroom.

"I think it is a brave thing you are doing," Kara said quietly to Eru as she followed her husband.

"Thank you," Eru smiled, but Kara had already left the room.

"I can't really blame Olo," Aymis said softly.

"Aymis!" Eru protested.

"Friend, I don't agree with him, but I think he has a good point. If we can't figure out a plan then we shouldn't pull innocent people into our own personal war."

'You're right,' Eru said in his mind, hoping Aymis would catch on. Fortunately she did, as Eru felt her concentration turn to him. *'Tell me everything that happened.'*

'I was afraid you would know what I was doing when I left...' Aymis began recounting her terrifying ordeal. Eru listened with rapt attention, letting his mind soak in every fact and start working on the implications of what she had discovered. By the time she finished her account, Eru thought he already saw a few vital elements to success. For the first time since they had decided on this goal, he felt a clear notion of what had to be done, and even a small sliver of hope. Eru smiled to himself, wondering who was right. Was it foolishness or optimism?

CHAPTER 23

ADDICT

*Broken Immortals are a truly tragic thing. Their gift domi-
nates their thoughts and they crave the euphoria experienced
when it rebuilds and restores their bodies. Unseized, their
gift heals just enough to prevent them the merciful descent
into a comatose state that any other person would have. The
result is a masochistic addiction that tears them, and anyone
unfortunate enough to care for them, apart.*

E ru seized a wealthy Baron from a passing carriage, whom he walked into
Olo's destroyed home. Eru could hardly believe the destruction of what
had once been a humble, albeit comfortable, home. Snow had swirled in, coating
most of the surfaces of the main room – a dry halo surrounding the wood stove.
Gruesome streaks of red ran down the wall from the window frame where Supe
had entered rather carelessly. Shards of glass and window framing lay strewn
around the small room with two gaping holes in the opposite wall. Eru stood
alone in the snowy main room, making sure everyone else stayed in the one
warm room. The Baron handed Eru his rather bloated billfold and coin purse.

"What was that all about?" Kara asked, having watched everything through
the cracked open door.

"A little compensation for your troubles," Eru said once he knew the Baron
was out of earshot.

"But–" Kara tried to protest before Olo interrupted her.

"You think you can buy our favor by stealing for us?"

"No, I will pass the misfortune of your ordeal on to someone with the means
to absorb the loss," Eru answered.

"Well, if you put it that way," Olo said. Eru sensed his quick capitulation and
knew Olo had always intended to take the money.

"I don't know," Kara objected.

"Kara, you need this, and deserve it," Eru responded.

"This is going to cost over two hundred Marcs to repair all of this," Olo said.
Eru doubted they had paid that much for the home, but he didn't really care
how much Olo asked for. Aymis and Kara both gasped at the large sum.

"Olo, please count out three hundred Marcs," Eru said. "I will know if you
take more."

'Eru, Olo's obviously taking advantage of you. Two hundred Marcs is ridicu-
lous, much less three hundred,' Aymis thought, giving Eru a critical look.

*'I know, but this can become another story about a generous, kind archos who
afflicts the nobility in behalf of those in need.'*

'I hope you know what you are doing,' Aymis relented. Olo took the money
with eager eyes, also noticing how much money remained.

"Why are you doing this?" Kara asked uncomfortably.

"Consider it our apology for everything that has happened," Eru answered. "I know the money is a poor compensation when it came at no sacrifice on my part," Eru continued. "I just want to make things right." Eru also had other motives, but he couldn't share those.

Olo would undoubtedly boast of his sudden good fortune, and how he conned this odd archos out of so much money. Ultimately, Olo's stories would plant more seeds, albeit with a few weeds. Such tales always evolved and grew with the telling, but Eru tried not to worry about that. For now he just needed the stories to start being told. The remaining money from the Baron would do a lot of good for some hungry and cold people, and buy a lot of notoriety at the same time.

'Eru, I don't know about taking that much money,' Aymis objected.

'The Baron will be fine, and we can do a lot of good with it,' Eru answered.

'It's just that it is so much money,' Aymis persisted.

'You are going to have to get over the fact that I have to take from someone to live, and realize that everything I am doing is for others. You'll feel better when you see people fed and clothed with this money,' Eru remarked. Aymis didn't say anything, but Eru could feel her discomfort as easily as Kara could see it on her face.

Eru let Aymis rest for the remainder of the morning, both for her arm's sake and her hangover. Olo, Kara and Anna left the destroyed home, bound for a nearby inn. Eru, Aymis and Supe stayed in Anna's room, though Supe had to go out to add wood to the stove in the other room several times. Most of the time Supe just sat silently, looking at Aymis or Eru with eerily empty eyes. Eru recognized someone who had been broken under archos dominion, though her resiliency as an Immortal left her in slightly better shape than most. By the time Aymis was able to get up, twilight's cold touch darkened the sky and the lamplighters had started their rounds. This deep into winter, sunset came early but it still made it feel like the whole day had passed. Eru commandeered a carriage and took them straight to a tailor's shop, hoping to get there before the owner closed his doors. Their carriage stopped outside with minutes to spare.

Eru knew he would have to seize Supe to get her out of the carriage in a timely manner. He felt health and awareness return to her mind as her incredible gift provided temporary reprieve from the cumulative trauma of her enslaved life. Despite her relief, it wrenched Eru's heart in terrible ways as he felt the unbelievable cruelty of her last fifteen years. Still, he welcomed a regular pair of eyes and ears that did not resent being seized.

The three of them climbed out of their carriage and walked into the shop. A bell rung with the door.

"We close in five minutes, so you had better make your selections quickly," the man at the counter called without looking up from his sewing. Eru saw several rows of coats hanging, recognizing skilled handiwork and evidence of several trained apprentices.

"I'll take them all," Eru said, feeling a bit self-conscious of his strange voice now that he heard it. The store owner looked up in curiosity over the strange voice and stranger request. As his eyes rested on Eru, his face filled with terror.

Please no, why would an archos want to steal all my wares? Eru heard his unspoken fear and felt the sinking feeling that hit the man's heart like a heavy anchor.

"Please, don't worry. I will pay you handsomely for them," Eru said, wishing he sounded more reassuring than he did.

"What? You ... talk...?" the shop owner asked, as the first wave of confusion sunk in over Eru's obvious aberrations from the normal archos behavior. Eru felt the fear in his heart lift slightly, replaced by bewilderment.

"Such a large order will take some time," the shopkeeper said. "My wife is home with my sick children. She will skin me alive and hang me on one of these racks if I leave late tonight."

"How about first thing tomorrow morning? I could use your help packing them all and handing them out as well. Can you do that for me?" Eru asked.

"Well, I can. I know this may seem odd... um... I know you could just take what you wanted, but I would appreciate some proof that you can pay for them. I must have at least one-hundred-and-fifty Marcs of inventory on hand," the shop owner stammered.

"We're good for it," Aymis said as she stepped forward and handed him seventy-five Marcs. "Consider that a deposit." She made sure to flash the extra large wad of cash. "There's another hundred-and-seventy-five when you help us distribute them tomorrow."

"Well, by the high Queen!" he exclaimed. Both Aymis and Eru cringed with his words, wishing people would stop calling Aitrox's attention to their efforts. "Where are my manners? My name is Ketu," he said as he extended his hand to Aymis.

"I would love to exchange pleasantries tonight, but I would rather not see your skinned hide as one that we hand out tomorrow," Eru said.

"Huh?" the shopkeeper said, completely missing Eru's strange reference.

"Oh, he means your comment about needing to get home to your wife," Aymis explained with a laugh. Eru's sense of humor came out in strange ways sometimes.

"Oh, I'll be seized! You're right!" he said as he put down his needle and made a dash for the door. "So, I will see you tomorrow morning then?" Ketu asked as he donned his thick coat and opened the door to leave, gesturing for them to step out in front of him.

"Actually, we need somewhere to sleep out of the cold tonight," Eru said. "Would you mind if we spent the night here?"

"I couldn't stop you if I wanted, and I don't have time to object," Ketu said as he stepped out and pulled the door closed.

"Well, that went well," Aymis said with a smile that Eru hoped he would never forget. He rarely got to see her when they talked, or hear her young, happy voice.

"Yes, it did. I am glad we have a place to stay tonight where we aren't imposing on anyone," Eru said.

"I am too, but it does feel kind of creepy," Aymis replied as she glanced around the dark shop.

"Well, let's make ourselves comfortable for the night," Eru said as he headed for the small wood burning stove by Ketu's work bench and sales counter. He grabbed a few of the thicker jackets along the way and laid them out to make a bed of sorts. He couldn't feel the difference from the hard floor except for a subtle difference in his mental comfort. Once he settled in, he released Supe again. It was a relief to have someone he could seize without all the negative backlash he felt, but he knew Supe had no chance of recovering if he continued to feed her cravings.

Unseized, she returned to her eerily silent self, sitting close to Eru with her blank unreadable expression. Aymis tried to avoid looking at her, feeling a shudder run down her spine whenever their eyes met. She had an idea what had reduced the poor woman to that pathetic state, and wanted as few reminders of it as possible. Still, all she had to do for motivation was look at Supe and she knew exactly what she was fighting to end.

When Aymis settled down for the evening, the pain in her arm flared up. She struggled to hold back the tears as she felt the throbbing in her arm. Eru had taken the time to work out a better splint, but nothing would stop it from hurting terribly. Part of her wished she had Supe's gift, but she realized that she never would have discovered the true goodness in Eru's heart then. Her arm could throb and hurt until the world ended, and she would accept it rather than lose that discovery. Supe and others could know Eru, but not as Aymis did. She closed her eyes with a smile, even as she trembled from the pain wracking her arm.

She slept fitfully at best, due to the pain. When she did fall asleep, it wasn't long before she moved in some unfortunate way and her arm's awful protestations pulled her back to consciousness. It would be a long night. It felt like time stood still, and she found herself longing for daylight so she could abandon the aggravating efforts to sleep. Sometime during this nondescript and eternal night, her eyes opened with a start as her arm slipped off her stomach and hit the coats under her. She choked back a shout with the impact, hoping not to wake Supe.

A faint orange glow still poured from the wood burning stove, casting its light onto Eru's form. He should have looked terrifying in the dim red light, but he held no fear for her now. Even his big, white eyes and splotchy skin looked kind. Strangely enough, the same features in other archos however struck terror into her heart.

"Supe, no!" Eru suddenly protested. Aymis's eyes darted around in search of the strange woman, finding her just in time to see Eru's reason for consternation.

The warm light from the stove glistened off a pair of scissors she grasped in her hand. Supe plunged them into her thigh with a gasp and sob, pulling them out and raising the now ghastly tool for another blow. The second blow never came. Eru saw the relief on Supe's face as the gaping puncture wound in her leg healed.

"Supe, what are you doing?" Aymis asked, as she watched Supe return to her usual empty expression. "Supe?" Aymis inquired again. Supe didn't respond. She just sat there hugging her knees and quivering like a struck harp string as a tear ran down her cheek.

CHAPTER 24

MAVERICK

Knowing I didn't have the luxury of never-ending life as Aitrox did, I couldn't hope to defeat her through my own strength. She was strong, but I knew she couldn't personally seize every citizen in Deor unless she had more archos under her dominion. I had to win the trust of the populace and weaken Aitrox's grip of fear over the city.

Aymis tried to get the image out of her vision, but the orange flash of light catching Supe's scissors just before they plunged into her thigh remained indelibly printed in Aymis's memory. It felt like something a cruel archos would make someone do, not something a person would do of her own accord. The thought of those heavy scissors, designed for cutting thick wool and heavy fabrics, bludgeoning a hole into Supe's thigh almost distracted Aymis from the very real pain in her arm. Aymis lay by the wood stove, her teeth clattering noisily. She just wished the long night would end and that she could get thoughts of Supe out of her mind.

Eru shared Aymis's discomfort and concern over Supe. Eru wished he could find a solution for Supe. For most problems, he could resort to seizing the perpetrator if dire circumstances required it. However, with Supe, every time he seized her it only exacerbated the problem. At the same time, he couldn't just let her suffer and bleed when she hurt herself. Maybe when Aymis recovered, she could watch Supe closely enough to help keep her out of trouble.

Eru sighed over the whole situation. His initial excitement to have a steady pair of eyes and ears he could use without guilt proved to be misplaced. Any chance Supe had to get her life back required that she be weaned from her addiction to her gift. He chided himself for even entertaining the temptation to seize her, clenching his jaw in frustration. Part of him said that Supe didn't even know to want her life back, and she did after all crave being seized. What could be so wrong with giving her what she wanted, when it served his needs so well?

No! Eru resisted that train of thought with a silent, internal fury. An archos ruined her and made her this way, and Eru couldn't let himself perpetuate that evil. Besides, Eru of all people, knew of the terrible pain that lingered in the background, skulking in the shadows of the addiction that dominated her. Supe's heart mourned her fallen state, but the relentless ache in her heart faded to the back of her awareness. Much like a factory worker whose mind tunes out the constant rhythmic din of the machines, unaware of it so long as it continues unbroken, Supe hardly noted the constant pain of her tortured soul.

Eru's heart ached for her, wanting to see her set free but feeling powerless to give her that freedom. Even at night, her sorry, wretched state robbed her of the peace of mind to truly sleep. Were it not for the innate resiliency provided by her gift, she would have been spared her plight by a broken mind. Instead, her mind remained permanently parked on that razor's edge, tantalizingly offering her escape while forbidding it to her. Could she recover? Eru had to hope so, to believe that the same healing that kept her from breaking completely could eventually bring her back.

Eru felt dawn coming as minds around the city stirred and woke. The gradual rising of minds to their state of wakeful activity had a strange beauty only an archos could possibly comprehend, a sort of telepathic sunrise. He sensed Ketu's anxious, uncertain mind approaching his shop, but Ketu wasn't the first to arrive that morning. Aymis heard the lock rattle and jostle as someone struggled to open the door. Finally, this terrible night was officially over.

A young woman rubbed her hands together vigorously as she stepped into the shop. "Hmm, Ketu left the stove burning again. He'll burn his shop down one of these days," she said, noting the warmer temperature but not the unexpected visitors yet. She hung up her coat, similar to the ones for sale, only hers was faded and worn from a few years' good use.

"Who are you?" she asked nervously when she noticed Supe and her haggard, ravenous eyes. She looked around for anything she could use to protect herself. Her eyes settled on the scissors, noticing the blood-stained fabric where they lay. "Oh, by Aitrox! Ketu!" she exclaimed.

"Take it easy, we are friends," Aymis said as she grimaced and sat up. Aymis's kind, unthreatening voice calmed the young apprentice slightly.

"How did you get in here?"

"We met with Ketu just before he closed the shop yesterday. We had an offer he couldn't ignore," Aymis said.

"Nice try. You have two minutes to get your things and leave before I call the city patrol."

"Please, don't do that," Eru said, counting on his odd voice to catch her attention. He felt the fear in her heart explode into terror as she recognized him as an archos.

"No! Please, by the maker, no!" she screeched frantically. The poor girl's mind ran through the most likely scenario to fit what she knew. Ketu lay dead behind the counter, and she would be next. Her breathing quickened and her eyes darted around her shop like something lethal lurked just behind the racks of coats. Then her eyes rolled upwards and she passed out.

A few minutes later, Ketu arrived, overcoming his own desire not to show up this morning. The thought of another hundred-and-seventy-five Marcs, and the opportunity to move all his inventory in a single day proved enough motivation to overcome his doubts. The archos never had seized him, after all, and he actually believed they would pay for his coats. He could hardly guess what motivated the creature. He nearly tripped over his apprentice seamstress, Tyra. He should have thought about the fact she would likely get there early to finish up her custom order.

"Tyra," he said gently as he touched her cheek and gently nudged her shoulder. "Tyra," he said again, giving her a gentle pat on the cheek. She opened her eyes with a faint gasp.

"Ketu! You're alive!" Tyra exclaimed.

"Of course, I am alive, why wouldn't I be?" he asked before realizing the likely cause for her lying on the floor.

"What's going on?" she asked, still quite nervous.

Ketu didn't feel much calmer, but he tried to project calmness. "Our, um, our customers are going to buy our whole inventory," Ketu explained.

"Right, and I'm the High Queen," Tyra said skeptically.

"I didn't believe it either, but you should have noticed by now that you haven't been seized. He never seized me either. And they gave me a deposit of seventy-five Marcs last night!" Ketu said almost excitedly.

"I don't know," Tyra replied dubiously.

"I hope your children and wife are well," Eru said to Ketu, deliberately interrupting their conversation.

"You see, have you ever heard of one that talks for himself?" Ketu whispered to her before turning his attention to Eru. "My youngest still has a pretty bad cough, but the two older children are improving."

"Hopefully, they get well soon," Eru replied.

"Thank you. What happened to my scissors?" Ketu asked as his eyes settled on them and a flash of fear rose in his mind.

"It's hard to explain, but everything's fine," Aymis said reassuringly.

"Did you kill an alley cat with them or something?" he asked angrily. "It's a disgusting mess!"

"I apologize, but like Aymis said, it is hard to explain. Let's get to business. We have a lot of coats and clothing to distribute today," Eru said, hoping he sounded determined and stern.

"Who are you distributing my coats to?" Ketu asked.

"The Sanche district isn't far from here; they certainly can use them this time of year," Eru answered.

"So, you're giving all of them away?" Tyra said skeptically.

"That's the plan, my friend. There are a lot of very cold people there, and your clothes will make a big difference to them," Aymis said.

"But that's insane!" Tyra objected.

"Why, we are paying you handsomely for your coats. They are ours to do with as we choose then, aren't they?" Eru retorted.

"Well, I guess," Tyra said sheepishly.

"Of course they are," Ketu affirmed.

"There will be another twenty-five Marcs if the two of you can help us match them to the recipients," Eru said.

"Well then, we have work to do!" Ketu said with an enthusiastic clap of his hands.

"Will you send for a large wagon, Ketu?" Eru asked.

"Tyra will at once," Ketu said, giving his apprentice a commanding glance as he spoke.

"Yes, of course," she said anxiously as she put her coat back on and stepped out of the shop. The bell on the door rang as she stepped out, and Ketu jumped to work. Aymis helped as best she could with her one good arm as they loaded up all the coats, being sure to organize them by size and style. Tyra returned a short while later, and the work of organizing their entire inventory began in earnest. After a few hours of hard work, the boxes were ready. The wagon arrived moments later.

Once the wagon stopped outside the shop, Ketu walked out and explained the situation to the driver. With the offer of more money than he usually earned in a week, he decided he would overcome his displeasure about his archos passenger and volunteer his services for the day.

"What's wrong with her?" Tyra asked with a nod towards Supe who watched the busy proceedings with her dazed eyes but sat still as a statue, except for the slight quiver in her hands.

"We are trying to help her, but it is complicated," Aymis said, giving Tyra a look that told her to keep her questions to herself.

"Okay, I get it. You have your secrets and I will leave them alone," Tyra answered defensively, lifting her hands in a gesture of surrender.

"Sorry, I didn't mean to be that way. It's just that I don't even really understand what is going on with her, but my friend is trying to help her."

"Well, he'll need Aitrox's blessing to pull something like that off," Tyra said with a snort.

"Don't say her name!" Aymis snapped.

"What's your problem?" Tyra retorted just as testily.

"Look, I am sorry for being so short with you. Let's just say we don't exactly want anyone calling her attention to our efforts."

"Well, no wonder you are so jumpy," Tyra said with a smile.

"It has not been easy," Aymis replied. *And we are just getting started,* she thought to herself. "Let's get this last box loaded up."

Silently, they finished loading the merchandise onto the wagon. Once everything was ready, Aymis asked Ketu to carry Eru out and help him settle into a spot on the wagon. Ketu didn't understand until Aymis reminded him that Eru couldn't see to guide himself without seizing someone. They rode the wagon into the Sanche District, drawing stares from the cold and dejected. Few carriages traveled these poorly kept roads, and even fewer wagons. They stopped the wagon in the middle of a square, drawing a few curious onlookers from their shanties and shacks.

"We have warm coats for those who need them!" Aymis called at the top of her lungs. Ketu repeated the call with his deeper voice that carried further. People now flowed into the square, seemingly coming out of every nook and cranny, and from under every piece of garbage. Soon the wagon had a sea of miserable, cold and destitute people looking at the wagon with a mix of longing and fear in their eyes. Aymis realized that the majority of the crowd's eyes rested squarely on Eru. As she glanced around from face to face, she heard a wide variety of thoughts, all centering on the same theme.

This is some sort of a trap.

First one to take a coat is seized no doubt.

I would rather freeze.

What, does the archos think we are stupid?

Aymis climbed from the wagon and walked towards a girl about her age whose clothes had more holes than seams. Her exposed skin looked blue, and she shivered violently. *No, get away from me you seized monster!* Aymis heard the protestation. Aymis tossed a coat in her direction, but the crowd shied away from it as if it were cursed.

Eru felt the sea of terrified minds. In the past, having hundreds of minds all reacting to his presence would have unavoidably resulted in several people being seized. Only with intense concentration did Eru manage to resist the weight of all their fearful thoughts about him. He had hoped to use this moment to leave the impression of a munificent archos in the minds of hundreds of people in one easy act. He couldn't say their response surprised him, but it disappointed him.

"Aymis, please come back to the wagon," Eru called. He felt the shock in a few of the minds that noticed that he spoke. Several believed it all part of his clever ploy, but a few started to wonder. Aymis turned around and climbed back into the wagon, wiping a tear off her cheek for the girl who had refused her coat.

"What can we do?" Ketu asked.

"Cover me with a few coats and we will go a few blocks away and try this again," Eru answered. Aymis helped him lay down in the wagon before covering him with one of their coats. The crowd parted in front of the wagon as it rolled from the square.

The jostling and bumping on the rough, neglected roads rekindled the ache in Aymis' arm. The pain muddled her thoughts and made her head spin. She watched the people return to their garbage heaps and shanties, regretting her inability to help them. She hurt for them with a pain almost as intense as the throbbing ache in her arm. A few people followed the wagons longingly. She felt in them a desire to hope that had been suppressed by the doubt of others around them. Aymis smiled to hide her aching arm and heart for those who followed the wagon.

Fortunately, they found another dirty plaza after just a few blocks. This time when the wagon stopped people spilled into the plaza like ants emerging from their colonies. She felt the confusion in the crowd, but not the same fear.

Aymis stepped down from the wagon gingerly, still reeling from her arm's protestations. She walked into the crowd looking for people who needed coats the most. They had about one hundred coats, and she wanted them to go where the need was greatest. A mother, not much older than Aymis, cradled her young boy in a ragged blanket, the only thing keeping the cold off both of them. Aymis put her hand on the mother's arm and whispered softly into her ear.

"Go to the wagon and ask Tyra to help you out," Aymis said.

"What do you mean?" she asked.

"We are here to help," Aymis said as she put a five Marc bill in her hand. The woman looked down at the money in disbelief, seeing more there than she had earned in her life. Aymis felt her thoughts of protest, but also felt her desperation overpowering her pride as she smiled timidly and broke from the crowd.

Tyra looked her up and down, sizing her up, then called a size and style to Ketu. He jumped to the appropriate pile of coats with a smile and tossed one to Tyra. She caught it and helped the young mother put it on. The smile on her face warmed every heart in the square. Even Supe, who sat in the wagon with her usual uncomprehending gaze, smiled as she watched things unfold.

Eru smiled with a joy that sprung from the happiness of others around him. He could get used to days like this. Ketu and Tyra worked enthusiastically, radiating their pleasure like a large hearth in a cold room. Eru had feared for Aymis, expecting a chaotic rush to the wagon once their intentions had been made clear, but it never came. Instead, the onlookers stood and watched hopefully. Several even started helping Aymis select people who needed coats the most.

Suddenly, as Eru's mind moved through the hopeful, longing minds in the crowd, he recognized someone and found a new sense of purpose.

'Aymis!' Eru called, touching her mind just short of seizing her to get her attention.

'What do you need, Friend?' she asked.

'There is someone here to whom I want you to give the remainder of the cash,' Eru responded.

'What?' Aymis asked in disbelief.

'It's Jordan,' Eru answered.

'The lamp maker?' Aymis asked, shock showing in her mind and on her face. Eru had never told her about Jordan's plight, but she knew of it from the times she had seen into Eru's soul and sensed his greatest regrets.

'Yes. Please find him,' Eru implored.

"Can Jordan, the ex-lamp maker, come to the wagon please?" Aymis called. A quiet murmur ran through the crowd. Aymis heard choruses of disbelief at the random, seemingly omniscient inquiry. The murmurs in the crowd grew louder as a haggard, beggarly man emerged and approached the wagon. Tyra sized him and helped him get a new coat on as Aymis worked her way through the press of onlookers. People bumped her broken arm unintentionally, but she pressed on, ignoring the pain. She reached the wagon just as Jordan turned to rejoin the crowd.

"Wait," she gasped breathlessly, grabbing the side of the wagon with her good hand to steady herself against a rush of dizziness. Jordan turned around slowly, an almost guilty look on his face.

"Yes miss?" he asked nervously. Aymis saw in his eyes and in his mind the hardship that had whittled him down from the once kind, optimistic shop owner. Pity filled her heart, and she wholeheartedly agreed with Eru's decision.

"My friend wants you to have this," Aymis said as she pressed the billfold into his hands discretely to keep the crowd from noticing. No doubt, he would fall among thieves if they knew he had that kind of money on him.

"What is this all about?" Jordan asked.

"My friend wants to make things right. He cost you your shop and your home. Please accept this as his apology," Aymis said.

"Who are you talking about?" he asked, still not understanding. The notion that the archos that lived under his porch could have been anything but a sinister monster had never even approached the fringes of his thoughts.

"My friend lived under your porch," Aymis said quietly. Jordan took a staggering step backwards, gasping in disbelief. Tyra steadied him, a concerned look on her face.

"How did you know about that?" Jordan asked.

"He is the one who made this possible."

"I don't... that's not possible," Jordan stammered quietly.

"Believe me when I say that your loss is one of his deeper regrets. Please accept his help." Aymis said quietly. Jordan's now worn and stained face creased with thought and Aymis felt his mind fight through the doubt and confusion.

"I don't believe it!" Jordan exclaimed, smiling with a dazed and confused look in his eyes.

"Jordan, I would feel a lot better if you accepted a ride with us to make sure you get out of this part of town safely," Aymis said, discreetly.

"Whatever you say, miss," Jordan answered uncertainly.

"There's just one thing," Aymis said nervously.

"What?" Jordan asked.

"You would be riding on the wagon with him," Aymis replied.

"Who?" Jordan said, comprehension eluding him.

"My friend, the one who lived under your porch, and your current benefactor," Aymis answered.

"Oh, I see," Jordan said. Aymis felt the jolt of fear hit him like a lightning bolt. She heard him contemplating his odds of getting out of the district safely. She hoped for Eru's sake and his own that he would accept the ride. A few tense moments passed. Aymis felt like every person in the square waited with baited breath on his decision, though few had even noticed their discrete conversation.

"I think I would like to see him again," Jordan said. Aymis exhaled the breath she hadn't realized she was holding. She felt Eru's heart skip a beat with his acceptance. She could only imagine how important this moment was to him, a chance to make one of the dark moments in his life right. Jordan climbed onto the wagon and sat there with an enormous smile as he watched them finish distributing their remaining coats.

With the last coat given out, Eru flung off his covers and called out to the crowd as he sat up, "Know that there is one archos in this world who cares for the downtrodden," Eru warbled with his unpracticed voice. He had never tried to yell, and it came out rather unusually. The exclamations of surprise from the onlookers erupted to a deafening volume as Aymis and all the others on the wagon covered their ears.

The wagon rocked and bounced its way out of the Sanche District with a small, enthusiastic crowd following them and shouting praises his way.

"Praise the Maverick archos!" someone shouted, and the name stuck. The chants of 'Maverick archos' followed the Wagon for several blocks before the crowd dissipated and returned to the unfortunate constellations of garbage and cardboard they called their homes. Eru actually laughed with glee when he first sensed the name they had given him. The Maverick archos was born.

CHAPTER 25

LEGENDARY

I have plenty of things to be ashamed of in my life, but there are also times when I knew my mother would be proud of me. Had my father been alive to see times like that day giving away coats, perhaps even his jaded heart would have felt softened. My mother's great wish for her son was that he would be a great force for good. Little did she know her son would set out to become a legend.

E ven as the group returned to Ketu's shop, Eru could feel the stories beginning to spread. Like all rumors, the stories grew and evolved with each
telling, and each evolution gave Eru new ideas to work with. The stories spread
quickly, for they brought a smile to the face of the teller and the hearer both. In
a city so long oppressed by Aitrox's evil, his simple act felt like a splash of fresh
water on a coal miner's sooty face.

The wagon rocked gently on the cobblestone streets as they made their way
back to Ketu's shop. Eru felt the pleasure in the rest of the passengers on the
wagon. Even the driver quietly chanted "Maverick" with a grin, before shaking
his head and mumbling, "My wife will never believe this."

Ketu, ever the businessman, worked over plans to use this to his advantage.
Soon his shop would be called Maverick Suits and Coats, complete with a
beautiful new sign.

Jordan sat on the cart, almost as silently as Supe, but Eru heard the flurry of
thoughts running through his mind. He had been granted early parole from his
life sentence of destitution and misery by the very creature he held responsible
for his fate. He still didn't know what to think about it, but slowly the clouds
of anger melted away as he watched Eru interact with the world. Jordan could
see how Eru avoided seizing others, and had to hear him speak several times to
believe it. Slowly, his mind accepted the truth of his unbelievable circumstances,
and the monster under the porch became something different in his mind.

Supe however remained vacant as always, her eyes wandering as purposelessly
as Eru's. Eru knew her heart had been warmed by the day's events, but he
wondered how much she comprehended. He felt her hunger growing, and
guessed that the quivering in her hands had spread. Aymis, in fact, had noticed
her trembling, taking a moment to wrap her own coat around Supe's shoulders,
assuming her to be cold. Aymis didn't know that Supe's innate resiliency made
it so the cold hardly touched her.

The wagon's jostling subsided as they left the poorly maintained streets of the
Sanche district. The sun had set, and the evening traffic of workers going home
slowed their progress. Eru sensed the sudden change in Supe's disposition, and
knew he had to act immediately.

Eru seized the driver of an oncoming carriage and pulled his wagon to a jarring halt. The wagon slid on the icy road, colliding with the curb and tilting precariously before righting itself. At the same time he seized Ketu, who sat on the wagon next to Supe, and grabbed her just as she thrust herself off the wagon. Eru, through Ketu, did his best to keep Supe from jumping off the wagon, but she struggled and fought back with more strength than he had expected. Her fingernail tore a gash across Ketu's cheek, and she squirmed out of his arms before Eru knew what happened.

Supe landed poorly, breaking an ankle with her fall and crying out from the pain. Had Eru not already stopped the oncoming carriage, Supe would have been terribly trampled. Instead, she landed in front of a startled horse, and her sudden presence, and painful screams only made things worse. Frantic, panicking whinnies drowned out Supe's screams, as the horse reared up and flailed its front hooves. Eru rushed Ketu to Supe's aid. Despite her own bad arm, Aymis immediately, and voluntarily jumped from the wagon as well. The two of them managed to drag Supe out of harm's way – not before the horse's pounding hooves did a number on Supe's arm, however.

"Wool-headed fool of a woman!" Ketu exclaimed as soon as Eru released him. "What in the fiery depths were you thinking?" He raised his hand to his cheek, where three red lines of swelling stood out. One had dug deep enough to draw blood, but not enough for it to flow anywhere.

"Hurry and get back to the wagon," Eru called. Supe's wretched cries of pain added to the ruckus of angry shouts exchanged among the drivers in the ever-growing back up they had caused.

"Ketu, will you please help Aymis and Supe get back into the wagon?" Eru asked. "Tyra, you too."

"Sure," Tyra said.

"So you will seize me, but not the women?" Ketu grumbled angrily.

"I'll seize you now!" Eru snapped in response, feeling no desire to explain himself.

"All right, I'm going!" Ketu answered, but Eru knew Ketu wondered why Eru hadn't just seized Supe to stop her. Ketu lifted Supe into his arms, doing his best to sooth her cries despite the angst he felt towards her. Tyra pulled Aymis to her feet with her good hand and walked her carefully back to the wagon. The whole chaotic sequence took no more than two minutes, but it succeeded in casting a shadow on an otherwise perfect day. The wagon driver flicked the reins and his wagon creaked into movement.

"Why didn't you just seize the wool-headed girl?" Ketu asked as they started moving.

"You don't give an alcoholic more wine to relieve her withdrawal," Eru answered.

"I don't understand," Trya said with furrows of confusion on her face.

"That makes two of us!" Ketu said bitterly.

"She's addicted to being seized," Aymis explained as she stroked the hair away from Supe's forehead. Supe continued to shake violently, with tears streaming down her cheeks. Her ankle looked terribly broken and dark bruises marred her arm. On one bruise in particular, a sharp line of crimson remained just under the skin as if threatening to break from its prison in revolt. The arm looked painful but paled compared to the demolished ankle. Had she tried to walk on it now, she would have been walking on the side of her foot. The sole of her shoe actually faced outward.

"That's insane," Tyra responded.

"There's nothing addicting about the experience, believe me!" Ketu said, casting a sidelong glance to Eru.

"That's because you don't have her gift. Remember the bloody scissors?" Aymis asked.

"What about them?" Tyra responded.

"Supe has a gift. She is called an Immortal because she heals immediately when an archos seizes her," Aymis explained.

"That's preposterous. I haven't heard something so ridiculous in my whole life," Ketu said.

"No, it's not," Tyra said thoughtfully. "I remember my mother talking about the miracles she saw at Congregation. I always thought it was some sort of trick or illusion."

"It's not an illusion. The Aegendi are the secret behind every so-called miracle," Aymis explained.

"Well, why doesn't he seize her now and end her suffering?" Ketu asked, his voice softening as he saw her wretched state in a new light.

"You may think it cruel, but I don't want to reward her behavior. Every time I seize her, it only reinforces her addiction," Eru explained.

"She's not a dog you are training! She's seriously hurting!" Tyra growled.

"Believe me, Tyra, I know. Her mind has nearly been destroyed from decades under her old archos master. She doesn't understand much right now, and I only hope that her mind will gradually heal with time unseized."

"Can't we do something? It just feels so cruel to let her suffer," Aymis asked.

"Please. I can't bear to have you of all people accusing me of cruelty. When we get back to Ketu's shop, I will do what I can for her," Eru said with a clear note of hurt in his unusual voice.

"I am sorry, Friend. I didn't mean it that way," Aymis said as she continued to sooth Supe like a mother comforting an inconsolable child. She knew Eru meant well, but that didn't stop the pain she felt for the poor, wretched woman. Aymis sat next to Supe, scarcely noticing the throbbing in her own arm any more. "It's going to be okay," she whispered softly into Supe's ear over and over.

They made their way back to Ketu's shop silently. When the wagon stopped, Ketu and Tyra carried Supe indoors somberly. Aymis descended with the assistance of the driver, giving him a grateful smile. Jordan took it on himself to pick Eru up and carry him into the coat shop.

"So, you have moved from a lamp maker's to a tailor's shop?" Jordan said with a smile.

"It has been a long and difficult road for both of us, Jordan," Eru responded.

"I never could figure out why you didn't take my food when you were hungry," Jordan said thoughtfully.

"I had taken enough from you. I hoped to lessen the misfortune of my presence. I am so sorry for what happened to your home," Eru replied sincerely.

"It's all made right now," Jordan said as he set Eru down on the coats by the stove.

"No, I cannot compensate you for your hardship," Eru answered.

"Just keep doing what you are doing," Jordan said. Jordan walked out of the shop with a content, peaceful look on his face as he stepped into the night and out of Eru's life.

"I need to seize someone so I can attend to Supe's ankle. Who is willing?"

"I will," Aymis said.

"Not you Aymis," Eru said. *'It will be too hard for you to see everything she has gone through.'*

"And why not?" Ketu asked irritably. "You favoring your friend?"

"It's because of my gift," Aymis spoke up in Eru's defense.

"So you're an Aegendi too? What is your gift?" Tyra asked.

"I am called a Reader. When my friend seizes me, I can see everything in someone's life. There is no keeping a secret from me. Even unseized I can hear people's thoughts."

"So what am I thinking right now then?" Ketu asked skeptically.

"'I could sure go for a bowl of my wife's crab soup,'" Aymis answered immediately.

"Well, that was random," Tyra said with a smile.

"That was the point," Ketu said quietly. "I agree with Eru. It shouldn't be Aymis."

"What, do you have some secrets to keep, old man?" Tyra asked teasingly.

"We all have secrets," Aymis said, noting the discomfort in Ketu's countenance.

"Fair enough. It seems that I am the only one who hasn't been seized so far. I'll do it," Tyra responded. Something about seizing a volunteer lessened the bitterness of the experience for both Eru and Tyra.

"That's odd, I thought it was a much worse break," Eru said with Tyra's voice as he inspected Supe's foot. Her severely swollen ankle had some discoloration and a slightly misshapen bulge on the outside, but there was actually little for Eru to do now besides immobilizing the joint. The bruising on her arm looked lighter with no traces of threatening crimson.

"What are you talking about?" Aymis asked as she came to take a look. "By the High, um, I mean, that's impossible. Her foot looked like it was growing sideways out of her ankle."

"It must be her gift," Tyra's voice spoke Eru's thoughts. "Do you have any Aspen bark extract or other pain remedies?"

"Not here, unfortunately," Ketu answered.

"Then there is not much I can do for her, but we will need to impose on your hospitality for another night," Eru said.

"You can stay at Maverick's Suits and Coats as long as you want."

"I like the new name," Tyra said with a smile as Eru released her.

"I would like to commission a suit from you," Eru said.

"What do you need a suit for?" Aymis asked.

"As word has been spreading, people have started talking about the almost angelic archos dressed all in white," Eru said with a smile.

"It's brilliant! I will make you a white suit with tails, and a silver top hat!" Ketu exclaimed.

"A white top hat. I want silver wings embroidered or painted onto the back of the outer jacket," Eru responded.

"Do you think you are up to that Tyra? Can you embroider the wings for me or will I have to contract that out to someone?" Ketu asked teasingly.

"Hrmph. If I couldn't do it, you certainly could. Don't worry, it will be spectacular," Tyra responded.

"Why wings, Eru?" Aymis asked.

"Because they represent freedom, and because the rulers hate birds," Eru replied.

"Why do you say that?" Tyra persisted.

"Haven't you noticed how almost every wall and roof top has spikes on it? It's like they don't want a bird to land anywhere in the city. I think the rulers would make the trees grow thorns if it was in their power," Eru answered.

"So the Maverick will have wings! It's perfect!" Ketu declared.

"I intend to fly as well," Eru said confidently.

"How will you do that?" Tyra asked.

"I saw people appearing to fly during worship services at the citadels," Aymis began thoughtfully. "It's brilliant! You are going to use a Wizard!" Aymis said excitedly.

"It will be amazing," Ketu said as the mental image of the painting he would commission grew and evolved.

"No, it will be legendary," Aymis corrected him with a smile.

"That's the idea," Eru confirmed.

Aitrox couldn't help but chuckle as she watched the rebel Streetborn's amusing efforts. The last few years of her rule stood out from the mundane, undistinguishable blur of the years before. This Streetborn had shown her many new and exciting things. He had a flare for the dramatic: she would give him that.

She could hardly believe what she felt in her own city. Small slivers of hope rose from the slums and ghettos of all places. Just as incredible was the fact that they placed their hope in an archos! Part of her almost felt envy for this Streetborn, for he had something she would never have. People would never fear him like they did her, but they would love him like they never could her. She preferred the delicious fear of the vermin beneath her. Why would she want the love of such miserable pathetic creatures?

Sitting on her gilded throne, Aitrox wanted to clap for the wonderful entertainment this Streetborn put on for her. Everything unfolding before her felt like a masterfully scripted play, incorporating elements of comedy, and drama. The best part was that she already knew the ending, and she loved tragedies.

CHAPTER 26

Secrets

I knew better than to believe we had won any significant victories, yet. Aitrox tolerated us for reasons beyond my comprehension, but I knew better than to think she considered any of our efforts the least bit threatening. I feared the day Aitrox would more aggressively oppose us, yet I also longed for it as well. In a sense, I wanted her to validate my efforts by fighting against them. Those days were an odd mixture of relief and frustration; relief because we hadn't yet reached *the terror I knew to be coming, frustration because of our implied insignificance. I knew we desperately needed a way to escape Aitrox's penetrating awareness, and a way to shed a light on so many of her secrets.*

"It's magnificent," Aymis said as she helped Eru put on the suit.

"May I see it?" Eru asked.

"Well, of course! What kind of a question is that?" Tyra said with a laugh.

"You forget what seeing entails for me. Would one of you willingly let me use your eyes?" Eru clarified.

"Just keep it quick, please," Ketu grumbled in consent.

Eru smiled like a kid in a candy shop when he inspected the craftsmanship. Ketu's workmanship and Tyra's embroidery put them on a short list of master tailors. The suit almost glowed with spectacular brilliance. The embroidered wings practically came to life on his back, glistening silver in the light. Eru couldn't have asked for anything better.

"He loves it," Aymis said, reciprocating the smile she saw on Eru's face.

"It is an exquisite creation. I will have payment before the day is out," Eru said as he released Ketu.

"That won't be necessary," Ketu answered.

"We can't accept something so grand as a gift," Aymis objected.

"You paid us handsomely for our inventory. Consider this a bonus," Tyra said with a smile.

"Any good word you can put in for our shop wouldn't hurt either," Ketu interjected.

"Ketu! You're shameless!" Tyra teased.

"There's no such thing as bad publicity," he winked in reply.

"Well, I won't be wearing it all the time, just when the Maverick is up to his philanthropic exploits."

"That's a shame," Ketu mumbled.

"I can't always be the saint and legend. Besides this won't be the easiest thing to keep clean, especially during the winter."

"I can think of a few noblemen who would love to scrub it for you," Aymis said with a laugh. Tyra and Ketu chuckled at the notion. Eru smiled at the reference.

"Please help me change back to my regular clothes now."

They all obliged, helping him as they would an invalid rather than Eru seizing one of them. Aymis buttoned up his shirt and weathered vest before replacing the iron bar around his neck. They had washed it, but what appeared to be rust was actually the lingering stains from Tero's death.

'Why do you insist on wearing that?' Aymis asked as she put it on him.

'Tero obviously felt there was some reason to wear it,' Eru reminded her.

'He was a monster who wore it for show,' she replied.

'We don't know that. The rulers forbid iron for a reason. Maybe it enhances our abilities.'

'Well, have you felt any stronger for wearing it?'

'I wouldn't have known I was wearing it without you letting me know,' Eru confessed.

'It gives me the creeps. I wish you wouldn't wear it,' Aymis said.

'It is too soon to tell if it is going to make a difference.'

'Every time I see it, I think of that terrible night – of our first kill. How long do you plan on wearing it?' Aymis asked.

'OUR first kill? His blood is not on your hands. If I haven't noticed anything by the time the snows melt, I will stop wearing it. Is that acceptable?' Eru asked.

'I suppose,' Aymis sighed. At this time of year it always felt like snow held the city eternally hostage, and the thought of spring felt as impossible as liberation from Aitrox. Outside, the snow swirled and blew in the wind as if to reaffirm its unflinching rule over the city.

"He hired your builders today," Rono's assistant, Jano informed him.

"Of course he did," Rono replied, secretly celebrating the news. When he first got news of the strange new archos the people called Maverick, he saw both an opportunity and a threat. Every time the white coated creature appeared, he spent a small fortune helping the poor. As the banker to many of the city's wealthiest nobility, Rono worried that the Maverick might call on him some day to acquire more funds. In the meantime however, he had set about trying to make the most of the archos's tendency to spend. He had recently organized a small building company and set up their office close to the Oak Hollow slums. That investment had just paid off handsomely.

"You have some accounts to balance," Rono said curtly to the assistant.

"Yes, sir," he replied as he quickly left Rono's office. Rono returned to his own affairs, reading a rather dry report he had commissioned about the viability of a new canal to the wheat farms to the south. It appeared to be a wise move given Rono's connections in the construction business as well as his partial ownership of some of the largest farms. He didn't get far into his reading before a disturbance outside his office interrupted him.

"Call the city patrol!" someone shouted from the other room.

"What good would it do?" another employee at the bank rejoined. Rono got up from his desk and headed to the bank lobby.

"Greetings," said a young, archos dressed in a brilliant, white suit, and an equally pristine top hat. Rono could hardly believe that an archos just spoke with its own voice, even if it sounded quite odd. "If everyone stays calm, and avoids any rash thoughts or actions then you have nothing to fear," the archos continued.

"And what brings such a fine gentlemen to my establishment today?" Rono asked, trying to remain calm. Perhaps the archos simply needed to open an account. Rono knew such a hope to be highly unlikely.

"I just hired a construction company to build a school and repair several roads in the Oak Hollow District." The archos paused for effect. If Rono didn't know any better, the creature was taunting him. He should have known that the archos would detect the connection. "I need some funding to fulfill my portion of the contract and to staff the school." A quiet murmur began among the bank employees.

"I don't see how I can help you," Rono replied.

"Please, Rono," the archos began. "I know exactly how much money you have on the premise, as well as the balances of each of your client's accounts. Don't think I would come here without doing my own research." Rono's face paled as he contemplated everything the archos may know about his business dealings. "I would prefer you bring me ten-thousand Marcs voluntarily."

"I will do nothing of the sort," Rono answered angrily. Then it happened. The vile thing seized him. It had been years since Rono had been seized before. Time had dulled the recollection's intensity. Rono knew he had to make the archos seize him or face the wrath of his clients. At least now he had witnesses to verify that he had indeed been seized. Rono gathered the money from the bank's vault room and brought the bag to the archos. A young lady, who had gone unnoticed until that moment stepped forward to take the rather heavy bag.

"Thank you. Have a wonderful afternoon," The archos said as he released Rono and left the bank. Rono couldn't help but admire the spectacular embroidery on the back of the little villain's suit. The sight of the silver wings glistening in the sunlight was the last Rono ever saw of the demon.

"Jano, my office, now," Rono growled after the archos left.

"Yes, sir," Jano said as he hastily stood and followed Rono. "This is a disaster!" he exclaimed after he closed the door. Rono nodded but didn't say anything immediately. He sat in his chair and looked at the fine wood grains on the arm rest. Jano knew the look when his boss was deep in thought. Finally he broke the silence.

"It definitely will make some things difficult, but it isn't as bad as you might think," Rono said thoughtfully.

"Sir, I respectfully disagree. Our clients will have your hide."

"I need you to draft a letter to Lords Hamilton, Penro, and Rollings. Inform them that the Maverick archos seized me and forced me to hand over thirty-three-hundred Marcs from each of their accounts."

"Lord Penro will be livid. He won't care that you were seized, and he is a dangerous person."

"Oh, he will be just fine. He knows I could ruin him. In your letter to him, inform him that if he, or anyone else attempts to exact retribution on my establishment that certain things will come to light. That should be enough to remind him of our *arrangement*."

"Still, sir, we just lost an awful lot of money today."

"No, my clients lost a lot of money today. I will get almost all of it back as the archos spends it with the building company I had set up."

"If word reaches Penro that the archos spent their money with your firms, I don't think there will be anything that will stop him from having you killed," Jano warned.

"You are right. I will need to get to work hiding my connection to those companies, but that can be taken care of. They will never know the secret," Rono said trying to project more confidence than he felt. In a city ruled by archos, secrets were terribly hard to keep.

Eru and Aymis made use of his spectacular white suit on several occasions, drawing larger crowds and stirring up a greater response with each philanthropic moment. The moments almost attained an element of spectacle as people flocked to see the legendary and elusive Maverick in his now-famous white suit and hat. With his growing reputation, Eru also increased the scale of his efforts. As he grew in veneration and praise among the working class and poor, he also grew in infamy among the nobility. Of course, Eru deserved their loathing, having expended thousands of Marcs of their money to feed, clothe, educate, and house the poor.

Shops that had benefited from Eru's business started displaying a small silver wing on their window as a gesture of pride and support. Other shops started showing the outline, as an invitation or supplication for the Maverick to do business with them. Aymis could hardly blame the shop owners for extending the invitation. Any shop Eru visited typically cleared a higher profit in one day than they usually did in three months.

Eru's spirits rose over the months until it became more common to see a smile on his face than not. As winter's grip slowly faded, the world also showed signs of warming due to Maverick's growing legend. He had never lived in a world where any positive sentiment existed towards the archos. To feel a growing sentiment of admiration and even affection for him exceeded his strongest childhood longings.

The temperatures gradually warmed, and the first touches of green showed on the trees and gardens as the snow receded. After the long winter in the smothering, lifeless blanket of white, even the sickly green of lawns that hadn't seen the sun in months felt vivacious and bright. Aymis anticipated the spring with its accompanying rejuvenation of the world, almost forgetting about Eru's promise with the iron. Still, she wasn't about to complain, nor did she feel surprised, when Eru remembered and honored his promise.

"Isn't spring beautiful?" Eru asked Aymis one morning as they woke in the home of a metalworker where they stayed as guests.

"It felt like winter would never end," Aymis responded.

Supe watched them blankly as always. Eru felt encouraged by her mild improvements in the past few months. She hadn't hurt herself or tried anything dramatic for several weeks, but her hands quivered almost constantly.

"Well, I have seen no reason to continue wearing the iron," Eru said with a note of disappointment in his voice.

"So you'll get rid of it?" Aymis said, not trying to hide her pleasure.

"No. It is time for me to explore another possible reason why iron is forbidden."

"What is that?"

"Well, if iron doesn't empower an archos, then maybe it has the opposite effect."

"Wouldn't you have noticed something?" Aymis asked, her brow furrowing in confusion.

"Well, it obviously hasn't hampered me by wearing it, but what if it is toxic to an archos?" Eru asked.

"Well, why would she ban iron over cyanide, arsenic or any other number of poisons someone could use against her? Besides, it would be impossible to poison a powerful archos anyway," Aymis answered.

"Well, there's only one way to know for sure. Please guide me to our host's workshop."

"I don't think I like where this is going," Aymis said uneasily as they made their way to the metal shop.

"Will you file the end to a point for me, or do I need to find someone else to do it?"

"I am sorry. I won't help you try to poison yourself."

"So what would you suggest?" Eru asked.

"Wait until we have another archos encounter," Aymis answered.

"I don't want to wait that long when the answer could be the key to surviving that encounter."

"What do you mean?" Aymis asked.

"Well, I have no way of measuring my strength against that of an enemy. It was providence that you found such a young and inexperienced archos at that congregation. What if that archos had been stronger? What if it had seized and killed me?"

"And how do you think that iron could possibly help?" Aymis retorted testily.

"I have no idea, but I need to explore all possibilities, lest we find ourselves unprepared when the rulers decide to fight back."

"All right. I see your point," Aymis relented.

"So will you do this for me?" Eru asked.

"What did you want?"

"File the iron to a point, but save the shavings."

"Okay, I'll do it," Aymis said quietly. Eru felt the fear in her heart; fear that her actions would make her an accomplice in his death. Eru refused to entertain the notion, feeling somewhere in his heart that an iron prick to his finger wouldn't be the way he died. He recognized the risk, but he felt the mystery pulling him. The mystery of iron felt like the first of many portentous secrets that Aitrox must undoubtedly harbor. Could it be the secret to her immortality? Finding the answer felt like it would be the least risky of his ventures.

When Aymis finished filing one end of the small bar to a point, she saved the filings before placing the bar into Eru's hand. "It's ready."

"I need you to let me know when I have drawn blood by pricking my finger," Eru said.

"This is crazy. Why don't you just seize someone?" Aymis objected.

"Because anyone I seize will prevent me from hurting myself." Eru remembered that terrible night when he had attempted to kill himself. For all he knew this sharpened iron rod could be every bit as lethal as the Deor River. He doubted it, but he couldn't risk any unforeseen instincts kicking in. He wanted to send everyone away, but he couldn't do it without some help. Aymis had focused on him enough to recognize all the thoughts that went unspoken.

"All right," Aymis said, surprised at the tear she felt welling in her eye. "Let's get this over with."

"Maverick, friend," Supe said as she walked over and touched Eru's hand. For the first time since her brief moments of semi-lucidity at Tero's death, she had spoken, and the emptiness in her eyes had been filled as if drawing from deep wells of concern reciprocated towards one who she knew cared for her.

Oko had stayed in hiding for just over a month before casing out another archos. In that time some surprising rumors had sprung up. Oko wanted to believe them, but wouldn't put anything past the duplicity and deception of the archos. For all he knew, this Maverick was a scheme to draw out Hiders and finish them off. Oko would teach them not to trifle with the hopes of the people. He would pay this Maverick a visit after he took care of his quarry tonight.

Oko's knife slit the throat of a Hawk Eye, the most immediate threat to his surreptitious movements. He had to move quickly now. He ducked as a projectile passed where he had been, piercing the now dead Hawk Eye with a gruesome splatter. Oko jumped back into the shadows and looked for any eyes that could see him. In his dark garb, the shadows were his home, and he knew they would not betray him. Oko scurried up the pillar in the citadel, scarcely making a sound. The stone around him burst and scattered debris as more deadly projectiles just missed their mark. Oko ran along the ledge and ducked behind another one of Aitrox's statues.

He indulged himself in a brief, satisfying fantasy where he found himself not behind a statue, but the real Aitrox, his knife ready for the kill. He smiled as he felt the satisfaction at drawing the blood of a goddess, but the urgency of his current plight didn't allow him to continue the pleasing daydream. Oko used one of his favorite tools for situations like these, pulling two small balls from his pocket and throwing them in opposite directions. They collided with a buttress and a wall before exploding with a flash on impact, and shot a weighted fabric higher into the citadel's rafters. The resounding boom the balls made on impact echoed through the citadel. The Wizard's retaliatory projectiles shredded the diversionary pieces of fabric, but Oko's eyes looked elsewhere.

He stayed in his spot, knowing his foe expected him to move before the ruses had been discovered. From his vantage point, he spotted the Wizard by following the projectiles back to their origin and by the movement of the Wizard's eyes foretelling the places where the next deadly projectiles would strike. Oko laughed to himself, recognizing a fairly amateur archos by such a thing. A clever archos knew they could throw things from anywhere, independent of the Wizard's location. The really dangerous archos would use other eyes to spot his targets, thus masking the source of the real threat completely. He liked his chances more with every moment.

Oko threw three star-like knives from his hiding spot, silently triumphing in his success as they found their mark. The three blades remained jutting from the Wizard's skull like axes notched into the side of a fallen tree. With the Wizard down, he knew his victory was a sure thing now.

Anxiously, he fingered his musket, a newly acquired weapon, relishing the anticipation of the dramatic victory shot. It had cost him half his iron to buy the illegal, and highly specialized weapon. He could hide it in almost any disguise, but its short barrel made it inaccurate except at short distances. In reality, his throwing knives were just as useful to him, but he wanted a weapon that could make a real statement when he killed an archos.

He remained hidden behind the statue long enough to ensure that no more Wizards remained to threaten him. Once satisfied, he made his next move, hooking a cord around Aitrox's neck, again envisioning something other than a statue, and lowered himself to the citadel floor.

Two people rushed forward at him, fury etched in their faces. The first approached with a dangerous speed, and Oko barely managed to duck the assailant's punch. His fist struck the wall behind Oko with a crash that sent chips of stone scattering, confirming Oko's suspicions. The Brute's strength mattered little to Oko, who brought a knife into his ribs. No amount of augmented strength could make a pierced heart continue beating.

As Oko's second knife whipped free, his second assailant stepped to block him with uncanny agility. Oko slashed for her throat, but she moved long before the blades could find their mark. His second slash missed by an even wider margin and he realized he had miscalculated. The archos rarely used Prophets in their miracles, making them extremely easy to miss in even the most meticulous reconnaissance. Still, Oko grumbled over the mistake.

Oko knew that fighting a Prophetess was suicide, but pride spurred him on. He couldn't give up now, when he could see his quarry behind her. He feinted a slash with one knife and slashed with the other. She completely ignored the feint, and easily dodged the real threat. Raising her dagger, Oko readied himself for defense. The Prophetess moved to strike. Oko dodged with skill he knew should have easily avoided her blow, but he only succeeded in placing his chest right in the path of her knife.

Oko screamed in pain and gasped for breath as the blade pressed mercilessly against the hidden mail under his garb. Heavier armor would have deflected the blow completely, but hampered his agility, and his ability to hide the fact he had protection. It saved his life, but still drew blood and hurt like merciless torture.

Then one of the Prophetess's knives caught his arm, ripping more than fabric, and the nerves in his arm added their clamorous voice to the agonizing chorus of pain. He felt the dizziness from blood loss setting in, and his usually steady hand wavered. When his knife fell to the floor with a rattling clang he knew he had to withdraw or die. Preferring the shame of defeat in exchange for a chance for victory in the future, with a loud boom, the room filled with smoke, masking his escape.

Janis saw the smoke both as it was and how it would soon be, a billowy sight. She knew her opponent could now escape, and part of her felt glad. Another part of her cried out in despair. *Please don't go! Please come back and kill me!*

CHAPTER 27

SLAVERY OR FREEDOM

As the Maverick grew in fame, I began to feel people's thoughts. Supe's calling me that name demonstrated how it had indeed become one of my names. I was Maverick the angel of mercy. I began to feel when people saw the wing symbol and smiled. I even began to hear people imploring to my name as if in prayer. I realized that I had created something dangerous — hope. I knew then that I couldn't fail them now, for the higher the climb the harder the *fall. Failure now risked thrusting the oppressed citizens to new depths of despair and hopelessness. No doubt Aitrox recognized this, and even encouraged my successes in small ways. Soon she would show me just how fragile hope can be.*

"That's enough, Eru," Aymis protested. Blood flowed from the palm of Eru's hand as the iron rod nearly poked out the other side. It almost made her vomit to see Eru do that to himself. Knowing an archos lacked human senses didn't lessen the morbid, creepiness of watching something like that.

"It's not doing anything," Eru answered despondently, but with no more alarm than one might have when unfurling the drapes on a beautiful spring morning.

"Yes, it is. It's staining the counter top."

"Where's Lord Penro when you need him?" Eru smiled, still pressing the iron into his hand.

"Eru, this isn't funny. Stop!" Aymis exclaimed, finally pulling his hand away.

"I thought I had."

"Don't go getting any ideas, Supe," Aymis said, giving her a knowing look. The life and awareness in her eyes hadn't lasted long, and now only a faint memory lingered like drops of water on the lawn after a storm. She just stared back, her hands quivering as usual.

"So the iron doesn't enhance nor diminish my powers. It doesn't produce any unusual harmful effects when used as a weapon against me. You saved the shavings, right?" Eru asked.

"Sure, I have them right here."

"Sprinkle some on my wounded palm, please."

"Eru!" Aymis exclaimed.

"Please," Eru rejoined with a tone in his voice that stopped all protestations. She knew that tone to mean he would do this, one way or the other. She grumbled as she sprinkled the shavings onto his glistening, scarlet hand. The filings stuck to the fresh blood.

"Anything?" she asked.

"I will need to give it some time so my body can absorb it. Did you use all of the filings?"

"Yes."

"Could you please grind up a small amount of iron into powder and mix it in a drink for me?"

Aymis wanted to protest, but knew she was powerless to stop him. With his mind set, he would continue this exploration until he died with an answer or felt convinced of his failure. "Maybe we are thinking about this wrong."

"What do you mean?" Eru asked.

"Well, all your experiments are about how iron directly influences you. The only way that would threaten a ruler is if someone managed to actually harm them. What if the iron is a threat for some other reason?"

"You do make a good point. Aitrox allows it in small quantities, almost teasing us. She maintains loyal nobility by letting them reap the profits from its inflated value. But, even they rarely have more than a pound of the metal at any given time."

"What do the rulers fear?" Aymis asked pensively. "They obviously aren't threatened by you, because they could control you if they chose."

"They fear Hiders," Eru said rather matter-of-factly.

"That's it!" Aymis exclaimed.

"You think that large quantities of iron can hide someone?" Eru asked.

"Well, it makes sense," she answered.

"I suppose it's worth looking into," Eru responded flatly.

"Eru, you were all enthusiastic and determined when it was your idea." Aymis rebuked him.

"You're right. I won't begrudge your clever thinking. Still, it is just a clever idea until we can prove it one way or another."

"Aymis, clever," Supe said with a smile. Aymis flushed red over the unexpected compliment.

"So, how are going to get that much iron? How do we even know how much we will need?" Aymis asked, firing both questions in rapid succession.

"It won't be an easy thing. The smugglers take incredible precautions when they move it." Eru let his thoughts wander back to the last blacksmith he had scoured even though it touched on the painful memories of the boy Jeo's fate.

Oko staggered out of the citadel knowing that his secret mail had saved his life. The pain in his chest lanced his mind with every breath, and he felt the world around him spin. He didn't make it far into the mild spring night before he had to duck into an alley and get off his feet. He kept a small kit of emergency tools and supplies packed in one of his pant pockets. A small vial of alcohol, a needle and some strong thread would serve him nicely for the arm.

He cursed his ill fortune at yet another failure. He had run out of proofs that he was a Hider, and as such his supply of iron was drying up. He still had a large enough stash to comfortably fund his efforts for some time, but the sudden dry spell made him nervous. Perhaps his ambition and pride was to blame. He could easily kill another Streetborn without risking his life, but they proved very hard to find.

Oko worked on stitching his arm silently, grateful for the mild evening. Shivering hands make for poor stitches. However, cold numbs the needle, so he felt every stitch uncomfortably tonight. He finished his last stitch and inspected his work. Soon it would be one of many scars earned in thankless battle. Nobody could know of his sufferings or his small victories. Of course Oko didn't pretend to be motivated by altruism, nor the money. Few people have the privilege of getting paid for doing what they enjoy. Oko, however, would do this just for the thrill of it. His immense wealth went largely untouched, serving him only as a means to an end.

Putting away his needle and thread, he tried to stand, but the pain in his chest foiled his effort. Staggering back to the wall, he slid to the ground with shallow, painful breaths.

"Oko, you proud fool," he muttered to himself. "Perhaps you should leave the rulers alone and go after another Streetborn."

"No. Streetborn are so boring to kill and tedious to track down," he retorted to himself.

"How about investigating this Maverick?" Oko smiled as he formulated a plan, and his hand wandered to his concealed musket. "That kill would be a spectacular kill."

The spring weather advanced, basking Deor in the resplendent beauty only life can bring. Trees blossomed, lining some of the more spectacular streets on both sides like nature's version of the red carpet welcome. The birds returned, and soon the clamor of the busy streets had the almost unnoticed addition of their music. Spring lifted people's spirits higher than normal this year as the stories of Maverick grew.

Eru however felt a small frustration mounting. He had watched several blacksmiths around the clock for weeks, but found no indication that any iron was coming. He knew for certain that one in particular had dealings with the metal, but nothing had happened for weeks at that shop.

Aymis reminded him that the time for Maverick to reveal himself was probably drawing near, but even so Eru felt hesitant. He needed something more to add to the legend, knowing that notoriety and fame craves the extraordinary. A simple repeat of his last showing would barely maintain the public adoration. He needed to make the wings on his suit something more than beautiful embroidery, but in order to do that he needed to find a Wizard.

Fortunately his archos mind allowed him to monitor three blacksmiths while searching the city for people whose thoughts rested on the Maverick. On this particular day Eru struck gold.

"Do you think the stories of this Maverick are true?" Volo asked his sister.

"I saw him! He fed thousands of people in the Morell District. He spoke with his own voice, and the most beautiful thing was that he was still only a young boy," Rose, his sister replied.

"What does that have to do with anything?" Volo retorted.

"If you heard the innocence in his voice, you would trust him."

"Yeah, and I'm the High Queen!" Volo said with a derisive grunt.

"Don't you remember what that man told you years ago?" Rose asked.

"How could I forget?" Volo replied.

"You have a gift, brother. In the hands of most archos it would do terrible things," Rose said enthusiastically.

"You believe I should meet this Maverick and risk being enslaved for the rest of my life?" Volo accused more than asked.

"You won't be! Please, brother, think of the good you could do."

"Let me think about it," he said to end the conversation. He had already made up his mind, and this Maverick character could be burned to ashes for all he cared. Still, he didn't want to hurt his sister, and had to admit he enjoyed seeing her so hopeful.

"Please, do think about it," Rose replied, giving him a knowing look. Just then a knock sounded on the door to their small apartment. Before she could open the door, an envelope slid in and stopped right at her feet. She bent down and picked it up.

"Who is it from?" Volo asked, unable to suppress his own curiosity.

Rose opened the envelope and nearly shouted her surprise. "Praise Maverick, it's from him!"

"Nonsense, you don't even know how to read! Give me that letter." Volo swiped it from her. The paper had the unmistakable wing drawn by expert hands. The ink looked like it would still smear with a careless touch. "I don't believe it!" Volo sat himself down as he read the letter out loud.

"'Volo...'"

"He knows your name!" Rose interjected.

"Hush, please," he said before continuing. "'I would like to entreat you to volunteer your services to my cause. It has come to my attention that you have a gift, and I am searching for one in particular. If you possess the ability to move things with your mind, your gift could be used for great things. Rather than seizing you, I ask that you meet with me and decide for yourself. I can offer no greater demonstration of my good will than that. I do feel obligated to inform you that once you are bound to an archos, no other can claim you. Some may say that a link to me is a worthwhile trade for the assurance that someone darker than me will not find and claim you. I trust you to guard the secret of my location with the utmost care. I will be at 235 Rue Way, room number B4, until tomorrow evening. Maverick.'"

"Oh, Volo! This is wonderful news!" Rose shouted.

"What's so wonderful about it?" he asked.

"He's real. You have a letter penned by his hand!"

"Well, actually it was probably poor John next door. I bet he is still trembling from the horror of being seized," Volo replied.

"He sensed our discussion. He has chosen you!" Rose continued, ignoring her brother's attitude.

"Well, what if I don't want to join his cause?"

"Would you rather hide in an apartment your whole life to avoid being taken by a normal archos?" Rose asked tenderly, as she put an arm around his shoulder. She knew all too well of his sleepless nights when the nightmares came.

"You are asking me to rush into a life of enslavement! I can't." Volo wiped a tear from his eye.

"It's not a life of slavery. It's a life of freedom from fear. Please, brother!" Rose said with a few tears of her own. Volo turned away from her silently. "Volo, if

Maverick didn't respect your wishes, he would have seized you already. At least meet him for yourself and then decide."

"No," Volo said curtly.

"Volo, you aren't the only one who sleeps in fear every night for your safety. If what Maverick said is true, then joining him would mean I could sleep soundly for the first time in years. Will you just talk to him, for my sake?" Volo turned to offer his final refusal, but the imploring look in his sister's eyes stopped him. He had never stopped to think about the weight of fear his gift must be on her shoulders.

"How can I refuse those eyes?" Volo said with a smile to hide his fear.

CHAPTER 28

RECRUITING

I took the responsibility of recruiting new people to my cause very seriously. As desperately as I needed Aegendi for my cause, I did my best to let them know exactly what they were volunteering for. I tried to let them know I was going to lead them into the maelstrom, and likely to their death. Of course, it is one thing to know a difficult road lies ahead, and another to actually walk that road. I knew that the same volunteers would probably never have joined if they truly comprehended what lay ahead of them.

Volo knocked on the door marked B4 with the sort of half conviction that matched his uncertainty. Maybe if he knocked softly enough, nobody inside would hear him, and he could leave on the pretext that nobody was home. Still, he had to knock hard enough that he could with good conscience tell his sister he had tried. *What am I doing here?* He asked himself several times as he raised his hand to knock one last time. The door opened before his knuckles touched it.

"You must be Volo," a young lady about his age said with a smile. Her dark hair hung down to her shoulders, and she had eyes he would never forget: beautiful, piercing and empathetic. He wouldn't have described her as beautiful, but she would definitely tilt the scales in favor of attractive. Her eyes radiated joy and hope. "I am Aymis." She offered him her hand, then gestured for him to come in.

"It's a pleasure to meet you," he said, not sure he meant it. She gave him a look that made him wonder if she could read his mind. He removed his hat and stepped inside. A few minutes ago, he doubted he could ever muster the courage to step into an apartment where an archos waited for him, but something about Aymis completely disarmed him. He looked around the unassuming apartment, unable to hide the surprise on his face.

"You expected something more?" Aymis asked with a knowing smile. Volo blushed. How uncouth of him to ogle at their simple apartment so obviously that she felt obliged to comment. "Please, don't worry. You have done nothing wrong."

"How..." Volo asked as his jaw dropped open.

"Now that's an expression anyone can read," Aymis said with a laugh, "but it's my gift to see into people's thoughts."

"Then are you seized right now?" Volo asked nervously.

"Oh, no. If I were seized I would know every last detail about you, down to your first word," Aymis said with a smile.

"I am terribly sorry Miss..." Volo trailed off, with a flush of red in his cheeks.

"Please call me Aymis. You can hang your coat up there if you'd like," Aymis said as she gestured to a hook on the wall. Volo did so and followed her into the next room. His heart skipped a beat when he saw the archos. Suddenly all of Aymis's smiles and hopeful eyes meant nothing and he nearly ran like a whipped dog.

"You are safe here, Volo," the grey-skinned boy with his large head and terrible blank eyes said. "Please sit down."

"You must be Maverick," Volo said as he remained standing by the door. Somehow, doing what the archos asked felt like a concession akin to being seized. Volo hoped he hid his surprise over how young Maverick was. Rose was right about his innocent voice, though she had never mentioned how strange his speech sounded. Something about it made the fiend feel less threatening – a clever ploy.

"My real name is Eru, though my friends use it with caution. I cannot guarantee I won't seize someone who uses that name. My friends often just call me 'Friend' actually."

"It's an honor to meet you, Maverick," Volo said.

"You don't want to be here." Eru stated it so bluntly, it felt a slap in the face.

"I came for my sister's sake," Volo said.

"You can go if you wish. Tell your sister you met with me and I wouldn't have you, if you wish."

"Friend!" Aymis said in surprise. "Please stay and listen," she said to Volo, pleading with her eyes. Volo started to wonder if he just had a soft spot for any female eyes, for once again a pair of beseeching eyes overpowered his fear. He still hadn't been seized. Maybe this Maverick really did respect his wishes.

"I owe it to my sister to listen to you, not just give her a token fulfillment of my word," Volo said as he sat down.

"Thank you," Aymis said with a small sigh.

"Are Aegendi so hard to find?" Volo asked as he saw the relief on her face.

"Without seizing thousands of people a day to test them for gifts, yes, it is very difficult," Eru answered.

"You are the first we have found," Aymis said.

"Then who is she?" Volo asked with a nod towards Supe, who he had noticed huddled in the corner. There was a wrongness about her that only added to his conviction to leave as soon as he could answer his sister's questions honestly.

"Someone I have taken under my care," Eru answered.

"A fine job you are doing," Volo retorted bitterly. What had he done to her?

"It is not what I have done to her, but what others of my kind did that has left her this way. She is an Aegendi, but I will not seize her even if my life depended on it," Eru responded, knowing that his survival instincts probably made that statement a lie. Still, he believed the intent behind his words and wouldn't take them back now.

"What happened to her?" Volo asked, unable to restrain his curiosity.

"She is called an Immortal. She heals very quickly, becoming virtually indestructible when seized," Aymis explained. "She was enslaved by another and tortured in the citadels. They used her healing gift to create *miracles* for the worshipers who came."

"I have heard about them from my sister," Volo said with a shudder. "Is that what will happen to me?"

"That is what happens when an archos seizes someone for too long. I killed her ruler, but it was too late for her," Eru answered.

"If you join us, that won't happen to you. Eru hates seizing others, especially his friends," Aymis explained.

"Why?"

"Would you enjoy slapping your sister in the face?" Eru asked.

"No!" Volo recoiled at the thought. "I see your point," he conceded after a pause. "So, what exactly is your cause that I would be joining?"

"To end archos tyranny for good," Eru said so nonchalantly Volo almost missed it. A heavy silence filled the room as the meaning settled on his mind. Maverick was insane, suicidal and utterly mad!

"You can't be serious," he said quietly. "You won't last a day."

"We have already lasted a lot longer than that," Aymis said proudly.

"You know what I mean. The minute they decide you're a threat it will all be over and you will be dead." Volo had to admit there was nobility to their suicidal quest. Part of him wanted to be a part of it, but not as badly as he wanted to wake up tomorrow.

"We know, and I don't want you having any illusions to the contrary," Eru answered.

"Why are you doing it then?"

"If you had experienced what my friend has, you would understand," Aymis said with a knowing look in her eyes.

"You speak as if you have shared Maverick's experiences," Volo said to Aymis.

"Through my gift, I have practically lived his life. I choose to fight back, rather than calmly accept fate, like cattle being led to the slaughter."

"You almost make it sound romantic," Volo answered.

"Oh, it is anything but romantic. If you join us you will probably die sooner than otherwise. Your days will likely be lived in fear. It will be a dangerous and violent path," Eru said.

"Well, since you made it sound like so much fun," Volo said bitterly as he stood up, "I think you will understand if I leave now. I can find my own way out." Aymis gave him another pleading look, but not even that could break his resolve this time.

"Friend, you sure sold him on the idea of helping us," Aymis said sarcastically but loudly enough that Volo could barely overhear her while getting his coat.

"It is not about selling someone on the idea of joining an adventure. I will not paint a pretty picture to hide the reality from him," Eru answered.

"I don't know. At that rate, we will only recruit Readers and the insane," Aymis said despondently.

Volo walked towards home in disbelief of everything he had just seen. An archos who would speak to him, and actually hated seizing others, was not even the strangest thing on that list. Did they actually believe they could win? He knew from the hope in Aymis's eyes that she at least found fulfillment in trying, but the whole thing was insane. At least he could tell his sister he listened to what they had to say. He walked the rest of the way home, trying to enjoy the budding spring morning. The air would have felt frigid with these temperatures in the summer, but after such a long, cold winter it felt refreshingly warm outside. He unbuttoned his coat to let the air cool him. He turned the key to his apartment and stepped in.

"Well?" Rose asked before he even had time to close the door.

"I met Maverick and listened to what he had to say." Volo gave her a look that should have ended the conversation, but Rose persisted.

"What did he say?"

"He's as cracked as an old vase."

"What do you mean?"

"He is trying to overthrow the archos!" Volo tossed his hands up in exasperation.

"What's so crazy about that? It's a beautiful idea," Rose objected.

"Are you serious? It's suicide. They'll be dead tomorrow." He grunted and folded his arms defiantly.

"You don't know that."

"Anyone in their right mind knows it!" Volo shouted.

"So, I guess you told him no," she said quietly.

"Of course. I don't have a death wish," he answered bitterly.

"Thanks for meeting with him. I am going for a walk." Rose stepped out the door before Volo could see the tear in her eye. She knew he still saw her as a little girl, and crying now wouldn't help that any. He still thought she couldn't read. He was mostly right, but she had managed to piece together most of the letter while he was gone. She should have known to expect his answer. Still, as she walked around the block, she couldn't stop her heart from fluttering with excitement. Just the thought of overthrowing the rulers made her want to sing. Her brother may be content living like this forever, but she wasn't. She couldn't stop thinking about such an audacious hope as defeating the archos.

She may not be able to do what her brother could, but she wondered if she had some other gift. What if gifts ran in the family? Volo had said that gifts are often unnoticed until someone is seized. Her brother had always sheltered her so aggressively, she could have a gift and be clueless about it. Volo may never forgive her for it, but the time for her to live under his wing had come to an end. She couldn't ignore the yearning for freedom that had taken hold in her heart. Pulling the letter from Maverick out of her pocket she struggled to work out the address again: 235 Rue Way, room 4B.

Volo waited for Rose to come back, hoping to pack a lunch and enjoy a picnic outside. When she took a bit longer than expected, he started packing a loaf of bread and a wafer of cheese. They didn't have much, but they could still enjoy the first real day of spring. He grabbed a small ground cloth and packed it. His stomach growled with hunger. The clock on the wall said two-thirty. Where was she? Once his mind recognized something amiss, another detail fell into place. He had left that letter out on their table, but it was gone. Rose had taken it with her.

"Blood and ash! He'll regret it if he recruits her!" Volo said as he ran out the door without even donning his coat or hat. Volo ran as fast as his legs would carry him. Foolish girl!

"You monster!" he shouted as he kicked in the door to the apartment breathlessly.

"Volo! Take it easy!" Rose ran to him anxiously.

"Give me my sister!" he roared.

"She was never yours to claim," Eru said calmly from the other room.

Aymis stepped to his side, a clear expression of concern or even fear etched in her face. "Careful Volo, my friend's instincts will prove deadly if you let your anger go much further."

"I am taking her with me!" Volo shouted, brushing Aymis's hand from his shoulder like he would a fly. He grabbed Rose and pulled her towards the door.

"Volo! No!" Rose screamed. She fought back with surprising strength, sending him across the walkway and into the wall of the apartment across the way.

"You're coming with me, sister." He stepped forward again, fury burning in his eyes. Suddenly the fury subsided and his body eased. The sudden change took Rose by surprise, but she guessed what had happened. A second later, the tension in his body evaporated and he stepped backwards with a dazed but angry look in his eyes. "You seized me!"

"I will not let you violate Rose's right to choose!" Eru called loudly enough to be heard outside. "If Rose wishes to go with you that is her choice, but you will NOT take her by force." His young voice carried more command than one would have guessed.

"Brother, you're saved now. Maverick has seized you, so no other archos can as long as Maverick is alive!" Rose looked so happy at the notion that he had been seized that Volo wanted to slap her. *Didn't she care how much that experience hurt?*

"As long as he is alive you say?" Volo asked quietly.

"You are sealed to Maverick, and safe now," Aymis said.

"It seems I have to join your cause now." Volo stepped back into the apartment. He would never forgive Maverick for pressing him into his service, but someone had to look after Rose. He would never forgive himself if his sister died.

CHAPTER 29

REMINDER

Everything appeared to be falling into place. Volo's gift as a Wizard would prove invaluable, but I also discovered that Rose was a Brute. It felt a cosmic irony that the gentlest person in all of Deor had that gift. This meant I had four Aegendi, if you counted Supe. Many of the rulers with their Congregations couldn't claim that many. I should have been more careful. Flying too close to the sun is a dangerous thing. I thought I already knew the extent of Aitrox's cruelty. She *would quickly send me a reminder to never underestimate her.*

A large crowd gathered in the Mondero Park. Word had spread for a few days that Maverick would be blessing the people here today. Despite the park's considerable distance from the deepest ghettos and slums, it would serve his purposes well. Maverick's fame would draw the needy from throughout the city, as well as thousands of curious onlookers.

Oko blended in with the crowd to watch and learn. Today was mostly about reconnosance, but he fingered his musket eagerly, hoping that a chance may just present itself. He twirled his favorite cane gracefully to hide his anxiety.

"I bring blessings to welcome the return of spring and with it hope!" an unusually high voice called. Oko looked around for the voice but couldn't expect to find it in the crowd.

"I bring blessings to welcome the return of spring and with it hope!" a different voice repeated, followed in quick succession through the entire park. They sounded distinct enough in their inflections and intonations that he almost wondered if the speakers were seized. This archos was very skilled.

"There! It's Maverick!" a woman close to him called as she pointed into the sky. Hundreds of astonished faces turned upward as their eyes centered on a figure in the sky. In the bright sunlight of that spring day he almost glowed radiant white. Oko gave him credit for having a flare for the dramatic.

Suddenly a whole troupe of dancers sprung into amazingly choreographed movement. Four separate groups burst into life, one in each corner of the large park. Cheers and applause erupted from the crowd, but the sight sent chills down Oko's spine. This archos must be one of the highest rulers to control hundreds of dancers amidst everything else, and have each dancer doing such a distinct part of complex choreography. Maverick, it seemed, was beyond him. Then again, Oko loved a challenge.

Oko worked his way through the crowds to get a closer look at his newest target. Prudence demanded he do some serious reconnaissance before taking down a target like Maverick. What was Aitrox playing at? Why would she let one of her most powerful underlings do something like this? It didn't make sense, but he couldn't deny the incredible hold Maverick had on thousands at once. Oko feigned astonishment as he watched his prey soar above the crowd. He had seen archos use Wizards in a wide variety of ways, but he had to credit this one for a bit of creativity. The cheers of the crowd subsided to a hush as Maverick descended. The throng cleared for him with that unnerving unison, leaving him alone in the center of the park.

"Maverick's hand reaches to those in need," Maverick spoke. Oko could hardly believe it. Why in all of Deor and by the unknown gods would an archos ever speak with his own voice? Many repeated his words, again making Oko almost believe the speakers weren't seized. Something didn't feel right.

Maverick raised his hands dramatically and several large tables flew into the park. He managed them with a choreographed skill that likely indicated several Wizards working in concert. The crowd cheered in astonishment at the feat, but Oko's blood went cold. When the tables landed, hosts of servants manned their positions while others brought out packages of food, clothing and other essentials. Those poor enough to admit their need in front of such a large crowd came forward first, but before long anyone could walk up and receive a bag of potatoes, a bushel of flour, a sturdy pair of pants and a shirt in the right size. Each recipient even received a small cart to carry their goods home.

At the end of each table, doctors spent time with the sick. After a long hard winter, the lines for their help stretched far into the crowds like sad, pathetic serpents. Oko searched the crowd for signs of the many Aegendi that must be working to pull off the feat. An event of this scale would have cost many noblemen their entire fortunes to pull off. The fact that this Maverick could simply commandeer a small army and all the resources to do this almost sent Oko running. He may as well try to kill Aitrox herself.

Despite his fears, Oko couldn't help but smile to see so many needy people helped. It rattled him to see an archos who did anything other than oppress and traumatize. Then again, he obviously had no compunctions about seizing others, and Oko had heard how terrible that could be. Still, Oko couldn't help but wonder if the world wouldn't be much better with Maverick running things.

As if to demonstrate his absolute confidence in his abilities, Maverick let people come right up to him. Oko watched as he conversed with people as they received their gifts. Maverick's smile almost felt genuine. His duplicity infuriated Oko. He worked his way closer to the archos to get a good look at him. Maverick was surprisingly young, or perhaps just small of stature, for a being with his command and power. He looked completely at ease with the chaotic yet orderly celebration that demonstrated his vast intelligence.

Oko made sure to stay in the crowd, using it as his cover. He still hadn't spotted any obvious Aegendi and almost felt like he could walk right up to Maverick and kill him now. The temptation pulled at him like a roasted turkey beckoning to a starving man. As he got closer, recognition hit him like a thunderclap and he stopped dead in his tracks. A few feet away from Maverick, he saw the Prophetess that had nearly killed him a short while ago.

Of course, this archos probably ruled several underlings. That made sense enough, but with a Prophetess so close, Oko would have to be very careful. Then his eyes followed the gaze of the Prophetess and he saw another unwelcome face. It was that Reader! He almost died the last time he saw her. He quickly inspected Maverick to see if his suspicions would be confirmed.

He chided himself for not seeing it sooner. Being a master of disguises himself, he should have seen right through the trappings and spectacle put on by this Streetborn. The world felt full of impossibilities today, but Oko's pride would not let him slink away. This Streetborn had almost killed him last time they met.

Janis watched in awe as her friend Eru orchestrated the menagerie. She would have smiled had her domineering master given her the allowance. Aymis was in good hands. That realization only made the task she knew she would do that much more painful. There could only be one reason why she was here. She thought a silent prayer to the unknown gods that her daughter Aymis would forgive her for killing Eru. She wished she could do something about it. Maybe the unknown gods would spare her, and let Eru kill her.

Her master moved her through the crowd expertly. Under happier circumstances she would have found it a thrilling experience to see the world in a strange convergence of future happenings and the present. While seized it all made sense as she saw what someone would do a few moments into the future. She watched the dancers as her master casually had her participate and blend in to the crowds. Their dance felt all the more beautiful when she saw the future of each step and its perfect fulfillment moments later. She saw the smiles on people's faces and offered her silent congratulations to Eru for such an amazing feat. It broke her heart to know that she would end it all.

Her eyes settled on Aymis and her heart skipped a beat. Aymis helped someone with the kindness her mother always admired. She had become so much more than her mother. *Please let her forgive me*! Janis felt her steps move towards her daughter. Her lips moved and she called to her daughter with joy in her voice.

"Aymis!" Janis exclaimed, wondering what her master was up to. Whatever it was, she knew it couldn't be good. Thankfully her daughter didn't hear her through the press of the crowd. "Aymis!" she called again, and saw her daughter's head lift in search of her. Janis felt her fist clench on one of her daggers as she watched in terror as Aymis ran to her. *'Aymis, NO! Run!'* She screamed with her mind, hoping her daughter would hear her plea.

Aymis could hardly believe Eru had pulled this off. They had practically emptied the coffers of several noblemen to fund this. She almost expected to see Counts Moure and Salle lining up for a hand out. They had, after all paid for all of it, albeit they required some persuasion.

Aymis distributed the gift packets nervously. A celebration like this felt like too blatant an affront to the rulers to go unnoticed. Eru was confident, but Aymis doubted. Were they really ready for open conflict? Despite her concerns, she couldn't help but get caught up in the celebrations and merriment. She of all people could feel the hearts lift with every help package.

"Here you go, miss," she said warmly as she put a bag of potatoes on a woman's cart.

"Maverick, bless you!" the woman exclaimed.

"Aymis!" She could hardly believe what she heard through the crowd.

"Mother?" she asked as her head turned up. "Mother!" Aymis ran to her with eyes only for her. She had thought she would never see her again.

'Aymis, NO! Run!' her mother's voice slammed in her mind, stopping her in her tracks. She felt the terror in her mother's mind and knew something was terribly wrong. She turned to run, but a firm pair of hands grabbed her. She smashed her elbow into the person's stomach but he held her firm. Before she could do more, her mother's dagger pierced her chest.

"Mother!" she gasped as she felt warm liquid running down her ribs and saturating her clothing. The last thing she saw before her vision left was her mother's stoic gaze, but she sensed the utter terror and sorrow in her mind. Telu's warning had proven right. She would die in the service of an archos after all.

"Noooo!" Eru's childhood falsetto cried out a heart-wrenching, piercing note. Panic struck the crowd directly around the murder, but the majority of the celebrants continued the festivities in tragic ignorance. Eru immediately found the archos responsible and seized him easily. He wanted to obliterate him, erasing every last trace of his existence. Had he possessed the means, he would have removed him so thoroughly from the universe to undo every last act he wrought on the world and bring his Aymis back to him. His awareness searched for her, and he knew beyond a doubt she was gone. Her murderer would suffer for this. He held on to the monster for the time being, waiting until he could concoct a death worthy of the crime.

"Aymis!" he screamed as he seized a few observers to guide him to her side. He ran to her body, scooping her up into his arms. His pristine white suit absorbed her blood greedily, but Eru felt it appropriate. Maverick died today. Rising from his grave was Eru, the god of war.

"Bravo!" Aitrox exclaimed through several people she controlled. She hadn't enjoyed a tragedy like this in all her years ruling. None but her could understand the pleasure of wrenching the pen from a playwright's hand and changing his triumph into a tragedy as she had just done. The best part of it all was that this was only the beginning. This Streetborn seemed an infinite pool of entertainment to draw from. The fun had only just begun.

Interlude
Point of No Return

J ante returned to his aerie with a young rabbit in his talons. His eyas, still downy and vulnerable chirped hungrily. Jante rested his kill on the nest floor, and his mate, Ela, worked with him to feed their offspring. Jante hardly felt that he deserved to have been granted the privilege of bearing an offspring considering his failure ten years ago. To the vyeshen, the balance of nature came before all else, even procreation. No vyeshen had died in uncounted centuries, and thus no offspring: until now.

The memory of Jenu's death still burned intensely in Jante's mind. The craving for metal still hummed quietly as well. Jante had needed the decade to work his life threads and quiet the terrible pull that substance had on him. Shanje too had needed the time to modify the threads that had created such an unexpected vulnerability in the vyeshen psyche. Jante had offered to assist; they both knew Jante's skill to be unmatched. The mere fact that Shanje considered the offer showed how disconcerting he found the vulnerability. Vyeshens' life threads were their own, sacred and off limits to the others. Changing one's own threads bordered on sacrilege, departing from the perfection Phoenix had helped them attain. Only in the face of such a perilous vulnerability would the population at large embrace changing their species again.

Jante wondered if fate had spared the vyeshen race that terrible day ten years ago. A vyeshen cannot hide anything from another and the influence of Jante's and Shanje's memories of metal swept through their population like a plague. Had they all returned, the power of their combined experiences may have been too much. The last decade had been a terribly trying time for their kind. Each vyeshen mourned the loss of the eighteen with a deep, powerful sorrow. At the same time, great focus was needed to adapt their life threads and lessen the allure the memory of metal had in their minds.

Shanje and Jante had suffered the worst, having actually been exposed to the metal. First hand experiences always sat more powerfully on the mind than anything a vyeshen could relate via mental sendings. However, Shanje and Jante were two of the most skilled at modifying life threads. Jante had expressed his concern about the ability of some, but the council held firm. Jante was not to touch another's threads without their explicit consent, which would never be granted. Thus, the power of the addiction varied greatly from one vyeshen to the next, but Jante could feel it lurking in every vyeshen's mind.

Jante had been chosen to rear an eyas specifically because his weakness to metal's allure had been so effectively subdued. Thus, he could pass that trait on to his offspring. A poignant and intense mix of emotions stirred in Jante's heart as he watched Shenta eat the small pieces of meat Ela lowered into his delicate beak. Joy sung a powerful song in Jante's heart as he reveled in the beauty of life, his life, passed on. Shenta's vibrant downy body almost appeared ablaze in the morning light, and Jante's heart swelled with love and pride to see his offspring growing and thriving. At the same time, Jante wrestled with fear for his offspring's future. Shenta had inherited the vyeshen weakness for metal.

The alluring pull of Jante's memory still tugged at him. It always would. Sometimes, it was all Jante could do to keep himself from flying in search of the humans, just to see it again. If Jante had been chosen to rear an eyas, then that did not bode well for many of the vyeshen. Jante desperately wanted to protect his offspring from this plague, but one thing was for certain. The humans were spreading uncontrollably, and Shenta would someday be exposed to them, and their metal. What kind of future awaited Shenta? How could Jante possibly hope to raise his young to honor Phoenix and preserve nature's balance when the humans' unharmonious influence spread unchecked?

Perhaps, had the vyeshen discovered their vulnerability a few centuries earlier, they could have been better prepared. They could have adequately destroyed the weakness before being exposed to it. Such wishful thoughts served nobody, and Jante had no choice but to admit that the vyeshen were not ready to face the humans again.

Jante returned to his nest, and nuzzled his beak affectionately against Ela's neck. Shenta chirped a greeting, looking expectantly at him. Jante did not disappoint his youngling, flipping a shimmering trout his way. Shenta snapped the wriggling fish out of the air. His joyful, grateful response elicited a quiet trilling from both Jante and Ela. Trout were a special treat. Jante had deliberately taken the detour to the lakes where they spawned, needing time to settle his mind before returning to his family. The vyeshen council had decided what to do about the humans. Jante had no doubt that something had to be done, but he saw no path forward that didn't strike fear into his heart. Despite his trip to the lake, his fears had not settled much, and Ela could tell immediately.

Ela reached out for her mate, offering encouragement support and empathy. She had no need to ask what troubled him. Jante's mind and heart always laid open to all the vyeshen, and nobody knew his soul like his life-mate Ela. She had been with him since before the vyeshen had fully rooted out aging and disease.

There had been a time when they had expected to die together in old age. Come what may, she would be by his side.

Jante welcomed her in, hiding nothing of his fears or concerns as he let her know about the proceedings of their gathering that day. In acknowledgment of their dire situation, the council had sent out exploring parties – one in all four directions. They searched for a new location for their aeries, a recourse they desperately hoped to avoid. They had returned with dire tidings. They had nowhere to go. The explorers confirmed what Shanje had long suspected. Vast oceans surrounded them on all sides. To the North, the ocean could be reached with two days' hard flight. Jante had first discovered the humans there what seemed like an eternity ago.

It took the explorers longer to find the ends of land in the other directions, but the furthest one could go before the land ended was just a week's flight away. Making matters worse, human habitations scarred the land in all directions. The human plague continued to spread, and the vermin now actively encroached on vyeshen habitat. All the vyeshen could feel the discomfort and imbalance in the threads of life around them. Already, the vermin had begun clearing trees and even damming rivers near their roosts.

The vyeshen could not hope to openly confront such large numbers. It had taken the council many long hours to arrive at a plan. They couldn't get close enough to safely manipulate the human's life threads, but human thoughts could be touched at a safer distance. Jante and Shanje had been chosen to use the dreams of human younglings to lure them away from one of the smaller settlements. At the same time, they would subtly taint the adult's dreams. If Jante and Shanje could get the different human herds to turn on each other over the disappearance of their young, perhaps the species would regulate its own population.

Starting a war between human herds was only one of their objectives. Jante needed the opportunity to study the human threads in depth. Hopefully, the vyeshen could find a weakness or strategy they could employ to bring the human plague in check. The plan would take decades, if not centuries, to bring to fruition – time Jante doubted the vyeshen had.

"Papa! Help me!" the boy screamed. Jante understood the words, more by virtue of the boy's thoughts than the sounds he made. It was too late for the boy. Jante already had him in his talons, and his pack was far away, well beyond hearing. Abducting the human young had almost gotten mundane over the years.

The council's plan had been remarkably successful. They had captured several hundred younglings, and then watched with fascinated attention as the human herds turned on each other. Typically nature's balance came from a symbiotic relationship between various species. Humans apparently worked differently. When in a herd, the creatures' appetite for violence and destruction often seemed insatiable. Jante had never before found a species so capable and willing to destroy itself. It had almost proven too easy to get them to nearly drive themselves to extinction.

Yet, as the years passed and Jante grew to comprehend the human's life threads, he began to second guess their actions. Despite himself, he found much to admire in the way the creatures saw the world. They had an intelligence that, despite years of study, felt completely alien to the vyeshen. Humans were the first species, excluding the vyeshen themselves, that had practically unlimited potential. The human mind could do things a vyeshen could never hope to comprehend. Similarly, the human mind would never comprehend much that a vyeshen found second nature. At times Jante mused over the possibilities if human and vyeshen were to work in partnership.

At first, Jante had found pleasure in capturing the human young. That was before he grew to comprehend how deeply the humans experienced life. Their emotional nature served the vyeshen well as clashes between herds so quickly escalated, like fire catching a dry field. However, Jante couldn't help but wonder what it would be like to feel so deeply, to love so profoundly. For a while, each abduction broke his heart. Jante knew that the vyeshen only partly grasped the sorrows they inflicted on such emotionally vibrant creatures. Jante had refused to be the one to abduct the young at first. Shanje hadn't minded, clearly not sharing Jante's reservations. Finally, Jante joined in untel he became numb, jaded to the plight of the human young and unwilling to acknowledge the suffering he caused.

Jante saw his loyal friend flying just below and to his side. Shanje's gorgeous plumage shimmered and played with the growing light of sunrise. *'Hello old friend,'* Jante seemed to say as he neared.

Shanje returned the greeting, unable to hide his patient, yet slightly condescending amusement at Jante's sentimental thoughts. Shanje would never see the humans as Jante did. No vyeshen comprehended the human threads as fully as Jante did, but Shanje came close. *'Pondering about the humans and their virtues as always.'*

At times, Jante wished he could hide his soul from the other vyeshen. Shanje's gentle tone of condescension and mild rebuke felt friendly in comparison to how most received him. Only his mate Ela, and Shanje welcomed his company these days. Even Shenta, his own offspring, felt ashamed of him. Jante no longer felt the sting of Shanje's mild rebukes, just gratitude for his friendship. *'Patiently staying by my side despite all I can do to drive you away.'*

Shanje quietly and quickly chirped, the vyeshen equivalent of a small chuckle, in answer to Jante's reply. Then Shanje's thoughts quickly jumped to an idea that this night raid had stirred in his mind. Rather than drive the vermin to extinction, why not harness them. *'You aren't the only one who recognizes the potential the humans have.'*

Jante couldn't help but wonder just how much the allure of metal had guided Shanje's thoughts. Shanje's simple suggestion had been enough to awaken that quiet humming in the back of Jante's mind. For a moment, the thought of humans crafting metal on behalf of the vyeshen thrilled Jante. Then he remembered how quickly the substance had driven Jenu and the others to their deaths. No, the vyeshen species was not ready to face that temptation. *'The idea is too dangerous.'*

Shanje didn't share Jante's concerns. Perhaps a part of him did, but excitement over the possibilities his idea entailed overpowered the quieter voice of concern in his mind. *'You are letting your concern for the humans cloud your judgment.'*

Jante couldn't hide the sting of Shanje's rebuke, nor could he conceal his anger at the insincerity behind it. Shanje knew that concern for the humans had nothing to do with his objections. Shanje noted the offense, and the two flew on in figurative silence. Jante knew that Shanje could still see his thoughts, were he to try, but neither desired the other's company at the moment. Thus, Jante was as alone with his thoughts as he could be.

Given a century for the vyeshen to further subdue their vulnerability to metal's allure and Shanje's idea would have merit. Unfortunately, the idea had taken hold now, and given Shanje's enthusiasm, Jante knew exactly how it would affect his flock. He knew Shanje had crossed the point of no return.

Fortunately, it would take time for the vyeshen to perfect any efforts to harness the human's threads of life. Jante knew exactly what he would spend that time doing. He first needed to completely subdue his own metal-lust. Then, if the others would not listen to him, he would do the unthinkable and violate the sanctity of his brothers' threads. It hardly mattered if he was branded profane and an outcast.

Jante glanced down at the human child. The boy had succumbed to exhaustion some time ago. Jante couldn't help but wonder what new horrors awaited this child. If he guessed correctly, the kinds of changes Shanje had in mind would be terrible indeed. Jante saw a dark, tragic future ahead for both human and vyeshen, and knew that his actions had already put them on that path. *'Oh, Phoenix, what have I done?'*

PART III

CHAPTER 30

CLOSELY GUARDED SECRET

What can I say about Aymis's murder? There are no words to convey the sorrow or the fury it stirred in my heart. If there was a way to distill the connotation, intensity and meaning of all the sorrowful words in our tongue and others into a single word, it may have come close.

Losing her felt like the sun had just died. All the warmth, hope and love in my life went cold and only dark thoughts of revenge remained. I will forever mourn her loss, but I came to find some consolation knowing she had been spared the dark and terrible days I knew to be ahead for the rest of us.

E ru clutched Aymis's body like doing so would bring her back. He longed to have his own senses, to feel her weight in his arms. He pressed his face to hers, wishing he could feel something, anything about her. His tears flowed freely, running down his terribly tragic face and falling onto her lifeless cheeks. His sobs and moans broke the hearts of those who heard them. Part of him wanted to never release the eyes that looked on Aymis's lifeless face, but his stronger part couldn't bear the sight.

Holding the archos under his dominion, Eru immediately perceived a troubling fact. The vile creature was not Aymis's true murderer. Aitrox had seized the wretched creature specifically because he had enslaved Janis, and then she discarded him. Eru never could have seized Janis's captor if he had been under Aitrox's power. No, Aitrox wanted Eru to know who the real murderer was, but there were many layers to her cunning at play. She knew that Eru couldn't pass up the chance to free an Aegendi as valuable as a Prophetess, yet Janis would forever remind him of Aymis's cruel death. Eru knew that this terrible defining memory would be stirred up by his power every time he seized Janis. Eru was nothing more than a novelty to Aitrox, a new source to satisfy her sadistic hunger for suffering.

Eru had no qualms about killing Janis's captor before seeking the void. Doing so liberated Janis from the monster. Eru sensed Janis's sorrow, almost commensurate with his own. She knelt by his side, wailing her terrible sorrow for the loss of her precious daughter. Her freedom should have been a moment of unbelievable joy and relief, but all of that was lost now. Her hands held the knife that had killed her own daughter. Never would she be free from the terrible images and sensations of Aymis's death. Her rational mind knew her daughter's blood didn't belong on her hands, but that couldn't change the terrible fact that it still felt warm and moist on her fingers right now. Her rational mind could never blot out the heart wrenching sight of her own hands wielding the knife that pierced her daughter's heart.

Janis wanted to scream at everyone in the park. A small crowd had gathered to watch with morbid curiosity. She felt their eyes on her as unwelcome intruders in her grieving. They could never know what this day meant, and had no right to stand around gawking in their ignorance. At the same time, the majority of the festivities continued as if nothing had happened. She didn't know whom she hated more, the few who stopped to take note of the tragedy, or the hundreds who went about their merry making in ignorance. She wanted to scream at them, and berate everybody who left with their care packages. She felt this flurry of emotions, but lacked the strength or conviction to act on anything that required doing more than shedding tears and bemoaning her sorrow.

This was all Eru's fault. Had he left her daughter alone, none of this would have happened. He had been foolish to draw Aitrox's attention on himself, and reckless to drag her daughter into this. That vile, conniving creature shouldn't have been born. Fury and rage boiled in Janis's heart as her fist clenched the knife, still glistening with her daughter's blood. Eru didn't even stir as she stood and raised the knife to strike. Then, through her tear-blurred vision, she saw the tragic creature in a true light.

She saw the creature tortured with grief and self-blame for her daughter's death, tragically mourning as he clung to her limp body as if he could revive her with his love. His once pristine, magnificent suit now stained crimson, a vibrant reminder that Aymis had willingly followed Eru despite the risks. Suddenly it struck her that Eru never seized her, even as she raised the knife to strike him down, and all of her hatred melted away. She could never understand the strength of Eru's will in that moment, but she knew that he would rather have died than betrayed his love for Aymis by killing her mother – even in self-defense.

Through blurry eyes, she saw her friend also mourning a terrible loss, and she found room in her swollen heart for empathy. A small stirring of pride and joy mingled with her grief to see the way her daughter had touched others, even an archos, and left the world better. Her eyes turned upwards when someone's shadow fell on them. Someone had the audacity to cross that unspoken sacred barrier that held the onlookers at bay. With angry eyes and a scowl on her face, she prepared to berate the thoughtless observer, but recognition quelled her tongue and filled her with fear. She thought she had killed him.

Oko watched the events unfold with utter confusion. Why would Maverick's Prophetess turn and kill his Reader? Could another archos be trying to destroy a rival? Oko knew of the epic struggles between the great rulers and the less spectacular confrontations of others. Was this Maverick what his name proclaimed him, a rebel? Had he finally drawn Aitrox's attention? If so, this festival would likely turn into a blood bath.

Oko watched in bewilderment as Maverick's head lifted and he screamed his mournful cry. If Oko didn't know better, he'd think this Maverick actually loved the Reader who now lay bleeding to death on the ground. It almost looked like Maverick showed a moment of blindness and disorientation before several heads turned to guide him to her side. Had he actually left himself completely blind and deaf amidst such crowds? If so, then it cast a whole new light on the celebration. If this Maverick had inspired such an event rather than compelling and willing it, then Oko had grossly misjudged the creature. Still, such a thing hardly seemed possible from an archos.

Seeing the boy cradling his Reader in his arms defied everything Oko knew about the archos. Oko had never thought of an archos as human, much less as an embattled child. He hadn't imagined an archos capable of such depth of feeling. Seeing Maverick's suffering shed new light on Aitrox's cunning, and her capacity to make even an archos suffer.

"My child!" the Prophetess moaned in a tragic sob. Oko's heart skipped a beat as those words revealed the terrible craftsmanship behind the unfolding scene. Oko no longer doubted that Maverick was an enemy to the rulers, nor did he doubt the pleasure Aitrox derived from her little masterpiece. His eyes settled on Maverick with a new appreciation. An enemy of the rulers was his ally, and this Maverick's worth far surpassed the value his fingers could bring in iron.

Oko dried his eyes, and worked to muster the courage to introduce himself. Separating himself from the crowd of gawking onlookers would be risky. Prudence dictated that he wait for a better moment, but his violent, lonely life never allowed a moment of tenderness. His heart pushed him forward despite his better judgment.

He stepped forward and walked to Maverick's side. He put a hand on Maverick's shoulder, but it went unnoticed. Of course it would go unnoticed, Oko realized. Maverick had no senses that could touch him. A shiver ran down Oko's spine with the realization that he stood so close to an archos who remained completely oblivious to him. His hand itched for a dagger, but he suppressed his hunger for blood. Enough had been spilt today.

The disparate expressions in the crowd vanished, replaced by a conformity that Oko had learned to recognize. Had this been a trap? A quick glance at Maverick and the Prophetess told him otherwise, but that didn't change the fact that hostile eyes rested on him. Oko leapt to action, grabbing the first assailant by his wrist and swinging him in the path of others just before they got close enough to tackle him. Usually Oko felt no hesitation to cut down someone under archos control, but he knew Maverick wouldn't have wanted it. More violence would destroy the purpose for the day.

"ERU!" the Prophetess shouted.

Oko swept his leg in a low kick, dropping an assailant as he ducked the arms of another. Rolling to the side, he stood up with a deliberate thrust. His head smashed into the chin of another, knocking him backwards and leaving him unconscious. Oko ran into the crowds as the festive atmosphere dissipated before the spreading screams of alarm.

More attackers turned their gaze his way, and Oko feared his knives would draw blood today after all. Just then a scrambling riot broke out, as those who advanced on Oko were tackled by others. Oko sheathed his knife and used the moment to escape. He knew of an entrance to the sewers right in this very park.

His stomach nearly wretched at the thought of the sewers, but at least he could control that environment.

The chaos around him spread like a fire in dry grass. Tables toppled and potatoes, carts and stacks of clothing scattered everywhere. The merriment changed to panic as the riot grew. He shed his outer disguise as he fled. With his appearance changed, he changed his tactics, throwing himself into the fight rather than fleeing. Oko's well-placed fist dropped one of the brawlers as his elbow collided with another. His battle hardened hands ached with each blow. He would need some ice tonight, assuming he lived long enough that it mattered.

Oko continued to use the crowd for cover as he made his way to the sewer entrance. He pried open the sewer lid quickly before climbing in. As he expected, his stomach clenched and his head spun with the smell. Closing the lid he dropped into the darkness and waited for his eyes to adjust. The vile liquid swirled around his ankles. Oko listened intently for the sounds of pursuit, but none came. His first thought was to follow the sewers and make a clean escape. It seemed that this Streetborn lived under constant surveillance from Aitrox. How could that be without Maverick realizing it? He knew Maverick wouldn't have dared do everything he did if he knew how closely she watched him. Had she found a way to hide her surveillance from other archos?

How could that happen? The only way to hide from an archos was to be a Hider. Unless, well, what if she seized a Hider? Could his gift work that way? That would of course imply that seizing a Hider was possible, something he had always assumed was not. Oko had to know. The possibilities that would open to his and the Maverick's cause were too valuable to ignore. Oko turned around with a sickening slosh. If he guessed correctly, he would find another manhole just on the edge of the park in this direction. He found it quickly and waited for the chaos to subside slightly before emerging.

Oko ducked behind a toppled table and grabbed a pair of pants. He shed his boots, stockings and pants, glad to be rid of the foul smelling clothes. Nobody noticed his brief immodesty, but Oko didn't care who saw his calves and undergarments. He pulled the pants up with a grunt. They fit poorly, not even reaching his ankles, and they squeezed his waist mercilessly. Oko now discarded his vest, smeared some mud on his shirt, and tore it in a few places. Adding a smattering of dirt to his face and ruffling his hair, his metamorphosis took only a few minutes. He had to get moving. If he lost Maverick, it may be months before he found him again.

This day turned out to be one of the most diverting in Aitrox's long unchanging rule. Along with the pleasure and entertainment she had extracted from the foolish Streetborn who called himself Maverick, she had also uncovered a closely guarded secret. She had expected Maverick's actions to draw the attention of the heretics, but they took an incredible risk by sending spies from one of their hidden sanctuaries. She seized the heretic spy and scoured him with pleasure. In his mind she found secrets he himself had protected by bloodshed – one less hidden sanctuary to worry about.

Aitrox didn't consider the heretics her enemies. A toothless cat was something to be laughed at, not feared. She had to admire their tenacity and cunning to keep secrets even from her. Still, prudence, or paranoia, dictated that she move to crush this small sanctuary. She moved with such lethal, immediate force that it drew her attention away from the utterly defeated Streetborn. This heretic sanctuary, a closely guarded secret, would be destroyed in a matter of minutes. No one in Deor was allowed secrets. No one but herself, that is.

CHAPTER 31

UNDENIABLE FINALITY

I discovered the true meaning of loss. This was the kind of loss that I would feel anew every morning. This was the kind of loss that can never be restored. For most people the ache dulls over time, remaining a constant influence but sparing them the brutal intensity of the initial moment. An archos mind however possesses the capacity to remember perfectly, and be in multiple moments at once. I knew that

I would forever remain at Mondero Park with Aymis's body in my arms. Part of me wouldn't have it any other way.

Eru seized Janis at her bidding. *'Help him!'* her mind exclaimed. Eru used her eyes to see threats to the Hider before they happened. Her gift filled him with awe as he bent time to his will. One moment, Eru would preemptively divert an attacker's knife with a carefully placed push from Volo. The next, he would seize two or three people and create an opening for the Hider to slip through a forming trap. Part of Eru wanted to let this dangerous enemy die. Instead, Eru helped him escape. He would have time for questions later. This Hider had tried to kill him on more than one occasion.

It has begun, Eru thought darkly. He had known the time would come, but had hoped for more time to prepare. The dark road ahead looked all the darker without Aymis at his side. He should have been more cautious, but he'd been caught up in the thrill of building his legend. Aymis had tried to warn him, and his failure to listen cost her life.   He had been a reckless fool to call so much attention to the legend of his creation.

'Stop doing that to yourself!' Eru heard Aymis's voice in his mind. *'Stop blaming yourself for things you couldn't have known or controlled!'* He remembered that precious rebuke on the night they met. His love for her prohibited further indulgences in self-reproach. Maverick died today, but his work would continue. Aymis's death didn't end the suffering of the poor, or the oppression from the archos. Without some means to escape Aitrox's penetrating eyes, his tactics would have to change.

'Eru, we have to get out of here,' Janis thought as the Hider finally escaped.

'No. I won't leave her,' Eru thought, forgetting that only Aymis would have heard his response. With the Hider gone, Eru released Janis, returning to the unfeeling void.

"Eru, we have to go," Janis said, out loud this time, Eru hearing the thought behind the words perfectly. The crowds had thinned, and the disorder cooled to a simmer. Fortunately, nobody besides Aymis had died, but hundreds nursed broken jaws, noses, and arms. The festive din of celebration had changed to the disconcerted ruckus of fear. It sounded similar to the ears, but could be clearly discerned by the heart.

"I won't leave her," he said, remaining by Aymis's side amidst the clamor.

"It is not safe for you here," Janis insisted.

"I won't leave her," Eru repeated.

Oko made his way back to the center of the park, hoping Maverick would still be there. Likely he had left some time ago. If so, then Oko would pick up the trail immediately. It wasn't the first time he had tailed this archos, but his motives could not have been more different. He could hardly believe the notion that he might surrender his gift and actually experience being seized. "Well, I'll be seized," he mumbled under his breath with a new meaning. How many times had he said that with his own ironic twist?

He knew better than to separate himself from the crowd again. He saw his first encounter with Maverick in a new light after today's happenings, and realized Aitrox was watching him even then. If they couldn't escape Aitrox's eyes, then they may as well just hand themselves over to her brutality now.

He pushed through the throngs cautiously, knowing they were just on the verge of panic. Reaching the spot where he expected to pick up the trail, he couldn't believe what he saw. The shocked masses still respected the bubble around the dead body, where Maverick remained as unmoving as a statue.

The Prophetess's supplications fell on deaf ears in more than the literal sense. She tugged at his stained suit coat as her bloodshot, teary eyes tried to avoid her daughter's pale, lifeless cheeks. Maverick's grey skin almost looked like stone for how still he remained. The Prophetess was right, though: they needed to get out of there.

"Eru, we have to go," she said again.

Eru, that was his name. Recognition swirled in Oko's mind, the same Street-born that had survived the most creative and fanatical attempts Oko had ever witnessed. "Eru, please seize me," he said, remaining an indistinguishable member of the onlookers.

"I will not leave her," Eru replied.

"Eru, please seize me," he said a bit louder, as he stared intently at the boy. Curse the unknown gods, he could hardly believe Maverick was so young. The Prophetess's eyes turned on him, but his latest disguise worked all too well. He averted his eyes, staring at Eru instead. Oko had never imagined he would find himself wanting—no, needing—an archos to notice him. He had spied on countless archos in the past, always grateful for and confident in his invisibility. He nearly turned and ran at the thought of shedding such a rare and precious gift. Could he really surrender his freedom so easily? Yes, he had to do it. Intermittent assassinations could never make a difference. Perhaps with Maverick, he could do more. "Eru, seize me!" he said again.

The Prophetess heard him that time, and turned to look at him. A quick start of surprise flashed in her eyes as recognition settled in. "Eru, he's back, and he wants your attention," the Prophetess said kindly. Eru's head lifted in response, looking like an animate grey statue. Oko felt him then, like a presence standing outside a locked door. There are times when someone does something without understanding the means, as Oko did now. He simply willed that effectual door open, yielding himself completely to the archos.

"Eru, seize me!" he called one last time, then it happened. Oko felt him enter with a mind, an intelligence so vast it penetrated to his most hidden thoughts and memories. Despite Maverick's magnanimous heart, his presence terrified Oko like nothing he had known. He tried to turn and run, even though he should have known better. To feel even his own limbs bent to serve another added to the terror. What had he been thinking?

Then Oko felt another faculty or sense only available to the superior intelligence of an archos. Through him, an archos could protect others from the influence of all other archos. The realization played on Oko's heart with a poignant harmony of excitement and jealousy. His immunity to archos control had made him special. Now, by surrendering that gift, others could experience that freedom and safety. Were it any other, Oko would have regretted his choice, but Maverick had the potential to win greater victories than Oko ever could alone. Oko would have smiled if Maverick had allowed it.

Eru felt a presence open to him, calling him with enough enticing force he could scarcely resist. In his current state of mind he had no desire to do so and he seized the phantom presence. Immediately he perceived the differences. He had seized a Hider! It shouldn't have been possible, but it had happened. When Eru recognized the gift, he felt the power presented to him, and his mind could think to use it for one purpose only. With this power, there wasn't an archos in Deor that would be safe from Eru's justice.

The implications both thrilled and terrified Eru at the same time. He wasn't foolish enough to think that Aitrox hadn't also made this discovery. How long had she been watching him with invisible eyes, and possibly even hidden Readers? She likely knew every last detail of his plans and aspirations. Only Readers could find Hiders and only then by their conspicuous invisibility. That must have been how Aitrox had spotted Oko both times he approached Eru. Such a powerful secret also explained why Aitrox had tried to kill Oko rather than risk Eru making this very discovery. Fortunately she had failed. Eru felt a flush of relief like someone who had been exposed to the harsh desert sun his whole life, finding shade for the first time. This was his chance to escape and truly disappear.

The thought of one of Aitrox's Readers lingering and witnessing his grief over Aymis's death disgusted Eru and spurred him to leave. He seized his friends, Volo, Rose, Janis and Supe, who had each spread through the crowd to avoid detection. Next he seized a commoner close by, who picked up Aymis's corpse, and their small crew disappeared into the scattering crowds. They moved in unique directions, scattering in haphazard and random movements.

"With your leave, Piru, we need a place to spend the night," Eru said to the stranger opening his door.

"Maverick? Come in!" Piru said, though his face communicated shock, and misfortune.

"I am sorry to impose on your home," Eru said just as Aymis's body arrived in the hands of the man who carried her.

"Well, I'll be seized! What happened?" Piru asked as he saw the corpse. Seeing the tears welling in Eru's eyes, he knew better than to hope for an intelligible explanation. Eru's tragic eyes and his blood soaked clothing told the story well enough. "By Aitrox, he loved her!" Piru exclaimed under his breath. Luckily, Eru had already wrapped the man in the Hider's protection. Let the man blaspheme her name. She deserved it.

"You aren't going to bring her in are you?" he asked. "My wife will have a heart attack, and my daughter would be terrified."

"My apology. I couldn't just leave her to be trampled by the crowd," Eru responded. He had picked this home, the residence of a successful potter, for a reason. She deserved a proper burial, but circumstances didn't allow for it.

"Well, I won't have my daughter left for the alley dogs!" Janis said as she arrived and Eru released her.

"I am sorry miss," Piru said, looking down and away from her eyes.

"Would you permit us to burn her body?" Eru asked.

"My potter's kiln is at your disposal," Piru said with a slight bow of his head.

"I don't know," Janis said, as new tears filled her eyes.

"It's really our only option. We can't give her a proper burial. You can spread her ashes however you wish," Eru said as gently as he could. She didn't say anything but Eru felt her consent as she nodded.

"My shop is around back," Piru said. They followed him through the well-kept space between his home and the next. In this part of town, this space served as a small garden rather than becoming an alley for mischief and refuse to pile up in equal amounts. Piru gestured for them all to stand back as he opened the kiln with a long hooked pole, raising his hand to shield his face from the heat. The bright orange glow filled the shop with a harsh light. Light and delicate as Aymis's body was, the potter still had no tools for putting something so heavy into the kiln while it burned at its high temperature. Fortunately, Volo's ability served the need perfectly as Eru lifted her from her bearer's arms. Her lifeless body had a spectral appearance as it floated towards the kiln.

"I love you Aymis. I am so sorry I couldn't protect you better," Eru said. He had no idea if any essence of Aymis still existed to hear his words or if he spoke the words for his benefit only. He wouldn't take them back either way, but his heart imagined Aymis awaiting him with his mother, Ama. That thought, shrouded in questions, couldn't quell his grief.

"Aymis, you made your mother so proud. Your courage and hope for..." Janis couldn't finish her thoughts as the tears choked out anything intelligible.

Eru watched through Volo's and Oko's eyes, determined not to waste the last precious moments when he could see her before her body began to burn. Eru removed his coat, and any other articles of clothing that bore the stains of her blood. By the time he finished, Eru stood nearly naked, with crimson stains on much of his grey skin. Unabashed by his immodesty, Eru threw the clothing into the fire.

The fires in the kiln kicked to one last furious holocaust before slowing to a subdued steady burn. Before much longer the fires subsided and only ash remained. That was when it hit Eru with undeniable finality. Aymis was gone. Eru fell to the ground by the kiln and wept bitterly.

CHAPTER 32

NOT ALONE

I faced a pivotal moment as the flames consumed Amys's body, and the room grew dark. Her smoldering remains seemed an appropriate symbol for my burning hunger for justice. The growing darkness was a type of the darkness that I felt trying to consume me. It would have been easy to let that darkness win, taking me down a path much like that my father trod. The line between justice and vengeance can be blurry when you lose someone you love. I knew Aymis would not have wanted that. My reasons and methods for fighting mattered just as much as the fight itself. Aymis's death marked a moment of choice for each of my friends, and I owed it to them to respect that. Supe would hardly understand the offer to leave, and wouldn't forsake the chance to be seized again. Still, I couldn't use her gift under any but the most unusual circumstances. Rose's gentle heart deserved the chance to leave. Violence didn't become her. I expected Volo to leave like a caged bird. The thought of continuing with just Janis and Oko disheartened me, but at least I knew I could count on them. I could feel Janis's conviction to continue her daughter's cause, and knew enough of Oko's hatred for the archos to know he was with me.

"Everyone, please gather close and pay close attention," Eru said. Through Oko's eyes, he watched as his small group of friends drew near. "As of today we have become a threat to Aitrox. Before Oko joined us, she had no reason to fear us."

"I don't understand," Rose said. "How does Oko change things?" Eru realized that nobody but he had any idea yet about Oko's gift.

"Oko has a very rare gift. He is called a Hider, and as the name implies, that means he is undetectable to the archos mind."

"Then how in all of Deor, did you seize him?" Volo asked.

"Oko offered his mind to me, and somehow that made it possible. While I hold him, I can hide all of us from Aitrox and any other archos." Flashes of excitement and joy pulsated through the hearts of each of his friends as they each realized what that meant.

"So, we are safe!" Volo exclaimed with a relieved sigh.

"Not really, Volo. While I have Oko seized, we are safe, but I will have to release him, and when that happens, we are in grave danger. Aitrox tolerated us when she could control and predict us. If she finds us while Oko is unseized..." Eru let the thought hang.

"Then you can't ever release Oko!" Janis said.

"I agree," Volo said, glancing nervously at the Hider.

"Volo, if our friend never releases Oko, he will be burned out. You know that," Rose objected.

"Better than all of us getting killed," Volo rejoined.

"How do we even know he will let our friend seize him again?" Janis asked.

"Janis asks a fair question. For the time being, I believe that Oko's desire to destroy our enemies is strong enough, and he knows the possibilities that are unlocked by working with us. With that being said, he, just like any of you, is free to abandon our cause if he chooses."

"You can't let him leave!" Volo protested, raising his voice in anger.

"I will not force *anyone* to help us."

"But our lives depend on him!" Volo rejoined.

"Our lives depend on each of your gifts. Volo, would you have me hold your sister a prisoner against her will?" Eru asked.

"No, of course not," Volo relented quietly.

"I will need to release Oko soon to give him a break. It is terribly important that we all be careful when I do." Eru said nothing about the greater need he felt to return to the void. Only then could he properly mourn for Aymis. He knew that those he seized couldn't see into his mind as he could theirs, but he never felt alone with his thoughts when he held others.

"We are ready," Rose said as she looked to each of the others. They nodded their assent.

"Very well," Eru said. He had Oko breathe a sigh of relief and leave the room. He knew he couldn't really release Oko just yet. Inevitably, the first thoughts in each person's mind focused on Aitrox in ironic reminders not to do just that. Only as each person drifted to sleep did Eru finally feel he could release Oko.

Alone with his thoughts, his mind relived every precious moment with Aymis. Their time together had been too short. His powerful intellect allowed him to repeat the memories perfectly. He could almost ignore the pain and continue in blissful delusion until his body crumbled to dust. At least part of his mind could do so, but the terrible memory of her death held too much sway to be brushed aside, and that dreadful moment also replayed in his mind with brutal intensity. Still, Eru knew he would forever crave the void now as a sacred refuge from the realities of the harsh world.

Oko sighed in relief as Eru released him. He understood why people feared and loathed the experience. The thought of being seized again nearly drove Oko to run away, but he knew that together he and Eru would achieve amazing things. Oko almost smiled at the thought, but Eru's presence had bludgeoned open memories he longed to be free of. Oko settled himself uncomfortably on the tile floor and rested his head on his arm. Closing his eyes, he tried to sleep, but the tingling in his hand and the ache in his hip from the hard floor made it difficult. Finally, sleep took him back to the memories he would rather forget.

Oko, the child, woke on the hillside where he and his father tended sheep. The Oko of present day groaned and turned in his sleep, but the dream moved mercilessly forward. Silhouetted against the full moonlight he saw his father sitting eye to eye with a haunting eagle-like creature.

"I don't understand," Teko, his father, said. His head lifted and he locked eyes with the massive wyvern before speaking again. "You want me to abandon my only son? You believe he's a Hider. That's preposterous!" The grass stirred with the powerful blast of massive wings as the creature lifted off into the night. Through the bright light of a full moon, Oko discerned the lack of feathers on its wings, though feathers still covered much of the body and head of the mysterious visitor. Its wings looked more like bat wings, their semi-translucent membranes allowing the moonlight to pass as if through a fog.

"Father," Oko called, "what was that about?"

"Go back to sleep, son."

"But what did he want?"

"I said go back to sleep!" Teko snapped irritably. Oko pretended to oblige, but sleep eluded him the rest of that long night. His mind raced over the possible implications of his father's words. *What if his father DID abandon him, as that strange beast had apparently mandated? What if it had placed an enchantment on his father? What if...* The uncountable permutations of that awful question continued to race through his vivid imagination until the rising sun called him to work with the herd.

"Father, you won't leave me, will you?" Oko asked nervously as they worked together to shear another sheep.

"What would make you ask such a question?" Teko asked awkwardly.

"I heard you talking to that thing last night."

"Then you heard me tell it I didn't believe anything it told me," Teko said, looking his son in the eyes with conviction.

"But it didn't say anything. It just looked at you."

"I heard it speak, though its beak never moved."

"What did it tell you?" Oko asked, almost cutting a sheep's ear off with nervous inattention.

"Nothing," Teko answered, but he couldn't hide the lie in his eyes.

"Please, father I have to know," Oko said, sounding years older. His father saw the determination beyond his years and relented.

"He told me that you are a Hider."

"What does that mean?" Oko asked.

"Do you remember what I told you about *them*?" his father asked, placing a unique emphasis on the word 'them'. "Hiders are legendary people *they* cannot touch."

"He believed I was a Hider!" Oko exclaimed. "I'll be seized, that's incredible!"

"It's ridiculous. They don't exist. Don't you think on it, son, or you'll be seized for sure. Watch your sheep, son," Teku said firmly as Oko's shears wandered. Something in his father's tone ended the conversation, but not the visions of glory that filled Oko's head. They finished shearing the sheep and left it to join the rest of the herd in its nudity. When they finished their work for the day, Oko jumped on the back of the wagon as they rode into town. After a hard winter, the sheep's thick wool would fetch a good price this year.

Oko's imagination envisioned grander things than fresh cream and a bag of sweets, the usual reward his father gave him after a successful haul. Instead he imagined a new life of adventure. He saw himself as one of the legendary bandits from old stories. He would move like a shadow in the night, using his knife to destroy wicked archos. He would be the people's hero, freeing them from archos tyranny and slaying even the mighty Aitrox herself. As they rolled into the small town of Tarseilles, the realization hit him. He had not been seized, even as he imagined himself slaying archos.

"Father!" he exclaimed.

"What is it, son?" Teko asked.

"What if it is true?" Oko inquired, an eager light in his eyes.

"Don't ask such things."

"But what if, Father?"

"Then I would have to leave you forever," Teko said with a shakiness in his voice that Oko had never heard before.

"But why?" Oko asked.

"Because I could lead them to you. They would use me as a tool to get to you." Suddenly Oko's visions of a glorious future felt the first cold dousing of reality.

"I see," Oko said morosely.

"Please, you are lucky to not know what it is like to be seized. Don't let this foolishness be the cause for you to lose that innocence."

"Yes, Father," Oko said obediently, but a small spark of hatred kindled in his heart. He had heard stories of the archos, but they felt like nothing but stories.

Imagining them torturing his father, the only person he had, in order to get to him, infuriated Oko.

"That's a good boy," Teko said as he ran his hand through Oko's hair playfully.

The small town of Tarseilles had maybe a thousand residents; small enough to go largely unnoticed, yet large enough for the rulers to station one archos there. In such a small town, their ruling archos had probably seized each person multiple times. The shadow of that domination crushed the light in their countenances, leaving each resident dim and lifeless. No wonder his father had chosen a life among the sheep. How Oko hated the beings that could reduce people to such dark, hopeless beings.

Oko had no friends in town, but anything felt more exciting than the long days with nothing but sheep's stupid calls. Today, however, he saw the lively village's activities in a different light. Even his father's countenance darkened as their wagon moved further into town. Why hadn't Oko noticed it before? Their wagon drew into the center market, and Oko saw the archos Veru. People averted their gazes and scurried away from him like beaten puppies. The archos took the finest cut of beef, a bushel of apples, and a bottle of expensive wine. Oko felt the fury for these people, who lived under a quashing blanket of fear.

"I will kill you," Oko said quietly as he stared at the archos. Tarseilles would be freed of their archos today.

Father sold their wool for a particularly good price, and the smile on his face showed it. He pocketed it contently as he examined his old worn shoes. "This year I will finally be able to get me some new shoes."

"Our wool sold well this year, Father?" Oko asked.

"Yes, Oko," Teko said as he tossed him a full copper coin.

"What's this for, Father?" Oko asked, with bulging eyes.

"You're old enough to choose what you wish to do with your earnings."

"But a full copper coin?"

"I told you our wool sold well this year," Teko said with a wink. Oko turned and ran with a smile. He had never held so much money in all his life. He could buy ten cups of cider, a full batch of sweet bread, and a bucket of cream with this money. He ran to the confectioner's shop eagerly, but the thought of Veru quelled his appetite. He stopped cold in his tracks outside the shop, fingering the coin in his hand. His father gave him this coin because he was a man now. Candy and sweets were not becoming to a man, especially not a man with a mission.

It didn't take him long to find the blacksmith in such a small town. The smoke rising from his shop and the ringing of the hammers guided him straight to it. He stepped in with a rapidly beating heart, but he hoped his anxiety didn't show.

"What can I do for you, boy?" the blacksmith asked. His thick hairy arms and broad shoulders intimidated Oko, but he was a man now.

"Do you have a knife for sale?" he asked, trying to add depth to his voice.

"A boy like you, whose voice hasn't even cracked yet?" he said with a laugh. Oko grunted at the insult. Apparently he hadn't done so well sounding older.

"I can pay."

"Come boy, a knife will cost you more than a few pennies," the smith snorted and turned to his work again.

"I have a full copper coin!" Oko said, stepping forward and waving the coin proudly.

"Well now, you didn't steal it, did you?" the smith asked.

"Our wool sold well this year," Oko growled.

"And what does a shepherd boy want with a knife?" the smith asked dubiously.

"I want one to cut my apples with. What does it matter to you?" Oko asked angrily.

"I don't sell dangerous weapons to children," the smith said with another derisive snort.

"I am not a child!" Oko yelled.

"Then tell me the real reason you need a knife."

"We also have a pig that needs slaughtering, but our only good knife broke over the winter," Oko lied.

"Heh, you should have bought your first one from me. There, was that so hard?" the smith asked. He turned from his hammer and anvil and stepped into another room. He returned with a small utility knife. "Let me sharpen it for you." The smith sharpened it on his grinding stone with the casual expertise of a man who had worked metal his whole life. Oko watched in fascination as the hot sparks flashed from the blade with an angry grating noise. The smith sheathed the blade in a leather scabbard and handed it to him in exchange for the coin. "Be careful with it, boy."

"Thank you, sir," Oko said with a triumphant smile. He had done it. He ran from the shop before the smith could change his mind. He knew the smith wouldn't have believed a boy to have bought that knife with murder in his heart, much less the murder of an archos. It was the beginning of his illustrious legend. He would live both lives, the unassuming shepherd boy would be the perfect cover. It was perfect.

Oko already imagined himself a legendary bandit, or cutthroat. He imagined his movements, the graceful stealthy movements of a lioness on the hunt. The people who passed smiled at the child's innocent play as they watched him duck behind a crate or passing wagon, remembering the days when their biggest concerns were the imaginary monsters in the town square. Little did they know that Oko stalked a real monster, and that serious look was the precursor to real bloodshed. He returned to the market hoping to find Veru. He was not disappointed. Oko pushed through the crowd. Finally he reached the invisible barrier that everyone, except Veru's entourage of three, respected.

Oko watched those three with fearful eyes. They moved with an uncanny unity of purpose, almost stepping in unison. He maneuvered until he was behind his prey, then mustered the courage to strike. His hand clenched on his knife, but the handle felt slick in his sweaty palm. What was he thinking? This was murder! No, this was justice! This was heroism!

He sprang across the boundary and closed the distance between himself and his quarry. Fortune favored him that this archos had no Prophets or Readers. Veru's Brute and Wizard were not equipped to protect against such a surprise attack, but surprising an archos should have been impossible. Oko unsheathed his dagger and jumped on the archos's shoulders. With a quick slash the knife slid across its neck in a brilliant splash of crimson. The monster crumpled to the ground like a tent that had lost its poles.

Screams filled the market as people scattered in every direction. Oko looked at his first victim, and first victory, with a mix of pride and disgust. He saw the blood on his hands, and could hardly believe himself capable of such a feat. Looking up, his eyes met with his father's and a chill ran down his spine. Father knew he was a Hider now. Oko could never see his father again.

"I am sorry, Father," he said quietly as he turned and disappeared into the town.

"I am sorry, Father," Oko mumbled in his sleep, but nobody in Piru's home heard him. The quiet apology repeated through the night until the light of dawn woke him from his sleep.

"I hope everyone slept well," Eru said. Everyone yawned and nodded their confirmation except Janis and Oko. Janis grumbled and rubbed her bloodshot eyes as she looked at the floor. Oko said nothing. "I am offering you your freedom today," Eru said to the group.

"You have always respected our choice," Rose said.

"I know, but we stand at a crossroads this morning. The path I will take will be dark and terrible, with small hope of victory."

"I will follow you!" Janis said with a fire in her eyes that drove away the grogginess like dew before the sun.

"So will I," Oko said.

"Oko, the things I wish to discuss must not be discovered. Do I have your leave?" Eru asked.

"Yes," Oko replied. The return of Eru's presence felt like a blow to an already battered face. Immediately, Oko's protection covered the thoughts of all in the home, and hope filled Oko's heart. For the first time since he had left his father, he was not alone.

"I will destroy Aitrox. Oko's gift is the secret weapon that allows me to hide whomever I will from archos dominion. Volo, Rose, your gifts will be incredibly valuable, but if you wish to leave, then you may. It will be worse than any of us can imagine. I will not hide that from you."

"Rose, we should leave," Volo said as he looked her in the eyes.

"No, brother. I believe in Eru," Rose answered.

"But, can you kill for this cause, Rose? I don't want to see your kindness drowned in blood," Volo responded.

"Yes, I can do what I must." Rose looked at her brother with conviction in her eyes. For the first time, Volo saw the woman behind those eyes, and he knew she could not be shaken. "I am with Eru."

"Then I am as well," Volo said quietly. She saw in his face an unspoken question and knew he wondered if he was the only sane person among them.

"Eru, friend," Supe said with a nod.

"Wonderful. We have work to do." Eru hid his relief that Volo and Rose had both stayed by his side. He needed their gifts to be the sharpened tools in his hands. Above all, he felt grateful. He may have lost Aymis, but he was not alone.

CHAPTER 33

Skirmish

There are many things in life that you think you understand,
and feel prepared for, only to realize later how naïve and
ignorant you were. I had experienced death and despair,
and thought myself prepared, or at least informed, for the
days ahead. I was wrong.

A crowd gathered for another one of Maverick's charitable giveaways.
Rumors had spread since the last spectacular festival, and a nervous hum
resonated within the hearts of all who waited. A somber attitude had settled on
the whole city. It would seem Maverick had either snapped, or had always been

playing games. Even those who had never braved one of Maverick's events had felt the hope engendered by the stories and basked in the glow of others who did go. Losing hope in the goodness of Maverick felt like a return to the deep of winter. Some quietly claimed that Maverick was a victim of a terrible tragedy, or that he had finally drawn the attention of the rulers. It hurt less to see Maverick as just a devious archos finding new ways to play with the people, than to see him as something truly special that Aitrox had destroyed.

The smaller crowd that gathered today consisted of the desperate and the foolishly optimistic. Just because Maverick had snapped once, didn't mean he would do so again. Others simply refused to let their hope die on nothing more substantial than hearsay. Desperation showed on the faces, in the posture, and in the voices of the majority of those who waited for Maverick today. They had that expectant look in their eyes, though exactly what they expected was unclear. For them, a quick death, and a good meal, held equal appeal.

A wagon rolled down the street with a tarp that covered the goods like wrapped presents. Sitting in plain sight for all to see, Maverick's white coat and top hat glistened in the sun. He smiled, a magnanimous smile that put many at ease, then his driver called, "Come and receive the blessings of Maverick!"

Something about that voice assuaged all the fears of the onlookers. They felt an inexplicable desire to please the driver of the wagon, and they gathered like hungry puppies before the master's dinner table. Then the tarp flung off the wagon, revealing several armed men.

Arrows flew, dropping victims with terrible screams of pain. The archer either possessed an uncanny sort of luck to never quite miss his target but never kill them, or a morbid accuracy. People fell with arrows piercing their limbs, or jutting from their sides.

Another man jumped from the wagon, landing in the middle of the crowd. In their panic nobody noticed how he had jumped at least twenty feet from a stand still. With a terrible grimace on his face, the Brute grabbed his victims and crushed them with no weapon but his own hands. He worked with terrible skill, mutilating or ripping limbs from their sockets, or crushing rib cages like balsa wood. Some died quickly at the Brute's hands, but most retained the capacity to groan, moan or wheeze their agony for some time. Others leapt from the wagon with swords or daggers, working through the panicking crowd, slashing to inflict pain, suffering and a slow death.

Maverick's murderers worked through the crowd, randomly sparing one person or another. In a matter of minutes, terrible screams and groans filled the air. Only four people out of the hundreds who had gathered remained physically untouched but mentally brutalized.

"Behold, the blessing of Maverick!" the cart driver said with his terribly compelling voice. "Go and make sure that everyone knows how Maverick cares for his people!" The four who had been spared felt the power in those words. They would do anything to please that voice, or even the memory of it. With his command to go, they scattered like cockroaches before the light. Their terror of Maverick and the death he wrought could only be surpassed by the pleasure they felt every time they obeyed that voice and spread the word of Maverick's cruelty.

Satisfied that his work here was done, the archos in the white suit and top hat smiled as he willed his underlings back under the tarp, and the wagon rolled into a new neighborhood. A few blocks further down the road, a smaller crowd of curious onlookers emerged from their shanties and piles of garbage and his work continued. It was only the second stop on what would be a long and fruitful day.

'Behold the blessings of Maverick!' Eru felt the thought hit his awareness with foreboding weight. Soon he sensed the tragic wake of death and destruction an archos left in his name. People lay dying, though the reprieve of death would not come quickly. He felt the archos, and perceived his cruel use of a Hawk Eye and Brute. Immediately he reached to seize the fiend, but met a foe his equal if not his superior.

"What's wrong, Eru?" Janis asked as she saw his brow furrow in anger.

"An impostor is murdering people in the name of Maverick!"

"Mother-forsaken Aitrox!" Oko snapped.

"Can you seize him?" Rose asked.

"No, he's too strong for that."

"You can use Volo's gift guided by someone's eyes near him," Oko said. Eru heard Oko through the foggy obscurity of others' minds. His words registered in minds Eru could see, and reached him like a story in its second telling.

"He's terribly strong! Oko, I need your leave!" Eru exclaimed.

"Seize me, Eru!" Oko answered. He felt the protective fortress engulf them just in time. He could feel the onslaught of this powerful enemy like waves battering the barriers for a harbor. The barriers held easily enough, but it left him no doubt what would have happened without them.

"Curse Aitrox for her cunning! It was a trap," Eru said with his own voice, despite having Oko under his dominion.

"Volo, people are dying. I need your gift," Eru said. Volo nodded, but Eru would have seized him regardless. This was not a time to be squeamish about the tools he had.

From behind the safety of Oko's protection, Eru could operate without fear. He quickly seized a few pairs of eyes just in time to feel an arrow strike the arm and then the knee of his host. Eru screamed in pain before blocking it from his mind. A few pairs of eyes focused on the villain in the white coat.

Eru used Volo's gift to grab an arrow and guide it with deadly precision for the archos in the white coat. To his dismay an Immortal intercepted the arrow, adding a gruesome splatter that reached the pristine blank canvas of the archos's white suit. The Immortal pulled the arrow out, the barbed head extracting flesh and tendon. Soon the wound vanished.

How had that happened? An Immortal shouldn't have had enough warning to stop an attack that came from the stealth of Oko's cover. Unless the archos had a Prophet. Eru mumbled a few angry curses, knowing how much a Prophet changed the game.

"Janis, I need you," Eru said. She too nodded her assent, but it wouldn't have really mattered. It took Eru a moment to sort out how to use her gift through other eyes. Fortunately, Janis's gift could work through any eyes Eru controlled if he focused hard enough. It would have been better to have her on location, but he would have to make do.

Janis's vision revealed a bewildering and indecipherable blur of events, like seeing a thousand futures at once. The visions overwhelmed even an archos mind, and left Eru powerless to stop his enemy's brutal slaughter. Moments later, comprehension filled Eru's mind. For every future action Janis's gift foretold Eru, the opposing Prophet had a response, creating an unending blur of confusion. The conflicting Prophets nullified each other, but his foe possessed the benefit of immediacy and therefore clarity. Being forced to use Janis's gift through another pair of eyes meant that ultimately the advantage fell to his opponent.

Furious at the impasse, Eru resorted to brute force. With Volo's gift he pulled cobbles from the street in a rising circle surrounding the wagon and brought them in with terrible force. Each stone struck a different target, crushing through the wagon's wheels, the frame, and the passengers with equal indifference. Shards of wood, appendages and rock chips exploded in all directions. The destruction of the cart was absolute, leaving the impostor Maverick, and his Aegendi, dead.

Eru had hoped to feel some satisfaction with his first small victory. He had, after all, proven that Oko's gift enabled them to defeat a greater foe. However, his seized pair of eyes surveyed the carnage with such terror that Eru knew who had truly gained the victory today. Aitrox could afford to lose the lives of her archos, but Eru could not afford to lose the hearts of the people. Already he felt the stories of Maverick's treachery spreading like wildfire. He may have killed one archos with his Aegendi, but how many innocent citizens had died before the imposter was stopped? Eru may have put down one monster, but in the eyes of the people he sought to protect, he knew that Maverick had just become like other archos: an omen of death.

Eru thought he had been prepared for Aitrox's cunning and wickedness. He had felt hope with Oko's newfound ability, but he sensed the foolishness of that optimism now. He had only begun to stir the brew that Aitrox had prepared in response to the challenge. Now that he had openly confronted her, Eru realized he faced a being beyond his ken with secrets and malice he could never hope to match.

All he could do now was alleviate the suffering of those who lay dying in the streets. Eru went about that work with a sickening knot in his stomach as he silenced one groaning victim after another. There was nothing else he could do for them. The skilled power of the dead archos had ensured that each wound would be fatal. It didn't take long for Eru to seize each dying victim and end their misery. He felt the agonizing pain of each one's injuries as he seized them almost as intensely as his regret for failing them. It had been so long since he had seized another to kill them. It hardly mattered that he did so out of mercy now. When the grim work was done, and the street remained deathly quiet, Eru buried his face in his unfeeling hands and wept.

CHAPTER 34

No Backing Down

*Warfare with the archos proved to be full of surprises.
Having Oko's gift lent a dangerous overconfidence to each
strike. I learned quickly not to underestimate the cunning
of my enemies. I had to fight them with no mercy, for
they would show me none. The harsh nature of the conflict
threatened to jade me. I started to view my friends as assets
instead of people. Life was becoming dangerously like a game*

of chess, where you may callously sacrifice your rook to gain a tactical edge.

"Y ou, the faithful, must do more to remain in Aitrox's favor," a booming voice called in the citadel.

"Praise Aitrox's name forever!" a fanatical voice exclaimed.

"Praising her in the citadel is not enough. If you sit idly by while others betray their goddess, you betray her as well." Everyone in the citadel knew what the archos was talking about. Many even guessed at the source of the newest stories about Maverick and his killing sprees. Of course, most in this congregation came for reasons other than devotion to Aitrox. They couldn't have cared less if the spokesperson declared that the sky was red and the sun shone black. The zealots, however, soaked up the new message with rapt attentiveness.

"No! I would never betray my High Queen!" someone exclaimed. Eru knew that person to be unseized as he observed the proceedings. The ruling archos had kicked into a higher frenzy, holding congregations more frequently and drawing larger masses. The same message echoed in all the spacious citadels. Eru had pushed Oko hard in response. Congregations served his purposes as much as they served Aitrox.

"Then go! Punish the faithless curs who give their hearts to evil!"

"Down with the faithless!"

"Glory to Aitrox!" The crowd had worked itself into a fervor, mostly artificially induced, but Eru could feel its influence on the indifferent. Eru's time to act had come.

"Down with Aitrox!" someone under Eru's control shouted. Without realizing it, most of the congregation shouted their approval of the changed message. Eru didn't waste time musing over their response. As expected, the blasphemy infuriated and surprised the citadel's archos. Confident in his superior strength, he had assumed himself safe from Eru's petty warfare. He had welcomed the fall of his rivals, believing himself to be above such a fate. Eru had sensed the same thoughts in several archos before he killed them. The windows in the citadel exploded inward, innumerable glass daggers converging on his target.

Eru knew of the Wizard his foe possessed, so it came as no surprise to watch as the shards of glass hung suspended in the air surrounding the target archos. Without his Wizard to protect him, the pieces of the stained-glass would have been dyed a new scarlet. Eru kept the force applied through Volo's gift, which in turn kept his foe's Wizard occupied. The crushing pressure on the glass caused it to crack and crumble with an eerie crunching sound. Rose, who had remained in the congregation under Oko's protection, now sprang into action. She pressed the button on the walking cane Oko had loaned her for this strike.

Rose moved to thrust the cane like a spear. With her strength, such a throw was as effective as a javelin would have been. However, Janis had seen how it would have turned back on its path and impaled Rose. Janis's prophetic sight saved Rose's life, and revealed a layer of cunning Eru hadn't anticipated. His foe's wisdom in hiding a second Wizard nearly won the battle for him. If Eru couldn't disable one of the Wizards, he knew he would lose the conflict and send his Aegendi to their deaths.

Instead, Rose sheathed the blade again, and moved through stunned crowd as inconspicuously as possible. Eru had hoped to finish this strike without killing anyone, his target archos excepted. The opposing Aegendi were not only innocent, but invaluable once their master was dead. Now, however, Eru's first priority became disabling one of the Wizards. So long as his foe had the advantage of two Wizards, the risk of losing the conflict and all of his Aegendi loomed large. Without Oko's protection, Eru or some of his own Aegendi would likely be dead already.

Janis's eyes followed Rose through the throng. Fortunately all the futures she beheld simply involved bumping into other shocked onlookers as she made her way to the front of the congregation. She should have an unimpeded path to the Wizard on stage. The intensity in her gaze reflected Eru's desire to finish this fight. If that Wizard fell, Eru would win for sure. The suspended shards of glass suddenly veered off course, cutting through Rose's body before she could reach her target. Fortunately, Rose's death happened only in Janis's prophetic vision. Simply by adding another vector of force to the suspended glass, the extra Wizard in the crowd would have killed her.

Eru took a cue from that foresight and changed the direction of the force he applied to the suspended glass in time to divert it away from and around Rose. She stood like a tree amidst a flooding torrent, with deadly glass flowing around her. Sadly, the diverted shards of glass stabbed, sliced and pierced many innocent bystanders. The ensuing panic and chaos that erupted in the citadel filled Eru's awareness, but he would regret the innocent deaths later. The chaotic response proved a perfect opening for Rose. She leapt from among the onlookers with the unnatural velocity provided by her powerful leg muscles. Her cane struck the Wizard's skull with a brutal crunch. The cane shattered, but so did the Wizard's eye socket and cheekbone.

Rose's body lurched to a stop in midair as the Wizard caught her. Suddenly she shot upwards with terrible speed. Eru immediately focused Volo's gift on her, but she didn't stop. The man on the stage had been a diversion! How had Eru missed it? Both Wizards remained hidden in the masses. Eru scowled over the failure. Rose flew upward, shooting towards the stone ceiling as if she were falling to the ground instead. With two Wizards pushing up, Volo's single opposing force felt useless. Eru pushed her out to the side, sending her flying out through one of the gaping holes where the massive stained glass windows had once been.

Fortunately for Rose, the two Wizards in the citadel lost sight of her as she sailed into the night sky. Eru set her down gently a block away. Rose sprinted back to the conflict. She moved like a blur in the night, attaining speeds unimaginable for regular human limbs. She closed the distance quickly and leapt high into the air, soaring back through the empty window into the citadel.

Eru sent many more objects towards the archos on the stage, but each one was deflected, as he expected. Eru put Janis's eyes to work, hoping to spot the Wizards in the citadel. This foe, however, worked his Wizards with an expertise Eru had yet to attain. Even Janis's enhanced foresight offered no signs of who could be a Wizard. Janis moved against the flow of people like a salmon swimming upstream. Soon, her contrary behavior brought her squarely into the focus of her enemy.

Projectiles flew her way – everything from stray shards of glass to tiles and bricks. Fortunately, Janis saw everything long before it threatened her, and avoided each attack with a casual ease. Unfortunately, the deadly objects struck other members of the terrified throng. Janis occupied the attention of one Wizard while Eru used Volo to draw the attention of the other. Rose grabbed a piece of the broken window frame and hurled it at her foe. The bent, distorted brass shaft spun on its axis, swinging like a woodsman's axe in the air. It flew with speed and accuracy, striking the archos across the ribs, its momentum carrying the archos with it and crushing him against the back wall.

Eru desperately wished he could find his foe's Aegendi. Being unable to seize the archos or locate the Aegendi meant they would disappear. Most likely, they would choose freedom if he found them, but the night's strike demonstrated how useful a second Wizard could be. Were Aymis around to help, finding the Aegendi would have been simple. Eru suppressed that thought immediately. He missed her for reasons far more important than the tactical help her gift would have provided.

Elsewhere in Deor, Oko gently swung the reins to get the carriage moving. The horse's hooves clopped quietly on the cobblestones as it drew Oko and Supe to the first rendezvous point. Oko dressed and acted the part of the driver, while Eru extended Oko's gift of protection to the crew. Eru remained concealed inside the carriage for the whole operation. The carriage never came close to the citadel, and Eru guided each member of the team to different rendezvous points in the city blocks around the latest strike. One by one they all climbed into the carriage.

"Five down, a few thousand left," Janis said when Eru released her as she entered the carriage. He felt her determination and the sense of satisfaction. She would never forgive the rulers for the death of her daughter.

"Has it been five?" Eru asked.

"If you count the one who posed as Maverick," she replied. The carriage rocked slightly as they turned a corner.

"I wasn't counting them at all," he remarked. The carriage door opened and Rose climbed in. Eru released her now that he had her back in safety. Janis saw the bewildered fear in her eyes and Eru sensed the same.

"I am sorry, Rose," Eru said.

"I thought I was going to die. Thank you for saving me, Friend."

"I am sorry that you were the one who made the kill. I had no other way," Eru continued.

"I still can't believe how strong..." she said quietly, looking away from Janis and falling to silence. The quiet clop of hooves outside and the creaking of the carriage frame filled the silence, as if the normally unnoticed sounds relished their moment in the spotlight. Janis put her arm around Rose's shoulder to offer some comfort. They rocked to a creaking stop as Volo climbed in.

"You monster!" he exclaimed at Eru. "You almost got my sister killed! If you ever..." he stopped himself, recognizing the dangerous ground his anger put him on.

"Volo, he saved me! You saved me!" Rose said.

"This is madness," Volo said with a scowl.

"Why are you here then?" Eru asked.

"Because you brought me back to the carriage," Volo answered, unwilling to answer the real question.

"If you want to leave, I won't stop you."

"Rose, let's go. This is suicide." Volo looked at her, desperately hoping she would listen to him this time. She looked back, and Eru sensed the temptation in her brother's statement. Her mind would forever remember the way her strength had crushed that archos and shattered someone's skull. Such things don't sit well in a heart as gentle as hers.

Eru knew that losing them would likely mean their cause ended tonight. He needed their gifts desperately. Part of him wanted to seize her and ensure that Volo's command met with a refusal. Of course that would in turn mean he would have to keep her seized indefinitely to hide the deception. The thought of breaking Rose ended the temptation immediately. He couldn't afford to think of his Aegendi as chess pieces. He had to be better than that. They trusted him to be more than that.

"No," Rose said. Eru breathed again.

"But..." Volo objected.

"Eru warned us about days like this. I believe in what we are doing," Rose interrupted.

"With each archos we defeat, the ruler's grip on the city weakens," Janis interjected.

"You can mind your own business," Volo snapped.

"She's right, Volo," Rose said, giving Janis an appreciative smile.

"We barely escaped tonight. We can't just keep doing this," Volo persisted.

"If you want to leave, Volo, then I will not stop you. But if you stay, I need to know I have your support," Eru said with determination in his young voice.

"Rose?" Volo said, glancing her way tentatively.

"I am staying," she said with more strength the second time. Volo sighed and fell silent.

Eru didn't need hearing to sense the heaviness of the silence in the carriage. They had faced another superior foe and emerged the victors. Eru, however, felt the failures of the night more than the victory. Again he had failed to find any new Aegendi. Likely, Aitrox would soon assimilate them into her network under another ruler. He wanted to hope they would find freedom, but he knew better than to let his hopefulness lead him to underestimate the goddess.

More disconcerting than the fate of those Aegendi was the fear for Oko's well being. Some days, Eru had to use Oko's gift from sunup to sundown. Oko always volunteered, fueled by his insatiable drive to defeat the archos. Already, Eru could feel the effect of prolonged seizure wearing on Oko. His zealots all lasted months before showing signs of breaking, but the Aegendi were different. Using an Aegendi's power took a heavy toll on their minds.

If things kept going at this pace, Eru feared Oko would break in no more than a week. He guessed that a broken Aegendi becomes less powerful. The diminishing of Oko's gift would make things difficult, but Eru had more important objections to breaking his team. Oko may be the most vital tool at his disposal, but he was also a person and a friend. Despite his fears for Oko, necessity forced him to keep him seized even now. Thoughts of the recent battle still raced through his crew's minds, and would bring death down on them immediately without Oko's protection.

"Eru, kill bad archos," Supe said quietly. Eru hoped he was right in seeing slow improvements from her. Perhaps her gift could slowly bring her back to full awareness, a deliverance none of the others could hope for if they ended up broken. He couldn't afford to use them up and cast them aside like spent candles.

He pulled the carriage to a stop in front of a nobleman's estate. They had earned a day or two of comfort. Oko opened the carriage door and they stepped out and stretched their legs. Eru climbed out last and took the lead towards the front door. He pulled the bell, hearing its clear note through Oko's ears. The door opened on the silent hinges typical of a well-kept estate.

"What do you want?" a servant, who had assimilated some of his master's elitist bearing, asked.

"We will stay in this estate for the night. It is your choice how that happens though," Eru said. Eru extended Oko's covering protection to the servant as a precaution.

"Maverick?" he asked in shock, shedding the arrogant tone immediately. "Praise the maker, you are real."

Hearing the name Maverick stung Eru's heart, returning a part of his mind to Aymis's terrible death. That name would forever reopen that wound. Still, this man had not yet given up on the good stories about Maverick. "I am Maverick, yes. We need a place to sleep. Will you let us in?"

"Well, I'll be seized! You actually asked me? I knew it! I knew the stories were true. Come in!" he exclaimed, all ostentation gone from his voice. "Are these your friends?"

"Something like that," Volo said as he stepped into the opulent building. The scowl on his face quickly disappeared as his eyes wandered around the immaculate home. "We should stay in places like this every night," he mumbled to himself.

"Are you going to make my master clean the washroom? Maybe he could scrub the servant's outhouse," the servant said eagerly.

"We will see," Eru said with a smile that hid the poignant mix of pleasure and pain that memory brought with it.

Once everyone made it inside, Eru released Oko. He had been under his control for over five hours. "You deserve a rest," he said. Oko said nothing in response. Back in the void, Eru had no senses that could notice the exhausted look in Oko's eyes, or the slight shakiness in his hands.

Eru paid close attention to each of his friends while in the void. Without Oko's protection, wandering thoughts from any of them could prove fatal. Even his own thoughts needed to be disciplined, but Eru couldn't get Volo's objections out of his mind. Could Eru really justify taking his friends into such danger with no real end in sight? How much did he gain with each attack? If anything, today's confrontation only proved that despite Oko's protection, the more powerful rulers still posed significant threats. He was still woefully unequipped to take on Aitrox.

Perhaps the best he could do for all of his friends was to simply escape. Aitrox, and her ruler subordinates kept an almost omniscient watch over the entire Deor Empire. Even small farming settlements and outposts remained under her close scrutiny. They would have to leave the Empire, which meant sailing across the sea. Cartographers and astronomers he had seized knew the world to be round, and surmised that other lands must exist out beyond the shores of the Deor Empire. Yet sailing away would prove impossible.

Aitrox permitted barges and small craft to carry goods and sail the waters close to shore, but nobody in Deor knew the waters beyond the coastal shorelines, and no vessels existed that could venture into that unknown. With his Aegendi, and Eru's wealth of knowledge, he could build a seaworthy ship quickly if avoiding detection weren't a priority.

No, for the time being, Eru saw no hope in escaping. Eru felt much like an exhausted mountaineer trapped high on a cliff. Continuing to struggle felt impossible, but it offered better hope of survival than attempting to back down.

Aitrox no longer smiled as she watched the wretched Streetborn undermine her power. The impudent brat had become a nuisance, but still she needed him just a while longer. He would never know how she had quickly intervened, seizing the archose just long enough to give the Streetborn's Brute a window of opportunity for the kill. She had to be subtle, but she needed the Streetborn to have some notable successes. She could feel the vyeshen in her city, nebulous and vague. She needed the Streetborn to draw their attention and draw them out.

Suddenly Aitrox felt the return of the Streetborn's mind, knowing he had again released his Hider. His feeble attempts to remain concealed almost made her laugh. Part of her wanted to seize him now and end this whole game, but that would only give the vyeshen more time, and time was a dangerous gift to allow them. No, Aitrox knew she needed to let the game play out. Soon enough it would all come to a head. There was no backing down now.

CHAPTER 35

COWARD

We had defeated five archos, but there were thousands more, and the small success only made me realize how far we had to go. Each victory weakened the rulers as an organization, but it would be years before we achieved a noticeable difference. Not expecting to live that long, I hadn't thought to plan accordingly. I needed to find some way to keep from using up my Aegendi like candles burned *at both ends. Oko suffered the weight of my power the most, being the one whose gift I had to use almost constantly.*

"I am worried about Oko," Rose said quietly to Eru as she watched the Hider leave.

"Yes, my control sits particularly heavily on him," Eru said.

"Maybe we all need some time to recuperate," Rose pondered.

"Our enemies aren't resting," Janis replied with an eager hunger in her eyes. Eru perceived a similar hunger in her heart, belying the fact that she seemed stretched thin.

"Janis, be careful. I just released Oko. He needs a rest." Eru felt the wear on his own mind as well, but chose not to mention it. A few days' rest would do them all some good.

"So are we going to stay here for a while, then?" Volo asked expectantly.

"Try not to destroy the place," Eru said with a smile.

"Of course not," Volo said, as he pocketed a silver candlestick from one of the decorative tables.

"And no stealing," Eru said in response.

"You are going to take the nobleman's money anyway!" Volo objected.

"I take only what we need, and I use it to help others. If you were taking with more munificent motives I would feel differently," Eru responded.

"Munificent?" Volo asked confusedly.

"It means kind and unselfish," Janis explained, catching an angry glare from Volo.

"And what about all of this is kind or unselfish?" Volo growled as he put the candlestick back down and walked away.

"I am sorry about my brother," Rose offered timidly.

"Why are you apologizing? He is his own person. Besides, his feelings are genuine and he has some valid points," Eru said.

"How can you say that? We are trying to help others," Rose replied.

"There is nothing kind about war."

"You may be right, but you are one of the most unselfish people I have ever met. My brother is the selfish one," Rose said.

"He is making the same sacrifices you are, just with different motives."

"I guess," Rose said.

"Please, take a moment to remind everyone to discipline their thoughts. I need to give Oko a break, so we will be vulnerable for a while."

"Good point. I will go tell the others," Rose said as she walked away. During their short conversation, each person in the team had wandered to their own corners or rooms. Rose found Janis in a large closet full of gowns and other fine clothes. Janis fingered the gowns with a strange look in her eyes.

"You would have looked beautiful in this one dear," Janis said quietly to herself.

"Janis, are you okay?" Rose asked. Janis looked up with a start, as if waking from a daydream.

"Oh, Rose," Janis said with an embarrassed smile, like a girl who was caught with her hand in a sweets jar. "I was just admiring the gowns."

"Is there anything I can do for you?" Rose asked.

"Thank you, but I just need some time to myself," Janis answered.

"I understand. I am just passing a message from our friend. He asked me to remind everyone that we won't have Oko's protection for a day or two, so we need to be careful," Rose said as she left Janis alone with the gowns.

You don't understand, Janis thought as Rose left her with the dresses. Janis picked another and held it up, as if sizing it against an imaginary person.

Rose thought she heard quiet, mournful sniffles behind her as she left Janis alone. In the next room over, she found Volo spread out on a large feather bed as if he could somehow absorb more benefit from the bed by touching every last square inch. His greasy, long hair and dirty clothes would have left the Count, who owned the mansion, furious.

"What are you doing?" Rose asked curiously.

"It's so soft," Volo said with a happy sigh.

"You're filthy. Some servant is going to have to work hard to wash the bedding when we leave," Rose said.

"You're just as dirty."

"But, I am not ruining someone's bed," Rose rejoined.

"Hey, we have been sleeping on floors and beat-up couches for days. I am going to enjoy this."

"You could at least take a bath first," Rose retorted.

"Oh, that sounds great," Volo said as he stood up and stepped into the bathroom. The pristine white bedding actually showed a grimy silhouette where he had been. "Rose, come here!"

Rose followed him into the room, gasping in surprise at the incredible bathroom. Carved flowers adorned the rich wood cabinetry. The walls had been painted by a skilled artist, almost transporting Rose to a lush garden with all the vivid, lifelike details. A beautiful statue of a woman held a watering can over the tub area. "I wonder what that's for," Rose said.

"Watch," Volo said as he turned a knob and steaming water poured from the statue's watering can. "It's even heated!"

"Well, I will leave you to enjoy being watered," Rose smiled. "Oh, our friend wanted me to remind everyone that we won't have Oko's protection for a day or two. Be careful." Rose stepped out of the garden and back into the real world. Behind her the sound of falling water, and Volo's contented sighs, echoed out of the washroom.

Rose found a room to claim, and closed the door behind her. As if the closing door meant the day had truly ended, exhaustion rushed over her. She could hardly believe it when she noticed this room had a dedicated washroom as well. She stepped in and saw a completely different theme. Carved doves and robins graced the countertop and rim of her small bath. The painted walls took her high into a sunset-colored sky. She almost felt like a bird in flight. The thought transported her back to the day's terrors at the citadel and the terrifying flight the Wizards had taken her on. Under opposing Wizard forces, she had feared her ribs would crush or the breath would be squeezed from her lungs like a deflated balloon. With a shake of her head, she snapped her thoughts back to the present.

She turned on the water and smiled as she noticed the clever design for her shower: a carved cloud that adorned the ceiling and incorporated itself almost indistinguishably into the paintings. Once she saw the water falling from that carved cloud, Rose decided she had the better of the two rooms.

Rose decided she liked the experience of being rained on more than she had thought she would. Eru had exposed her to terror and fear like she had never known, but it also gave her a taste of opulence and luxury beyond her wildest imaginings. Bathing had always been an arduous task, having to draw the water herself. Bathing under a constant, comfortable flow of warm water felt heavenly compared to the cold, stagnant water of a tub. It made sense to have the dirt and sweat washed down the drain rather than sitting in it. Reluctantly, she finished bathing – but only because the water began to cool off – and found some clothes to sleep in. She climbed into the bed, and realized why Volo had had such a content look on his face. She hardly had time to think about it before she fell into a deep sleep, completely spent.

Eru sat on the couch in the main room as the sun set outside and the minds around him slipped into sleepiness. He had picked this estate after sensing the Count's absence. Likely the owner hadn't returned from a winter villa in the southern coast of the Empire. Naturally he would be furious when he returned and found his mansion had been violated. Eru had no desire to spend the few days they needed to rest with the constant rancor of an indignant Count eating away at him. Eru sensed the pleasure and wonder in Rose's heart as she took in the opulent settings, much as Aymis had done in Penro's estate. The similarities hadn't escaped Janis' notice, and her sorrowful memories played their own mournful song on Eru's heartstrings .

The memories of Aymis burned brightly, and painfully. He would forever cherish those times, even if they reminded him of everything he had lost. However, Eru had to focus on other things tonight. He needed to figure out how he could protect Oko. The further they got into the war, the more important

Oko's gift would be. Before long, the constancy of the conflict would reflect in their casual thoughts and they would need protection at all times.

Eru remembered something now, rebuking himself for letting the conversation fall to the back of his thoughts. His mind had compartmentalized all memories connected to Aymis, avoiding them and the grief they brought. Now, however, he remembered one of their last conversations and their theory about iron. What if iron actually could provide them with a true sanctuary, something more sure and lasting than Oko's gift? Oko's protection felt a welcome escape from oppressive fear like a tent from the elements. It offered a needed escape, but had a feeling of impermanence. If only Eru could gather enough iron to do some experiments. Suddenly the knowledge he gained from Oko of the Hider's large store of the contraband metal felt terribly important.

After Oko's consistent protection, he felt incredibly naked and exposed. The night seemed unusually empty, but the sparse population density in this part of the city would explain that. Compared to their usual locations where people stacked into apartments like fish in a tin, the blocks of expansive estates were like a barren wasteland. Only Supe's mind remained conscious, if it could be called that. As always, Supe lingered near him, desperately longing to be seized.

Suddenly, pain and alarm flashed in Supe's mind like a bolt of lightning. Something ripped through her abdomen, splattering the tapestries and carpets with her blood. Eru seized her immediately, and her wound closed. He felt her euphoria as her gift filled her with the vigor and health of a thousand athletes in their prime. He could hardly believe what he saw through her eyes.

All the furniture in the room around them lifted and flew towards him with terrible, deadly momentum. How had he missed such an obvious attack? Then it occurred to him. He had assumed Aitrox controlled a Hider. Why wouldn't she use the same tactics on him? Somehow he just expected her to let him fight his war until she got bored enough to seize him. Seeing how the entire room swirled in a maelstrom, he realized the scale of his blunder.

Eru seized Janis, yanking her from sleep with desperate violence. He ran her into the room, anxious for her gift to keep him alive. Her eyes guided Eru's movements as he managed to dodge the end table, then a candlestick and a falling chandelier. Supe blocked or absorbed the impact of several other threats, recovering to full strength almost immediately. Releasing her in this cyclone of deadly objects would kill her, and her gift had saved Eru's life several times already.

Volo and Rose woke of their own accord with the clamor of the ambush. Eru seized them and put them to use immediately. No doubt the Aegendi behind this attack was close, but Eru couldn't feel anyone other than his own Aegendi. Hider! Eru's heart skipped a beat at the realization. Without a Hider of his own, he had a terrible disadvantage. Just a few hours ago, he had enjoyed the fear he sensed in his opponent as he himself enjoyed this advantage. Tonight, Eru had no idea where Oko had gone, and had no means to even the odds.

Volo looked out his window, and saw several people watching the mansion through the brass bars of the fence. Volo's power yanked the pointed bars apart and thrust them at the watchers. The improvised spears impaled two or three of the assailants, but the opposing Wizard quickly shifted his attention to stop Eru's assault. With the Wizard's attention occupied, the chaos in the mansion subsided. Eru had Janis leap out the window, crushing spring flowers with her landing. Janis moved through the gardens with the confidence granted by her gift. She grabbed a stray bar from the broken fence and smashed it into the Wizard's shoulders. The Wizard didn't even flinch, a clear indicator of archos domination. With another savage blow, he fell dead and the attack ended.

Eru breathed a sigh of relief, though he could only guess why the attack had been so limited. If Aitrox considered him a real threat, she would have seized him rather than sending such a meager assault his way. It galled him to feel how she played with her prey, so comfortably in command at all times. She lost a few Aegendi in her attack, but thanks to her Hider, the archos escaped. Still, she may have unwittingly revealed a truth about her Hider. By Eru's reckoning, no more than five people had been hidden from him during the assault. Eru could hide over three times that many through Oko. Had Aitrox broken her Hider? If so, Eru had a slight edge, and a clear warning. He hoped Aymis had been right. He had to get to Oko's iron and find out. Where in all of Deor was he?

Oko noted the street and number of the mansion – not that he would need help finding it. He had never met Count Pillay, but his wealth was legendary. Oko suspected that much of the iron he had helped smuggle ended up in Pillay's hands. Oko walked down the wide, empty streets without fear. Thieves and cutthroats never ventured into this part of the city, and Oko could handle any if they did. He needed some time to himself.

Had he done the right thing, to surrender to an archos? Together they had already accomplished more than he ever could alone. Oko just didn't know how much longer he could do it. He felt like something inside him was on the verge of snapping. He had faced death in uncounted scenarios, but that never scared him. Something about the fate he could feel coming terrified him. He felt like a shell, as if part of his soul had already been sucked from him. Maybe it was just his cowardice facing the fear of being seized. He had always prided himself in the inviolability of his will. Maybe he just felt the loss of that part of himself as he surrendered it to a greater need.

Oko could hardly believe his own trepidation. He had found an archos that actually wanted the same thing he did. Together they could do the impossible, but it hadn't been at all like he expected. He missed the thrill of the hunt, and the triumphant feeling when his weapons drew archos blood. Oko's power to hide them all was far too valuable for Eru to put him in harm's path during an assault, but part of Oko missed the heat of battle. Perhaps that was why he had loaned his favorite weapon to Rose. At least that way his weapon might get to kill again.

Oko realized he had given up more than just his freedom from archos dominion. He still had that if he wanted it. All he had to do was walk away, and never look back. Suddenly, the empty street called to him with intoxicating appeal. Down that street, a life without the misery of archos control awaited him. Down that street, the thrill of the hunt and the rush of the kill awaited him. His heart ached with longing as he contemplated a return to his old life. He would be free to be the bandit and hero of his childhood fancy. Wasn't that why he had killed his first archos? Wasn't that why he had left his father?

Oko sat on the curb, staring at the cobbles in the street. They were laid out in an intricate pattern, making the streets themselves a thing of beauty to compliment the spacious estates. His eyes settled on the stones, as if he expected to find something meaningful in the smallest details of the stone texture. Nothing had turned out like he had expected. As much as the return to his exciting and relatively simple life appealed to him, he knew the fate that awaited him down that path. Only inexplicable luck had forestalled his death a few times already.

Oko felt torn between two paths, like a traveler left to ponder a fork in the road. Down one road he saw death at the hands of an archos. It looked full of excitement, triumph, and loneliness. The other path offered greater successes and camaraderie, but something dark and terrible seemed to loom just beyond the bend. Suddenly Oko perceived a third choice that almost went unnoticed with its bland simple future. What if he just left it all? He had enough iron to build more than a comfortable life. What good would all that wealth do if he just continued to hoard it like a greedy old miser? Something about that option terrified him more than the other two. He saw himself dying, an old lonely dotard. He would lie alone with his wealth to contemplate how he had forsaken his father, then abandoned the very goals that had justified that choice. That path felt easy, comfortable and terrifying. It meant admitting defeat. It meant that everything he had gone through went to waste. It meant he had left his father and had nothing to show for it. "I did not leave you for nothing. I will bring the archos to their graves, or find mine," he repeated to himself, as he had done on many difficult nights.

Oko sat on the street corner contemplating the three terrible options before him. He had always fancied himself a brave man, until now. He sighed in frustration and muttered, "Oko, you coward," over and over.

CHAPTER 36

FREE YET PRISONERS

I had grown accustomed to the security my awareness provided. Finding myself in mortal danger without even the slightest premonition truly terrified me. I understood the shock and terror my tactics inflicted on my enemies, and for a moment I pitied them. That feeling never lasted long. The memory of their black hearts that had never shown an ounce of pity or mercy quickly soured my empathy and turned it to loathing.

E ru returned to the void, where he couldn't feel his throbbing heart or heavy breathing. Aitrox had actually staged a counter attack. Only a stroke of luck spared them. Had the Wizard managed to hit him rather than Supe first, it would have all been over. The experience gave him a new appreciation for the power of surprise, an experience as foreign to an archos as love or friendship, but far more dangerous.

Eru knew that staying in Pillay's estate could cost them their lives, but he felt he had little choice. If he lost Oko, then they may never find each other again. Life without Oko meant furtive, surreptitious activity and constant fear. It meant necessity driving them to leave no trail that a Hider could follow. Ultimately it meant certain defeat coming at them like a runaway carriage on a steep hill. Staying for another day had its risks, but Eru needed to give Oko time. He only hoped the man would return.

Eru offered freedom to everyone on the team, and he did so with honest intent. However, the mystery and helplessness he felt about Oko left him scowling and clenching his teeth when he thought about it. For any other Aegendi in their small crew, Eru felt a hidden security that he could always get them back. Losing Oko felt different. A smith who misplaces his hammer in his shop knows he will find it soon enough, but losing the same tool because it falls out of his wagon somewhere in the city is different. Ironically, the very gift that empowered Eru and his friends could leave them when they most needed it.

He hadn't expected the notion of losing Oko to hurt as much as it did. Only now did Eru recognize the camaraderie that had been forged in their short time together. They had defeated enemies that should have been beyond them. Nothing could take that away from them, or break that bond of friendship. Now that Eru recognized it, he could see its unmistakable imprint on the hearts of each team member. Even Volo, for all his irritability and anger, harbored a sense of pride and accomplishment. They were almost like gods for the things they could do. If they lost Oko it would all come crashing down to the ground like a bird with clipped wings. The second he released Oko, he disappeared into the aggravating unknown. Where was he? What was he thinking? Would he come back? Eru wanted to break something. Everything he knew about Oko pointed him to answers he wished he could change.

Eru knew Oko like nobody else ever would. He knew everything the man had been through, and given up. As powerful as Oko's hunger for archos blood was, he also had a sense of pride in his individual achievements. He bore the suffering of his solitude and loneliness like a soldier wears a medal signifying a wound in battle. Deserting them and returning to his solitary life felt as natural and right to Oko as a black widow eating her mate.

'*Kill him!*' Eru felt the thought with terrible immediacy, and with such strength he knew he should have picked up on the precursors long before. Had Aitrox attacked again so soon? Similar violent intentions surrounded him, battering his resolve to stay in the void like a fortress under siege. Eru hadn't lost control of his instincts for so long; he had almost forgotten the horror of the experience.

Eru seized one man after another, plunging their knives into their own chests, or cutting their own throats. The horror of the sight through their eyes could only be surpassed by the dread in their hearts. Eru quickly discerned that these phantom attackers shouldn't be his enemy, but he couldn't hold back his instincts as one after another died by his power.

"Please, I mean you no harm!" he screamed in his youthful voice. "Stop attacking me! Please! I don't want to harm anybody!"

He felt the surprise in their minds to hear an archos who actually spoke. As the meaning of his words overcame their surprise, their deadly hostility slowly faded and Eru managed to avoid slaying the last attacker. The seven or eight others weren't so lucky. Their blood stained the rugs and floors, adding to the scene of destruction left by the previous attack.

"But, if you meant us no harm, why did you kill them?" the man asked, barely holding back a sob as he saw his friends' corpses still bleeding before him.

"I am sorry for what happened, Sonu," Eru said, addressing the man by name. Sonu said nothing, a maelstrom of confusion and heart ache raged in his mind. "There are times when my instincts control me as mercilessly as I control an attacker. After years of struggle, I have managed to rein it in to some extent, but a sudden ambush of hostile attackers was more than I could handle. It had been so long."

"What do you mean?" Sonu asked tentatively.

"They would have killed me if they could have, and that set forces in motion I can only occasionally control. If a doctor strikes your knee, it flinches. The violent reflexes I have are almost unavoidable when spurred."

"How do I know you aren't lying to me?" Sonu objected.

"Well, usually the fact that I have learned to talk rather than seizing someone to speak for me goes a long way in proving my sincerity," Eru rejoined.

"I don't trust you," Sonu said suspiciously, but Eru perceived far more than the words Sonu spoke. The man harbored a deep secret, one his friends just died trying to protect.

"If I wanted your secrets, I would have them, but I assure you that we have a common enemy," Eru answered.

"What are you doing here?" Sonu asked. Again, Eru read far more than the words spoken. Sonu refused to believe Eru had simply happened upon this place.

"My team needed some time to recuperate. I felt they deserved a few days in comfort after all they have done," Eru said.

"Your team? What are you talking about?"

"I cannot explain right now. Not without a critical team member who I am waiting for."

"What do you mean?" Sonu persisted.

"Well, I could probably make you understand without alerting our common enemy, but your thoughts would probably get us both killed," Eru answered.

"I understand. I may talk to you again soon," Sonu said as Eru sensed him turning to leave. Eru probed the man's mind as much as he could without seizing him, hoping to answer a few questions. Suddenly the man disappeared, as if he had just fallen off a cliff. By the maker, what had just happened? Had Eru not known better, he would have thought the whole strange sequence to have been a hallucination or dream.

Eru had little notion of how much time passed as his mind mused over Sonu and his mysterious disappearance. Sonu's enigmatic vanishing act drew enough of his attention to provide some relief from his concern about Oko. Eru almost failed to notice when several cautious minds appeared nearby. Eru focused his attention to them enough to discern their thoughts and converse with them.

"Please, come with us," Sonu said to Eru as he entered the devastated room. Eru felt the shock hit the minds of Sonu's three silent companions. Being told what to expect hadn't prepared them for the sight of their friends lying dead. Seeing a young archos sitting there, with an inconspicuous serenity on his face amid such destruction capped off the shocking scene.

"Should I seize one of you, or will you carry me?" Eru asked.

"What about your team? Can't you seize one of them?" Sonu asked.

"They are resting," Eru answered.

"Besides, anybody he brought with him would have to be placed under the same oaths we are," Sonu's companion said before turning to Eru. "We would put you under oath if we didn't think it would be disastrous to try."

"What oath is that?" Eru asked.

"Never to leave our sanctuary, unless you have earned the privilege," Sonu said.

"Well, I would refuse, for reasons I cannot share," Eru answered.

"We know, and we couldn't enforce the oath anyway," Sonu's companion answered.

"Then why are you taking this risk?" Eru asked.

"We cannot answer your question out here," Sonu answered evasively.

"I understand. I will not compel any of my team members to take your oath, so you will have to carry me. I imagine you would rather not have me seizing anyone and possibly learning more than you are comfortable with," Eru said.

"Judging by the fact that you haven't seized any of us yet, I believe you can be trusted to seize one of us. However, I would rather carry you than be seized," Sonu said as he hefted Eru with a grunt. Eru felt the tension in their minds, but it didn't surprise him. He was an archos after all, and they had a portentous secret. Eru hardly dared believe his own suspicions, smiling brightly despite his wishes not to show his anticipation.

While in the void, Eru could only guess where Sonu carried him. From the thoughts of Sonu and his companions, he gathered that they remained in Pillay's estate, but likely had entered a different wing further away from the street. A few minutes later, the presence of hundreds of people flooded his mind as if a dam had burst. Suddenly, the massive, empty estate became a bustling hive, packed mostly with sleeping minds. It felt similar to the crowded apartment complexes. In rooms they passed on both sides, Eru felt them all around, many dreaming fretful nightmares of being discovered.

Most who had found their way here willingly subjected themselves to an imprisonment for freedom from archos tyranny. Rumors had reached them of a rogue archos, but most felt the notion as preposterous as claims that the sun rose in the west and set in the east.

"You are using iron to hide people?" Eru guessed.

"Yes," Sonu said. "So long as we remain here we are free, free in a prison of our own making."

"It's an amazing secret," Eru said with a smile.

"Yes, it is," Sonu answered somberly, and suddenly Sonu's darkest moments gained context and clarity to Eru. Eru's mind now pieced together the details leading up to the moment Sonu slew his son. Sonu's son had grown up in the sanctuary and didn't believe the archos existed. In his mind, the archos were fictitious demons created to control their population and keep them in fear. His son chaffed against the life in prison, and longed to be free. He and a small group of rebels had tried to escape. Sonu, as one of the chief officers in the sanctuary crushed his own son's rebellion, and killed his only son. What else could he have done? Had his son left the sanctuary, he or one of his followers would have eventually been seized, and hundreds would have died.

Eru had felt similar tragedies in the heart of each attacker he had seized a short while ago, but the immediate terrors he inflicted on them had pushed them from his mind. Now, as he felt the touch of similar horrors in the hearts of many, the memories of the recently killed returned. Even here, people lived in the shadow of the archos. True to what Eru had come to know of his kind, even the shadow of the archos touch sowed death. "I will destroy Aitrox," Eru said with a growl.

"And how will you do that? Outside these walls, she is an inescapable goddess."

"I have discovered a very rare kind of Aegendi known as a Hider. He cannot be seized without granting his consent, and when he is seized, I can hide others. With his gift, I can gain the element of surprise," Eru answered.

"You will need more than surprise to defeat Aitrox. Your quest is suicide," Sono rejoined.

"As was your attack on me tonight, yet you still went through with it," Eru rejoined. "Why did you try to kill me?"

"When we heard about an archos so close to our borders, we panicked. It was rash, and foolish, but we had to do something to protect our people."

"So you rushed to your death hoping that surprise would be enough," Eru responded. He could see the desperate reasoning behind their attack, while recognizing the tragic futility of it all. Was his battle against Aitrox any different? Surely, the element of surprise would never be enough to destroy her, not without a whole legion of Aegendi. Perhaps these sanctuaries represented a better path to freedom – escape.

"It was a necessary risk. Aitrox has crushed other colonies. Ours is the largest, and the strongest. We have survived for twenty, hard years," Sonu answered.

"It was a waste of lives to attack me like you did. You should have tried to talk to me."

"And risked divulging our secret to a hostile archos?"

"And what if I had killed all of you?" Eru asked.

"You aren't the only one who has a Hider," Sonu said proudly.

"Then by the maker, why didn't you send him out to kill me?"

"He is away purchasing provisions for the sanctuary, and we couldn't risk waiting for him to return."

"Surely, waiting would have been worth avoiding the needless deaths," Eru protested, trying to stifle his own growing dislike for Sonu.

"Casualties are an inevitable fact of war, and make no mistake we are at war. I will not have you lecturing me about things beyond the reckoning of a boy!" Sonu snapped, apparently picking up on Eru's contempt.

"A boy!" Eru shouted back. "I have memories and knowledge from enough lives I could be centuries old! I have destroyed enough lives to know not to take it lightly, and to tread carefully where death is involved. Every person who dies leaves behind a wake of sorrow and broken hearts that you had better be ready to answer for. Would Kepu's wife accept your explanation for his death?" Eru asked, pulling the name of one of his latest victims for impact.

"Kepu was like a brother to me," Sonu said softly. "You would do well to know I didn't make the decision alone. He agreed with me. We all volunteered."

Eru felt the truth to Sonu's thoughts, sensing the desperate hopelessness that drove them. Even protected by iron, fear of the archos stifled their life and held them prisoner. They all volunteered because death at least meant freedom from constant fear. Yet Eru sensed a subtle, faint change that prompted him to ask, "Why did you bring me here? Why not wait for your Hider to return and have him kill me?"

"Because we are at war, and you can win that war for us," Sonu replied.

"I thought you said that trying to kill Aitrox was suicide," Eru rejoined.

"It is if your only tool is the element of surprise. Without us, you will never have the resources to threaten Aitrox. Without you, the many Aegendi who have found their way to our sanctuary are impotent and useless. When we realized that the rumors of an archos who is fighting on our side are true, and that he was the one at our doors, we had to act. You need us, and we need you." Eru could hardly believe what he was being offered. He almost shouted for joy before another sobering realization calmed his elation. He found himself in a terrifying and beautiful place in this sanctuary. Here, people were free, yet prisoners. Here people were tools, or pieces on a chess board. Suddenly, Eru had an army of Aegendi at his disposal, and a safe base of operations.

"Still, it was terribly risky to bring me here. I cannot guarantee I will be able to protect your people from myself when they discover an archos in their midst."

"I believe it was a risk worth taking. If we squandered this chance, the best we could hope for is a perpetuation of our imprisonment before eventually being discovered," Sonu replied. Despite dawn still being several hours off, word of Eru's arrival had already begun spreading, stirring a few of the light sleepers from their fitful sleep to confront their greatest nightmare – an archos in their refuge. Things were about to get ugly.

CHAPTER 37

DISSENSION

This sanctuary was a truly remarkable and terrible place. Here families loved and shared moments, free from archos intrusion. Here parents killed their own children to protect the sanctity of their home. Here people could sleep without fear of the trauma of being seized. Here people lost sleep fearing discovery and retribution. All of these terrible contradictions existed because of the archos, so it goes without *saying that my presence in the sanctuary was anything but welcome.*

"**S**onu, you fool!" someone in the gathering crowd shouted. The large ballroom served as a common area. Sonu set Eru down in a chair and turned to face the people.

"You're going to get us all killed!" another shout affirmed. A murmur of agreement filled the ballroom.

"I am a friend," Eru said.

"Right, and wolves eat grass," someone objected sarcastically.

"If he meant us harm, he would have seized people," Sonu objected.

"And how do we know you aren't seized?"

"Sonu's seized!"

"Get him!"

"No! I am not seized!" Sonu objected, but it did him no good. Nothing he could do would prove that he hadn't been seized.

"No! Please!" Eru exclaimed, but his young voice couldn't break the growing panic. Eru felt fury grow to an inferno, and nothing he could do short of seizing nearly fifty people would save Sonu. That moment of indecision cost Sonu his life as he received the sharp end of several daggers. Sonu crumpled into the arms of his brother, whose knife was lodged in his stomach.

Fury and disgust filled Eru's heart. He wanted to seize every person in this sanctuary in his rage. How many other innocent people had died under similar circumstances? Eru sensed the anger of the mob turning towards him like a fire hungry for fuel. If he didn't do something quickly, more people would die.

"Stooooop!" Eru shouted. He hoped each person would see reason. "You killed him! Please stop before more innocent people die!" Eru felt his words settle into their ears, as the realization of what they had just done struck several people. Sonu's brother still held his body, looking into the now lifeless face with confusion and regret. One by one people's eyes met, and Eru felt the unspoken question. *I'm not seized. Is anyone else?*

"He's crying," someone said, directing everyone's attention on Eru. Eru felt the intense focus of several minds, and just managed to resist seizing them. Fortunately, his time as Maverick, drawing crowds to admire and focus on him, had given him practice. Yet, being left to face intense, angry and terrified minds all turning on him in unison nearly overpowered his discipline.

"Careful, I don't want to seize anyone," Eru said.

"Sonu, no," his brother Tenu cried out as his fear subsided, and he realized Sonu may not have been seized.

"How do we know we can trust you?" another person asked.

"Each of you knows you are not seized, but you have no way of knowing if your neighbor is or not. I wish there was something I could do about that," Eru said.

"Why have you come here?" Tenu asked bitterly.

"I didn't know about your sanctuary. I brought my team to Pillay's estate because it appeared empty and my team needed rest," Eru said.

"Your team?" someone asked. Eru sighed, realizing that he would have to explain things all over again, but he knew better than to tell them he had already explained it to Sonu.

"I have, well, had, a small team of Aegendi. I am afraid I may have lost my Hider."

"Hiders are Aegendi too?" a woman asked.

"Yes. If a Hider is willing to be seized he can allow it, and an archos can use his gift. With a Hider's gift I can hide many more people."

"You mean, I could safely leave the sanctuary?" she asked.

"Don't get any ideas," Tenu said.

"Well, not permanently, but I could at least go for a walk in the park? I could see the flowers and feel the breeze!"

"Shery, that's enough." Tenu said firmly. "There are more important things then smelling flowers at stake here."

"Actually, I disagree," Eru objected. "Even with your help, assuming you will give it to me, I don't expect my struggle against Aitrox to end well. It may well be that giving people a few pleasures, and letting them feel human again, is the most important thing I accomplish."

"Then you'll do it? You will use a Hider to give us a chance to go outside?" Shery asked anxiously.

"No, he will not," a new voice said authoritatively. Everyone in the ballroom deferred to the man who had just stepped into the room. Eru however heard his words only as they registered in the minds of others around him. The sanctuary's Hider had arrived. Eru perceived the way others deferred to the man and knew the Hider to be the ruler of the estate.

"Forgive me, Count," Shery said quietly.

"So, the famous Maverick pays us a visit?" Pillay said. "I thought you would be older."

"So, you're a Hider?" Eru asked.

"How do you think I got so much iron?"

"Then you will help me?" Eru asked.

"Why would I help an archos? I am not about to let any archos seize me."

"But, sir!" Tenu objected.

"You're lucky I don't kill you," Pillay said. Eru heard the words through several listening minds.

"Please, don't say things like that within earshot of others. You have no idea how terrible my instincts and reflexes can be," Eru said. He felt the surrounding crowd recoiling from him as if he had a plague.

"You are dangerous. Your coming here could destroy everything I have fought to build," Pillay said angrily.

"But he is fighting our enemy!" someone protested.

"In a battle that cannot be won."

"I say it's better to fight!" Tenu said.

"So did Sonu," Pillay said so calmly one would not have known Sonu's warm body still bled a few feet away. "A lot of good it did him."

"You mother forsaken..." Tenu growled.

"Watch yourself." Pillay cut him short with a dangerous look as their eyes met.

"Forgive me, Count," Tenu said as he ducked his eyes to avert his gaze.

"Just what is it you have built?" Eru asked angrily, answering his own question before Pillay could speak. "Rather than living with the chance of losing the right to choose momentarily, you take it from people for the rest of their lives. In place of the fear of being seized, people here live in fear of discovery and reprisal. Is what you have here really worth protecting?" Eru felt the question work its way into people's minds, like a worm struggling to push through hardened soil.

"Everyone who found their way here chose freedom; freedom from your kind, and the wicked invasion into his most private and sacred moments. Most found my sanctuary, driven by the terror of having been seized. They would rather die than be seized again," Pillay rejoined.

"It's easy for you. You can leave!" Shery objected.

"And you see how often I take that privilege. The only reason I go into the world is to acquire more iron for your protection. There is nothing out there for any of us."

"There is fresh air!" Shery rejoined.

"There are flowers! There is the Deor River!" another person called. Several others spoke their affirmation. Those born in the sanctuary composed the majority of the enthusiastic supporters of the sudden insurrection.

"Would you trade that for safety?" Pillay asked. "Flowers, and a polluted river?"

"They can have both," Eru said. "With your gift, you could give people the chance to feel alive. You could give people a break from their imprisonment."

"And what about your own Hider? Why don't you use him?" Pillay rejoined.

"Because I don't know where he is. Our fight has taken a heavy toll on him," Eru said.

"So, you used up your tool, and you need another one? You expect me to eagerly volunteer to be used up like a candle?"

"I had to protect my team, at times for full days. Even releasing him at night was a risk. Now that we have a shelter, it would be different," Eru answered.

"A shelter I risked my life to build," Pillay said.

"I never claimed otherwise. You have created something amazing here, but it's not what you claim it to be. From here we can really make a difference against Aitrox."

"No, you can't! You cannot beat Aitrox! She has ruled unchallenged for hundreds of years. She has several hundred archos and a few thousand Aegendi. You think that this small group with maybe twenty Aegendi can possibly win? You will get us all killed," Pillay said. Eru recognized the truth in Pillay's words. He wanted to protest and continue the argument, but several hundred lives mattered more than his ego.

"We all know Aitrox will find us and destroy us someday. We can either skulk in here, or we can fight back!" Tenu protested.

"I am with Maverick!" someone from the crowd called. The enthusiasm that name invoked in others juxtaposed the pain it stirred in his own heart. He wished the name could forever die, but knew it would not. Tenu's objection brought the answer Eru had been looking for. This argument had nothing to do with his pride or ego. It had everything to do with these people's right to choose. Their ultimate fate may be set in stone, but Pillay sought to dictate the path to that end with archos-like domination. Eru couldn't stand for that.

"You have always had the power to choose, so you know nothing of what it means to have it taken from you. If you did, you wouldn't run your sanctuary like a prison, controlling these people as much as any archos," Eru answered.

"But it is better this way," Pillay said with a growl.

"Says the one man here who is still free," Eru said.

"Huzzah for Maverick!" someone called. Much to Eru's surprise, the call repeated through the crowd until everyone Eru could sense joined in. He couldn't see into the Count's mind, but he could easily guess what he was thinking.

"Your blood won't be on my hands. You're all fools!" Pillay turned and pushed his way through the crowd to leave. With Pillay's angry departure, the enthusiasm in the group lessened as many loyal to him tried to follow.

"Get away from me!" Pillay scowled.

"Sir," one of them protested.

"You'll get me killed out there! If any of you try to find me, I will kill you," he said as he left. *Not exactly the most affectionate of farewells*, Eru thought. Shery's eyes weren't the only ones who watched Pillay with jealousy. Eru felt people's questions as their leader left them, seemingly for good. Eru had no way of knowing if he would ever encounter Count Pillay again, but he hoped not.

"I don't suppose we have any other Hiders, do we?" Eru asked.

"Of course not. Why would a Hider need a sanctuary?" Tenu asked.

"Of course," Eru said to himself. Where was Oko? "Where is my team?" he asked, realizing that he could not sense them at all.

"I imagine they are still asleep in the front building," Tenu answered.

"But I can't..." Eru suddenly realized the unintended side effect of this sanctuary. While inside iron's protective field, he remained absolutely blind to the world outside. He had envisioned the protection offered by iron to be more like a fortress, giving him tactical advantages and allowing him to spy out his enemy's plans in safety. Instead it served more like a windowless room, leaving him completely unaware of the world outside. If Oko didn't come back, all the iron in the world would mean nothing.

Oko saw the dawn lightening around him, and realized he didn't even feel the need for sleep. The toll of being seized constantly already threatened to rob him of the pleasure of sleep and the freedom to dream. His mind felt spent, but his body no longer understood what it could do about the exhaustion. His eyelids didn't even feel heavy. For all the time he had spent contemplating the three terrible paths to choose from, he was no closer to a decision.

The streets in this part of the city remained still as the day dawned. None here needed to rush into work in the mundane shops and factories. Vendors, chimney sweeps, and street cleaners wouldn't make their way here for another hour at least. Still, Oko spotted a cluster of three people walking away from

Pillay's estate. The one in the middle walked with a familiar awkwardness, as if guided by another set of eyes.

Recognition kindled the fire of life in Oko's mind as he realized what he saw. An archos walked down the street with two pairs of eyes to guide him. In busier streets, two pairs of eyes would have been easy to avoid, but in the emptiness here, Oko felt as naked as a newborn. He would stand out like a lone tree in a field of corn. He quickly ducked behind brass fencing that lined the park. The bars wouldn't hide him, but he had nowhere he could hide in time.

What could an archos want in this part of town? Usually they left the nobility alone, considering them adequately controlled through financial means. This could only mean one thing – an attack on Eru. The fact that the archos apparently survived meant things hadn't gone well for Eru or the others. Oko's eyes watered at the thought of his friends all dead back in Pillay's estate. He hadn't had much opportunity to get to know them, but they had all risked their lives for the cause they believed in. During their evenings together, Oko's exhaustion had kept him from socializing, but somehow he felt a kinship with them that this monster had just destroyed.

Fortunately for Oko, his newest target walked without fear and his seized watchers remained focused on guiding their master's steps. Oko's heart pounded in his chest as his newest quarry passed just a few feet away. Adrenaline filled his veins, invigorating him as the thrill of the hunt returned. Jumping at his prey from behind, Oko grabbed the large archos head and snapped the neck with ease. A bloodless kill lacked the flare and excitement, but after so long it hardly mattered. Oko was alive again. He had avenged his friends, but their deaths decided his path for him. The road ahead felt clear, and for the first time in months, Oko smiled.

CHAPTER 38

SILVERTONGUE

It is easy to look back on Count Pillay with scorn, but he had done something noble and good. He just lost sight of what was truly important and lost control of his own creation. I do not doubt that his initial intentions were honorable. Otherwise he would not have taken such a terrible risk. There is a reason most Hiders cut all ties with anyone close to them. I would soon discover that protecting, feeding and

*hiding several hundred people is no small burden. I can
hardly believe Pillay had managed alone for fifteen years.*

"I can't believe he's gone," a woman named Tara said.

"He'll be back," a refugee named Jetu said.

"I don't know. I don't think I have ever seen him that way before. I think we should take shifts watching... What should we call you?" Tenu asked, turning his attention to Eru.

"My name is Eru, but you should be careful using it. I haven't seized someone for calling me by my name for a while, but it is a challenge every time. I like it when people call me 'Friend.' That is safer."

"Well, I think we should take shifts watching over our friend then," Tenu said.

"Do you really think that is necessary?" Eru asked.

"The Count gave his life to this cause for fifteen years. I don't think he will let it go easily," Jetu answered.

"But, do you think he would resort to violence?" Eru asked.

"I don't know. The Count is more of a schemer normally. Still, he is one of the few people out there who could actually harm you," Tara answered.

"You're probably right. We can't be too careful," Tenu said. "I'll stay awake for the rest of the night. Can one other person stay on watch with me?" Tenu asked. Eru sensed several dissenting thoughts, like 'Who put you in charge?' The thoughts seemed to vanish before Tenu finished his sentence, and several dissenters almost volunteered.

"I will," Tara said with a yawn.

"What about my companions?" Eru asked.

"We will fetch them in the morning. You did say they deserved some rest," Tenu answered.

"Thank you," Eru said. He had never had any need for guards, but he had never knowingly crossed a Hider before either. The realization that a man like Pillay could walk up to him and kill him made Eru nervous. Most archos kept people under their control constantly, making an undetected approach difficult. Eru had refined his awareness, and his prowess as an archos through the discipline of staying in the void, but it could end up costing him. Fortunately, the very differences that drove Eru to avoid seizing people also earned the trust of others. Eru remembered a time, a few years ago, when he had hid under a lamp maker's porch, and the thought of anyone volunteering to protect him would have been nothing more than a cruel joke.

Tenu remained awake through the night, but Eru wondered how attentively he watched. Tara soon drifted to sleep. Eru could feel Tenu's mild irritation at her snoring, and his attempts to let that irritation distract him from deeper, more painful feelings. Eru doubted there would be trouble tonight, and didn't have the heart to demand anything from two volunteers. As things settled down, and the uneasy stillness of a sleeping hive returned, the reality of Tenu's crime settled in. Eru knew without eyes or ears that Tenu sobbed over his mistake. He felt the waves of grief washing over him, bringing back memories of his own terrible loss not too long ago. At least Eru knew not to blame himself for Aymis's death, but Tenu would never have that luxury. Even Janis, who had been the archos' tool to kill her own daughter, could rationally, if not emotionally, forgive herself. Eru wanted to say something to him, but knew that words could offer no consolation, much less words from an archos.

Eru felt how Tenu avoided looking at him, and could hardly blame him. Tenu had, after all, killed his brother due to the initial terror Eru had provoked. It would have been better for Tenu's conscience if Eru had turned out to be the monster Tenu feared. At least that would have given some meager justification to his irrational actions. Tenu knew now that Eru represented hope, and a chance at freedom, but that realization only served to condemn himself further. Eru wished he could tell Tenu that he had acted appropriately for the knowledge he had, even if Eru didn't feel that way. A rational observer would realize that Sonu had returned to the protection of their sanctuary unseized after his first encounter with Eru, yet he voluntarily went back out. A moment's rational thought would have recognized how Sonu carried him, and how he spoke for himself to avoid seizing others. Tenu saw all of that now, but there was nothing rational about the panic of the mob. Tenu deserved blame for his brother's death, but this terrible *sanctuary* was part of the problem.

To Eru, even naming it a sanctuary felt cruel and dishonest. Eru didn't doubt that the sanctuary started out on better footing than it had grown to. However, over time the shelter became a prison and safety became fearful confinement. Fear gave Pillay power and warped his good intentions into something vile. Eru passed the night in the void, commiserating, rebuking and wondering. Would morning bring more trouble? Most of the people in the sanctuary had slept through the small spurt of panic. Eru feared that dawn would leave more people mourning the deaths of their loved ones.

Eru's thoughts fell back on the time when he lived in the villa with his zealots. He remembered how he grew to love the waking world, a sort of emotional sunrise. Today, he felt that sunrise as if it had storm clouds, ominous yet striking and unmistakable. As minds began to wake, the awareness of an unknown but terrible event spread. None who had witnessed the happenings dared broach the subject, as if the first to mention the archos presence would be assumed to be seized.

"Good morning," Tenu said, though he felt to Eru like he didn't believe it. Tenu's bloodshot eyes and red cheeks showed his grief to those who needed eyes to sense it.

"Is it?" Eru asked.

"That remains to be seen," Tenu answered. "This morning, the fate of our little colony hangs by a thread. If I didn't believe I could help, I would have killed myself last night."

Eru wanted to tell him that suicide would solve nothing, but the memories of his own failed attempts stayed his tongue. He had been in those depths where no escape seemed possible. In hindsight he would never have approved of that decision, but he would moderate the judgment he passed on others for contemplating it. "I see. I am glad you have chosen otherwise," Eru answered.

"Unlike most people here, I have never been seized. I came here with my brother after he had been seized and used to kill someone. It was a terrible thing, a random killing done simply for the amusement of the archos."

"So, why did you come with him?" Eru asked.

"Because I was terrified that a similar thing would happen to me. Because I wanted to support my brother. We have always been..." Tenu choked down a sob.

"I am sorry," Eru said, knowing how shallow and foolish his words sounded.

"Anyway," Tenu resumed after a pause, "I think I am an Aegendi."

"Think?" Eru asked.

"A higher percentage of people in the sanctuaries are Aegendi. When an archos kills a rival, there is a chance for the Aegendi to escape. It doesn't happen very often, but you can imagine how they would seek a safe haven."

"Why do you think you are an Aegendi if you haven't been seized?" Eru asked.

"Some of our Aegendi have seen hints in the way people respond to my suggestions. They think I may be a Silvertongue. When a Silvertongue speaks under archos control, his voice carries an intoxicating and powerful influence."

"Yes, I have heard and felt this. I should have known the effect was an Aegendi's power," Eru mused.

"Yes, but even unseized, a Silvertongue's voice can influence people. The escaped Aegendi have told me they can feel that influence in my voice. I could ask someone to punch his wife in the nose, and he would be tempted to do it."

"Well, that depends on the quality of the marriage," Eru joked.

"Hrmph," Tenu grunted in reply. Eru felt a pang of foolishness for the frivolous remark, in light of Tenu's immediate grief.

"Sorry," Eru said.

"A sense of humor won't be enough to calm people down when they see you. I think you are going to need my help," Tenu answered.

"You want me to use your gift to calm people this morning and prevent panic," Eru said.

"Yes. I wouldn't volunteer if it wasn't important."

"If people think you are seized, it will destroy my credibility and could get you killed," Eru replied. He felt Tenu's twinge of longing for that fate in response to his warning.

"Once you release me, I will deny I was seized. Between those denials, and the power of the gift it won't be a problem."

"Maybe not, but the difference would be obvious. Everyone would know you were seized," Eru responded.

"From what I hear, you could simply have me say I am not seized and they would believe it. You and I would be the only ones who know," Tenu responded.

"I don't know," Eru said nervously.

"If you don't, we will have another panic, and more people will die," Tenu continued. "Seize me, Eru." Tenu focused his gaze on Eru's blank white eyes and repeated the command several more times. Eru struggled to resist such a strong assault on the void, but it ultimately proved to be too much.

Eru's mental picture of the sanctuary had been something quite different from the scene that unfolded before him as he saw everything for the first time. His mind had felt the densely packed population and he had envisioned something more like the wretched neighborhoods in the slums. What he saw felt more like a refugee establishment that had overrun the entire wing of a castle. He had seen the front buildings of the Count's estate and knew grounds would be massive, but this exceeded his expectations.

The once ornate and lavish entryway where he had spent the night practically overflowed with stacked crates that covered opulence with stark functionality. The entryway led into a massive pentagon shaped landing with two or three rooms out each side. Stairs took you up to balconies and a second floor of rooms. A makeshift kitchen took up a quarter of the landing area, and rows of tables served as a dining area. Already, several of the morning cooks went about their assigned duties preparing breakfast. In a corner all the necessaries for a large and functional laundry room had been set up. A few people had risen early to beat the daily crowds and get their clothes washed, busily scouring their clothing against the wash boards.

None of the space had been left unused, converting the lavish loveliness into something entirely different, yet beautiful in its own way. The people under Pillay had at least united and made the most of everything they had. Eru had expected refugees to be content with survival, but here they maintained a decent standard of living by many criteria. Sure, space and privacy came at a premium, and each room was lined with bunk beds, but cleanliness prevailed. That isn't to say that every refugee marched with military discipline and predictability. Eru's initial impressions likening the sanctuary to a hive may not have been too far from the truth. Nothing remained still, and now that he had ears to hear, even the relative quiet of morning felt clamorous. Still, everything had an ordered chaos that bespoke unity and purpose.

Were it not for the fear that Eru felt heavily on people's hearts, he would have considered them content, if not happy. Seeing everything kick into activity, Eru suddenly realized the responsibility that had fallen on his shoulders with the Count's departure. All the time organizing and executing his massive festivals and gatherings would hopefully serve him well. Yet, those had been singular moments with time to breathe and regroup between each event. Every day here would probably feel like one of those gatherings, and these people would depend on him.

Eru knew he had to maintain the illusion of remaining in the void, so he had Tenu carry him. Tenu's experiences in the sanctuary instructed Eru about many things. Tenu had even been involved in the remodeling work, revealing the methods they used to make iron protect them. A room could not be considered safe unless it had iron bars in the walls. They spaced them about five feet apart, hiding them behind plaster and paint. The ceilings also had iron rafters spaced in a similar fashion. It must have taken Pillay years to amass that much iron.

Eru guided Tenu past the dining area and up to the balcony. The balcony circled the entire room and the second level had bedrooms where the majority of the refugees slept. Fortunately, those who had risen early worked with enough purpose to pay them little attention. It wasn't until he rang the bell on the balcony that everyone turned their attention to him. The bell was used to call attention for important announcements, and with the dark rumors of the night before, people had been expecting to hear it.

"Everyone," Tenu's voice called. Eru felt its effect pour out over every person in the sanctuary. He hadn't expected that simple word to have such an effect on the hearers, but he felt their adoration as they practically melted in his hands.

Every heart turned towards the speaker, and longed to gain his acceptance. They would do anything to hear another word come from his mouth, and his voice moved them almost as powerfully as archos compulsion. Not only that, but in their minds, Tenu couldn't speak a lie. That simple word 'everyone' had surprising effects. They were all part of this greater collective called "everyone", a fellowship that could never be broken.

With this gift, Eru would never have another enemy. Even the notion as preposterous as a kind archos would become truth to the hearers. The thought of every person under the sound of his voice loving him and longing to be with him struck Eru with tremendous force. For a moment, he wanted it so badly he almost had Tenu cry out that wish immediately. Then, however, he recognized the reality behind the effect it would produce. None of them could love him with the genuine truthfulness that had existed between himself and Aymis. Many of them would have felt ill-treated and manipulated when the effects of the gift wore thin, like something had been taken from them. This gift, called Silvertongue, was perhaps the most terrible thing in all the world. With Tenu's power, Eru could create throngs of zealots who would long to be seized. No, as much as a part of Eru longed for such adulation, he knew in his heart how wrong it would be. At least when he seized someone, they retained their identity.

Eru released Tenu, and both of them gasped, from relief. Everyone below still looked up at them with longing eyes, like children waiting for praise from their father. Eru now knew that he couldn't do what Tenu had proposed. Tenu's gift was far too terrible to be used, even if he believed it to be a just cause. For all the fear that churned in Eru's heart over the use of the gift for good, it couldn't hold a candle to the terrible realization that Aitrox had already made ample use of it for her own purposes. The imposter Maverick was likely one of many who had worked to turn the hearts of the people against him.

Armed with a power like this, Aitrox never had cause for concern as Maverick had waged a campaign of hope. At any moment, Aitrox could turn the entire city against him and negate all the good will he had struggled to build. Worse yet, at any time, Aitrox could turn whole districts of the city into zealous mobs, void of any identity or purpose beyond pleasing her Silvertongues. Eru knew enough about Aitrox to know the flood of death and cruelty she could unleash on Deor at her whim.

CHAPTER 39

STOLEN

Slowly, Aitrox's secrets began to unfold, but rather than illuminate the path ahead, they seemed to pull me deeper into confusion and fear. Iron, for all its promise, left me blind to the world outside. Silvertongues turned out to be one of her more deadly secrets. Some it would turn into mindless zealots, but its power became most terrible on the masses. Mob psychology is a mysterious thing: converting rational people into violent monsters. Add a Silvertongue's influence *to the mix, and a mob takes on a whole new and far deadlier personality.*

"Refugees," Eru called, refusing to seize Tenu, no matter how badly he needed his gift. It felt wrong to win allies through such a manipulative means. "I know you are here because of the evils of my kind. I am fighting to destroy that evil, and free Deor from Aitrox's oppression." Furrowed brows, blank stares and other looks of confusion came from the crowd.

"Is that an archos?" someone asked. Murmurs ran through the crowd like a gust of wind over a field of grass.

"You had better do something," Tenu said quietly to Eru.

"I will not use your gift to cull them and distort their sense of reality."

"That's an archos!" The woman's scream struck like a thunderclap. Thousands of subtle permutations of fear sprung up, summing to something truly terrifying in Eru's perception.

"Looks like you don't have a choice," Tenu said.

"Refugees! I am here in peace! Please!" Eru called in vain. Already he felt the panic growing to lethal intensity, still lacking direction. If anyone's fear threatened Eru then things could easily spiral out of control.

"Tenu's seized!" someone screamed. Hostile eyes pointed at him with lethal intensity. The tragic irony of the circumstance played out painfully in Tenu's mind as he saw himself in the situation his brother had been in a few hours ago.

"Eru, please!" Tenu begged.

"No!" Eru exclaimed. He would not use Tenu's gift, but he had only one other option left. It had been so long since he had tried to test the limits of his strength, he had almost no idea how much he could do on his own.

"Calm down! I mean you no harm!" Just over two hundred voices said in unison, as almost half the crowd settled to a controlled calm. Eru felt the pain and terror he inflicted on each person, and wondered if he could calm the crowd by slapping them in the face like this. Those remaining unseized took pause as the sight of hundreds of their friends seized ratcheted up the heat of their fear. It didn't take long before Eru had either seized or subdued everyone, but he found himself in a singular predicament.

"What are you going to do now?" Tenu asked as he looked over Eru's hand-iwork with his jaw agape. *Burn me, but he's just a kid!* Tenu exclaimed in his mind, forgetting that Eru heard thoughts, not voices. Eru would have smiled in better circumstances, but he needed every ounce of energy to focus on the problem at hand. The longer he seized the crowd, the more it hurt them and cemented his sinister nature in their mind. His power lent itself nicely to brutal domination, but proved woefully inadequate at eliciting cooperation.

"I am sorry, Jetu," Eru said as he relented to necessity.

"My friends, please be still," Tenu's voice called, cooling and soothing their hearts. Several under the sound of his voice fell into a half-asleep daze in obedi-ence to the command. Eru released everyone but Tenu as peace settled into the sanctuary.

"I am your friend. I seized you only to prevent violence. I have found my way here on accident, but know that I am working to free all of Deor from Aitrox's domination," Eru said through Tenu before releasing him. He could not, and would not use this power to directly recruit others to his cause. He knew that even the words he had said had probably unjustly bought him several volunteers.

"Who are you?" a single voice called, sounding coarse and unrefined in every-one's ears.

"I am Maverick," Eru answered with his own voice. It seemed he would never be free of that name or the grief it stirred in his heart.

"Long live Maverick!" Tenu called, thrusting his fist triumphantly in the air. His voice lacked the same irresistible appeal, but a trace of it still remained.

"Long live Maverick!" The call repeated more times than Eru cared to count. For better or for worse, he knew he had the loyalty of hundreds now. It hardly mattered that he had stolen it.

Ketu stepped into his shop with the sort of smile you might expect from a man who wore a fine silk coat and still had plenty of money in his pocket. He brushed the water from his expensive coat nonchalantly. Outside the spring drizzle picked up slightly, pattering on the window with a comforting sound. The silver wings painted on his new sign had done good things for his business. Tyra gave him a quick acknowledging glance, all she could spare as she supervised and inspected the work of the new employees. "Fix that seam," she said with a growl. "Nice work," she said to the next. "Double check your sizing, the shoulders look a bit small," she instructed another.

"Sounds like things are going well," Ketu said as he hung his hat on a hook. He took a moment to admire the painting he had commissioned. The artist had done a masterful job, casting Maverick in rays of light that made his white suit and top hat shine. He even captured Ketu's and Tyra's likenesses well, portraying them as they put a coat over a street urchin's shoulder.

"That's easy for you to say. You haven't been here for two hours already," Tyra sighed in response.

"You don't have to push yourself so hard," Ketu responded.

"You say that, but the orders keep coming in faster than we can keep up."

"So stop taking orders, or create a waiting list," Ketu said.

"If we make people wait that long, they will go somewhere else," Tyra responded.

"And is that such a bad thing? There will be plenty more where they came from. They practically break down our doors, after all." Tyra just grunted her response, the standard ending to the discussion they repeated at least once a day. Ketu had done well enough he could retire comfortably at any time. Tyra wasn't financially strapped by any means, but she couldn't relax yet.

Crash! A muddy rock smashed through the window, bringing a shower of glass and water in with it. A loud thump hit the door to the shop, nearly pushing it open. Tyra ran to the window to see what was going on.

"We've got trouble!" she said as her breathing quickened.

"What do you mean?" Ketu asked. The door to the shop fell open as people poured in, wild looks of anger and hatred on their faces.

"There they are!" one of the intruders shouted as he pointed accusingly at Ketu.

"What do you want from us?" Ketu asked as he backed nervously away.

"Faithless!" another screamed, spurring the angry mob to new heights. Not even the new employees were spared the wrath of the throng as they were pulled away from their work areas.

"Let go of me!" a worker screamed, thrusting his head back into the nose of his attacker. The assailant staggered backwards with a splash of red pouring from his nose and a lethal look in his eyes. Soon two others had the worker by the arms, dragging him out of the shop. His flailing limbs knocked tables and coat racks over. Tyra and Ketu received similar treatment on their way out into the rainy morning. Hundreds of people waited outside, some holding torches that managed to burn despite the weather.

"You're making a mistake! Please!" Ketu exclaimed.

"The silver wings on your sign are enough proof!" the self-appointed leader snarled, and the crowd cheered.

"But, look at this!" another lackey said as he brought the painting out into the rain. The water based paints streaked and smeared in the drizzle, but not in time to destroy the damning evidence.

"He's a supporter of the infidel himself! He even met him!" the ring leader cried out, and angry shouts ran through the crowd. Ketu looked through the mob and recognized several coats of his own making, likely handouts from that day. How could the same people who had received Maverick's generosity turn on him?

"Maverick helped us! He helped some in this crowd! What are you doing?" Ketu objected.

"Faithless!" they screamed. Ketu's words of protest only increased their fury as the masses converged on him. Ketu screamed in terror as he was pulled into the streets. Several of the mobsters threw him into the mud, soiling his fine shirt and knocking his head against the hard ground. He staggered and tried to stand before a savage kick to his ribs dropped him back to the muddy street.

Ketu groaned and stirred. He pushed with his arms in a vain effort to lift himself but fell back to the ground. Mindless but furious hands pulled him up and ripped the muddy shirt from his shoulders. Ketu's head hung weakly but fear shone brightly in his eyes. More angry hands ripped the rest of his clothes off, leaving him naked before the burning hatred of the crowds. Other monstrous faces accompanied a bucket that steamed with every drop of rain that fell into it. They poured the bubbling black pitch over his body, its quiet sizzle unnoticed over Ketu's agonizing screams.

Tyra and the other workers were at least spared the steaming tar, more likely due to a shortage than any feelings of clemency from the mob. Their screams of protest and concern for Ketu added to the terrible wails of Ketu's agony. Soon, their cries of protest turned to screams of pain as angry mobsters violently beat them. Others threw their torches into the shop's broken windows. Before long, flames climbed out the shop windows and up the front walls. Unfortunately for the neighbors, their attached homes and shops soon caught fire as well. The rain fell on the fire in a futile attempt to subdue the growing holocaust.

"Curses to Maverick! Curses to the faithless who call him their friend!" A powerful voice called over the tumult. Even as Ketu writhed in agony, those words took hold in his heart. He deserved this for daring to affiliate with Maverick. Ketu trembled in agony as he tried to rise and join his brothers in their cause, but pain overwhelmed him, and he collapsed back to the muddy street.

"There are more faithless out there!" someone called.

"Let's show them the fate Aitrox has in store for those who betray her!" Angry cries to the affirmative echoed through the mob and they flowed away like a single amorphous entity. Ketu raised his head to watch as the mob left, wishing he could follow. Desperately he reached in their direction, longing to stay near that beautiful voice. Not far from him, Tyra wobbled to her feet and attempted to follow them before falling to the ground with a painful cry. Tyra crawled over to Ketu's black, steaming body. The swelling around her right eye left it closed. She touched him but pulled back with a hiss of pain. So hot! Ketu groaned quietly with slow, shallow breaths. Tyra wept bitterly as she looked at her boss and friend through her one open eye. The spring rain continued its vain attempts to extinguish the flames as they spread through several blocks of the city.

CHAPTER 40

LIVING IS AT STAKE

Even after less than a day in the sanctuary, a certain discomfort settled on me. You would expect the opposite, and in many ways the protection was comforting. However, in other ways I felt like an ostrich with my head in the sand. I hadn't realized how terrifying the unknown can be. Aitrox lurked outside, like a grizzly bear just outside the hunter's tent, held at bay by meager camouflage. I had no way to safely operate against her, but loathed every idle hour.

"Can someone please take me to my team members?" Eru asked.

"I'll take you!" About twenty people volunteered simultaneously. Eru tried not to cringe at their excessive willingness. He had practically converted them into zealots.

"Just three people, and only those who have authorization to leave," Eru responded. He felt the disappointment in several minds. Pillay had been wise to be cautious about those he let out in the open with their secret. Everyone hoped for sweeping changes with Pillay gone, but Eru wasn't about to disregard his prudence.

If anything, the first change people were likely to see would probably be hunger. Nobody knew all of Pillay's contacts he used to buy the food to feed hundreds. Eru didn't have access to Pillay's funds, meaning he likely would have to acquire money through his regular means, but how to buy and move that much food without drawing scrutiny?

"Tenu, you stay here," Eru said. Everything Tenu's gift represented made Eru's skin crawl. He couldn't fault the man for it, but that didn't change the fact that he didn't want him around. "Jana, Kilu and Rono, can you please take me?" Eru asked. He knew their dark secrets, and the blood they had all shed to protect the sanctuary, but he preferred their company to a Silvertongue. In some strange way, Eru felt a kinship with them. He too had blood on his hands, often due to impossible choices where no acceptable option presented itself.

Rono hefted Eru into his arms easily and the four of them set out. To Eru's senses, emerging from the sanctuary felt akin to a deep cave explorer's sudden return to brilliant sunlight, blinding, bewildering and refreshing. Unfortunately for Eru, the world he sensed had taken a terrible turn. Hatred and anger fermented throughout the city, directed towards Maverick and those who were affiliated with him. He felt the misery and sorrow that Aitrox had wrought through Silvertongues of her own. Ketu's shop lay in ashes, and Ketu barely fared better. Eru felt his pain and despair as a terrible low amidst the chaos.

Huge roving mobs felt like terrible hot coals rolling through the city and setting homes and lives ablaze. Their hatred for Maverick had reached that level where Eru had to struggle against his protective reflexes. He knew that revealing himself now would prove fatal.

More tragic, and perhaps more justified, was the hatred the innocent victims felt towards Maverick. He had brought this fate on them. He had dared oppose Aitrox, bringing down her stern cruel hand like an abusive parent. How could he have expected any outcome other than this?

Eru wanted to console the countless victims of Aitrox's cruelty. He understood the growing anger towards him. He knew Aitrox's nature better than most, and knew to expect reprisals. He had expected her to simply seize and kill him when she tired of his exploits. Oko's gift as a Hider had protected him from her fury, and Eru hadn't stopped to think how else she might direct her rage. Even so, he would not take the blame for her wickedness. She wrought death and misery whether or not any opposed her. It had to end, even if the road to liberation was dark and terrible. Still, his heart broke for each victim of her malice. The full scale of Deor's plunge into anarchy and terror flooded over Eru as his powerful archos mind emerged from the sanctuary.

"No, no! By the maker, no!" Eru exclaimed as all of the terrible sensations rushed over him.

"What's wrong?" Jana asked.

"Deor is burning," Eru answered with a quiet sob.

"What?" Kilu asked.

"Mobs are rioting, burning down homes and shops of anyone suspected to support Maverick," Eru said.

"That's terrible," Rono said. Eru felt each of them rein in their angry curses, hopefully early enough to prevent drawing any attention. He had chosen his companions wisely.

"There's nothing we can do about it right now. We should hurry so we can get back to safety," Kilu said, ignoring the angry glare from Jana.

"He's right," Eru said. "I need to get back to the safety of the sanctuary before the anger of the mob overpowers me. If I seize even one of them, we will be revealed. We must hurry."

"Quick, take him to the sanctuary! I will go find his friends." Kilu ordered. Eru wasn't surprised that he took charge, nor that Jana and Rono submitted like pups.

"Where are your team members?" Kilu asked again.

"Probably in different bedrooms in the main building," Eru answered.

"Just seize them and bring them here!" Rono snapped.

"No, I need to get back into protection, now!" Eru growled. The veins on his head bulged with exertion as he fought back his instincts. Meanwhile, the fury of the mobs rose to a terrible crescendo.

"Hurry!" Jana snapped. Eru could feel the fear rising in their minds. Fortunately, they hadn't ventured far from safety, and it took only moments to return to iron's protection.

"Thank you. Please, find my friends quickly."

"We will find them," Kilu said reassuringly.

"Please, give them a choice," Eru implored.

"There's only so much choice we can give them. Whether we tell them about the sanctuary at first or wait until they get here, doesn't matter. Once they know, they can't leave," Rono said.

"We'll do our best," Kilu reassured Eru.

Tenu approached the group. "What happened? You are back quickly."

"I had to get back to safety," Eru explained.

"What's wrong?"

"Angry mobs are killing my supporters and burning down entire districts of the city. My reflexes nearly gave us away."

"You did well to get back then," Tenu answered. "Where are you three going?"

"We still have to go find his friends," Jana explained.

"What? It's not safe!" Tenu objected.

"It is as safe for them as anyone. I was a risk because of my awareness, and the risk I might accidentally seize one of the mobbers. My friends are unsafe out there," Eru answered.

"Fine, go, but come back quickly. I don't like this at all," Tenu grumbled. Eru felt the threesome disappear, and his awareness of Tenu increased. Fresh memories of the intoxicating effect of Tenu's gift tantalized and invited Eru to seize him, even while the same thought sickened him. He felt the memory of people's adulation and acceptance like a rare delicacy's aftertaste. He felt the disgust at the falsity and wrongness of stealing their loyalty like a quiet voice telling him *no*. Never had Eru felt such a powerful pull to seize another, or such a vile revulsion at the thought.

"How much iron do we have available?" Eru asked.

"Not much. We recently added a room to the sanctuary. Why?" Tenu asked.

"Do we have a forge?"

"No. Pillay worked the iron himself, somewhere outside the sanctuary."

"We will need a forge inside the sanctuary, and I will need some iron to work with," Eru said.

"What do you have planned?" Tenu asked.

"I won't know until I can work the iron and learn what I can," Eru answered. He felt Tenu's curiosity pique, but Eru wouldn't say what he hoped to accomplish. He wouldn't get everyone's hopes up. Just having people construct a forge and decommission the new room to get him some iron would raise some eyebrows for sure. His powerful mind began working over the possibilities and experiments he would conduct. He had lots of work to do, but not much time.

Eru set the refugees to work immediately constructing a forge. A kitchen's oven would suffice with some modifications, though not without some substantial inconveniences. Even with the lingering effects of Tenu's gift, frustration rippled through the sanctuary with the news. Fortunately, Eru had scoured a blacksmith who had worked iron in what felt like a previous life. He still remembered the metal's unique properties. He knew the temperature he needed to soften it, and just as importantly, purify it. Most likely, Pillay had purified their iron already, but Eru would have to be sure.

Eru could hardly contain his anticipation to finish the forge, a chore that moved slowly at first as he tried to do it without seizing anyone. He eventually gave up such a ridiculous notion, and seized a volunteer to be his hands and eyes in the job. Converting the oven would require some clever improvisations, but Eru had the benefit of several vocations from which to draw knowledge. With the skill of a master mason, he worked the ovens' bricks to his needs. With the knowledge of a master leather worker, he created an improvised bellows from leather gleaned from one of the couches brought in from an unprotected room. It came together quickly, but Eru's anticipation showed in his twiddling fingers and excited smile.

It had been a long time since he had worked with someone's hands, and it felt incredible. Not since Jeo's last day alive had he worked with fire and heat, harnessing it to his needs. Had Eru been born a regular child, he suspected he would have found his way to a blacksmith's shop as an apprentice. Of all the vocations he knew, the primal experience of harnessing fire to put metals to use brought him the greatest satisfaction. Eru's excitement to return to the fire and anvil only partially explained his sense of urgency. iron had probably saved his life this morning, but Eru needed it to do so much more.

Eru focused so intently on his project, he didn't even notice as Janis, Volo, Rose and Supe entered the sanctuary. He hardly noticed their bewilderment as the implications of everything they saw settled in.

"We're free, Rose. Aitrox cannot touch us here," Volo said to his sister.

"It's wonderful," Rose answered.

"Rose, we don't have to fight any more," Volo said with a look of relief on his face.

"Eru needs us still," Rose rejoined.

"Why? We are free. I say we leave good enough alone."

"Do you think that Aitrox doesn't try to find and destroy places like these? You heard the warnings about protecting the secret. There is more fear than freedom in a place like this," Rose replied.

"But..." Volo protested.

"You do what you want, but this gives us what we need to continue the struggle," Rose said.

"Rose, stop!" Volo snapped. "This isn't you!"

"What isn't me?" she asked.

"All this talk of fighting and destroying Aitrox."

"How can you say that?" she asked in objection, not giving him time to answer. "It would be unkind of me to sit idly in relative safety when I have the opportunity to change the world."

"I knew you would say something like that," Volo said quietly.

"Volo, you are not so different from me. You put on an uncaring front, but you have stayed by my side through everything," Rose answered, putting a hand on his shoulder.

"I promised Father I would look after you."

"But, you believe in our cause," Rose said, almost a question with her tone of voice.

"I hate Aitrox, but I don't want to die."

"We all die," Rose said.

"Well that's a cheerful thought," Volo answered sarcastically.

"My point is that dying is not in question. It's living that is at stake."

"Did Mother tell you that?" Volo asked.

"I can think for myself," Rose chastised.

"It's living that's at stake huh? I kind of like that," Volo answered.

"If you call permanent imprisonment in a crowded shelter living, then be my guest," Rose said.

"Well, do you call fighting a losing battle full of fear and certain defeat living?" Volo asked.

"I call trying to make the world better living," Rose answered.

"Did Mom tell you that too?" Volo asked. "Hey, I am kidding!" he said hastily in response to her glare. "You really have grown up."

Janis ignored their conversation, absorbed in her own thoughts. She looked around silently, struggling to suppress the painful, hypothetical situations that a place like this had brought to mind. If only they had discovered a place like this sooner. The sudden notion of freedom from the archos threat hurt, with the pain of a gift that arrived too late for her daughter. To Janis, this place brought no joy. Only the realization that she could freely contemplate revenge, the only joy left to her, could bring a misunderstood smile to her face.

Supe looked around with her dazed uncomprehending eyes, but a smile settled on her face and the tension faded from her shoulders when she spotted Eru. "Eru, Friend," Supe said as she wandered through the crowds to him. Eru continued his work, unaware of Supe's approach.

"Bring me some iron," Eru commanded with his own voice. Tenu had anticipated the request, and brought the single unused bar of iron to him. By now, Eru had seized several people, and he had them working the forge with perfectly choreographed precision. Eru took the iron with one pair of hands while another worked the bellows to stoke the flames. People stepped away with raised arms to fend away the heat that Eru loved. With a few loud clanks the iron bent to his will. With more time in the heat, Eru had molten iron ready to be molded to his desires. "Let's see what secrets you can show me," Eru said with a voice laden with anticipation.

CHAPTER 41

COUNTER

Iron's ability to block the archos senses proved different than I had hoped. True, you could wear it and enjoy personal immunity, assuming you didn't mind a painfully conspicuous thirty pound helmet. Small quantities did almost nothing. In order to continue, I needed more iron, a lot more iron. We had iron, but it came at a high cost. Space was a rarity in our sanctuary, and it didn't go over well when I took a room away. With that much iron, I was ready to try *something risky. The war had begun in earnest. I couldn't work directly against the mobs without being exposed, but I had enough Aegendi to strike back.*

T he heavy afternoon rains doused the fury of the mobs, sending most of them home soaked and dazed. Unfortunately, the fires they had started couldn't be quenched so easily. It would be several hours before the flame's appetite for destruction would be sated. In the meantime, the scorched trail left behind quickly became a quagmire in the intensifying downpour. Thousands were left homeless, having lost everything in a terrible moment. Most stood out in the rain, having no shelter, and lacking the mental clarity to seek refuge. Tears ran from many eyes, but the rain concealed them. Husbands tried in vain to comfort wives. Children old enough to understand cried from the terror of the day, and those too young to understand followed their example willingly.

Despite the rain, the smell of smoke and fire filled the air, and the black, muddy ash seemed to find its way onto every face. Sorrow dominated the hearts of the people, but anger made a strong campaign for the runner up. Maverick had brought this upon them. Maverick had the audacity to provoke their High Queen. It was one thing not to love the goddess who controlled their lives, but who in their right mind would oppose her? Those who had shown support for him felt betrayed. Where was he when they needed him? Why didn't he protect them?

True, Maverick had never promised protection, and had warned everyone of the dangers of helping him. Yet, it was Maverick who stirred hope in their hearts: a dangerous emotion. Having never known it, they felt powerless to resist its appeal, and Maverick dispensed hope like candy to children. Maverick took them to new heights, only to abandon them in their time of need.

Eru didn't feel any of the festering malcontent as the large cargo wagon that concealed him and his Aegendi rolled by. The iron frame gave them a mobile sanctuary, the next best thing to having a Hider to work with. The heavy clouds hung so low, the tops of the tallest citadels remained shrouded in mist. The same heavy clouds concealed two dark, winged creatures as they followed the wagon. The heavy cloak that covered the wagon driver held the rain at bay. The wagon rolled through the ruined districts, not even eliciting a curious look from the downtrodden and destitute.

Tenu looked out at the scene of destruction, grateful the cloak hid the terrified look on his face. For all his talk about wanting to fight, he hadn't ever expected to do anything about it. Now he directed their war wagon to its first destination. Someone in the wagon handed him slips of paper with directions to their next location written on them. Tenu focused on the minute details of the two horses hauling the wagon to keep his mind away from thoughts that could end their operation before it started. The rain dripped down the horses' muscular shoulders as they strained to pull the heavy wagon through the muddy streets. Black sooty mud stained their legs, splashing with every step. He noticed the way one horse's ear twitched whenever a rain drop hit it. On occasion a shudder rolled through the beast's body as it shook water from its face. Tenu had never cared much for horses, but he was grateful for them now. Anything to keep his thoughts away from his fear.

Tenu read the next slip of paper. Twenty-three Miraye Boulevard was two blocks away, and very close to a citadel. Everyone on the wagon knew what awaited them at their destination, but he couldn't decide what scared him more, the thought of being seized by Eru, or making an open assault on a citadel. Only Aegendi volunteered, and their sanctuary had an unusually high concentration of Aegendi. Five Wizards, counting Volo; three Prophets, including Janis; four Immortals; three Brutes counting Rose, Tenu the Silvertongue and two Hawkeyes. The wagon rolled to the designated corner and Tenu read the next instruction: Stop.

Eru felt the fear in his volunteer army with particular intensity. Enclosed in this portable sanctuary, only fifteen people existed in Eru's world, and they filled his awareness completely. Rose, Volo and Janis knew what to expect, but the prospect of operating without a Hider's protection still cast a shadow of fear on the day's plans. Although everyone in the assault team had volunteered, peer pressure was the only thing holding some of them firm to their cause. If any of them could have known the fear that festered in their neighbor's heart, Eru suspected the whole wagon would abandon the cause. Without a Hider, Eru could hardly blame them. The wagon could get them to their destination, but they were taking a terrible risk.

Most in the wagon knew little of the risk that drew closer with every bump of the wagon. Every time the wagon stopped, Janis handed another set of instructions to Tenu from her place in front. Eru remained tucked under Tenu's bench, ready to pop his head through an opening next to Tenu when the time arrived. His experiments proved that he could sense the world outside unhindered once his head cleared the iron frame. For a brief moment his Aegendi would be lost to him, but they had their instructions to exit the wagon immediately. Finally, the wagon rolled to a stop and the terrifying wait ended.

"It's time," Janis said with a hungry and scared look in her eyes that fell short of inspiring the others. Eru popped his head straight up. An odd lump appeared in the seat cushion next to the driver as Eru's head pushed clear of the iron frame, the seat cushion kept Eru's head concealed. They hoped that concealing him as much as possible would buy them time, though Eru had his doubts. Eru waited to feel the return of his Aegendi. The awareness of the full world left him surprisingly disoriented after a week in his little microcosm. Even several hundred minds in the sanctuary couldn't compare to the bustling activity of the full city. He felt the pain and anger towards Maverick, calmed from its initial intensity but firmly entrenched in their hearts. He felt the furor of devotion kicked up inside the citadel as a Silvertongue worked his wickedness. The time to strike had arrived.

Despite the fullness of the world, and thousands of beings all around him, Eru felt terribly naked and alone. Where were the Aegendi? Why were they waiting?

"Go! What are you waiting for?" Janis shouted at them. Inside the iron frame, her efforts and her anger remained hidden from Eru.

"We can't do it," Royo, one of the new Wizards, said with a whimper.

"We aren't soldiers," another confirmed.

"We don't have a choice!" Janis growled. "Go!"

"Well, if you are so brave, you go!" Royo commanded.

"Fine! Rose, Volo, let's get this over with!" Janis said with a growl. Rose looked back at her with fear in her eyes.

"But we don't have a Hider," Rose said in a fearful gasp.

"Worthless, all of you!" Janis growled as she jumped out of the wagon. Eru seized her immediately. She saw the rest of the Aegendi remaining in the wagon, paralyzed by fear. A moment later, she saw a terrible future only a few seconds away.

"Yaaaaw!" Tenu screamed as he kicked the horses forward in a vain effort to escape what she had seen. Janis felt the powerful pull of his voice, and even that simple command filled her with a burning desire to kick to a full sprint. Apparently the power of his voice worked equally well on the horses, as they furiously pulled the heavy wagon, but it wasn't enough. A heavy piece of stone struck the wagon, just catching the back end. The wagon spun and toppled to its side. The passengers inside screamed with the sudden impact. Had the wagon been normally constructed, the impact would have demolished the whole back end, but the reinforced iron frame had undoubtedly saved a few lives.

Tenu fell to the hard stone without a scream, landing awkwardly. Janis suspected his arm broke with the fall, but he wouldn't scream while seized. "Get out now!" Tenu's voice commanded, and all the Aegendi willingly obeyed. Janis's legs carried her to the wagon, but her eyes scanned the citadel and surrounding buildings for any signs of another attack. Her arms pulled Eru from the wagon, and Tenu's eyes checked him for injury. Aside from some minor scrapes and bruises from the wagon's tumbling, he had fared well enough.

Janis's eyes saw several new attacks before they happened, but their five Wizards easily prevented them. Eru kept Janis behind to use her eyes as protection for their assault force. The toppled wagon would never see another ride, destroying a critical part of their plans. Eru had counted on keeping their wagon moving through the city to keep them hidden while he controlled the Aegendi. Immobility left them terribly vulnerable and exposed. Rose and the other Brutes each ripped an iron bar from the wagon frame and headed into the citadel with the unnatural speed their strength gave them. The Immortals led the charge, a terrible sort of shield against most threats. The Prophets also moved in. With Eru's powerful mind backing them, even the Hawkeyes became terrible weapons. No detail escaped their notice, giving them a different sort of predictive ability. They could see any threatening object as if time slowed down, and recognize the warning signs to any strike before it fell. The terrible task force moved in for the kill, but Eru hadn't counted on a single, terrible, yet simple tactic his enemy would employ.

Oko watched the angry mobs setting fire to his city with a dangerous edge to his anger. Even with Maverick dead, Aitrox would use his name for her wickedness, it seemed. It wasn't enough for her to simply kill him, she had to crush any spark of hope he may have sown. He clenched his teeth, hearing them grinding in his ears. He had heard of the Aegendi called Silvertongues, but never would he have guessed of their terrible power. He had even felt them on occasion, learning quickly to avoid any citadel that had one preaching. He almost found himself loving Aitrox after one sermon, only barely resisting their terrible influence. Perhaps his gift as a Hider had provided him some unusual resistance to their power, because that terrifying realization broke the influence long enough for him to escape.

Today however, fate had placed a new challenge before him. Aitrox had taken it too far this time. The archos driving these Silvertongue had to die. The maelstrom that filled the city made everything difficult. Avoiding the roving mobs, both for his safety and his sanity, slowed him. They flowed unpredictably, often cutting him off, and in several cases nearly setting the city ablaze around him. Someone with less skill in surreptitious movements probably wouldn't have managed, but eventually Oko made his way to the citadel.

By the time he reached it, the building practically burst with the crowds that swelled out the doors. People stood within, packed like cattle in a slaughterhouse. Usually crowds served his purposes, but the unpredictable nature of a mob gave him pause. He owed it to Eru to do this, and take this risk. He knew he would die someday fighting the archos. It may as well be today, and it may as well be in an attempt to protect the honor of his deceased friends. Oko pushed into the crowds, feeling them pressing in on all sides.

"Down with the faithless!" people called in so many different strains that the single sentence gave the false sense of active conversations. Nobody in the building said anything more than that, and even Oko added to the clamor to avoid notice. Oko hoped that the Silvertongues remained in the city going about their terrible work; better there than here. If he killed their archos, it would come to an end for now.

"You have done well!" a voice called, bringing the clamor to a quiet silence. Oko stopped in his tracks, content to bask in the approbation of that beautiful voice. He had done something wonderful, though he could hardly imagine what. It didn't matter, so long as that voice approved. How could Oko have possibly thought about destroying something so beautiful? So precious and even sacred?

"Down with the faithless!" they cheered in unison, and even Oko's voice carried conviction.

"What?" the voice asked, and everyone looked around like confused children. "Aitrox has smiled on us, and given us another chance to prove our devotion. Maverick is outside right now. Destroy him!" the voice called.

"Death to Maverick!" they screamed, bloodlust burning in their eyes.

"Death to Maverick!" Oko shouted. "Death to Maverick?" he asked aloud, as the realization settled in. "Maverick is already dead." The contradiction broke the voice's hold on him, and reminded him of his purpose. Seeing the pull the voice exerted on others, Oko again suspected that his gift offered him some protection from the power. Still, he felt the urge to run with the mobs and kill whatever unfortunate being had been labeled as Maverick. "Death to Aitrox," Oko muttered under his breath as the crowds rushed out the doors.

Outside, Eru's Aegendi advanced on the citadel, but the Prophet's vision warned them of the unexpected. Hundreds of furious, bloodthirsty people poured from the structure. Eru pulled each of his advancing Aegendi high into the air in retreat. The furious crowd ignored them, focused on the toppled wagon. Eru could feel the frenzy in their hearts and their lethal intent. His protective instincts took over, and the frontrunners hurled themselves to the ground to be trampled by those who followed behind. Still, the mob advanced with terrible speed.

Eru's Wizards lifted his team high into the air, just in time to save them from the clutches of the rushing mob. The vanguards stumbled as confusion and surprise tripped them up. They shouted angry oaths and threats up at Eru and his Aegendi. With the immediate danger passed, Eru hurled rocks through the citadel's windows and sent in his counter attack, all the while keeping the rest of his crew moving through the misty air. Then something he should have expected, but hadn't dared plan for, happened. The archos in the citadel had proven to be an equal enough match to Eru that neither could simply seize the other, but Eru should have known that Aitrox would be watching.

He felt her seize him with the terrible force of a tornado ripping up a sapling. All the pride and sense of his growth meant nothing against such might. He could live for centuries in the void and scarcely compare to her. Now it would come to an end, as he had always known it would. With Aitrox in control of his Wizards, they all plummeted toward rooftops several hundred feet below. Gravity, it seemed, would be all she needed to kill him.

CHAPTER 42

GASPING FOR AIR

Exactly how I survived this second encounter with Aitrox would remain a mystery for some time. For the time being, I operated in ignorance to Aitrox's enemies, believing them to be few and far between. Organized opposition had always seemed impossible, and the relative newness of the sanctuary to my world meant that all of its implications hadn't set in. Aitrox never feared the sanctuaries, knowing they posed no real threat to her. On this fateful day I caught a fleeting

and mysterious glimpse into the only thing Aitrox feared.
Fortunately, it saved my life as well as the lives of my
friends.

E ru felt Aitrox's presence in his mind like a raging lion among a herd of
sheep. The rooftops and pavement couldn't come fast enough. If Eru
was going to die, he at least hoped it would happen before she laid bare the
secret of the sanctuary. He had been a fool to try an attack without permanent
protection, but iron could never provide that. The best he could ever hope for
with iron was the ability to move in secrecy, a powerful tool, but not enough
against a being as intensely aware of the city as Aitrox.

Aitrox's hatred and wickedness left Eru feeling sullied, like a clean sheet fallen
from a drying line into the mud. Her presence in his mind sickened and repulsed
him as much as it terrified him. She saw all humans as insects. Some she could
put to her purpose like a farmer who knew the praying mantis to be a friend,
but most scarcely deserved her regard, and pests were to be crushed without
compunction. Eru felt her regard for him as she crushed him without thought
or concern. If anything, he had become a small stinging fly in her regard, never
a serious threat but something to loath for the small sting he could inflict. He
mattered so little, that simply letting gravity do the work seemed more effort
than Aitrox wanted to expend.

Eru felt the minds of all his Aegendi, and felt himself wielding their power
against his will. Apparently, Aitrox intended to keep his Aegendi alive to become
part of her innumerable army of slaves. That meant that their secrets would be
discovered soon enough one way or the other. Eru watched through their eyes as
their descent slowed and he plummeted away from them, quickly disappearing
into the mists.

Suddenly, Aitrox's presence vanished so abruptly it left Eru totally disoriented. He still retained control of his Aegendi, but the unexpected liberation
caught him completely off guard. Nobody he had seized could see him through
the mist and Eru had nothing to stop his fall. He quickly seized several people

from the angry masses surrounding the citadel and tried to find where he would emerge from the low hanging clouds, but knew he didn't have enough time. He didn't need sight, hearing or touch to feel the speed with which he toppled to his doom. Fortunately, the terrible holes he had poked through his ear back in Jordan's shop hadn't destroyed those delicate bones that provided him with an awareness of his orientation and movement.

It was only through that awareness that Eru knew something had changed. He felt his velocity slowing but had no senses available to discern how or why. Somehow, his descent slowed with enough force to jar his head and rattle his awareness of the world, but it was a decidedly better alternative to the sudden stop the rooftops or street would have provided. He thought he sensed a being of some sort near him, but the comprehension eluded him with a sort of foggy uncertainty he had never felt before. It reminded him somewhat of how he would perceive an animal, though he had never found one with enough innate intelligence to feel this clear, yet nebulous, to his mental sight.

He realized he had come to a complete stop now, triangulating his location as best he could through his connection to several people he had seized. Several eyes looked in his general direction in time to catch a fleeting glimpse of a large dark shape vanishing back into the mists above. What had just happened? Why did Aitrox suddenly let him go? What had stopped his descent?

Aitrox returned, seizing him with a fury he had never known. He had grown in her estimation from being something to eliminate at her casual leisure to something menacing and fearful. Whatever it was that just happened terrified her and as a result gave Eru hope. Fear implied vulnerability, an attribute he had never before associated with Aitrox. If only he could understand what she feared and why. So many secrets, but he realized now that secrecy implied vulnerability as well. So many secrets meant so many weaknesses. Iron had proven to be a weak link in her practically invulnerable armor. How did the other mysteries she guarded so carefully relate, and how could they be discovered and put to use against her?

Eru didn't feel his own hands at his throat, but that innate awareness of his being told him what was happening. He felt his capacity dimming, surmising correctly he would soon be unconscious. Eru didn't have much time left.

Then something severed her connection with him like a swift clean cut of a guillotine's blade. Eru gasped for breath physically and mentally, relishing the freedom he hadn't expected, leaving him dazed, sputtering but at the same time intensely aware of the unexpected new lease on life. What was happening?

Eru tried to put his Aegendi to good use, but Aitrox returned with the same furious intensity. The terrifying cycle continued with the regularity of waves battering a lone rock at high tide. It felt similar to a man being repeatedly dunked in water, brought to the point of suffocation and pulled out at the last moment. Even if Eru had the capacity to endure such battering indefinitely, something had to be done about the angry mob that had now spotted him. He felt their lethal intent moving towards him, but never had enough time to act on as the cycle of seizure and liberation continued.

"There he is!" someone shouted, pointing.

"Death to Maverick!" another exclaimed with a lethal fire in his eyes. Supporting cheers rolled through the masses as they moved closer. Soon they surrounded him, but even the Silvertongue's power couldn't overcome a lifelong dread of archos so easily.

Oko fought the flow of the crowds like a fish swimming upstream as he pushed through the doors into the citadel. This would be the riskiest moment for him, but Oko felt compelled to move forward. Innocent people would not die because of his hesitation.

If he survived this moment, Oko knew he would need time to sort out his unexpected behavior. He had killed many innocent people to protect his secret. His brief time with Eru had changed him more than he would have guessed, but Oko didn't expect to live long enough to reflect on this change. He pushed through the door with reckless abandon. A small mass of people circled his prey, forming a human shield. Their eyes moved with that uncanny unison that he recognized instinctively. All of their eyes settled on him, and he knew he had been detected. Oko ducked behind a statue of Aitrox just in time. Something collided with the door behind him, blasting through it and leaving a grey hole into the dim rainy world outside. Another smashed into the statue, breaking Aitrox's arm off at the elbow. The rush of the moment filled Oko and he smiled. Let the hunt begin, he thought.

Oko knew he could not win this fight, especially with only two daggers, a far cry from his usual arsenal. He had no hooks or ropes to free him from the two-dimensional world gravity imposed on all but birds and fish. He had to keep moving, knowing that a crafty archos can curve projectiles around obstacles with their Wizards. If he stayed in any one place for long, the Wizard would find him. Oko braced himself to take a leap, hoping to catch his foe by surprise and find new cover.

The windows to the citadel exploded, the clamor of the shattering glass ringing in Oko's ears. He reflexively ducked and put his hands up protectively. Cobblestones from the street outside smashed into the tile floors of the citadel, leaving a trough of broken tiles in their path. Not far behind them, several people flew into the citadel, moving with the full freedom Oko longed for. Their arrival couldn't have come at a better time. Oko watched as a tile fragment burst through the first person to land with a gruesome, crimson spray. The person barely staggered, but kept moving forward. An Immortal! Oko could hardly believe it. He had heard of the epic struggle between rival archos, but had never expected to be caught in the middle.

Things didn't look good for his prey now. By Oko's count he saw at least two Immortals, two Brutes and likely one or two Prophets. Oko couldn't guess why an archos with so many Aegendi would bother with an obviously inferior opponent, but he didn't pretend to understand the insanity of the ruling archos. A familiar looking young woman brandished a twisted iron bar, moving with the speed and strength of a Brute. She stopped short of smashing through the human barrier.

"Rose?" Oko asked himself. He didn't dare draw too much attention, but he could hardly believe his eyes. Could it really be Maverick outside? How was that possible?

Oko watched in disbelief as several more Aegendi flew in through the broken windows. He had never seen so many at a time. Oko knew he had his answer now. Eru couldn't possibly have marshaled so many Aegendi in such a short time. Oko may have killed the archos that killed Eru, but that archos must have been an underling of one of Aitrox's higher ranking rulers. His heart went out to Rose, Janis, Volo and even Supe for the fate that must have befallen them. The thought of his friends enslaved by an archos set his heart ablaze. Any indecision evaporated before the fire in his heart. Oko knew he had no chance against this new foe. The fact that this newcomer sent this many Aegendi in spite of the horde of angry people outside meant he likely had more Aegendi to protect him. Oko didn't care.

The spectacular, chaotic battle between the archos gave Oko the perfect cover. The greatest threat to him now was the barrage of lethal debris cast back and forth by the opposing Wizards. It was impossible to predict when they would come, or in what direction each object would be deflected. Fortunately, Oko closed the distance quickly. Oko cut his way through the wall of people protecting the archos, cutting them down like a gardener trimming errant branches. In a moment his prey fell and the unity in the wall of people dissipated. They scattered in terror, some falling to the sides of those Oko had just slain. He had seen similar sights many times before, and heard their mournful cries uncounted times. This time, however, it sunk into his heart unlike any time past. Eru wouldn't have wanted that for them.

Oko filed the regret away for now, not expecting to live long enough to think on it more. Oko had a new target now, and a new goal. He would likely die before getting close to the archos assaulting the citadel, but Eru's friends – his friends – deserved freedom. Daggers in hand, he bolted for the exit.

Blood stained Oko's vest, hands and shirt. Such a conspicuous sign of murder wouldn't serve him well, but he didn't have time to worry about it now. Outside, he saw a toppled wagon and a swarm of people surrounding it. Suddenly, several people plummeted to the cobbled streets roughly, but not hard enough to be lethal. Oko recognized Janis, and memories of his last encounter with her deadly predictive power. She almost killed him the first time.

Janis looked at him, and excitement, even relief flashed in her vision. The next moment, anger and lethal intent hardened her gaze. She took a few steps in his direction before stumbling. Catching herself quickly, she looked again at Oko, desperation in her eyes.

"I need you, Oko!" she exclaimed. The lethal glare snapped back into place, and she dashed in his direction. What was going on? What did she mean? Could her words even be trusted? As Janis neared, Oko saw her dagger and knew there would be no dodging her first slash. No amount of skill could surpass the power of a Prophetess under archos control. Janis's arm recoiled in preparation for the murderous strike when the lethal intent vanished from her eyes and the blow never fell.

"Oko, please. Open your mind to me!" Janis exclaimed. "It's me, Eru!"

"Eru, seize me!" Oko called. He never thought he would welcome the return to archos dominion so fully.

CHAPTER 43

ESCAPE

Oko couldn't have revealed himself at a better time. I can't say I have ever felt so relieved to seize someone before. Aitrox, however, was furious, and we weren't out of the woods. Aitrox feared me now, and she would not rest until I was dead, along with any associated with me. My mind always knew I could never win this battle, but it took longer for my heart to accept that truth.

E ru acted quickly once he had seized Oko, pulling himself and his Aegendi under Oko's protection. He felt Aitrox slam into that protective barrier, but it held firm. Unfortunately, Aitrox wasn't about to leave it at that. With the speed of a snake's strike, the circle of angry bodies collapsed on him. Fortunately, Eru had seized several of those closest to him, and he put them to use protecting him. They curled over him, shielding him with their bodies against the furious onslaught. Eru's heart felt sick as an indistinguishable mass of hands clawed, punched and choked the life out of people he literally used as human shields. Aitrox's underlings peeled them away from him like layers of an onion.

The swarming mob under Aitrox's dominion scattered before the force Eru brought to bear with his Wizards. They flew outward, smashing into buildings, or coming down on the spiked rooftops. Eru's Wizards held the next wave of people at bay with less lethality. He lifted the entire team into the mists, grateful for the heavy cloud cover. They had made their escape, and achieved their objective, yet he wasn't about to celebrate a victory. He had to get back to the sanctuary before it was too late.

Eru spread his Aegendi out, not wanting to risk losing everyone should they be discovered. He flew them through the mists, spreading them through the city, as far as his strength allowed. Walking in fog, a relatively two dimensional experience, could be disorienting, but flying in it proved to be even worse. After several near collisions with buildings and rooftops, Eru begrudgingly slowed the pace slightly.

Every second lost gave Aitrox more time to crush the sanctuary she undoubtedly discovered when she seized Eru and gained access to his Aegendi. For most of his new recruits, the sanctuary had become a fundamental part of who they were, and Eru had picked up on it the moment he seized them. Aitrox would not have missed a secret like that. Logic warned Eru not to go back to the sanctuary, but he couldn't abandon all the people there, nor deny the sliver of hope that he could save them.

The thick mists condensed on the skin of each team member, grasping at them with a cold, probing touch. Eru felt the touch of death in the air, fearing that Aitrox's handiwork hadn't come to a close yet today. As they neared the sanctuary, the senses of each person brought unwelcome tidings. A touch of smoke filled their nostrils and stung their eyes.

Eru cautiously brought his team closer to Pillay's estate, lowering the Hawkeyes through the mists to see what he could learn. Even the mists felt like a strange, overwhelming experience through a Hawkeye's heightened senses. He felt the touch of every miniscule droplet and the small transfers of body heat into the water. The swirling impenetrable conformity of the mists came to life in their powerful sight. Eru sensed the ripples and eddies in the clouds, seeing how the mists flowed almost like a fluid. With their eyes he saw the smoke's imperceptible taint like oil mixing with water.

As the Hawkeyes emerged from the mists, the sudden rush of details pushed even Eru's powerful mind as every nuance from the spiked roofs to the soot collecting on the chimney filled his senses. A few hundred paces away, the glowing fires of their sanctuary still burned in defiance to the soggy weather. Eru heard the roaring flames and felt the intensity of the red glow searing his vision. More terrible than the crackling flames, and the hissing of rain falling in the heat, were the tragic screams of people in their fiery grave. The Hawkeyes' perception differentiated each cry, bringing the pleas of people who Eru knew with the intimate knowledge only an archos could have. Eru felt the hopes and dreams of each voice smoldering, and sensed in this moment the fulfillment of their greatest fear. Every cry wrenched his heart, as people who trusted and depended on him burned due to his folly. The children's painful cries harrowed his soul the worst of all.

The outer wall of the estate collapsed with a rumble. The front facing buildings had none of the iron in them, but Aitrox's malice showed no prejudice in her hunger for destruction and death. Further in, the collapsed building still burned, a few glowing frames sizzling as water fell on the warped, glowing iron. A few moving forms emerged from the flames, and Eru's heart skipped a beat. Could there be any survivors?

The powerful senses of his Hawkeyes seemed capable of filtering and focusing according to his wish, bringing every miniscule detail of the burned escapees to his attention. Jana's singed hair and raw scalp left her almost unrecognizable.

An even more disfigured form held his arm around her shoulder as they staggered out of the holocaust, sputtering and coughing through the smoke. Eru thought the other may have been Jetu, but not even the Hawkeye's senses could discern any identifying features. His chest moved slowly and his feet dragged.

Just as the two of them emerged from the inferno with a sad mix of relief and misery, an unseen force thrust them back into the flames. Jana's faint cry shouldn't have registered over the ruckus of fire and rain, but it sunk into Eru's heart like a lead brick. Eru scanned the surroundings; Aitrox's Aegendi had concealed themselves well.

Eru knew their blood was on his hands. Pillay had warned them only days ago, and Eru had ignored him. Eru's arrogance exposed these people to Aitrox and got them killed. Could he have saved them by evacuating the sanctuary before he set out for the attack? Such questions mattered little now, but Eru doubted any would have willingly left. The only way Eru could have saved them would have been to abandon his goal to destroy Aitrox. How many more innocent people would he expose to Aitrox's brutality in his quest for the impossible? All the best intentions in the world couldn't protect them, nor could they assuage his anger and regret. He had traded the lives of people who relied on him to kill a single archos. It sounded like something Aitrox would have done.

Eru withdrew all his Aegendi, not knowing exactly where to go. Seeing the iron frames sag and collapse into the fire reminded him of how badly they needed a safe place to rest. Oko had protected them for almost an hour, and Eru could feel the strain building. At the same time, he knew that none of them could be trusted with their thoughts in a time like this.

He had always tried to respect the privacy of those he seized, however impossible that had proved in practice. Every person he seized revealed their defining moments instantly, often uncovering their most intimate secrets, but only a deliberate scouring would reveal others. Eru believed Oko had his own cache of iron, but had respected that secret until now. If Oko knew what iron could do for them, he would willingly volunteer it no doubt.

Eru brought Oko and himself down into an alley where he sensed a sleeping drunk sheltering under a few scraps of board and fabric. Hopefully, his clouded mind wouldn't reveal them to Aitrox.

"Oko, thank you for coming back," Eru said, hearing his own voice through Oko's ears. On a better day he would have felt proud about how far his speaking had come. "You saved all of our lives. Please let me save you now."

'I won't leave you to die again. I thought you were dead; that's why I left,' Oko answered in his mind. Only when Oko was seized could Eru see into his thoughts, allowing them to communicate like Eru could with any other. Eru already had Oko's conviction and the reasons he had left, but it still felt reassuring for Oko to deliberately express his loyalty.

"I know. If I released you now, Aitrox would destroy us all in an instant, but there is a way I can give you a break," Eru replied.

'How?' Oko asked, doubting Eru's words despite himself. It felt too good to be true.

"Iron. It can block the awareness of an archos. That's how we launched our assault without being discovered."

"Iron? So what do you need from me?"

"I need you to guide us to your iron," Eru answered.

"You don't know? But I thought..."

"I would have to scour you to take that knowledge. I couldn't betray you like that."

'I have a small warehouse on 56 Deor River Plaza,' Oko thought in answer.

"But that's right across from Aitrox's own citadel!" Eru exclaimed in disbelief.

'Would you expect anything less from me?'

"Well, it does have your flare for the dramatic," Eru said with a slight chuckle. "Hiding your contraband iron right under their noses."

'You need to kill the drunk,' Oko's stern thought hit Eru like a slap in the face.

"No, enough people have died today."

'Then break him, but this secret cannot get out,' Oko answered with an angry edge in his thoughts.

"Only I could hear the location. I wouldn't let you speak it out loud after all."

'Eru, you aren't thinking clearly. You practically told anyone with ears where it is.'

"No, I didn't!" Eru protested.

'How many places could someone hide a large stash, right across from Aitrox's citadel?'

"You have a point, but I won't kill him," Eru protested. With those words, the man stirred in his shelter, fear igniting in his heart at the realization that an archos stood so near him. Rather than kill the poor man, Eru seized him, and brought the man under the protection of Oko's gift.

As twilight settled over the city, the heavy clouds slowly flowed away, leaving the city dripping like a drenched rag and smelling of that odd mix of freshness and stirred up refuse. Depending on how the evening breeze stirred, a given breath could be invigorating and the next a blast of vile odors. Eru had a constant menagerie of pleasant and foul scents presented through his Aegendi scattered throughout the city, all discretely converging on the address Oko had provided. As the sun set, Eru caught the first glances of the sky, and the crescent moon. It felt a terrible mistake to head towards Aitrox's own citadel. Such a location could never become a fulltime sanctuary, and moving the iron to a suitable location without getting caught would prove difficult.

In the growing darkness, the towering complex loomed over Oko's secret stash like a hostile giant slumbering. Eru knew that Aitrox never slumbered, and had likely devoted hundreds of her underlings to the search for him. Whatever it was that had happened when she'd seized him had terrified her. At first, the thought of her fear gave him hope, but now he knew what it really meant. Until now, Eru had been unimportant, something to be humored or tolerated. Nobody tolerates or humors something that terrifies them, much less a being like Aitrox. Eru still didn't understand the reason for her fear, but he knew better than to take it lightly.

Aitrox's citadel cast a shadow of fear on the surrounding blocks, and those with means avoided these streets. Even the poor refused to set up their shanties here, but the utility of the land so close to the river couldn't be ignored by merchants and manufacturers. This suited Oko's purposes perfectly, as he had acquired an old, run-down warehouse across from the citadel. Proximity to the river, and the sewers combined with the regular movements of goods from the surrounding warehouses made it the ideal place to hide his iron. Such extreme proximity to Aitrox's citadel meant he could acquire the building at a bargain. The building looked abandoned, with boarded up windows and a sagging roof. Cracks snaked up the outer brick walls, and the doors on the main entry looked ready to fall off their hinges.

Hundreds of terrible statues of Aitrox stared down at them from the citadel walls just on the other side of the river. Eru felt the fear in every one of his Aegendi as they each slipped into the building. He arrived with Oko last of all, but had already put the crew to work. They couldn't possibly work a forge without drawing attention to themselves. Instead, they stacked the bricks of iron to create several pillars about three feet tall. They laid a piece of wood on top of the makeshift shelter and framed the outside edges with the iron bricks. To test the effectiveness of the makeshift structure, Eru willed Janis to crawl under. He lost his hold on her immediately, meaning the shelter would work.

Soon Eru had all the Aegendi safely tucked under the shelter except Oko. He used Oko's eyes to guide him into the shelter, losing his hold on Oko but feeling the returned awareness of each of his Aegendi. He felt their fear, sorrow and grief growing as the realization of everything they had lost settled in their minds. Alone in the void, Eru had no ears to hear the mournful sobs, but he felt the loss in their hearts. Eru knew that their losses fell on his shoulders. In one terrible day they had lost their homes, their families and their security. The claustrophobic makeshift shelter only reminded them of what they had lost. Their sobs continued into the night, made more terrible by the tangible fear of being hidden so close to Aitrox's citadel. Eru couldn't have chosen a more terrible shelter for an archos. In the makeshift hut only Eru's small team existed, filling his senses with their terrible grief and offering nothing to distract him. Eru embraced their sorrow and let it wash over him as penance.

During the long, miserable night Eru's thoughts solidified around the hard, cruel lesson he learned with the fall of the sanctuary. His failure to protect the sanctuary showed that fighting Aitrox inevitably brought death and sorrow to innocent people, all for an impossibly small chance for change. Was it really worth it? He knew now that they couldn't possibly win. Rationally, he had understood that fact long ago, but the emotional acceptance had never really come. On this terrible night, surrounded by those who grieved the deaths of everyone they loved, Eru's heart accepted the impossibility of the task. Aitrox would hunt them mercilessly now. If he attacked another archos, Aitrox would come after them all with a vengeance. It wasn't just the proximity to her citadel that filled Eru with a sense of foreboding. They had found a momentary escape tonight, but so long as they remained within Aitrox's reach they would never be free, and the people of Deor would never be safe from Aitrox's wrath.

Aitrox watched Pillay's estate burn down, finding no comfort in the flames or the death screams of the refugees. Today's happenings took her back to a time she had almost forgotten, back before she became a goddess. Her enemies had changed dramatically since then, and for the first time since the liberation, she felt afraid. She had managed to draw the vyeshen out of hiding, but their adaptations had caught her off guard. This changed everything, and this change gave her an entirely new feeling: fear.

Aitrox knew she would not find release from this fear until Maverick had been destroyed. He may have escaped this time, but Aitrox would take him seriously from now on. Part of her felt a pang of regret over the thought of destroying her latest diversion. He had provided a nice change from the routine, but the day's events reminded her how dangerous change could be.

CHAPTER 44

REGRETS

In some ways, this was the darkest time in my life. Losing
Aymis would forever hold a unique status in my history,
but that loss gave me the perspective to understand the
heartache I was responsible for now. I knew what it meant
to lose the only person who loved me, so I understood
the devastation I had wrought for the Aegendi from the
sanctuary. Alone in that makeshift shelter, I felt their pain

as if they were the only beings in the world, which wasn't too far from the truth for me due to the iron.

'W hat are you going to do now?' Janis asked in her thoughts. Eru didn't answer. *'Eru, what are you going to do now?'* Janis expected the use of his name would snap his attention to her, but not even that worked. Of course, with an archos you had none of the usual cues to tell if you had its attention, but Janis had enough experience with Eru to have a fairly good idea. Lying on her back, in the darkness, on the hard warehouse floor, she couldn't have seen Eru if she wanted, but there was a feeling in the back of her mind when Eru's thoughts rested on her.

She made no effort to hold back her tears. She hadn't lost any loved ones today, but the quiet sobs and curses from the others stirred memories of the day she lost Aymis. In some of the cries she heard despair quashing any desire to struggle. In others she recognized the first sparks of the same fire that drove her. Eru fought Aitrox to stop terrible days like this from happening again, but Janis's motives differed. She fought Aitrox for a simpler and perhaps selfish motive: revenge. The positive side effects of destroying such a wicked goddess offered additional incentive, but they were only fuel for the overriding need for vengeance.

She wondered how many of the newly recruited Aegendi would follow Eru after today. Surely those who felt similar to her would follow gladly, but if she guessed right, most of the new recruits were broken and useless now. Short of seizing them around the clock, Eru wouldn't be able to count on them, and Eru would never do that to another. To do such a thing would betray everything Eru stood for, and defile the cause Aymis died for. Were revenge his driving motivation, the intensity of his loss would have spawned a ruthless hunger for retribution that would have made him terrible indeed. Fortunately for all their Aegendi, and for all of Deor, Eru struggled for different reasons.

Janis's tears flowed as she remembered Aymis's kind heart, and knew that her hunger for retribution wouldn't be what her daughter wanted. She felt the pain of those around her now, yet her heart would gladly push others to such depths for vengeance. She cried for what she had let herself become, a person as dark and hate-filled as the one she sought to destroy, a person who would gladly see others suffer to satisfy her needs, a person her own daughter would be ashamed of.

Janis rolled her head slightly to move the ache of the hard floor from one spot on her skull to another. Similar aches built on her spine, and lower back, but their cramped shelter offered little room to move. She tried turning to her side, her hips brushing against the low wood roof of their shelter and leaving slivers in the fabric of her skirt. She rested her head on her arm, but realized quickly that couldn't last long. The tingling in her hand grew to sharp piercing sensations as discomfort in her shoulders and hips flared. After only a moment, she returned to lying flat on her back, finding it to be the least unpleasant option. The Aegendi next to her seemed to be working his way to similar conclusions as he fretfully stirred and jostled. Then, without any warning, he was no longer there.

"What are you doing?" Oko's voice said angrily.

"I have to get out of here!" came the panicked response.

"No, Paul!" Paul's wife Sara exclaimed. "Wait!"

"Get back under the shelter now!" Oko commanded. Janis heard Oko's footsteps nearing.

"No! I have to leave. My daughter may still be..." Paul's sentence stopped, interrupted by the almost imperceptible sound of a knife puncturing his chest. Janis heard the quiet gasps of his last breath preceding the thump of his body falling to the floor. Janis felt warm liquid seeping into her sleeve, and nearly threw up.

"You killed him!" Sara screamed.

"He almost got us all killed!" Oko said.

"Who are you to decide? Why are you allowed outside this prison?" Sara persisted, her words garbled by her wretched sobs.

"For now, we have to live by the same precautions you did back in the sanctuary, or we will all die," Eru interjected. His voice brought the uproar to a quiet murmur. "This little shelter is a terrible thing, but it is keeping us alive. I am so sorry for your loss, Sara."

"None of this would have happened if Pillay were still in charge!" Sara shouted, and several of the others mumbled in agreement.

"Keep the noise down! This warehouse isn't exactly soundproof," Oko snapped.

"Or what, you'll kill us like you did Paul?" Sara retorted.

"Yes," Oko answered casually. Janis had forgotten how cold Oko could be when it came to protecting his secrets.

"You mother-forsaken monster!" Sara growled.

"How many people have died to protect the secrets of Pillay's sanctuary?" Janis asked, unable to stay quiet any longer. "We are more vulnerable now than ever before. If one of us leaves right now, we would be discovered in a heartbeat."

"But, all of those who died to protect Pillay's secrets died in vain! Maverick threw their sacrifices away. You're no different than all the rest!" Sara turned her attention to Eru with her angry accusations. Janis knew Eru well enough to know the pain those words would cause him. Sara couldn't have chosen a crueler accusation to level at Eru.

"He is nothing like them!" Volo objected, catching Janis and several others off guard.

"Volo, this isn't your argument," Rose said chidingly. "You haven't lost your family, friends and now your lover. Sara has." As if Rose's words reminded Sara of her loss, the anger in Sara's voice burned out, smothered by the return of her sorrow. Her accusing words stopped, but her crying would continue for the rest of the night.

"You didn't volunteer to help a monster. I won't have others say you did," Volo said more quietly to his sister.

"Volo, you don't have to stand up for me all the time. I can look after myself when I see the need," Rose answered.

"Well, you must be blind then," Volo said irritably.

"Volo, calm down please. She has been through a lot. Let it be," Rose said with a stern tone. Volo grumbled and fell silent.

Janis hardly felt the discomfort of the hard floor, conspicuously aware of the emptiness beside her and the warm liquid that continued to seep through the fabric of her clothing. Despite her best efforts to convince herself it was only water, the awareness of the liquid's true nature dominated her thoughts. She had never gotten to know Paul. Knowing that he had loved someone, and that Sara now mourned his death just feet away, added a terrible cruelty to the sensation of the warm liquid staining her skin. Janis passed the rest of the night in silent tears, not for the person she had become but for the sad, terrible world she lived in.

Oko worked as quietly as he could, moving Paul's body and cleaning up the mess. Sara no doubt would want to give him a proper burial, but Oko wasn't going to give her a choice. She couldn't hate him any more than she already did, so it hardly mattered that he dumped the body in the river. Oko hated this job. Most of those he killed could be left in the streets or alleys for some other unfortunate soul to take care of. Still, Oko had disposed of his fair share of corpses without the discomfort and regret he felt tonight. Paul's body hit the river with a conspicuous splash, the only noise Oko made through the whole task.

Oko wiped a tear from his cheek with a start. Tears? Had Eru changed him that much? The last time Oko wiped a tear from his cheek was the first night he had slept alone in the forest. There was no room for tears in this world. His time with Eru had changed him, had changed everything. Oko killed, believing that the only way to beat the archos was to fight by their rules. Eru had proven just how wrong such a notion was. Winning by Aitrox's rules would only ensure that another devil took her place.

Oko couldn't figure out what his issue was with Paul's death. Paul would have gotten them all killed. Just taking the time to ask him what he was doing had been foolish, but Oko had never doubted before. Doubt gave him pause, and pause could mean death. Oko stepped back into his warehouse and grabbed a mop to continue cleaning up the grisly mess. His tears continued unabated as he worked.

You're no different than all the rest! Eru kept hearing Sara's angry accusation over and over in his mind, and the words sunk deep into Eru's heart. Now of all times he missed Aymis the most. She never tolerated the indulgence of thoughts like that. Eru knew all the arguments in his defense, having reviewed them for self-assurance on many occasions, but they always meant more coming from her. Aymis had loved him enough to keep him grounded in times of self-doubt. She had had faith in their goal. What would she tell him now? Hadn't Eru been the one to warn her that the road ahead would be darker and more terrible than she could guess? Hadn't he tried to send her away? Now he found himself seeing his own warning coming to fruition, and he looked to the memory of a dead loved one for answers? What would have happened had Aymis come to him with these questions?

If Eru didn't have the answers to those questions for himself, what was he doing? Aitrox would destroy them. He knew now how certain that fate was. Was that what he wanted? Was that what he wanted for everyone on his team? Should he throw their lives away? So long as they remained in Deor, they lived on borrowed time, but there was a reason people came here.

Squalid living conditions, rampant poverty, and crime seemed a fair price to pay for the lowered chances of being seized by an archos. Eru knew from Oko's memories how heavily a single archos dominated a farming village. In villages that small, Eru would have no place to hide. Even the countryside with the farms and herds would mean certain discovery and death. He would have to live in the deep wilderness to avoid detection. What would be the point?

Eru knew the answer right away. He no longer could justify continuing the struggle at such a terrible cost to innocent people throughout Deor. It was his foolish insistence to keep fighting Deor that destroyed Pillay's sanctuary. Continuing to fight would only lead to more deaths before the inevitable defeat.

Who knows, maybe if they traveled far enough, they could find a place where nobody knows of the archos, a place free from the terrible fear and oppression of his kind. Even Aymis, with her loving acceptance of Eru, had occasionally shown a tinge of fear around him. Eru had never dared imagine a place where archos and terror weren't synonyms. Such a place likely didn't exist. Even his imagination lacked the capacity to create such a place, but the prospect thrilled him. The thought filled him with loathing for this city and everything it represented. From the filthy mud in the alleys and the polluted Deor River all the way up to the spiked inhospitable rooftops, everything in this city showed evidence of Aitrox's touch. Eru could hardly wait to get out of the city, as far from Aitrox and everything she represented as possible. Of course, one question loomed large in his mind: how were they going to get out of the city undetected?

CHAPTER 45

FEAR AND DOUBT

Aitrox's domination had always felt as immutable a fact as the blue sky. I felt that fact ingrained in every mind I seized. She dominated the mental landscape like the oppressive sun in a sandy desert. The densely populated city offered some protection. I knew that leaving Deor would be dangerous, but felt we had no choice. If we stayed in the city, it would only be a matter of time before Aitrox found us. Leaving Deor would either end things immediately or *give us a chance at a life of freedom. Of course, we first had to get out of the city.*

E ru had little sense of time in the iron shelter, cut off from the world full of minds noting time's passing. Sorrow and pain surrounded him, fiercely intense without the background noise of the rest of the city. Even Supe took notice.

"Paul, dead," Supe said quietly.

"Supe, be quiet please," Rose said.

"But Paul... Paul dead?" Supe asked. She said nothing more, though her own tears added to the painful chorus.

Without ears of his own, Eru's awareness of the noise of Oko's work came only through the irritation and discomfort it caused to those around him. Eventually the irritation was replaced by relief as Oko improved their makeshift shelter enough for people to sit up and stretch. By that time, the first hints of daylight seeped in through cracks in the doors and window shutters- cool blue slivers in the darkness. With Aitrox's citadel looming outside, the direct sunlight wouldn't touch the windows until late in the day. Still, the gradual return of light signaled an end to the night they all wanted to forget.

"What are we going to do now?" Janis asked. Eru felt her hunger for action.

"Does it matter?" Sara asked despondently.

"As soon as we leave this prison, Aitrox or that murderer will get us," another new recruit said.

"I am going to leave the city," Eru said, knowing the shock it would generate.

"Eru, that's insane," Volo objected. "We would be found for sure!"

"Who's to say we will get caught?" Eru objected.

"The first archos to see us will seize us for sure," Volo answered.

"Sure, without Oko to hide us. But with Oko's help, Aitrox's senses can't find us. If we stay clear of villages and farms, we will be fine."

"But, we can't do that to Oko," Rose said.

"We will only need his protection for a few days. Once we are far enough into the countryside, Aitrox's senses may feel us but she won't be able to locate us."

"You don't know that," Volo objected.

"I am an archos. I know how our senses work. She won't be able to find us," Eru answered.

"But she's not a normal archos!" Volo answered angrily.

"No, but she is not an all-knowing goddess. Her power is in numbers. Away from her underlings she can't touch us."

"What do you hope to accomplish by leaving the city?" Janis asked.

"We can't defeat Aitrox, and continuing to fight her will only cause more death and sorrow. I should not have needed something as terrible as the destroyed sanctuary to make me realize that. The best I can hope for is to find a place where nobody has heard of the archos, where we can start a new life outside of Aitrox's shadow."

"Eru, what has gotten into you? We need to destroy Aitrox!" Janis said angrily.

"Aitrox will crush us the next time we make a move of any kind," Eru rejoined.

"Then we will die trying!" Janis growled.

"I won't, and burn me alive if I will let Rose knowingly go to her death!" Volo objected.

"But, why would it be any different next time? We have the advantage! We have iron to hide our movements, and now we have Oko again!" Janis persisted.

"Aitrox never feared us until now. She seized me, and something broke her control over me. I felt her confusion and fear over that unknown. She thinks it is something I have discovered. You can rest assured that she will bring her full power down on us at the first opportunity," Eru answered.

"We have to keep fighting! I won't give up!" Janis exclaimed. "You always said you knew it would end this way. Are you backing down now? Are you running away?"

"Janis, calm down," Rose said.

"My mind is made up, Janis. The destruction of the sanctuary was a wakeup call. I have been reckless with the lives of others. I will not repeat that mistake again. I will not sacrifice others with no chance of success. How would I be any different from Aitrox if I continue, if I so casually throw lives away for nothing?"

"How can you give up?" Janis asked. *'How can you give up on Aymis's dream? Did she die in vain?'* Only Eru could hear her continued barrage of questions, but everyone could see the tears on her cheeks and the fiery determination in her eyes.

"Aymis's dream was to find a place where people could be free of the archos. Her dream was not a brutal death at Aitrox's hands," Eru retorted.

"You coward," Janis said quietly.

"This isn't about Aymis at all, is it?" Eru retorted, letting his own emotions get the better of himself. "This is about what you want: revenge. You want to pay Aitrox back for what she made you do." Janis said nothing. All around them, some averted their gazes, others chewed fingernails nervously, or fretfully fidgeted in unconscious response to being caught in a conversation they wanted nothing to do with. "Janis, you can come with me as I search for the place Aymis dreamed of, or you can stay behind and die trying to kill another archos. Ask yourself, which of those options would Aymis want you to choose?" Janis remained silent, but her breathing slowed and she nodded slowly. She would leave with him.

"I think starting a new life sounds wonderful," Rose said to break the awkward silence.

"I'll come too. Where would you be without your older brother?" Volo said.

"I will follow my friend, Eru," Supe said, sounding more coherent than ever.

"What about us?" Sara asked, practically through clenched teeth. Eru felt her loathing for him, and couldn't blame her. In a few short days, he had destroyed everything she had in her world.

"It is your choice. Any who wish to stay must promise not to leave this iron shelter until tomorrow morning."

"Why would we want to do that?" Sara said testily.

"Because, Sara, as long as I am alive, another archos cannot seize you and claim your gift. I know you hate me, and I deserve every bit of your anger. But your only chance at freedom is in my escaping the city. Aitrox likely has Readers throughout the city searching for any clues to my whereabouts," Eru explained.

"If Eru is discovered, then you *will* be seized and enslaved by Aitrox," Oko interjected from somewhere outside the shelter. Eru felt the shock of Oko's words in Sara's heart.

"Oko is right," Eru continued. "Aitrox will certainly seize me and hunt each of you down."

"Then don't leave!" Sara said with a quivering voice and eyes on the verge of panic.

"If we stay in Deor, then that will be our fate; whether it be tomorrow, or a week, or a month. The only way I can spare you from Aitrox's cruelty is by leaving. I have to try," Eru answered.

"He is right, Sara," Rose said as she reached out to sooth Sara. Sara jerked away.

"I can't stay here," Sara said quivering, as her eyes fixated on the blood stains from her slain husband. "I can't!"

"Your other option is for me to seize you so I can hide you until I am far enough away to lose hold of you," Eru offered. Sara said nothing in response, but Eru sensed her consent.

"What about the rest of you?" Eru asked. The quiet murmurs from everyone felt like an indiscernible blur of voices to those who relied on ears to understand. Eru however easily discerned each answer. The answers split the group pretty evenly, some preferring the shelter to being seized again, while others shared Sara's loathing for this place. Eru didn't feel surprised that none of the Aegendi from the sanctuary wanted to leave with him. He couldn't blame them.

"Oko, are you there?" Eru asked.

"Right here," he answered.

"We need a way to get out of the city," Eru answered.

"You happen to have asked the right man, but it won't be fun," Oko said.

"What do you mean?" Janis asked.

"Iron smugglers are very creative about the routes they use in and out of the city, but we cannot be too particular."

"Sounds fantastic," Volo said ironically.

"Not the word I would choose," Oko remarked.

Within an hour, Oko had a collection of supplies assembled for the six of them: Eru, Janis, Rose, Volo, Supe and himself. Oko had his own thoughts about Eru's new idea. How could they hope to survive in the countryside? Without tools and expertise to hunt they had no way to gather food. Oko remembered the hard days after his first kill. He had survived, but just barely. The thought of keeping all six of them alive felt like a death sentence of a different kind. The rational, self-preserving side of his mind screamed at him to leave now. Eru wouldn't even know until he was long gone.

Oko didn't know what had gotten into him. It went without saying that ignoring your survival instinct would get you killed. Not long ago, Oko would have left this archos and his desperate band of followers to their fate. Truthfully, he probably would have slit the Streetborn's throat. He could hardly believe that he now willingly cast his lot with Eru despite every reason not to. Just as unbelievable to Oko was how certain he felt of his choice as he finished packing the final backpack. With everything ready, Oko ducked under the shelter and opened his mind to Eru. He had made his choice. The last thoughts he had to himself dealt with the incredible difference between fear and doubt.

Eru immediately extended protection to the six of them, as well as Sara and the other refugees who chose to leave the shelter. They all shared his relief to be out of that uncomfortable hut as Eru had them all stretch their legs and limbs. He scattered the refugees throughout the city, seizing carriage drivers to move them more quickly. Part of Eru hated watching his Aegendi scattering into the masses, never to be seen or seized again. All that power lost, but it was for the best. Outside the city they would only be more mouths to feed. At least he had his true friends with him still.

Oko's mental instructions led them across the street and down to the shores of the Deor River. The pungent smells from a sewer draining into the river filled their nostrils, and Eru understood the plan. Even the heavy rags Eru wrapped around each person's face did nothing to hold the rank odors at bay. Eru felt the furious objections rising in all their minds. Despite their protests he agreed with Oko's assessment that the sewers probably would be their best bet to escape undetected.

This close to the river, the currents in the sewers flowed with enough strength to make walking in the disgusting liquid difficult. Even with Eru's ability to filter the inputs that reached him, the combined power of six people's senses nearly overwhelmed him. According to Oko's memories, they had about five miles of this – to think that he had made the run hundreds of times! No amount of money could have tempted Eru into this experience. Eru kept his thoughts focused intently on the goal, holding on to Oko's memories of the first euphoric steps into the fresh air as he exited the city. The smugglers had dug several tunnels, joining into the existing sewers to get them undetected to just about any point in the city.

Most of the underground sewer pipes were too small for human traffic, funneling any smugglers through some of the common passageways. Oko's choice of a warehouse location made perfect sense when considered in light of their secret underground network, being so close to an exit from the network. Oko knew the network only so far as it served his purposes, but Eru could make several guesses and extrapolations. If he guessed right, a fork in the tunnels could take him close to Pillay's now destroyed estate.

Eru pushed each of them onward, fighting against their nausea as each person's steps made sickening slopping noises in the foul waters. Every step brought them all one step closer to their ultimate goal: freedom.

Pillay's shoulders ached with the weight of his latest load of iron, but other more pressing senses dominated his thoughts. He felt the vile liquids squishing between his toes in his shoes, and the repulsive odors made him wretch. With his connections and power, he hadn't had to run these routes for some time, but that was before Maverick had dealt him such a serious setback. It didn't surprise him that his sanctuary had been destroyed so quickly or so brutally.

He may have lost his sanctuary and most of his iron, but Pillay's successes came by always moving forward. However, this latest stroke of luck haunted him, filling his nights with restless dreams, and his waking with notions of revenge. He had heard about the power struggles of the archos. Maverick's unconventional approach disarmed the unwary, but Pillay had known better. Once the monster had found his sanctuary, the end result was inevitable.

Pillay's stomach churned with the terrible odors that filled his nostrils with each disgusting step. Pillay's eyes burned with the disgusting vapors, and his head spun for lack of clean breathing air. Maverick had put him back in the mire. Each sloshing step added to the anger he felt growing towards Maverick. Pillay knew himself to live a life of privilege, but it had nothing to do with wealth. He belonged to a far more exclusive class, who enjoyed the privilege to think whatever they pleased. Despite himself, Pillay found himself dreaming of killing Maverick for everything Maverick had taken from him.

As if on cue, the sound of steps echoed down the sewer towards him. Not wanting to reveal his large iron haul to a competitor, he ducked into a tight side passage and waited for the oncoming smugglers to pass. He could hardly believe his eyes when he saw the hand fate had dealt him.

CHAPTER 46

No Room for Miracles

I had compelled people to do some pretty uncomfortable things, but nothing that had overwhelmed their capacities and strained my resolve. Aitrox may not be an all knowing goddess, but she influenced everyone's actions like a large boulder in a small stream. She didn't have to seize someone to make him do awful things. Everything anybody did reflected her terrible influence on the world. I only hoped

that our trek through the sewers would be the last thing
Aitrox would drive us to do.

E ru kept the team moving forward, though the conditions strained his control over them. Only with the greatest concentration could he quell the chokes and gag responses in each of them. How Oko had ever made it through these tunnels without passing out would forever be a mystery. If they kept up the pace, they would be breathing fresh air before too long. For now, Eru just had to take one step at a time, one bend in the sewers at a time. Oko took up the lead, followed by Rose, then Volo. Next came Supe, who remained close to Eru, and Janis came last. The swirling sewers came alive in unusual ways through her prophetic vision. The usually chaotic, unpredictable eddies in the disgusting currents felt both ordered and more chaotic as she saw the present and future of every ripple, drop and disgusting splash.

Janis's eyes saved Eru's life around the next bend. Her eyes saw the attack in time for Eru to duck, but not completely escape Pillay's ambush. His lunging slash would have caught Eru square in the ribs, but instead the knife cut a nasty gash in his bicep. Of course, Eru lacked any sense of pain at the blow, but immediately he lost his hold over several people. Three of the Aegendi he had scattered through the city were lost to him now, as well as Volo, Rose and Janis. Blood poured from his arm, a dark, ghastly streak in the dim light. Eru had no choice but to use Supe to take the next attack.

Pillay's knife cut a gash down Supe's torso with a gruesome flourish. She grabbed his wrist, stopping his hand before the next blow could fall, and his knife fell into the sewage. Her wounds closed quickly, but Pillay's added size and strength gave him the advantage as he roughly threw her aside before directing a savage swing at Eru. He knocked Eru's head against the wall with a fierce blow to his face. Eru struck the brick wall with a heavy crunching sound, sliding down against the damp bricks until the foul waters swirled around his waist. Unconscious, he lost hold of all his Aegendi.

"Eru!" Supe exclaimed, rushing to his side. "Eru, friend! Eru, hurt!"

Oko and Supe stood in a disoriented stupor at their unexpected release. Fortunately, Janis had already recovered from her release, and she barreled into Pillay, knocking him off his feet as her shoulder struck him square in the chest. He fell over with a splash, his arms flailing. Oko jumped on him, grabbing Pillay's scalp and pushing his face under the surface of the foul liquid. Pillay's arms and legs thrashed and kicked violently, splashing the disgusting liquid all over them, but the strength soon left him. It felt like an eternity before Pillay's body went limp and the thrashing limbs plopped lifeless into the flowing sewage.

"Eru!" Janis exclaimed, lifting him out of the water. His small frame made lifting him easier than she expected. Blood soaked his entire right side, and his breathing was faint. "He's lost a lot of blood."

"This means we are vulnerable!" Rose exclaimed.

"Quiet! Don't think about it!" Oko commanded angrily. "Control your thoughts!"

"I don't understand. The bleeding has stopped," Janis said.

"That's good. Let's get moving," Oko said, taking Eru into his arms as he spoke.

"But, I don't understand!" Janis exclaimed.

"Oko's right. Now's not the time. Let's go," Volo said through his choking and sputtering. Without Eru holding back their reflexes, each of them succumbed to the sewer's overwhelming influence.

"Eru, friend. Eru alive?" Supe asked as she followed so close on Oko's heels she almost tripped him up on several occasions.

"How much farther?" Rose gasped.

"Don't think about that! Just keep moving!" Oko growled through clenched teeth. Rose found herself wishing she hadn't opened her mouth to talk, with the terrible taste it left in her mouth. Rose stumbled, wishing she didn't have to catch herself with her hands, but preferring it to the alternative. Volo's strong arms scooped her up and swept her back to her feet.

"Come on sis, we have to keep moving," Volo said through clenched teeth of his own. Rose said nothing in response, concentrating on two things: taking her next step, and getting out of this terrible place.

Aitrox kept at least a thousand Readers scouring the city non-stop for any sign of Maverick. Hundreds of Hawkeyes scrutinized the city's faces and streets for him. Whatever it was that Maverick had discovered terrified and enraged her. Nobody had ever escaped her when she had them seized. If Maverick had discovered how to cut her hold over him, maybe he could cut her hold on others. She had never imagined such a thing possible, but Maverick seemed to do a lot of impossible things. Up until now, his unexpected accomplishments didn't matter. For uncounted years, her secret remained safe, impregnable and utterly unknown. Maverick's discovery wouldn't matter so long as her secret remained unknown, but losing one layer of security made her uneasy. The utter failure of her Readers and Hawkeyes only added to her sour mood.

'What? What happened? He let me go already? But he can't be out of the city yet!' Aitrox heard that thought amidst the hundreds of thousands of minds her Readers brought to her awareness. She focused the Reader's attention on that thought and her frustrations vanished. She almost laughed at the irony of the situation. Maverick had been hiding right under her nose until just a few hours ago! Now he was leaving the city! She practically had him now.

Sara and all of the Aegendi Maverick had recruited needed to be taught a lesson. Death would be too generous. Once she killed Maverick she would take each one into her service and teach them what it really meant to be Aegendi. Part of her almost regretted the end to the cat and mouse games she and Maverick had played over the years. Ever since her last great victory centuries ago, killing her enemy's god, life had been mundane and void of challenge or triumph. She didn't think anybody could give her that sense of challenge again. Destroying

Maverick represented a return to the numbing uniformity only an immortal could comprehend.

Just to reassure herself of her secret's safety, she had one of her servants grab a ceremonial blade. Running it down the length of her arm, she watched with pleasure as the wound closed before the eyes she controlled. Aitrox caressed the vibrant fiery feathers that made up her gown. For thousands of years those feathers had remained downy, soft and beautiful, another witness to her original triumph, and the safety of her secret.

"Is he going to make it?" Rose asked timidly as they stopped to catch their breath, concealed in a small copse just outside the city. She breathed in deeply, relishing each breath of fresh air. They all reeked of the sewers, but luckily a slight breeze brought fresh air their way.

"How should I know?" Oko snapped irritably. "We need him back soon though."

"Who attacked us back there?" Oko asked.

"I didn't get a good look, and I only saw him briefly back in our sanctuary, so I can't be sure, but I suspect it was Pillay," Janis said.

"Pillay was a Hider?" Oko asked.

"You didn't know?" Volo replied.

"Why would I know? It's not like it's a secret we are open with for obvious reasons," Oko answered.

"What are we going to do now?" Rose asked.

"Be careful," Oko cautioned. "I worry that you may be too used to protection. We should all focus on simple things until Eru is back with us."

"Eru, will be okay?" Supe asked quietly as her concerned eyes studied him like her life depended on him.

"Stay here, and for the unknown gods, be careful. I am going to make sure we got out unnoticed," Oko said as he ducked out of the brush.

Janis watched Oko leave them, doing her best not to wonder what their chances were for surviving with the unexpected turn of events. She studied Eru's wounds, marveling that he had somehow survived. The deep gash in his bicep looked like it had severed some major arteries, but no blood flowed from the wound. His hand looked pale, lifeless and slightly shriveled. His breathing remained shallow, but steady. His disturbingly large eye sockets had blackened from Pillay's fierce blow to his face, and a discolored bump showed where his head had struck the wall. How could such a young, fragile looking person survive such injuries?

"Don't move," Oko whispered as he ducked back under the bush.

"What's wrong?" Volo asked.

"There's a patrol coming. Stay silent, stay still, and pray to whatever you pray to that there are no Readers or Hawkeyes in this patrol."

"Were they seized?" Janis asked.

"Shhh!" Oko hissed angrily.

Moments later, the sound of footsteps drifted their way with the breeze. The ominous silence hung over them like a guillotine's blade. Surreptitious footsteps drew nearer, adding to the threatening atmosphere.

"Clear over here," someone said just a few feet away from them.

"Clear here," another call repeated ten paces in the other direction. The breeze kicked up slightly, rustling the leaves and stirring the blades of grass on the hillside.

"What is that terrible smell?" the voice ahead of them and downwind asked.

"We aren't that close to the sewers are we?" another voice asked.

"How many are there?" Volo whispered.

"Just three," Oko answered as he ducked outside the copse. Volo followed.

"Volo, wait!" Rose whispered, following behind him. Janis and Supe remained, and even Supe's face showed some awareness of their danger.

Oko hadn't found himself in such a delicate, dangerous situation in some time. Stealth came far easier in the structured, regular world of buildings and citadels. Out in the wild, the random unknown elements like an unnoticed twig or territorial squirrel could foil the best efforts. Buildings followed patterns and common distances that didn't exist in the natural world.

Fortunately, nature remained his loyal friend as he successfully snuck up behind the nearest patroller. He had no knives on him, having left his packs and gear hidden back in the bush. Oko, however, didn't need a weapon to kill, snapping the man's neck from behind before he could make a sound of warning.

"Hey you!" a voice called. Had Oko been careless? His head turned in the direction of the angry call, realizing right away that he remained unknown. Unfortunately, Volo and Rose couldn't say the same. "What are you doing out here?" the patrolman asked suspiciously. "Why do you smell like a donkey's backside?"

Oko saw what he most feared, the subtle change in the man's eyes that could mean only one thing: Aitrox had discovered them. Oko abandoned any efforts at stealth, charging Aitrox's underling for the kill. "Get the other one!" Oko called to Volo, pointing as he closed the gap. Volo looked around, momentarily caught in an uncertain stupor. Oko leapt into a kick that carried his full momentum into the blow. His foot struck the man's jaw so hard it knocked his head back with an audible crunching snap. The man staggered backwards a step but didn't look phased.

"Great, an Immortal," Oko grumbled.

Volo's hesitation ended abruptly as Rose charged the other patrolman. Seeing his sister taking on a man far larger than her sparked his protective instincts. He couldn't let the man hurt her. "Rose, no!" Volo exclaimed as he rushed after her. He caught her by the shoulder, pushing himself ahead of her and throwing his hardest punch at his foe. He lacked the disciplined technique Oko had developed over a lifetime of training, but a brother protecting his sister shouldn't be underestimated.

His foe caught Volo's fist in the air, and practically ripped his arm out of its socket. He picked Volo up with one arm and threw him to the ground with a crunch. "Volo!" Rose exclaimed. She jumped on the man's shoulders, scratching at his face. Adrenaline, combined with the added strength of her latent gift, enhanced her furious assault. Her fingers dug deep, leaving gashes running up the man's face, but pain meant nothing to a Brute under Aitrox's control.

Oko knew they had lost. Had they not run into the Hider in the sewers, they probably would have made it away clean. Without their gifts enhanced through Eru, they could never hope to overcome an Immortal and a Brute. Even if they did, Aitrox now knew their location. Barring a miracle, they had a few minutes left to live, and Aitrox's world left no room for miracles.

Oko ducked the knife slash of his foe, skillfully disarming his opponent and claiming the knife as his own. It did him little good against an Immortal, but at least a knife in his hands couldn't hurt him. In another quick, skillful move, he slashed up and across his opponent's torso. To his surprise, the wounds didn't close immediately. The Immortal staggered backwards, pain, shock and even a notion of relief in his eyes. The look vanished as quickly as it came, and the long laceration closed. Oko moved in again, taking advantage of the moment's pause. His next strike nearly beheaded his foe. He had seen Immortals recover from worse, but his opponent fell to the ground, never to stand again.

Volo struggled to climb to his feet in spite of the screaming pain throughout his body. He looked up in terror as his foe pulled Rose from his back like she weighed nothing. He held her with a single arm, lifting her over his head. Suddenly, his arm wobbled and Rose fell on top of him, sending him toppling to the ground under her. Rose's weight fell squarely on the ribs of the Brute, squeezing the air out of his lungs and quashing his cry of pain. Volo heard the crunch of breaking ribs. At least Rose would be safe for the moment.

"We have to get out of here," Oko said as he ran to Rose's side. "Are you all right?"

"I am fine. Help Volo," Rose answered.

"What happened?" Janis saw them returning and emerged from the copse, carrying Eru in her arms.

"I don't know," Oko answered.

"Volo, are you okay?" Rose asked. Volo just groaned before collapsing. "Volo's hurt!" She said frantically.

"Janis, help Rose with Volo," Oko said as he took Eru from her. Janis obeyed without question and the two of them helped Volo to his feet. Fortunately, neither of his legs had broken, but they suspected he had a broken arm, a few broken ribs, and a severe concussion. He groaned and looked around with dazed, disoriented eyes.

"We have to keep moving," Oko said as they headed away from the city. He knew they didn't have much time, or much hope in reality. They had only been struggling along for a few minutes before Aitrox's underlings returned. They dropped in from above, landing in a circle around them. All ten of them looked on Oko with that unified gaze he hated and feared.

Suddenly, the unity in their gaze vanished, replaced by confusion and disarray. In the same instant, a dark, terrible blur swooped down picking up one of Aitrox's Aegendi with its talons and soaring back into the sky. Two more vanished in a similar fashion, just as quickly. It didn't take long before Aitrox's Aegendi had been destroyed or scattered. Five monstrously large, dark beasts landed and surrounded Oko and the others, eying them with sinister aquiline eyes. Had the ghastly looking creatures not saved them, Oko would have thought their situation had gotten a lot worse. *What were these things, and what did they want with Eru?*

Interlude
Uprising

It was gone. The constant pulling in the back of Jante's mind, the unyielding, alluring voice that had been his unwavering companion for years was gone. Jante had only succeeded in rooting out the final flawed threads with the combined help of his mate, Ela. She, too, had found freedom from the insidious hold metal had on her mind. It hadn't taken long once they agreed to work together. Something about inviting her in and accepting her touch on his life threads made a remarkable difference.

Jante felt as free and jubilant as the day he first flew. Part of him wanted to lift off and soar the open skies to celebrate. Ela nuzzled the feathers of his neck affectionately, sharing in the joy at their newfound freedom. For the moment, that joy would not be sullied by their mutual fears for the rest of the vyeshen. Yet, the very path to their freedom bode ill for the rest of his kind. Jante could never hope to make such a difficult change to others uninvited. In fact, he would need their active participation. The other members of the council would never consent, or take part.

Jante had witnessed a terrifying transformation in the minds of many vyeshen, Shanje included. It was as if they had surrendered to metal's pull on their mind. It started simply enough. What could be the harm in exploring the possibilities to harness the human plague? Yet, with each of Shanje's small successes, the façade faded. Now, neither Shanje nor several of the vyeshen council denied their interest in enslaving humans for their metals. After all, human metallurgy could serve the vyeshen in powerful new ways they claimed.

Sheer numbers made it impossible for Jante to root out this addictive vulnerability from the entire population, at least not in the time he had. Jante had hoped to at least free the more powerful members of the council. Let those who guided the entire species at least do so without the constant metal-lust clouding their minds. Only now that Jante had truly silenced it, did he realize just how incessant and strong it had always been. He simply had grown accustomed to ignoring it.

Time was running out. Shanje and a few others were having remarkable, terrifying success with the human young they experimented with. Some had been transformed into sinister creatures with pasty skin, milky, featureless eyes, and wickedly keen minds. Others had been left untouched, subjects on which to test the new creation's powers. Jante discovered a new meaning for terror – trauma in the hearts of those poor children.

Jante at least found some solace in the fact that the human test subjects did not suffer long. The first controllers, as they came to be known, only survived for a day. The unchanged children killed the atrocities at the first opportunity. It had been easy. In order to grant the human mind such controlling power, other capacities had to be sacrificed, leaving the controllers terribly vulnerable. Shanje would not give up so easily. He had tasted the potential of his idea, and an almost maddening drive pushed him forward.

Subsequent batches of human children, Jante had given up counting, marked iterative *improvements*. Gradually the controllers became more powerful, more perceptive and more dangerous. The protective instincts and reflexes Shanje began introducing to his creations terrified Jante. What if a controller turned on the vyeshen? At the rate Shanje was empowering the controllers, such a happening could prove catastrophic, but Shanje would not listen to Jante's warnings. He bristled with anger when Jante questioned his decisions. Shanje insisted that his plans to control the controllers would protect them.

Jante did not share Shanje's confidence. None of the vyeshen wanted direct involvement with the controllers, finding them even more distasteful than regular humans. Thus Shanje set out to craft the emotional make-up of the controllers to suite the vyeshen goals, making them crave vyeshen approval while despising other humans. Shanje never did appreciate the profound intensity and complexity of human emotions. Jante still hadn't puzzled out the balance between the influence of his life threads, and his experiences on his own soul. The thought of trusting the emotional groundwork Shanje laid not to change and shift during a controller's life felt like utter insanity to Jante.

As Shanje's devilish crafting of the controllers neared completion, the vyeshen turned their efforts towards infecting real human population with the seeds to birth them. This proved far more complicated a puzzle to solve, and for a time Jante hoped that the entire scheme would come to naught. Many more years unfolded as Shanje continued to abduct subjects. Abducting humans mature enough to bear young was far more difficult;, another delay Jante welcomed. Still, Shanje's obsession never wavered as decades passed.

Then one morning Jante felt it. A tremor of excitement and anticipation rippled through all the vyeshen in the aeries. Shanje had done it. The first *naturally* born controller had just been created. The only thing to mar Shanje's victory was the unavoidable death of the mother.

That morning, Jante and Ela felt truly alone in their sorrow. They remained in their nest, watching the celebratory acrobatics of hundreds of their brothers. Powerful shrieks of triumph and excitement filled the morning air. Jante understood a portion of their jubilation. Some feared that manipulating the herds through their dreams could not last forever. Driving the humans to violence made those who survived that much more adept at destruction, as the creatures devised ever more impressive ways to kill. Many viewed Shanje as their savior, having created the means to finally protect them fully from the human threat.

Those who felt relief at Shanje's triumph were ignorant of the dangers, but their celebrations were not the ones Jante mourned. It broke his heart to see how many celebrated for a different reason. The lust for metal had consumed the hearts of most of his kind, until Jante no longer recognized many he once called friends. True, they looked the same as ever with their fiery plumes and keen talons, but their souls were no longer vyeshen. Jante felt the loss of his old friend, Shanje, most profoundly.

In sorrow he turned to the only soul he could trust, grateful that none of the other vyeshen even bothered to pay them any mind. He did not want their polluted souls to see into his or Ela's hearts any longer. Part of him desperately clung to hope that he could still save his race. Perhaps he and Ela could find a way to blunt the controller's power.

Ela immediately warned Jante of the very real danger such a notion posed to them. Had another vyeshen discerned such a goal in his heart, they would have been cast out or killed. Despite her fears, Ela shared Jante's hopes and aspirations. *'Be careful my love.'*

Jante recognized Ela's wisdom. They couldn't possibly pursue such a dangerous plan. It wouldn't take long before their goals were laid bare to the other vyeshen. They would be discovered before they could do a thing. *'Was it truly so hopeless?'*

Ela's audacious and brilliant response caught Jante completely off guard. What if they could hide from the others? Ela did not mean hiding in some cave, physically removed from their people. Such a plan would serve nobody. No, she intended to hide mentally. What if they could hide some of their being from the others? It would be a challenging change to make to their threads. Years ago, before Shanje's quest to control the humans began, such a thought would have repulsed them both. However, now the idea felt as liberating as subduing their metal-lust had been.

Jante's heart leapt at the idea his mate had just shared. They would need time and space to change their threads, away from vyeshen minds that could discover them. The hardest part would be hiding just enough to conceal their plans, while still presenting enough mental presence not to rouse suspicions. All around them, the vyeshen celebration continued. For the moment at least, Jante and Ela were practically invisible. There would be no better time to slip away.

Ela could hardly wait to leave. Together the two of them left their roost, wondering what they would find when they returned.

Jante made no efforts to hide his fear and trepidation from Ela. He could now. The two of them had finally succeeded. He had feared that such an ability would harm his relationship with his mate. Ironically, the very fact that he *could* hide things from her, made their absolute openness with each other that much more meaningful. She left her heart open to him, except when they practiced and fine-tuned their new skill.

It had taken a year to work their change to perfection. Now they could choose to compartmentalize their thoughts, hiding parts of their being from each other. Even practicing with Ela felt... wrong, but Jante would feel no such reservations with the other vyeshen. His race had lost its way and no longer deserved his openness. By now, Jante felt like he would have to hide more of his true self from the vyeshen than he could ever share with them. He couldn't even trust any other than Ela to know where they had been for the last year.

Jante hoped that the colony would believe the story they had worked out together. It had been no secret that the two of them despised the controllers, and the thought of enslaving humanity. Thus, they decided to claim that they had attempted to cross the vast, salty waters where the land ended. After a year of failed attempts, they had been forced to concede defeat and return. The whole idea seemed preposterous to Jante, but they had one thing on their side. No vyeshen had ever been capable of lying to another before. The others would have no reason to suspect, assuming Jante and Ela succeeded in hiding their true memories. After weeks of practice, Jante felt as ready as he could be.

It wasn't the fear of being discovered that filled Jante's mind with dread. It was the prospect of confronting what his kind had become that terrified him. How much further into the abyss had his brothers fallen? Could the two of them possibly hope to reclaim their race? Part of Jante's heart wished that he and his mate could simply escape. More than once, he had contemplated doing exactly what they would tell the vyeshen they had tried. The two of them could just fly towards the rising sun until they found new lands, or they fell exhausted to a watery grave.

Hell – Jante had no other way to describe his life back with the vyeshen colony. The constant need for secrecy weighed on his soul oppressively. Most of the time, the two had to hide much of their soul even from each other. Occasionally, they would risk opening up to each other, but only late at night when they could be reasonably certain all the others slept. Such opportunities felt like refreshing gasps of air in the suffocating webs of deceit they now wove.

None of the vyeshen suspected them. Shanje even had welcomed Jante back, grateful that his old friend had finally come around to see reason. Now Jante worked at Shanje's side *perfecting* the controllers, even as Shanje's wretched creations drove the enslaved humans mercilessly. It had not taken the vyeshen long to enslave the nearest herd of humans after Jante and Ela had left. With that triumph, the vyeshen fall from grace was utterly complete.

By the time Jante returned, his people's hearts had truly and completely forgotten Phoenix. Many covered their glorious, sacred plumes with glistening metal. Their thoughts constantly rested on the next metal masterpiece their slaves could produce. The controllers' powerful minds enabled the enslaved humans to create truly magnificent works. Even to Jante, who no longer felt the lust for metal that once plagued him, the work of the seized slaves filled him with awe. Yet in his heart, nothing the slaves could do could ever come close to the splendor and glory he had once beheld in his god, Phoenix.

All vyeshen get the privilege of visiting Phoenix's roost once in their lives, when they come to full maturity after their first century of life. It had been so long ago for Jante, but he would never forget that glorious day. It pained him most of all when he realized that his offspring Shenta would reach that momentous age soon, and that the date would come and go without a thought for him. Only the splendor of the slaves' metal craftsmanship mattered to Shenta now.

Jante loathed every moment lending his unsurpassed mastery of the threads of life to such a terrible cause. Jante had to lend enough meaningful help to avoid any suspicion and Shanje knew the kind of mastery he should bring to bear. Thus, he could not avoid taking part in making the controllers ever more powerful, and ever more difficult to kill. It had been some time since a slave had killed a controller, but it still happened on rare occasions.

Fear was Jante's constant, secret companion. Doubt gnawed at his heart relentlessly. Was his effort to undermine the controllers and save his people going to be enough? His awareness of the danger the controllers presented only grew in time, and he feared that his unwilling contributions could doom his kind. Having to undermine the controllers secretly meant he had to be slow and subtle, where Shanje had abandoned any subtlety or delicacy in his work on the controller's threads.

In time Jante hoped to make it impossible for a controller to seize a vyeshen. None had tried yet, and Shanje believed it to be impossible, but Jante knew otherwise after learning the controllers' weaves. Correcting that oversight in the controllers' weaves would take a long time, so Jante started with a few weaker protections in the meantime. First he worked to ensure that a controller's mind would struggle to change its own threads if one ever did seize a vyeshen. Were a controller to gain unbridled access to enhance its own threads, then all would surely be lost.

Even as Shanje had Jante work to constantly enhance the controller's ability to seize others, Jante worked to subtly and carefully undermine that power. He had to do so with great caution, lest Shanje discover the changes and undo them. Over time, he subtly diminished the controller's ability to control others in the presence of the metal Shanje craved. Shanje would hopefully never notice that the controllers outside the mines no longer could seize a slave deep in the mountains. The mines production continued uninhibited, due to the abundance of controllers in those dark, hellish shafts.

In Jante's spare time, he and Ela worked on protecting themselves from the controllers. If they had been free to work together, the change would have been a simple extension of their ability to hide from the vyeshen. Unfortunately, the times when they could share all their thoughts openly were rare enough that they had to work alone. They hoped to eventually hide their minds completely from the controllers, but they couldn't risk hiding themselves more fully from the vyeshen, lest they be discovered. Gradually Jante's mind grew harder for the controllers to discern, but his mate, Ela lagged behind.

Jante returned to his roost just as the sun approached its midday apex in the sky. He bore a large goat in his talons. Ela had returned with several large fish in her claws, a special treat. He knew the reason for her high spirits, even if they could not share their thoughts openly right now. Jante could read the relief in her body, and saw the glimmer of triumph in her eyes. He felt it, too.

Their efforts to save their race were far from complete, but he felt relief to know they at least had a contingency plan. Neither of them relished the idea of using the mines as an emergency shelter, but it was a start. Come what may, at least the vyeshen would not be completely destroyed if the controllers revolted. That small victory felt like the world had been lifted from their backs. The goat and fish made for an excellent celebratory meal.

'I am Aitrox, and you are free!' Every vyeshen heard that proclamation. It had happened. A controller had rebelled.

Jante immediately opened his mind, knowing that all the vyeshen had to know everything he and Ela had been doing. As their eyes met, their thoughts also converged and they immediately understood what they must do. The two of them took flight, ignoring the half-eaten goat, and the morsels of fish.

Jante felt the panic rippling through the vyeshen. Indeed, he shared in the growing dread at the unfolding events. As Jante approached Shanje, he let his thoughts rest so forcefully on his poor, foolish, lost friend's mind that he couldn't possibly be ignored. For a moment, Shanje's mind struggled to comprehend everything Jante was telling him. The shock and scope of Jante's deceit, something Shanje hadn't even dreamed possible, felt as impossible as the ensuing chaos amongst the vyeshen. Fortunately, Shanje recognized the reality that Jante's actions would likely save their kind.

Jante had fixed his mind so intensely on Shanje, that he almost missed the approach of another tortured vyeshen soul. At the last moment, he felt Shenta's terrified soul as his offspring dove from the heights, intent on killing him. Jante did a tuck and rolled to the side, feeling Shenta's talons graze his neck as they passed. His youngling's heart screamed with dread and sorrow as an external will, Aitrox, drove his body.

The usurping controller did not know how to wield the vyeshen body like she could a human's, but she also attacked with a reckless abandon of one who cared nothing for its own well-being. After all, what was the life of one vyeshen to her? If Shenta died while she drove his body to fight others, all the better.

Shenta floundered as he missed on his attack. Jante and Shanje used that moment to take flight. The two spread out, hoping to reach as many other vyeshen and direct them to the mines. When Shenta recovered, he immediately took pursuit of his father. Around him, the skies above the vyeshen aeries erupted into chaos as vyeshen locked in combat with each other. Any time a seized vyeshen managed to lock in combat with another, the usurping controller won regardless of the outcome. If the seized vyeshen died, this demon, Aitrox, simply seized the survivor.

The message to retreat to the mines spread through the vyeshen flock quickly, and those that could were now turning in the direction of the mine entrance.

It was not far, but under current circumstances, any distance felt like miles. Jante's son relentlessly pursued him, but the two were evenly matched in terms of speed. In the distance, Jante spotted Ela, also making a rapid dash for the mines.

Suddenly, a newly seized vyeshen crashed into her, and the two spiraled out of control. Jante shrieked in terror, as he turned and dove to intercept them. He could not let her be killed, or seized. She was everything to him. Losing her would be a fate worse than a thousand deaths. Fury raged in his heart, as he dove for the floundering pair of vyeshen. Ela felt his approach, always so remarkably in sync with him regardless of circumstances. At the perfect moment, she rolled in the air, exposing the seized vyeshen to Jante's talons as they dug deep into the bird's blazing torso. Jante felt the poignant mix of terror and relief in his prey's heart. Rala, a proud member of the vyeshen council, died grateful to Jante for freeing her.

Shenta's talons slashed across Jante's back moments later. Fortunately, Aitrox remained fairly clumsy with her new tools or Jante would have died in his son's talons. Pain shot through Jante's body, but the slashes were not serious. Ela had not missed Shenta's approach, and she skillfully snagged his leg as he passed. Shenta's momentum jerked her violently, and Jante heard the loud snap of her leg breaking from the torque. Ela screeched in agonizing pain, as she released her son. The tactic worked however, as she had changed her son's trajectory, sending him full speed into the sharp rocks of the steep mountainside, now perilously near. Shenta would never fly again.

Jante could see the mine's entrance now. So agonizingly close. They had to get there. Ela saw it as well, and steeled herself to make the desperate flight. Jante knew how every stroke of her wings filled her with pain, but at least her broken leg didn't ground her. Then Jante felt her. Not Ela: Aitrox.

He felt the usurping controller feeling after him, and perceived her surprise that she hadn't been able to seize him yet. Blazing Phoenix, he had to get into the mines! She was strong, far stronger than Jante had thought possible for a controller, and the glimpse he caught of her heart filled him with fear. This controller had completely shed the emotional trappings Shanje had built to protect the vyeshen. Jante suspected she had done so long ago, and had only been waiting for the right time to strike. Again she reached for him, and Jante could not quite explain how he eluded her grasp. Then she seized Ela, and Jante despaired.

Terror and pain filled Ela's heart as the usurper forced her to hunt her love. Aitrox drove her on mercilessly, seeming to relish the pain Ela's broken leg inflicted. The two shot through the mine's opening and plunged into the darkness. Jante's body glanced off a stone wall and he skipped and rolled along the shaft floor. Ela followed a similar, painful trajectory tumbling to a stop just a few feet away. Jante could hardly move, but he could feel how much worse Ela's wounds were. *Phoenix, help me!* Jante pled in his heart. They had to get deeper into the mines. Then, perhaps Aitrox would lose hold of his love.

Jante hobbled over to Ela, not caring that a hostile being inhabited his mate's body. She was so battered and wounded, that even this usurper could not make much use of her. Flying in this impenetrable darkness would do him no good. In fact, Jante hardly knew what he hoped to accomplish, but he refused to give up.

Jante clasped Ela's leg with one of his talons, and pulled with all his might. The two of them scraped along the rocky mine shaft floor, moving just a few feet with each thrust. Jante felt the pain he caused Ela with every pull, but he refused to let her die under this usurper's dominion. He would die before giving up. With his next thrust, his prayers were answered. The two of them toppled over the edge of a shaft, plunging deep into the heart of the mountain.

Relief flooded Jante's mind as he felt Aitrox lose her hold on his mate. She was free. Jante flapped his wings with his strength, doing everything he could to slow their fall. The two crashed into the shaft floor with a sickening crunch. Jante's wing had broken, as had a rib and one of his talons. Ela had hit first, but miraculously the impact had not killed her. Jante knew, however, that she only had moments left to live.

The two opened their souls and shared in their terrible, tragic, yet beautiful last moments. She could never thank him enough for getting her free from the usurper's grasp, despite such incredible risk. His wisdom, kindness and love had made the uncounted centuries together a joy. She did not want to leave him, but she could do so with no regrets, and that was perhaps his greatest gift to her.

Jante would forever feel that Ela had given him infinitely more. Ela was his life, his true constant and loyal friend. She knew his soul like no other, and loved him for who he was. She had faith in him when the rest of their flock spurned him. She loved him, when others felt him a fool. Always, she accepted him. Without her, he never would have had the strength to act as he did, or to impart wisdom to anyone.

Moments later, Ela's soul went silent and Jante knew she was gone.

PART IV

CHAPTER 47

THE VYESHEN

My encounter with Pillay nearly proved disastrous. I hadn't had such a close call with death since that time back in Jordan's shop. I should have thought to be aware of other Hiders in an established smuggling route. My rescue finally revealed Aitrox's enemies to me, but it wouldn't be long before I discovered the dark truths about the vyeshen. You might think that Aitrox's enemies would be a force for good in contrast to her oppressive evils. You might think that *finding a capable, organized resistance would have given me hope. It did at first. Yet, it quickly became apparent that the vyeshen were a dangerous ally, especially for an archos.*

J anis felt the pain mounting in her shoulders, and the chill of the wind began to hurt. The world drifted lazily below them, making it look like they weren't moving, but the strong wind from their flight told her otherwise. Strong grey talons wrapped under her armpits, clamping like cruel vices. She kept reminding herself that this creature didn't intend to hurt her. At least she hoped they meant no harm. Why would they have rescued her otherwise?

"My shoulders hurt, can we please take a break?" Janis asked, but the giant creature flew on as if she hadn't said anything. At first she would have thought to describe it as a massive eagle, but that didn't feel right. The giant animal's feathers spread sparsely over the massive body. Grey skin blended in with the dark feathers in a scattered patchwork. Massive eyes peered out over the world, but she had the distinct impression they were almost blind. They flew with a supreme awareness of everything around them, but their dark eyes seemed blank and lifeless. A sharp hooked beak matched the dark skin and feathers. The wings surprised her the most, with strange finger-like appendages fanning out at the primary joint in the wing. In flight they remained clenched in a fist, but the fingers seemed unique, as if designed for a specific purpose. A long, flat, featherless tail fanned out and rippled in the wind as her captor flew. Their bellies had an unusual leathery texture.

Janis didn't know the countryside well enough to have any idea where they were headed. She only hoped that she would be put down soon. The pain in her shoulders nearly overcame her capacity to think of other things. "Please, I need a break. I am sure that the others do, too!" Janis shouted into the wind. If the creature carrying her had any ears, it had to have heard her. She wondered how much these creatures shared in common with Eru. Did they even need ears to hear her? She didn't know how, but she knew the thing understood her. It made no outward indication of understanding but somehow she felt it, but that failed to ease her mind. The creature didn't mean her harm, but her pain seemed to please it. The flying beasts made her skin crawl.

She tried to keep her mind off the unyielding and almost unbearable pain in her shoulders and the growing fear she felt of the thing that had her in its grasp. In the few moments she managed to think on other things, her thoughts unfailingly returned to Eru. Occasionally his bearer flew into her field of view, and she watched him dangling in the claws of another of these dark creatures. He looked dead, but she refused to believe that possible.

"Please, do we have to hang from your claws like your latest catch? I would gladly take my chances riding on your back over this!" Janis begged. She knew it would do no good, but the pain pushed her to irrational desperation for relief. This time, she felt an undeniable response from her bearer. She felt his anger hit her with some sort of psychic force, every bit as real as a blow to the face. The strike left her unconscious, granting her an escape from the pain.

For the first time since his unconsciousness back in Jordan's shop, Eru returned to the world of sleep and dreams that normal people visited every night. As he slept, his archos body worked to heal his latest wounds.

"Eru," Aymis said. Bright sunlight rimmed her hair, giving her an angelic look, and the friendship and love in her smile warmed his heart. Was this what death was like?

"Aymis, what is this?" Eru asked.

"You shouldn't be here," she answered with a look of concern on her face. Despite the concern, and a sense of disappointment he felt in her heart, the longing to stay and be with her mattered most.

"Why? I don't want to leave. Did I die?"

"Eru, I can't make you go back, but if you give up, Aitrox will remain in power for thousands of years."

"But, I can't defeat her! I will only kill those I care for most, like I did you," Eru responded.

"You are the best chance humanity has," Aymis answered.

"But, I just want to stay here with you," Eru responded.

"I will be here waiting for you. Is this the way you want to end your dream - OUR dream?" Aymis answered.

"I can't do it," Eru answered quietly.

"It's not just yours and Aymis's dream," a vaguely familiar voice said. As Eru struggled to bring his eyes into focus, he recognized the features of his mother, though he had only seen her in that first dream back in Jordan's shop.

"Mother," Eru gasped.

"Eru, you have made me so proud," Ama said. Eru felt the love in her voice, saw it in her eyes, and sensed it dominating her emotions.

"Why are you proud of me? I killed you, killed your husband, led Aymis to her death and hundreds if not thousands of others," Eru said.

"Eru," Aymis said, giving him the look he rarely saw, but frequently felt; the look saying clearly how she hated it when Eru did this to himself.

"You have done something no archos has ever done. You have loved and lost. You have inspired hope in the hopeless. You have fought against the evil inside you, and largely overcome it. I couldn't be more proud of you," Ama said.

"I don't know what to say," Eru said, feeling his cheeks flushing and tears running down his face. He felt his own tears on his skin. If this was what death was, it felt more like life than his usual time in the void. Something about the immediacy of his own senses shocked and surprised him.

"Say you won't give up," Ama said.

"But, I can't win," Eru responded.

"You don't know that," Ama replied.

"So you are saying that I can win?" Eru asked.

"No, I don't know if you can or not, but if you stop trying then you have answered the question already," Ama answered.

"We can't make you do anything. If you choose to stay here, you have certainly earned a rest, but believe me, you will be much more fulfilled in the end if you continue your struggle," Aymis answered. Eru felt a truth in their words that meant the world to him. Ama's love, and her pride in his achievements, would not change if he chose to stay. Similarly, this choice had no bearing on Aymis's feelings for him. That realization however contrasted to his own heart. Staying now would mean spending forever with his own failure, not necessarily a failure to defeat Aitrox, but a failure to see it through to victory or the bitter end. Eru owed it to both of them to go back. Somehow, knowing they waited for him made going back easier.

"I will go back," Eru finally answered.

"Eru, one last thing. Be careful with your new allies. They cannot be trusted," Ama said. With those words, Eru felt consciousness returning, pulling him back into the world without senses of his own. Somehow returning to consciousness and life felt more like the opposite.

He felt the awareness of several vague, dark beings around him. He guessed correctly that each of these beings carried one of his Aegendi, and him. Pain, confusion, fear, and bewilderment swirled in the minds of each of his friends, even the unconscious ones. Janis slept in a deep subconscious state where dreams and sentient thought cannot penetrate. The being that carried Eru had a strange fogginess about him, something Eru's awareness had touched on a few times in the past. It reminded him of other intelligent animals, though he could sense the deeper sapience of something at least as intelligent as any person or archos. He suspected he could seize the thing, but Ama's last warning held him back. Seizing an untrustworthy ally unprovoked wouldn't help relations.

Eru felt the being turn its thoughts on him, communicating through images and impressions rather than words. Eru understood immediately. This was a race that had no spoken language, but their minds bore some similarities to the archos. Eru felt the communications clearly, unconsciously translating impressions into words and sentences.

'Don't put too much weight behind your dreams,' the being told him, through a series of emotions that conveyed the message with far greater clarity and intensity than any words could. *'Dreams are of your mind's own creation, nothing more than the connections in your brain firing randomly.'*

'No, that's not true. They told me things I could never...'

'They told you what your heart most wanted; rather convenient, don't you think? Do you really think the mother you killed would wait to receive you? Do you think she loves you, an archos?' the being said. Eru felt the reason behind the voice. He knew enough about the human mind to know how often people believed what they chose to believe. Why would an archos be any different?

'Be careful with your new allies. They cannot be trusted,' Ama's voice repeated in his head.

'You are wise not to trust easily, but you should apply that mistrust more liberally. Do not trust your feelings so willingly,' the vyeshen that bore him said.

'My feelings are what have led me to where I am now. I feel the wrongness of Aitrox, of my people and our power,' Eru retorted.

'Logic demonstrates the wrongness that a parasite should dominate and oppress for millennia,' his captor said. Eru sensed something far deeper than impartial logic behind the being's desire to fight Aitrox. Even though it endorsed a distrust of feelings, deep powerful emotions motivated all of its actions. Everything Eru sensed harbored a hatred for Aitrox, and all the archos, but no human had the capacity for hatred to match this being. Almost equal to its hatred for Aitrox, these beings hated all the archos, and even humans with a similar zeal.

'Why did you save me?' Eru asked.

'We have a common enemy,' came the reply.

'But, I can feel your hatred for me seething just under the surface. How can I trust you? As soon as you don't need me, you will kill me,' Eru answered.

'No. We did our job too well when we created the archos. Even we cannot kill you,' the creature replied. Eru felt the pain in that last response as his mind filled with the terrible recollection of the countless people who had tried to kill him, especially his father. He knew without a doubt what the creature meant, that trying to kill any archos was suicide, even for them. The first part, however, left Eru completely bewildered.

'Created the archos? I don't understand,' Eru said.

'We have lived for generations under the shadow of our past. I saved you because you represent the culmination of our efforts to change our greatest mistake. You, too, are our creation,' the creature answered.

'What are you?' Eru asked.

'Humans once called us the vyeshen,' Eru felt the interpretation of the feelings that translated undoubtedly to humanity in the creature's mind. Rats, cockroaches, pigeons and other pests enjoyed a similar classification in its mind. Eru saw the packed squalor of Deor through his perception, saw the polluted rivers and deforested hills, and understood the blight humanity represented to him. Humans, rats, he barely bothered to differentiate them.

'Vyeshen, what does that mean?' Eru asked.

'It means creature of change.'

CHAPTER 48

TALES FROM THE PAST

Did the vyeshen create the archos? The one who rescued me claimed that to be the case, but it seemed impossible. Did the vyeshen create ME? That notion also felt preposterous, but I had to remind myself of everything I didn't know about them. The list of things I knew felt terribly small, but first and foremost I knew I couldn't trust them. They hated humans almost as much as the archos, and were powerful enough for Aitrox to fear them. I needed them, and they obviously needed me. Already, I felt the growing question looming in my thoughts. What would happen once the nature of our relationship changed?

E ru had nothing to judge their trip by, lacking senses beyond that internal awareness of his body in space. Without sight to watch the land floating below him and without touch to feel the wind on his face, he only had the impressions he could sense in those around him. The discomfort, uncertainty, and impatience of his friends rubbed off on him, and Eru too found himself longing for the flight to end. Eventually, his uneasiness won out and he seized Rose to gather what information he could.

He felt an almost immediate response hitting him with a painful and violent force. Nothing had ever assaulted his awareness in that way before, and it caught him completely off guard. The blow immediately severed his hold on Rose before he could see anything.

'You will NOT seize your Aegendi in our presence without our consent!' his captor commanded, impressing the command on his mind with cruel, unyielding force.

'Oh, you saved me when Aitrox seized me!' Eru said, understanding filling his mind. As always, the reply came through impressions, thoughts, and images rather than actual words, unfolding the details from the past.

Shanje, the vyeshen who now carried Eru, clung to the alley wall, his recently adapted fingers on his wings finding holds in the stucco. The leathery underside of his tail exuded a sticky substance, clamping it to the side wall. It had taken a few centuries for the adaptations to finalize, affording them concealed landing places in Deor despite Aitrox's spiked roofs. Now Shanje held to the alley wall with ease, watching the cart that concealed Eru and his team. Shanje should have known to expect their puppet to behave irrationally. Without his Hider, he would be leading his team to its death. Saving him would risk everything they had worked for over centuries, but losing him meant starting completely over.

Shanje didn't share their puppet's concern for the welfare of the humans, but he needed them. Shanje loathed every moment spent in this vile place, despising the adaptations he had crafted to operate here covertly. Over a thousand years of hiding in caves had rendered his eyes almost useless in the daylight. He preferred it that way, hating the sight of the vermin that poured out of the buildings, swarming through their squalid streets. He knew enough through what he felt. Despite Shanje's hatred for everything touching humanity, he had worked hard to ensure their puppet would feel the opposite.

Shanje felt the fear in the iron wagon that carried his puppet's team, a painful reminder of his lost friend. It was not the first time, nor would it be the last, that Shanje's heart would burn with regret over the fate he had brought upon his friend, upon all the vyeshen. Jante had been right all along. Now, Shanje found himself clinging to the wall, an abomination and outcast. He deserved this fate, but that did not make it any easier.

Shanje's small team had their schemes crafted meticulously over centuries. Only his team had adapted their minds to make them harder for an archos to detect – a sort of mental smoke screen. At the same time, they crafted ability to cling to smooth walls, hiding in the shadows of the alleys where Aitrox never thought to look. Even their grey patchwork of feathers and skin served as a sort of camouflage against the smoke-stained alley walls. On a few occasions she came close to finding them, but a quick severing blow to her Reader or Hawkeye avoided discovery. Aitrox had never seized one of his team, but they had plans in place to get out safely should it happen.

The thought of leaving this city and these pathetic people to their fate had some appeal, but he couldn't bring himself to give up on his redemption. The thought of his race being condemned to life in the caves felt like a fate worse than life surrounded by these urchins. So Shanje clung to the wall, observing Eru's wagon, sharing the fear that emanated from the Aegendi. Shanje should have anticipated this decision by his puppet, but creating those feelings of benevolence and concern didn't mean he understood them.

Heavy clouds made it easy to observe his puppet's maneuvers today, hiding him from human eyes but doing nothing to obscure his own senses. Without a Hider, Eru was as good as dead though. The wagon rolled up to the citadel, and the moment of truth arrived. Aitrox wasn't using her typical games in this fight, but she still showed a flair for the ironic. Using a Silvertounge to turn the people of Deor against their only true champion was just like Aitrox. Eru's attack unfolded exactly as Shanje had expected: Aitrox seized Eru and threatened to destroy the culmination of Shanje's plans and dreams.

Breaking Aitrox's hold over Eru proved far harder than Shanje had anticipated. By the time he succeeded, Shanje knew Eru wouldn't have time to find his Aegendi and stop his fall. Shanje tucked into a dive, honing in on his target by sono-location in the heavy mists and cloud cover. Shanje barely caught Eru in time, grabbing his shoulders with his talons, then wrapped his body with his tail before thrusting upward with his wings to slow their descent. Had he caught him only a moment later, they would have hit the street together with lethal force.

With his puppet safe, Shanje knew he had to get back out of sight before one of Aitrox's underlings could zero in on him. He had no desire to put their escape strategy into practice unless he had to. Shanje reached out to the rest of his team, all of whom waited just above the roof tops. If Aitrox seized their archos again, they would need to work together to break her hold before she could kill him. Fortunately, Eru's Hider made an unexpected return.

The Hider's return gave them the chance to retreat. They had already played more of their hand than they should have, and Shanje had underestimated Aitrox's strength. Their actions today prematurely revealed their involvement with Eru, undoubtedly drawing Aitrox's full attention and wrath their way. One way or another, their struggle would all come to a head soon.

'Just what are your plans for me?' Eru asked, trying not to feel too angry at everything Shanje had revealed. Shanje had saved his life twice, yet he couldn't help feeling anger over the thought that somebody had been manipulating him. Shanje claimed to have created him. Eru didn't know if he really wanted to know Shanje's plans for him.

'You are going to help us destroy Aitrox,' Shanje answered.

'What makes you think I will help you?' Eru asked.

'I made you for this purpose. You will help us. It's in your nature,' Shanje answered.

'How dare you claim to have made me! You don't even know me!' Eru snapped back. Shanje's answer told another tale from the past.

Again, Eru saw a narrative of Shanje's surreptitious observation unfold. Eru recognized the subjects of Shanje's story immediately. The sight of his parents together played a painful song on his heartstrings. Telu returned from his day at work as a merchant's accountant. It paid well enough to keep his family out of the slums, a fact Shanje appreciated. Shanje had picked this couple with care, not comprehending the depth of the emotions Telu and Ama felt, but knowing he would need his archos puppet to be exposed to such feelings from the beginning.

Shanje could hardly believe he was deliberately adding to the archos population. Shanje had to work with whatever tools Aitrox gave him. If things worked as he hoped, Aitrox would never see their plans coming. Why would she have thought to remove the vyeshen's ability to convert a normal fetus into an archos in the womb?

Shanje didn't understand this couple, which is exactly why he had chosen them. They loved each other with the kind of intensity he hadn't thought could exist under Aitrox's thumb. In three generations of searching the city, Shanje had not found another woman who possessed such an indomitable hope and unconditional love for others. Despite himself, Shanje almost found himself caring for her, but he always quickly put those feelings to rest. Caring for a human! Shanje couldn't believe the thought ever crossed his mind.

Ama felt different, truly rare. Shanje regarded her like a jeweler valued a rare gem. One such as her wouldn't come around again for hundreds of years. Just as a jeweler has to take his tools to a one-of-a-kind gem, breaking it to make his masterpiece, Shanje knew his masterpiece would destroy this rare being.

Shanje could hardly blame her husband, Telu, for worshiping the ground she walked on. Shanje only hoped that her goodness, combined with Shanje's subtle influence throughout the pregnancy, could pass some of those attributes on to his archos. It was a fool's notion. Just the thought of an archos that cared for others defied everything they had been crafted to be. Shanje's goal to bypass generations of craftsmanship going into the archos' natures with a single birth flew in the face of every principle of change the vyeshen worked with.

At the moment of truth, Shanje almost lost his nerve. He didn't know if it came down to all his doubts about the foolishness of his plan, or a foolhardy attachment to the mother. After all, why would an archos ever help him overthrow the system where they were worshiped and empowered? And how could he ever let himself feel any compunction over the death of a human? Did a farmer feel pity for the pig he raised for the slaughter?

He overcame all those doubts in a moment of swift decision. Shanje and his followers would free his race from the caves and return them to the freedom of the beautiful blue skies. vyeshen were never meant to live in caves. He had nothing to lose, and redemption for all the vyeshen to gain. As soon as he knew the pregnancy would result in an archos' birth, he left. He knew he would have to return frequently to continue to influence the fetus. Shanje would have his puppet soon.

'You monster! You killed her!' Eru shouted at Shanje in his mind. He couldn't believe it. He refused to believe it.

'It had to be done,' Shanje said.

'Did it? I could have had a normal life! You killed my mother and destroyed my father, and you don't even care!' Eru wanted to seize the monster and destroy him right now. Shanje deserved it for all his meddling. Eru knew the details of the tragedies Shanje had wrought. Eru knew the depths of sorrow Shanje had sewn in Telu's life. Eru felt almost consumed with thoughts of what might have been. Telu hadn't always been the murderous terrorist who killed hundreds of people without remorse. His father had been a kind, loving man. The thoughts of being raised as a normal child with Ama as his mother and Telu as his father stirred deep emotions in his heart. That was the life he should have had. Shanje destroyed that.

'A few casualties are inevitable in war, especially if...' Shanje began.

'If we want to defeat a goddess. I know,' Eru finished the thought angrily.

'NEVER call her that!' Shanje replied with such force that it nearly left Eru unconscious. *'There are no gods or goddesses, especially not Aitrox!'*

'Why did you choose Ama? Why did you do that to her?' Eru asked bitterly. He knew his tears flowed freely, reminding him of his dream just hours ago.

'You know the answer already,' Shanje answered.

'But, you had no idea if it would even work. You killed her for a gamble!' Eru answered angrily.

'But, it did work,' Shanje answered. Despite Shanje's implicit confidence, Eru didn't know if he agreed.

'Why don't the vyeshen fight Aitrox?' Eru asked, sensing the pain his question caused Shanje, but not regretting it. Shanje's answer unfolded as the final tale from his past

Shanje and the rest of his flock had learned to survive in the deep confines of the mountains, but the yearning for the open skies almost drove him mad. Jante's wisdom had saved them, but he couldn't help but wonder if he had chosen the mines as a way to punish them all for their folly. With little else to occupy his mind except feelings of guilt, Shanje and most of the surviving vyeshen attacked their metal-lust with renewed vigor. Such a vulnerability would never pull them so low again.

In the darkness, the vyeshen rediscovered light. Their hearts returned to Phoenix. They had all forgotten him, and they had all failed him. Being forced to spend just under a century in purgatory while they waited for Aitrox to die felt like a merciful punishment for their sins. As the lust for metal slowly faded in the minds of each vyeshen, Phoenix's warmth returned in their hearts. They had all missed him so terribly.

Shanje woke with a terrified start, as did every vyeshen in their flock. They had all felt it. Phoenix was under attack, and to their shock and terror, their god was afraid. Every time Phoenix faltered felt like a vice crushing Shanje's heart, and every revival brought liberation and relief. Phoenix's harrowing ordeal dragged on, seemingly forever for the vyeshen refugees. Then it happened. Phoenix faltered, faltered but did not rise again. Their god was dead.

Phoenix's death shook Shanje and brought him lower than he could ever have imagined. It had been his fault. His sins brought about the death of his god. NO! Shanje could not, would not believe that. A god could not have been brought down by mere mortals. His god had failed them. Had Phoenix truly been a god, Aitrox would now be dead. Shanje's thoughts resonated with a small group of the vyeshen flock, earning them all banishment.

The vyeshen would not be so cruel as to drive the profane heretics from the mines, but it hardly mattered. Shanje and his band were dead to them: no longer vyeshen. The regard of the vyeshen mattered little to the heretics. Those foolish enough to cling to the worship of a dead god did not deserve their attention.

So the centuries passed with the vyeshen and heretics living together but growing further apart. Those who honored Phoenix would never leave the caves. To them it hardly mattered that Aitrox was immortal. The vyeshen were determined to join Phoenix in his grave. An eternity in darkness could never atone for the fate they had brought upon their god. The heretics on the other hand engaged in a fool's errand, to find a way to defeat Aitrox. As the centuries passed the heretics forsook their sacred plumes, growing to vile creatures that belonged in the darkness, becoming wyverns.

CHAPTER 49

UNDER THE MOUNTAINS

The more I learned about the vyeshen, the more uncomfortable I felt about them. I had never thought that anybody
but the archos could have such mental abilities. The vyeshen
mind worked differently, but I could feel their strength and
comprehend volumes of information from a single thought.
In my brief communications with Shanje, I knew the vyesh-
en hid a dark history. Shanje and I shared a common
enemy, and were uneasy allies for now. I couldn't help but

fear what the world would be like if the vyeshen came out of hiding.

E ru felt the fear in his friends' hearts amplify, realizing they were plunging into the impenetrable darkness of the vyeshen mines. Shanje and his part-ners navigated the tight confines and the spacious caverns with the same sense as bats, though they hadn't always possessed that ability. Almost as absolute as the darkness was the oppressive silence. Only the faint sounds of vyeshen feathers and beating wings disturbed the quiet.

As they neared the settlement, Eru felt the presence of hundreds of vyeshen growing clearer. Even without the effects of iron, sensing the vyeshen pres-ence this deep in the mountains would have been difficult. As the wyverns returned, anger and jealousy rippled through the vyeshen; anger at the heresy of the wyverns, and jealousy at the freedom their heresy gave them. To the vyeshen, the wyvern's abominable adaptations ranked them close to the humans in ignominy.

The spectacularly massive creatures truly didn't belong in the caves. Despite their ability to adapt their bodies, the vyeshen devoutly clung to their traditional form, an homage to their god. Fiery plumage served no purpose in the absolute darkness, and their large bodies and massive wings didn't serve them well in the caves. Only adaptations that didn't change appearance were accepted by the devout vyeshen, allowing them to navigate the dark caves via sonar, but little else. Shanje and the ten or so wyverns, however, had broken the mold with their deviant tails, spotty dark plumage, and highly adapted appendages on their wings.

Along with the hundreds of vyeshen, thousands of people, if they could be called that, lived in the settlement as well.

'Humans! There are people in your settlement?' Eru asked in disbelief.

'Their ancestors were humans,' Shanje answered with disdain; included in his reply came a glimpse into a history of slavery and servitude. The slaves' minds had been changed, as had their bodies, under vyeshen influence. Confined to this dark prison, their eyes resembled the blank, useless eyes of the archos. They

too navigated the darkness with sonar, a necessary sense the vyeshen had given them.

'Slaves! They are your slaves!' Eru answered angrily.

Shanje's answer didn't even grant them that level of dignity, making it clear he thought of them as a farmer regards livestock. They lived on the cavern floor amidst the refuse that the vyeshen let fall from their lofts amidst the stalactites. Eru nearly threw up, realizing that the vyeshen had adapted these slaves to subsist on the meager nourishment they could derive from vyeshen droppings. The occasional captured bat, or cockroach supplemented the wretched creatures' diets. Their minds had grown slow and dumb in the darkness with such a despicable diet.

Eru understood the interrelated nature of species. Bats shared a similar symbiotic relationship with cockroaches and dung beetles, but this didn't qualify as a natural symbiosis. These had once been people, and the vyeshen had reduced them to a role normally reserved for insects and vermin.

'You will not set my Aegendi down among the slaves. I will not have you placing them in such squalor,' Eru commanded.

'I wouldn't dream of it,' Shanje replied sarcastically. Shanje hardly felt there to be any distinction between filth in Deor and the squalor at the bottom of the cave.

'How did you do this to them?' Eru asked bitterly.

'We control the threads of life. It is how I created the archos, and how we created these things.'

Eru's powerful mind immediately comprehended the depths of the vyeshen power, and the breadth of its touch on the world. He saw how Shanje's mind could grasp the infinitely complex threads of each creature's life, threads so miniscule they repeated millions of times in every organism. Beyond that, the vyeshen – and wyverns – could navigate, comprehend and manipulate these threads.

'What are you doing here, abomination?' another vyeshen growled, addressing Shanje with obvious distaste.

'Working for your freedom,' Shanje answered.

'We don't deserve freedom from our failures,' he replied. Eru felt heavy sorrow and guilt in the communication between the two vyeshen.

'I did not come to debate this with you!' Shanje snapped. Eru nearly seized the new vyeshen, Jenshu, when their minds touched.

'You brought a godkiller into our sanctuary! How dare you!' Eru felt Jenshu's thoughts quickly turned away from him with the skilled discipline he hadn't experienced since Telu's death.

'You should see by now that he is different. The fact that you are not seized or dead should be proof enough of that,' Shanje replied calmly.

'Never underestimate Aitrox's cunning,' Jenshu retorted, seething.

'It is Aitrox who has underestimated our cunning. Everything is working according to my plans. She will soon regret everything she has done to the vyeshen,' Shanje answered, seemingly indifferent to Jenshu's anger.

'She is the punishment we have earned for failing our god. It is not your place to destroy Aitrox,' Jenshu replied.

'I will have none of that foolish dogma! Gods don't get themselves killed by a mortal. There are no gods. There is nothing mandating an eternal punishment for the sins in our past. There is survival and nothing more,' Shanje rejoined.

'Then we can survive in the caves,' Jenshu said.

'Enough! This is pointless. I have work to do,' Shanje replied.

'No, you don't. Bringing a godkiller into our sanctuary is the final blasphemy. I will see to it that you and that abomination are exiled.'

Eru felt Jenshu's departure like he was pulling his hand away from a hot flame. For all of Shanje's hatred for the archos and humanity, it couldn't compare to Jenshu's fierce disgust. Eru had felt that kind of unbridled hatred in his father, seeing uncanny similarities between Jenshu and Telu. Eru was grateful when Jenshu distanced himself and turned his thoughts to other things. Jenshu would cause trouble for Shanje, but Eru didn't know if that would be a good or bad thing.

CHAPTER 50

THINGS IN COMMON

At no other time in my life did I need the memory of Ama and Aymis to give me purpose more than now. Like it or not, Shanje had made my mother a martyr for the cause of defeating Aitrox. Aymis had died for that same purpose. Part of me wanted to forsake Shanje for what he had done, but I knew Ama would have given her life willingly to bring about Aitrox's downfall. The first time Shanje let me seize him, it was all I could do not to kill him. A wyvern's power under archos domination was truly remarkable.

The wyverns set Eru and the others down on a ledge high above the underground lake. In the absolute darkness, none of Eru's companions had any notion of their location, or the precipitous, fatal drop just a few feet away.

"Nobody move," Eru instructed all of them.

"Trust me, that won't be a problem," Janis said.

"Where are we? What is going on?" Volo asked nervously.

"We are in the vyeshen settlement. They are sworn enemies to Aitrox. They can help us defeat her." Eru couldn't bring himself to tell them everything. Having made his decision to work with the vyeshen, he didn't want to trouble his friends with his uncertainty. He missed Aymis terribly right now. Knowing he couldn't have hid his doubts from her, he would have had a confidant. He couldn't bring himself to burden any of the others. He felt their terror nearly driving them to insanity as it was. If they knew everything he knew, it could break them.

"I hope you are right!" Rose responded.

"How can they help us defeat her?" Janis asked.

"I don't know yet," Eru answered truthfully. Shanje must have a plan, or he wouldn't have brought them here. There was still so much Eru didn't know about the vyeshen. Maybe the wyverns had some other adaptations that they could use when they attacked Aitrox. However, Eru sensed that Shanje operated on borrowed time, and that Jenshu's threats were very real. It gave Eru a small sense of respect for the monster that had killed Ama and destroyed his chances at a regular life. At least Shanje had enough conviction to willingly sacrifice everything in his fight for redemption. Somehow that thought lessened Eru's loathing for the creature slightly.

"I don't trust them," Volo said. "For all intents and purposes, we are their prisoners."

"They are our allies, not our enemies," Eru responded.

"That's not the impression I got," Janis said uneasily.

"Me, neither," Volo replied. Eru felt similar affirmative thoughts in each of their minds. Even Supe felt doubt and uncertainty about the vyeshen.

"Look, I understand your doubts. The vyeshen hate humans, and they hate the archos even more. However, they did save us from Aitrox, and they need us. For the time being, they are on our side," Eru said, hoping he sounded more confident then he felt.

"How can we trust them?" Volo asked.

"We can't, but Eru's right," Oko answered. "For now we have no choice, and they need us, or they wouldn't have saved us from Aitrox." Just as he finished speaking, a quiet rushing sound from large wings heralded the return of a wyvern. Eru felt Shanje's return, but none of his friends even had a name to put to any of the vyeshen. That fact alone added to the fear and mystery they felt about the vyeshen. Eru felt each of them grow tense, thinking about the dark, fearful creature somewhere nearby.

'I am going to weave your life threads. In the past, I worked subtly and slowly to avoid notice. That is not a luxury we have now. Understand that I am putting my life in your hands,' Shanje said to Eru. Eru sensed the deeper implications to his statement. Shanje was gambling that he had crafted Eru's nature well enough to protect him. Doubt nagged at Shanje's heart, for he had gambled on such emotional conditioning in the past, and lost.

A shiver ran down Eru's spine, not physically – for Eru would never have felt that – but this tremor penetrated to the deepest recesses of his soul. He found no words to describe the feeling of a foreign presence creeping through the very essence of his body. He had known feelings of violation and vulnerability when Aitrox had seized him. This was different, but so terribly the same. Shanje crawled through the essence of his life, capable of destroying him with one misstep, and comprehending his nature profoundly.

Never before had Eru had to fight so hard not to seize another. Never had someone's focus so purely and powerfully consumed him as Shanje's did now, and never had that act so perilously endangered Eru. He almost wished to just give in. The demon that crawled through his soul had killed his mother and condemned him to a life as an archos. How many lives had been ruined through this meddling monster's actions? Yet Eru knew that Ama would not have wanted that. He knew that Aymis wanted him to push forward, even if it meant working with this demonic creature.

Eru and Shanje had two things in common, their mutual hatred, and an even greater hatred for Aitrox. Both had hoped to find answers and keys to defeating Aitrox in their uncomfortable alliance, yet neither of them could really offer anything groundbreaking and new to the other. They needed a way to penetrate Aitrox's secrets, to see deep into her soul. It was their only chance at defeating her, a slim chance at best.

Without a Reader, they couldn't hope to delve into her mind. Eru hadn't imagined how crucial Aymis's gift could have been now. As much as he missed her terribly, he was grateful she had been spared everything he and the others had gone through. He was equally grateful she would not have to confront Aitrox. Eru didn't know if he could have let her face such a confrontation, even though her gift would have been their only chance to find Aitrox's weakness, if she had one.

Eru's thoughts reached Shanje, *'I have an idea. Aitrox is terrified of the* vyeshen. *She is guarding a secret that she is afraid could be exploited to destroy her,'* Eru said. *'Give me the Reader's power, and I will find her secrets. I will find what she is hiding, and defeat her.'*

Despite Shanje's doubts, he had no better alternative, so he set to work on Eru's threads. The forcefulness of his presence on Eru's very being harrowed him in ways he could never hope to describe. An archos could not feel physical pain of his own, but this experience hurt unlike anything Eru had experienced in another. Shanje pushed and shredded with brutal intent, sparing no time for the typically delicate, subtle and gradual changes. Even Eru's life of discipline and training to resist his instincts could not have prepared him for this new, terrible threat.

Eru seized Shanje, and instantly experienced the depths of Shanje's torment. Eru knew Shanje's guilt, a burning that could consume a thousand souls, insatiable and unrelenting. He knew the sorrow he felt when Ela had died, and how

Shanje had secretly loved a female that would never be his. Her death weighed heavily on his heart. Yet, nothing hurt as miserably as the knowledge that he had squandered the friendship, trust and loyalty of the one who turned out to be the greatest vyeshen that had ever lived. Jante had always done right. Jante had saved the vyeshen from the destruction they all had deserved. It would have been right for Jante and Ela to have left this land, but they had refused. In the end, Jante had died to make their ultimate freedom possible.

How could Shanje ever hope to live up to such a standard? He knew he could not. Nothing he could ever do would bring back the hundreds of vyeshen who died because of his arrogance and greed. He was beyond redemption. Shanje feared death, but as Eru seized him, he accepted his fate – fitting that his final punishment would come at the hands of an archos. As Eru comprehended the full breadth of the vyeshen history, his hatred for Shanje almost vanished, and Eru just managed to restrain his violent instincts.

After recovering from the initially overwhelming experience of seizing a being who had lived for millennia, Eru's mind began to grasp the power over the threads of life. The beauty, complexity and marvel of the threads would have overwhelmed a human mind. Eru saw how the vyeshen's entire being had been crafted and built to navigate these threads with the confidence of a spider in its own web. Even the incredible power of the archos' mind was ill suited for this kind of task. Yet, through Shanje, Eru perceived the nuances that defined every one of his friends. The threads themselves established a complicated foundation that the vyeshen could change, but the tapestry of life experiences also wove a part of each soul's tale, and the vyeshen could not touch that.

Eru turned his focus to his own threads and felt immediately rebuffed. With or without Shanje's assistance, Eru could not comprehend the workings of his being. Through Shanje, he comprehended one of Jante's final saving acts, and Eru understood. Had Aitrox gained access to her own threads, no vyeshen would be alive. Her triumph would have been even more unassailable. As Eru recognized that he could not touch his own threads, he released Shanje. *'I am sorry. I had never felt such a force before.'*

Shanje replied more through images and thoughts about his history crafting the controllers, and his near perfect comprehension of the reflexes he had created. *'I knew it was coming. I am amazed you managed not to kill me.'*

Eru had to muster all the discipline from his lifetime not to seize Shanje as the work continued. He felt like a child being ravaged by wolves inside, vulnerable, unprotected, exposed. Several times his mind spun as Shanje's work altered the very way his brain operated. Any feeble sense of time that Eru had faded and Shanje's brutal harrowing of his being continued. Eru wondered if it would ever end. He wondered if he could last another second, yet last he did.

Jenshu's fury kept the rest of the vyeshen clear of him, a fact he didn't mind. Shanje's betrayal burned in his heart. Not since the days of Aitrox's rise had any vyeshen betrayed their own so deeply. To bring one of the god killers to their settlement! How dare he? It was the final heresy of the profane wyverns. The vyeshen should have killed them long ago. Leaving the wyverns alive had been a foolish refusal to accept their own eternal punishment. The vyeshen had let the profane outcasts live because they represented hope. The vyeshen did not deserve hope, and these heretics did not deserve life. They would kill the wyverns, and their god killer. When Jenshu realized that he had not been killed by such a careless thought, a thrill of excitement rushed through him. The god killer was vulnerable, and Jenshu would make sure to exploit this opportunity.

CHAPTER 51

LESSER EVIL

I always loathed my power, and the misery and death it wrought. I had always longed to be free of it, like a child longs to fly through the clouds. The clouds look soft and inviting but he is unaware of the cold temperatures and rough, turbulent air that makes the most spectacular clouds. If you were to grant a child that wish it would be anything but a joyous and comfortable experience.

E ru had long passed the point of declaring he could stand it no longer. He had reached such points, sort of artificial ultimatums, more times than he could count as Shanje ravaged his being to make the change. There was no endurance left. The agonizing experience continued, but the only part Eru played now was the simple act of not dying. If he could have died, he would have welcomed the escape. Then it ended.

"I don't believe it," Eru muttered out loud, hearing his own words through multiple pairs of ears even though he had nobody seized. Much to his disbelief, he even felt the faint echoes of his voice register in the ears of several slaves far below. The entire cave came to life for him, through the sonar senses of several vyeshen. Eru felt the cold, clammy rock against the skin of each of his Aegendi, and smelled the muggy, humid air through each of their nostrils. Janis had a runny nose, and the soreness in Volo's shoulders felt particularly intense.

"What, Eru?" Rose asked.

"Do you feel me in your mind?" Eru asked, too excited to care about how his voice cracked.

"No, you haven't seized me, so why would I?" Rose answered.

"It's incredible! I can hear everything you and everyone else hears! I can sense the caves as the vyeshen do! I can feel the stone your hand is touching right now, and I don't have to seize anyone to do it!" Eru practically squealed in his excitement. His elated exclamations fell on the confused ears of the slaves below.

"Then you're free!" Rose said, sharing his enthusiasm. Eru sensed her desire to hug him, held back only by the fact she had no idea where he was, or where the edge of their ledge was in the dark. Eru, however, had no such limitations, so he stepped to her and gave her an exuberant hug. He nearly squeezed the breath out of her lungs.

"Eru, that's amazing!" Volo exclaimed.

"I-I don't believe it," Eru stammered. Shanje had just granted Eru a gift he had never even dared dream could be possible. He could live without causing others pain. The patient acceptance of that repeated trauma that his Aegen-di willingly endured had been forgotten under the demands of their struggle against Aitrox. Now that he faced the very real prospect of never needing to seize anyone again, the thought of doing so felt repulsive.

"Eru, free?" Supe asked, her voice picking up on the infectious mood.

"Yes, Eru doesn't have to seize anyone ever again!" Rose exclaimed.

"But, you still will, won't you?" Janis asked, noticeably less excited than Rose, Supe or even Volo. Eru realized that he still had almost no idea what Oko felt. At least Shanje's sonar gave him a read on Oko's facial expressions, implying that he too shared Janis's concern.

"Why? I don't want to do that to any of you," Eru said with conviction.

"But, you will have to," Oko said.

"Oko's right. We still have to fight Aitrox, and that means you will have to use our gifts," Janis added.

"But..." Rose began to object.

"We were never fighting to free, Eru. We have been fighting to defeat Aitrox. I will be happy for you once Aitrox is dead and your freedom means something," Oko added, interrupting Rose's objections.

"How does this help us defeat Aitrox?" Janis asked.

"I don't know. This isn't what Shanje was trying to do," Eru answered.

"Who is Shanje?" Volo asked.

"Shanje is one of the wyverns that brought us here, an outcast vyeshen. It is their power that made it possible," Eru explained.

"So the vyeshen have a gift of sorts?" Rose asked.

"Eru can explain that later," Oko interrupted. "Why did Shanje do this for you? I assume that he is fighting against Aitrox, or he wouldn't have saved us."

"I asked him to make me a Reader," Eru answered, gradually calming down as he remembered their initial goal.

"Well, did it work?" Volo asked.

"I don't think it did. At least, I can't figure out how to do anything more than I have always been able to do," Eru answered. He tried to find Shanje, to ask him what had gone wrong, but the wyvern had already slipped away. The iron deposits in the caves made it impossible for Eru to reach him.

"So, what is our plan?" Janis asked.

"Well, once Shanje fixes this, I plan to discover what Aitrox is hiding. Hopefully it will reveal a way to destroy her," Eru answered.

"That's assuming that she has a secret we can exploit," Oko said cautiously.

"She kept iron, Hiders and the vyeshen secret because each posed a threat. Secrets are the key to her power," Eru replied.

"Not every secret she keeps has to be a weakness," Volo said.

"Volo is right. The savvy fighter keeps a few knives hidden in battle. Aitrox could have a few deadly tricks of her own that she is hiding," Oko said.

"And if you could know where your enemy hid his weapons, it would give you an edge, would it not, Oko?" Eru answered.

"It helps, sure," Oko said. "It is still a fool's errand, but if we wait until we have a better plan, we probably will never leave these caves."

"There is a problem," Eru said. "I didn't feel even the slightest tug when Janis said my name. What if I can't seize anyone now?"

"Don't be ridiculous!" Volo said. "How could you lose that? You're an archos."

"Their power to change life is very complex, and Shanje was forced to work very forcefully and quickly as he tried to make me a Reader. I honestly don't know what he might have accidentally done."

"Well, we had better find out," Janis said. "Seize me."

Eru tried, but failed. "I can't," Eru answered.

"What are we going to do?" Oko asked.

"Shanje will fix this. He has to," Eru said, not very sure of himself. For all he knew, Shanje had meant to remove his power to seize. Perhaps Shanje only needed him to gather information with his expanded senses. Shanje could, after all, sever an archos's hold on others, but Shanje had to know how critical Eru's Aegendi were – particularly Oko. Shanje and the wyverns, couldn't hope to defeat Aitrox with her hundreds or even thousands of archos she controlled. Without a seized Hider, Shanje's attack would end the moment it began.

"What if he can't?" Janis asked. Eru felt the growing tension and frustration in Janis and Oko. At the same time, he felt a churning mix of emotions in the hearts of Rose, Volo and even Supe. If Eru couldn't seize them, then their part in the battle against Aitrox was through. Eru couldn't blame them for feeling relieved, and even excited at the thought. At the same time, each of them felt a sense of uselessness, and failure.

"Then, maybe we can do what we left Deor to do in the first place," Volo said quietly.

"Maybe now that Eru has been freed, we can truly start over somewhere where nobody has heard of an archos," Rose agreed.

"You are forgetting about a pretty critical detail. We are trapped in these caves. We need the vyeshen to get out of here," Oko said.

"But, Eru can see like the vyeshen do," Volo objected.

"Only through their sonar, and only what they see. I could get us down from this ledge, but no vyeshen's senses currently reach beyond this cavern," Eru remarked.

"So, we need Shanje's help to get out of here," Oko added with a note in his voice that seemed to remind everyone that he had been trying to say that all along.

"That or another vyeshen," Rose said hopefully.

"I don't think that's likely. Maybe one of Shanje's followers, but I don't even know where they are," Eru replied.

"Just who are these vyeshen? Why are they here in these awful caves? What is this all about?" Volo asked, firing off questions in an irritable tone.

"It's a long story," Eru replied.

"We aren't going anywhere," Volo retorted.

"True. Well, it all started a very long time ago..." Eru began explaining the history, doing his best to summarize the vast history between vyeshen and humans in a reasonably brief period.

"Unbelievable," Janis muttered as Eru finished relating the tale.

"So, Aitrox used her captured vyeshen to create the Aegendi," Oko surmised.

"But, what about the Hiders? Why would she create them?" Volo asked.

"Aitrox didn't create the Hiders. The Hiders were Jante's final act of defiance. Even while seized a vyeshen maintains some autonomy over how he or she influences the threads of life. Jante managed to secretly create the Hiders even as Aitrox created all her other terrible tools."

"Does she still have any vyeshen seized?" Oko asked.

"As far as Shanje knows, she does not. If she still controlled vyeshen, the entire population of Deor would be an Aegendi by now," Eru answered. "Shanje guesses that Aitrox panicked when she discovered their Hiders, and killed her vyeshen slaves before they could undermine her power any further."

Oko broke in, "But, how did Aitrox survive until today without the vyeshen making her immortal?"

"Nobody knows. We know that she destroyed Phoenix, and somehow gained immortality by doing so," Eru answered.

"I don't know who I hate more, Aitrox or the vyeshen," Volo said. The others all nodded their agreement.

"Volo makes a good point. If we defeat Aitrox, what will happen when the vyeshen come back out of the mountains?" Oko asked. "What if life in Deor under Aitrox's domination was an improvement to absolute slavery under the vyeshen?"

"I hadn't thought about that," Rose said pensively.

"The vyeshen are not the threat they used to be," Eru answered. "The vyeshen tried to enslave humanity and couldn't without their slave drivers. That was when there were many more vyeshen. There are only a few hundred left now. We must first defeat Aitrox, then worry about the vyeshen." Eru chose not to tell his friends that humanity had hardly fared any better than the vyeshen. Aitrox had never let the humans spread far beyond the confines of Deor. To his and the vyeshen's knowledge, the humans, too, were just a tiny fragment of the people they had once been.

"It's clear to me who my enemies are," Janis said with icy, stern resolve. "The vyeshen didn't kill my daughter. Aitrox did."

"The vyeshen are the lesser evil, and I believe it is necessary to work with them in order to defeat Aitrox," Eru said.

"So, how do you fit into Shanje's plans?" Volo asked.

"You may be surprised to know that he created me, manipulating my mother's pregnancy and working to change my nature. I am in essence the culmination of his plans, and Shanje's greatest hope of defeating Aitrox. He is very powerful, and very cunning. You will not find anyone more committed to Aitrox's downfall then Shanje," Eru explained.

"But, can he be trusted?" Oko asked.

"For now, our goal is the same," Eru answered.

"I don't trust him, Eru," Rose said.

"That may not matter for much longer," Eru said nervously. "I think that the vyeshen have realized I cannot seize anybody. They are coming."

CHAPTER 52

TO SAVE AN ARCHOS

Shanje's mistake had granted me a gift, freedom from the need to seize others. I feared it also made me useless and disposable to him. Would he come to our aid now? The ledge where he had placed us offered some protection, but without Shanje's help, the vyeshen would kill us all.

The vyeshen's murderous thoughts burned in Eru's mind like a growing fire as they drew near. The oncoming vyeshen seemed to revel in Eru's vulnerability, acting like fascinated children taunting a chained predator. Each vyeshen filled his mind with its own horrendous imaginings for how he would die. The images of his death did not bother Eru, but their brutally graphic intent hardly discriminated between him and his friends.

"Everybody back!" Eru commanded, doing his best to herd his friends to safety. Eru remembered enough from what Shanje's sonar had revealed to believe they may find a small cavern of sorts back against the cave wall. It would be a tight fit, if they could squeeze through the gaps between a few stalactites. Being accustomed to the absolute precision and control of seizing others, his attempts to guide his blind friends quickly frustrated him. "No, no, the other way!" he growled as Volo nearly stepped off the ledge.

Jenshu drew near first, unwittingly granting Eru the senses he needed to herd his team back through the stalactites to shelter. He was accustomed to guiding bodies from a third person perspective, and his terrified friends responded to his newfound confidence well. Eru breathed a sigh of relief when Oko and then Volo made it through the gap between stalactites as Jenshu came within striking distance: only Eru remained exposed.

Jenshu's sonar gave Eru the cue he needed to know exactly when and where to duck. Jenshu's talons narrowly missed him, scraping and grating against the cavern wall. An angry shriek indicated Jenshu's surprise. Before Jenshu could recover, Eru squeezed through the gap, cramming into the tight confines with his friends.

Their feeble shelter felt full of knees, elbows and ribs. Jenshu shrieked angrily as he thrust his massive beak through the gap. His beak snapped shut just inches from Eru. Rose, Volo and Janis all cried in terror as the sounds of Jenshu's snapping beak, scraping talons and angry cries continued. Then Eru breathed a sigh of relief as Jenshu retreated.

Eru's relief was shortlived, as he quickly perceived Jenshu's plan. It would require an impressive feat of acrobatics for a creature his size, but Eru knew Jenshu could pull it off. He watched nervously through Jenshu's own sonar as the massive bird twisted in flight to precisely avoid the cave walls and hit the protecting stalactite at high speed. Jenshu screeched in pain, but the stalactite held firm. The protective stone cracked ominously on Jenshu's second attempt.

Fortunately, stone wasn't the only thing to break that time, and Jenshu had to withdraw.

Other vyeshen soon took his place, each one plenty willing to sacrifice their bodies to reach the profane god killer in their midst. Crack! The stalactite gave way. The crack echoed through the caves, followed by a rapid succession of splashes as the pieces of stone plunged into the lake below.

"Oko, hand me your knife," Eru ordered. Volo grunted as Oko's elbow knocked him in the chin as Oko contorted to reach his knife. Keeping it sheathed, he wormed his arm through the press of bodies extending the weapon in the direction of Eru's voice. Eru grabbed it just in time.

He quickly unsheathed the blade, slashing at the gaping maw of the attacking vyeshen. With one stalactite broken, the massive creatures couldn't get all the way into Eru's shelter, but they could reach far enough with their beaks to be dangerous. Oko's sharp blade cut the soft flesh inside the vyeshen's beak, splashing warm liquid on Eru. The attacker cried out as much in anger as pain as he withdrew. By now, there was no shortage of vyeshen waiting for their chance to destroy a god killer, and another quickly took his turn.

Eru thrust the blade at the next attacker, lacking refined coordination or technique. The knife sunk deep into the vyeshen's useless eye socket, and another pain-filled cry echoed through the mines. Eru's satisfaction lasted but a moment. The injured vyeshen jerked his head back forcefully, ripping the knife from Eru's hand. The blade remained lodged in the creature's eye socket. With another sudden contortion, the vyeshen snatched Eru's wrist with his talon.

"Hold me!" Eru screamed desperately. His cry hardly registered in the terrified minds of his friends. He could hardly blame them. He could imagine the horror to be crammed into such a claustrophobic space, listening to the violent cacophony around them, helpless and blind. "Grab me!" Eru screamed again. This time, Volo heard, him, and grabbed his other arm.

He caught Eru just in time. The vyeshen talon clasped Eru's wrist with terrible strength, digging into his flesh as the powerful beast pulled. Volo grunted as he pulled back with all his strength.

"Against the wall!" Oko commanded, with an undeniable authority. Volo hugged his body to the wall, and Eru turned his head, doing his best to guess Oko's intent. Boom! The power of that sound shocked Eru as he felt the actual pain it caused in every hearer's ear. He smelled the odor of burnt powder, wafting to Volo's nose. The hot metal barrel burned against Volo's cheek where Oko's musket brushed him in its recoil.

The force of the ball's impact thrust the attacking vyeshen away, its grip on Eru's wrist going limp instantly. Seconds later the bird's massive body plunged into the lake below, Eru's knife still lodged in the dead creature's eye socket. Oko had spent his only ball.

"I never guessed this thing would be used to *save* an archos," Oko said with a note of irony and pride in his voice. Eru hardly heard Oko, due to the ringing in every ear he could draw from. The ensuing clamor of vyeshen fury drowned out Volo's angry reply about his burned cheek. With nothing left to defend themselves, Eru knew the end had come.

Failure, it had been Shanje's constant hallmark. He had failed when he crafted the controllers, ironically succeeding brilliantly in all the wrong ways. He had just done it again. He had done what his puppet had requested, granting him the most powerful Reading gift ever seen, but doing so had destroyed his ability to seize. He had destroyed all his work to defeat Aitrox and free the vyeshen. His puppet was useless to him now.

Shanje felt Jenshu's sudden realization that the god killer in their midst could not seize him, and he knew that Eru would soon be dead. What did it matter now? Yet, a small voice in Shanje's mind cried out in protest. Jante never gave up. He never quit. But who was Shanje fooling? Through all the millennia he had tried to live up to Jante's ideals, failing spectacularly every time. Why did he always compare himself to the unattainable?

Memories of Jante filled Shanje's mind. There had been a time when Shanje strove for greatness, not out of competition or comparison, but because his friend inspired him. He owed it to Jante's memory to do the same now. Jante would have wanted him to fight on. He reached out to the rest of the wyverns, his small band of a dozen heretics and outcasts. Attempting to rescue the god killer was a suicide quest, but the resolve of each of his followers held firm.

A tremendous boom filled Shanje's mind with pain as they entered the cavern, each successive echo feeling like a repeat blow to his sensitive ears. Shanje could hardly believe his senses as he watched Shena fall lifeless into the lake. She had been Jenshu's mate. For a moment Shanje shared in the explosion of vyeshen fury. How dare that human kill a vyeshen? It took a concerted effort to fight back that anger. That human may have just saved all of the vyeshen. If Shanje succeeded, many more vyeshen would die soon.

None of the vyeshen noticed Shanje's arrival, blinded by their rage over Shena's death. Despite Jenshu's injured ribs and wing, he was the first to retaliate against Shanje's puppet. Shanje steeled his resolve as he swooped down, digging talons into Jenshu's neck. Using his adapted wings, he grasped a stalactite above him, and used it as a base to push against. With a furious swing he thrust Jenshu away. Jenshu crashed into a cave wall with a crunch. He floundered to the cavern floor, sustaining more injury with his forceful landing on the lake shore. Jenshu's tragic squawks of pain and terror wrenched Shanje's heart as the colony of modified humans swarmed him.

The other wyverns quickly came to Shanje's side, ready to defend him from the inevitable retribution of the vyeshen flock. Shanje felt grateful for their loyalty, but knew it would mean nothing. With Jenshu's death, the vyeshen retaliation would be far more than they could hope to withstand. His only hope lay in correcting the mistake he had made with his puppet.

At first, Eru had mistaken Shanje's arrival as merely another vyeshen intent on killing him. He could hardly believe it when Shanje actually killed another vyeshen to save him, an archos. Then Shanje's presence tore into Eru's life threads so powerfully it nearly rendered him unconscious. He knew what Shanje needed to do, but did not want it. He could not go back to the monster he had been, a creature that inflicted pain to survive. He had come to terms with his pending death. Death, a reunion with Aymis, felt welcome to him now.

The vyeshen flock swarmed Shanje's small group en masse, tearing the wyverns from the cave walls and ceilings. By sheer force of numbers, the wyverns withered before the angry assault. Shanje would die, and Eru could soon follow, knowing he had struggled to the end. Then, something snapped in his being, and Eru's protective reflexes took over. In a split second, he seized ten vyeshen, killing them by diving their bodies full speed into the cavern floor below.

Panic bolted through the vyeshen flock as Eru's merciless instincts continued the work of death. As the vyeshen retreated, Eru regained control. Shanje and one other wyvern had survived. Eru seized them, as well as Oko, intent on getting his friends out of this hellish place.

CHAPTER 53

HEALING

Shanje had saved us. I should have felt more grateful than I did. He saved my friends, who did not deserve to die in such a terrifying manner, but he had also taken my freedom from seizing others away. I had faced my death and accepted it. Death would have been a relief, an escape from the looming confrontation with Aitrox. I may have felt differently had Shanje acted to save one he cared about. Shanje's feelings for me were similar to a hunter's regard *for an expensive bow. I was a tool, a weapon and nothing more. Shanje had saved me so I could die on his terms. The same was true for each of my friends. For me, however, as the moment of truth drew near, I didn't know if I had it in me to lead them to face Aitrox.*

Shanje and Kelwu bristled at the indignity of being seized by Eru. Eru didn't care. They had both sustained injuries from vyeshen beaks and talons, but Eru could do nothing about that now. No matter what Shanje thought, Eru regarded the two wyverns as new Aegendi at his disposal. He quickly discerned how to utilize the wyvern's adapted mental attack to sever an archos's hold on someone. He also discovered that the wyverns could actually detect the unique threads in each Aegendi's being. They could pick an Aegendi out from the crowd, even Hiders, a power most archos would covet fiercely. If they fell into Aitrox's control, nothing could ever rise to challenge her again.

As they drew nearer to the cave exits, Eru knew he would need to hide everyone. He felt everybody's mind racing, still reeling from their terrible ordeal, and narrow escape. Even without direct thoughts about Aitrox, such frantic minds would likely draw her attention. Eru suspected that she had turned her awareness to the mines, hoping they would be foolish enough to emerge unprotected.

"Oko, I need you," Eru said into the darkness. Oko said nothing, but responded by letting Eru in.

Eru knew that being able to seize others again had saved their lives, but he still wanted to cry. Shanje's mistake had given him a taste of true freedom, only to have it taken away. He had let himself imagine the future that gift would have granted him, and it hurt terribly to lose it. Even in the unyielding darkness of the cave, everyone's senses had felt new, invigorating and exciting. Now, not even the vyeshen sonar interested him. Life felt sullied anew by his having to seize to experience it.

The vyeshen sonar guided them as Eru used Volo's gift to carry them out of the mountain. In the pitch black of the caves, Oko and Volo's senses added nothing useful, offering the feel of muggy cool air, the wooshing sound of flight in their ears and the occasional sound of the vyeshen wings. Eru used Shanje at the front of the group to pick their path forward. Kelwu took up the rear, giving Eru a view that ensured nobody collided with any walls or stalactites.

Finally, Eru saw the sliver of light indicating the opening to the outside world. The miniscule light felt painfully intense to the dilated eyes of each of his team members. The vyeshen felt it too, a vague awareness of light seeping through their almost useless eyes.

Eru felt the anticipation in each mind around him, surprisingly more in the vyeshen than anyone else. The vyeshen may have found a way to survive here, but centuries imprisoned in the caves, especially for creatures meant to soar the open skies, outweighed the loathing his team could develop in such a short time.

When they emerged from the cave, a vibrant sunrise greeted them. Their breathing billowed in foggy plumes in the chill of the early morning. He immediately made for the forest several thousand feet down the mountain. As they drew nearer, Eru spotted a lake, and remembered the parched throats and dry lips of his friends. Eru knew he, too, likely needed water, but didn't mind his lack of feeling in this case.

When they landed at the lake's shore, Eru released everyone, except Oko. He yearned to release Oko, wishing he could do so and enjoy nature's beauty through the others. That gift had been lost, and he needed to keep Oko seized for the time being at least. Perhaps, after the others settled their minds, he could risk giving Oko a break. Aitrox couldn't seize them so long as Eru lived, but they could lead her straight to him. For the moment, he wasn't willing to risk it. Truth be told, he could hardly bear the thought of returning to the void, as dark and empty to him as the caves had been for the others.

The void used to offer some semblance of serenity and peace to Eru. Now it offered the painful reminder of what he had lost. Eru felt the brisk morning air on Oko's skin, grateful that the lower altitude brought some warmth with it. The rising sun shimmering on the lake's surface reflected the granite rocks on the far side of the lake so perfectly he could hardly distinguish where the water ended. The deep greens of the pine trees felt vibrant and new. He wished more than anything to experience this moment through unseized eyes, but it was not to be.

Fortunately, none of the crew had been injured, besides Volo's buned cheek from Oko's musket. At first glance, Eru looked to have fared far worse, with gruesome red splashes across his face and torso, all of it vyeshen blood. Eru suspected he had a dislocated shoulder from the tugging match between Volo and the vyeshen. His wrist had a dark ring of bruises around it from the powerful grip of the talons. Eru worked his shoulder back into its socket through Oko's hands. The procedure would have been agonizingly painful for a person.

With his injuries cared for, Eru put Oko to work building a fire. Hunger gnawed at Eru's awareness. None of them had eaten anything since the wyverns had rescued them, an uncounted time back. Everyone else, excluding Oko, had already drunk their fill from the lake's clear waters. Once the fire burned strongly, Eru and Oko made their way to the shore for a drink.

'Are you strong enough to hunt?' Eru asked reaching out to Kelwu.

'I am always strong enough to hunt,' Kelwu replied, with happy recollections of successful hunts. He took to the skies immediately, with thoughts of the kill filling his mind. In such an open world, his sonar didn't serve quite as well, but the vyeshen could hunt as much through their feel of the threads of life as any other sense. It did not take Kelwu long to find his prey. He swooped in with his powerful talons and snatched a squealing goat away from a cliff.

Kelwu returned with his trophy, setting it down at Eru's feet before taking off to find another goat. *'Shanje and I are hungry, as well,'* Kelwu communicated playfully before he left.

"Oh, thank goodness, I am so hungry!" Volo exclaimed.

"We don't have much to work with, but I know a few things about cooking," Eru said through Oko, as he put Oko to use preparing the goat. Eru settled into a routine, doing his best to interact with the others as if Oko were not seized. Even with his seasoned crew, it seemed to ease their minds if the person he seized acted more like themselves than Eru.

"I could practically eat it raw," Volo replied ravenously.

"You may not want to watch if you are squeamish about blood,' Oko eyed Janis as he spoke. 'You are going to have to eat this, after all," Oko cautioned.

"I think I will go look for some roots we can stew up with the meat," Janis said. She wouldn't know how to identify anything edible, but she needed an excuse to get away from the butchering. She had witnessed violence and death many times since Aymis's death, but at seemingly random moments the sight of blood brought painful images to her recollection. Somehow, the innocent, helpless goat's death felt tragic, and the crimson stains on its grey-white coat brought back visions of her daughter's blood on her hands.

Volo could hardly look away, for all his hunger. "Can I help you?" he asked.

"Yeah, pull here when I tell you," Oko said, gesturing to a hanging piece of the goat's hide. Volo grabbed and pulled eagerly.

"Easy!" Oko snapped as he pulled his hand away just in time to keep his knife from slicing his thumb. "Wait until I tell you, or you'll yank my knife right into my hand."

"Sorry," Volo said sheepishly.

Supe sat with her feet in the frigid cold lake. She had the distant look in her eyes that had betokened her broken mind. As if she sensed Eru's focus on her, Supe turned towards him.

"Thank you," Supe said.

"For what?" Eru asked. He already had a good enough read of her thoughts to know, but recognized that she wanted to express it.

"For saving me. For letting me fight through the pain. For not seizing me except in the greatest need."

"You have made remarkable progress," Eru said.

"There are still times when I long for the feeling of my gift rebuilding my body."

"You know, your gift is probably why your mind has recovered so well," Eru answered.

"Please explain," Supe replied.

"An archos simply magnifies innate abilities. Most Brutes are stronger than normal, Readers are very insightful and empathetic, and Prophets have unusually good reflexes. I would guess that Immortals are very resilient."

"Perhaps, but it never could have happened without an archos as rare as you. My last archos, my son, only left me unseized when he needed me to be hurt for a miracle. He, too, craved the feelings I felt when he had me seized," she said with a flicker of pain in her eyes.

"It is an amazing feeling," Eru said pensively. Only one who knew pain like Supe did could possibly appreciate the rush of healing that came with it. Part of him understood why she would crave suffering. Even now, she sought it out. "Are you sure you should be standing in the water? The lake is frigid."

"Yes, it really hurts. I think that pain is a good reminder."

"Reminder?" Eru asked.

"That I am strong enough not to need my gift," Supe replied.

"You are stronger than you know," Eru said with warmth in his voice.

Janis walked and scrambled along the lake's uneven and rocky shore. Hunger gnawed at her, but she would wait until Oko called her back. Her emotions were close to the surface right now, probably as a result of their recent ordeal. She needed this reprieve, but she almost wished to be back under strain to take her mind away from her raw emotions. As she climbed over a boulder, she stumbled on Kelwu and Shanje.

Under normal circumstances, it wouldn't have been such a bad thing. Kelwu however had brought two more goats back from the cliffs, and the two of them were neck deep in their respective animal's ribs when she caught sight of them. Her eyes fell on them, and she felt their distaste, even hatred for her. They tolerated her out of necessity, but everything about them drove fear into her heart. Their blank useless eyes, dark skin and patchy feathers, sharp talons, cruel beaks, and even their visible battle wounds all terrified her. The carnage of their meal brought the memory of her own blood soaked hands vividly back to her mind's eye. Weeping, Janis turned away and ran back to her friends.

Janis sobbed unabashedly, hardly even caring if the others saw her in such a state. The memory of her daughter filled her. Ever since Aymis's death, Janis had been driven by revenge. Hatred and death had nearly consumed her until only one thing could have brought her joy – Aitrox's death. Aymis would have mourned the person she was becoming and Janis knew it. She had become too much like the vyeshen, cold and uncaring for life. It had to change. She had to fight Aitrox not for herself, but for Aymis. Seeing Aitrox's death shouldn't bring her joy; freedom from terror and oppression should.

Janis hadn't realized she had wandered so far, and had plenty of time to calm her frantic sobs. Tears still trickled down her cheeks as she returned to the aroma of cooked meat. She sat next to the fire, which felt great in the brisk morning. Oko poked a slice of meat with his knife, the only utensil anyone had, and handed it to her. Despite its lack of seasoning, tough texture, and gamy flavor, the meat hit the spot.

Janis chewed the meat pensively, emotions still painfully tender in her heart. She could hardly believe everything they had been through together. For all the darkness and fear, Eru's noble and kind heart offered so much hope and light. She had followed him out of hunger for vengeance. Only now did she begin to truly appreciate the archos she followed, to see exactly what it was that Aymis gave her life for. Janis's hatred for Aitrox had not wavered, but for the first time, she felt a different reason to fight. Oh, how Janis longed to share this peaceful moment with her daughter. She missed her so terribly, but that grief no longer led to anger. Janis had finally begun to heal.

Volo gave the first slice of goat to his sister, Rose. He hardly recognized her any more. She looked so gaunt, traumatized and battered. How had he let this happen to her? She accepted the slice of meat gratefully. What Volo saw when their eyes met shocked him; strength. Had it always been there? He thought back on the day they received that fateful letter. He had wanted to turn tail and run, but it was Rose who had the strength to hope. All this time Volo had imagined himself protecting his sister, when he had always needed her strength. Yes, her strength had always been there, but never so bright as now.

Despite Rose's weakened, battered body, the strength that burned in her eyes had grown incredibly. Volo was wrong to blame himself for everything that had happened to them. She had chosen to face the evil of the world head on. In a sense Volo had as well, though he always had implicitly put accountability for his fate on his sister's shoulders. A part of him wished the two of them had continued in their normal lives, having never met Maverick. A part of him wished that neither of them were an Aegendi. Life would have been so much easier.

Life before Maverick had been like living under a constantly overcast sky, dim but never truly pitch black. Maverick had shown them the bright light of hope, and the glory of struggle. He had also led them into absolute darkness, literally and emotionally. Even while Volo could never willingly face such terror again, he doubted he would accept were someone to offer to send him and his sister back to a life where none of this had happened, a world where nothing dared oppose Aitrox's oppressive domination of all life.

Eru could not feel the warmth of the fire, but he basked in the peace of the moment. Moments like this were so rare and precious. If only he could give Oko a moment's respite. Nobody but Eru could truly comprehend the depth of Oko's sacrifice. Even Eru didn't truly comprehend it. He shared in Oko's experience, but only Oko fully knew what it meant to surrender his will voluntarily to an archos.

Eru's thoughts wandered back to their escape from the vyeshen. Shanje had restored him to his normal self, but he had never given him the Reader's gift. Only now that his friends were safe, had he remembered to wonder.

'I did not fail this time,' Shanje seemed to say in response. The full communication carried so much more. Shanje would not have condemned so many vyeshen to die under Eru's control, had he not needed to save a tool far greater than a typical archos.

'I don't understand,' Eru replied.

'You have not returned to the void since you regained the power to seize,' Shanje reminded him. *'The void now represents a crossroads – a fork where you can choose how to direct your mind's awareness. Your awareness of the minds around you is so powerful now that you don't have to seize others to use their senses. I got that part right on the first try. However, I needed to reopen the channel that allows you to seize others, and finish building the channel that opens a more concentrated awareness to you. From the void you can choose to seize and dominate, to see through all eyes, or to absolutely and truly see one.'*

"You mean I haven't lost my ability to see without seizing!" Eru exclaimed aloud, his sudden outburst startling everyone near the fire. *'I don't believe it!'* Eru continued in his mind.

'You will need to know how to use your new power before we face Aitrox,' Shanje replied.

'But, I cannot release Oko out here,' Eru reminded him.

'Was I unclear?' Shanje seemed to ask impatiently. In reality, he reiterated a few key points, adding clarification. Shanje had made Eru strong, incredibly strong. He probably could not seize Aitrox outright, but she would never be able to seize Eru again. When the time came for their attack, Oko's gift still helped give them some element of surprise, but their survival no longer depended on it.

'Why didn't you tell me sooner?' Eru asked with a mix of irritation and exuberant joy.

'I had to be sure,' Shanje replied. It wasn't a question of Eru's strength, rather of trust. Shanje had to be sure that Eru could be trusted with the full measure of

power Shanje had granted him. He had largely made that decision the moment he returned to Eru's aid, sacrificing the lives of many vyeshen for Eru's sake. Yet, he had not been fully convinced. Only as Eru's haggard team recuperated outside the mines did Shanje come to understand. For the first time, he saw a glimpse of what Jante admired in humans.

Eru couldn't wait any longer. He released Oko, and felt the rush of everyone's senses fill his mind. How could he ever give this up again? Why would he ever seize another, or confine his awareness to the focus on just one soul? He knew he must, and so he turned his focus onto Shanje, coming to know the wyvern more thoroughly in that instant than he had ever known another soul.

Interlude

To Kill a God

Darkness, absolute and overwhelming. Pain, intense and agonizing. Jante sat in the pitch black of the mine shaft, but it was Ela's death that threw his soul into a dark abyss. The pain that screamed in his body from his injuries could not compare to the agony in his heart at losing her. His wounds provided the only measure he had of time's passage. Millennia ago when he had enhanced his healing abilities, he had not expected to need them as he did now. The gradual, but observable pace of his broken bones mending kept the oppressive darkness from driving him mad.

Jante sensed the traumatized souls of many other vyeshen scattered throughout the mines. Hundreds in their flock had died that day, and the usurper had enslaved at least fifty. A few she had seized had escaped her grasp when she drove them into the mines after her quarry. Once Aitrox realized the escape the mines offered, she changed tactics. Now, the enslaved vyeshen patrolled the entrances. The flow of incoming survivors had come to a stop about the time Jante's ribs fully mended, (approximately two days after her rebellion.)

Aitrox's power and cunning surprised even Jante. He of all the vyeshen should have remembered how the complex weaves in a creature's threads could sometimes result in unexpected aberrations. Nothing Shanje or Jante had done should have given her such strength, but the vyeshen had been foolish and arrogant to assume they could control life itself. From the moment of her birth, Aitrox had been working towards her goal of domination, patiently and cunningly playing off the vyeshen greed for metal. She had always kept her full strength hidden, letting Shanje and Jante make her stronger as the years passed. Fortunately, for all the vyeshen, her lifespan was brief. They would only be trapped in the mines for five or six decades at most, unless Jante's other failsafe proved inadequate.

Jante knew that they had already made many terrible mistakes in underestimating this usurper. She had at least fifty vyeshen under her control. Jante felt confident that she couldn't immediately put her vyeshen captives to use modifying her threads, but how long would that last? If she were to use those vyeshen to grant her immortality, then Jante and the rest of the flock would be condemned to an eternity in the hell of these mines. Jante could feel the controllers and their human slaves still working the mines. They remained oblivious to the rebellion outside, and Aitrox could not reach them here... yet.

The controllers in the mines had to be dealt with, but only Jante could hope to do so. Shanje had made them too hard to kill, even for a vyeshen. Only Jante could hide a part of his thoughts, and thus only he could plan to kill them. Even sharing his plans with another vyeshen could easily get it killed. Before he could make a move on the controllers in the mines, Jante had to conquer the darkness.

Fortunately, nature had already provided Jante a blueprint for living in the perpetual darkness. Modifying his own threads was always far easier if he followed the patterns he saw in nature. By the time his wounds had fully healed, Jante had copied the senses of the smaller flying rodents that inhabited the mines. His sonar did not compare to theirs, yet, but it was enough for now.

The other vyeshen in the mines had picked up on his thoughts, and had already begun working their own threads in a similar way. The thought of ending the darkness gave them a sliver of hope.

It felt wonderful to fly again, even in the claustrophobic confines of the mines. At first, Jante had to focus completely on navigating the tight, labyrinthian tunnels, but after a few hours of practice he could set about his primary objective – hunting and killing a controller.

The clanging of picks and hammers echoed through the tunnels as Jante neared a crew of working slaves. The clamor felt deafening with his heightened senses, but fortunately it did not interfere with his sonar. The light of their lanterns burned in Jante's eyes after so long in absolute darkness. The smells of humanity filled Jante's beak, but most of all, the misery of the slaves flooded his mind. Working a mine, even without the terror of a controller, had always been just a step away from hell. Jante located the controller, more by his mental senses than by sonar or sight.

The controller sensed him as well and Jante perceived the creature's hunger to please him. It had never had a vyeshen present it in the mines, and the unexpected visit filled the controller with curiosity and hope. Perhaps Jante had come to recognize it for such excellent production. The controller remained pliable and easy to control, as Shanje had designed it. Jante played off the controller's hopes, sending thoughts of praise and honor its way. Then he killed it.

For a brief moment, the humans that the controller drove paused. Then awareness of their freedom sunk in, and they turned on Jante. The hardened tools they used for working the mines now made powerful weapons, and the arduous labor had built their muscles to be terrifyingly strong. Fortunately, Jante had expected their attack. His furious shriek echoed in the mine shaft, piercing and painfully loud to the human ears. As they recoiled, hands covering their ears, Jante clasped the dead controller in his talons and made his escape.

Human flesh, particularly that of a controller, had a distinct taste, but Jante couldn't afford to be choosy about his food. It had been a long time since that last celebratory meal of goat and fish, and healing from his wounds had taken a lot out of him. The other vyeshen undoubtedly were equally as hungry. All of the vyeshen had crafted their threads to depend less on regular sustenance, but they could still starve to death with enough time. Fortunately, most of the slaves that worked the mines never left the abysmal shafts. Large stores of food had been laid up here to support the workers, and the controllers. Once Jante finished the controllers off, the miners and their food stores could sustain his flock for some time. Perhaps they could even modify the miners' threads, converting them into a perpetual food source as the humans had done with their cattle. Satisfied that Jante had puzzled out the means for his race to survive, he set about hunting the rest of the controllers down.

Shanje tried to convince him not to go. Jante however refused his counsel. The seized vyeshen no longer patrolled the mine exits, but no vyeshen other than Jante could safely leave. It would take them years to make the changes he and Ela had done together, and hide their minds from the usurper, and Jante doubted they could afford to wait that long. Shanje's most compelling argument had been the need their flock had of Jante's skill with the threads, but he could not hide the fear he had for his old friend.

Jante no longer felt much friendship for Shanje. Perhaps, if the feelings had been mutual, Shanje would have convinced him to stay. However, Jante would never forgive him for the fate he brought the vyeshen, for the loss of his beloved Ela. Indeed, Shanje's desire for him to stay only motivated him to leave. Someone had to destroy Aitrox. Jante could not guarantee that Aitrox would remain mortal, not while she had so many vyeshen under her control. He had proven he could kill controllers. It had been easy.

Jante made sure not to expose his realization that killing Aitrox would be different. Jante had exploited the controllers' craving of vyeshen approval to rid the mines of them. He could not do that with Aitrox. The controllers in the mine were relatively simple, naïve creatures compared to Aitrox's cunning intelligence. Jante had no guarantees he could kill her, but he had to try.

When Shanje realized he could not convince his old friend to stay, he offered to accompany him. Shanje knew all too well the sorrow he had brought his old friend. Shanje should be the one to risk his life to make things right.

Jante acknowledged Shanje's request, and made no attempt to deny Shanje's fault for their circumstances. However, were Shanje to leave the mines, it would almost certainly doom Jante to be caught and discovered. As desperately as Shanje craved redemption, almost as intensely as he still craved metal, acting on that craving now would only make things worse. If Shanje attempted to follow him, Jante would kill the fool for his selfishness.

Shanje could not hide the hurt Jante's response caused him. The truth always cut the deepest, and he could not deny the truth of everything Jante felt. He wished more than anything that it could be himself risking everything. If Jante died too, Shanje would never forgive himself. *'Be careful, old fiend.'* Shanje doubted he would ever share thoughts with his old friend again. Always, Jante had been the steady, wise influence. If he had listened to him more, everything would be different. Only as Shanje felt his friend's mind fade in the distance did he truly realize how much the vyeshen would miss him.

The light of the half-moon felt painfully bright in Jante's eyes as he exited the mine. The sheer granite cliffs seemed to glow a sepulchral, bluish tint in the night. The fresh evening air felt invigorating after so much time in the stale, dusty mines. A breeze pushed Jante higher, and he reveled in the return to the open skies. Far in the distance, he saw the empty roosts where his flock had once lived. He hoped they could return to their nests soon.

Jante did not feel the presence of any of the enslaved vyeshen. He had expected a trap, and didn't know for certain what to make of their absence. If anything, it did not bode well. If they were not watching the mines, the usurper could be putting them to much more terrible uses. Aitrox had been a controller at the forges, so that was where Jante chose to begin his search.

He felt her there. Aitrox's presence loomed over the forges' complex like a massive spider, waiting for prey to fall into her web. She had not felt him yet, something that gave him some small measure of hope. At night time, most of the humans slept, and the usurpers mind could spare more effort to feeling for him. Several times, she almost caught him, but he somehow managed to avoid her notice. Each time, he could feel it, the undeniable sense that you have eyes watching you, only much more powerful and terrifying.

Aitrox had not forgotten the one vyeshen she had not been able to seize. So long as he lived, she could not rest easy. She had pulled the hunting patrols back, hoping to lure her adversary into the open; hoping he would take the bait. It had worked. The realization of his folly did nothing to deter Jante. He understood now the game she was playing, but he had no choice but to press forward.

Then, he saw her below. He could hardly believe how young she was. She hadn't even reached human adolescence yet, probably younger than ten years old. She lounged comfortably in a hammock, while two vyeshen slept soundly by her side. Her black fingernails stroked the feathers on the back of one's neck as he slept. *Poor Ashte*. He did not deserve such a fate, reduced to being a trophy pet of such a monster.

Ashte's eyes snapped awake, having sensed Jante's notice. *Blazing Phoenix*! Yet, Jante knew he could not have helped such a thought. He should have known better than to leave it unhidden, but how could he suppress pity for the plight of these vyeshen. Jante knew the critical moment had come. Heedless of his own safety, he tucked his wings and dove straight for the usurper. He had gotten close enough. He might just have a chance to strike her down.

Knowing the moment for stealth had passed, Jante screamed a hateful shriek as he swooped down for his prey. His sharp talons spread wide, on a direct course for the young monster's torso. He plummeted from the sky with amazing speed. It would be over in seconds. Hundreds of human and vyeshen eyes snapped open and rested on him. The fate of both human and vyeshen hung in the balance as all these eyes watched. Jante felt the hope in their minds, as keenly as he felt the misery of their plight. He also felt their dread, and he knew he had failed. They all knew he had failed. This was exactly what Aitrox had wanted.

With so many eyes on him, and so many minds keenly focused on him, Jante could never hope to remain hidden from Aitrox's awareness. She let him draw close, painfully close, but she had always been in control. At the last possible moment, she seized him, and Jante learned the true meaning of hell.

Jante found one source of solace in his own personal torment. Aitrox had given up trying to enhance her own threads directly, but that did not mean his kind was safe. Over the years, she had used the vyeshen to create truly terrible tools. Jante had been the most effective tool under her dominion, and thus he had witnessed many of her terrifying triumphs.

People she seized could now do incredible things. Some had strength enough to hurl massive boulders. Others could move almost anything with little more than a thought from Aitrox. She had used Jante's knowledge of enhanced healing to create others that could instantly heal from just about anything. The most terrifying, however, were the ones that could see moments into the future. As the years passed, she drove the vyeshen mercilessly, building a vast army of these powerful tools.

Still, Jante held onto a shred of defiance. Aitrox had not realized yet that the vyeshen maintained a sliver of autonomy over their power on the threads of life. He dared not touch her, himself or another vyeshen. She kept such a close, wary eye on them. Instead, he secretly worked over the years to create his own tool among the humans. He and Ela had learned how to hide a part of their minds. Jante was determined to plant the seeds so that humans could hide completely from Aitrox.

His secret work moved painfully slowly. The attention he could give his hidden labor felt so meager. Perhaps it would be meaningless. He doubted he could finish before Aitrox aged and died anyway, but he pressed on still the same. This act of defiance was the sliver of his soul that he clung to. Without it, he would have gone mad by now. Many of the other vyeshen had. The strain of Aitrox's domination over the years had broken their minds. They still made excellent tools under her control. In fact, they were almost better this way. She could leave them unseized if she wished, knowing they would hardly move. The blank, empty look in their eyes broke Jante's heart. He owed it to them to press forward. Most of all, he dreaded ending up just like them.

Something was different. Different was good. It was welcome. No, different was bad. As insufferable as the indistinguishable blur of days, weeks and months was, at least it meant things had not gotten worse. With Aitrox, anything different did not bode well. Today, things were very different.

Jante had not been compelled to the pens where Aitrox kept the humans she intended to convert to tools. After he finished his morning meal, a few meager scraps of cow and sheep, Aitrox had brought him to the center of their complex. She had marshaled hundreds, maybe even thousands of her new tools. Jante guessed that she controlled so many by the use she made of about fifty controllers. All of her vyeshen had also gathered. Yes, this was going to be a truly terrible day.

One of the humans placed a harness on Jante's back, and firmly strapped Aitrox in. She drove him to flight, and then the entire gathering followed. Jante had hoped she would not be able to bring the massive army of her tools wherever they were going. Of course, his hopes proved ill-founded. The ones she used to move things with her thoughts could easily carry the entire throng along.

Terror filled Jante's heart as he imagined her making an assault on the mines. The remaining vyeshen would be decimated by such a force. Only as they flew past the mines entrance, deeper into the Phoenix mountains, did he breathe a sigh of relief. Then their true destination settled in and Jante could not help but feel a thrill of hope mingling with a sense of ominous foreboding. Aitrox intended to kill his god.

Jante desperately hoped that Phoenix would not answer the challenge, even as he hoped his god would. Could Aitrox possibly hope to defeat Phoenix? Even with such a marvelous force at her disposal, she couldn't possibly hope to defeat an immortal god could she? Perhaps she acted out of reckless desperation, driven to such madness by her looming mortality. This could be the day the terror ended. By sunset, Jante could be free. The vyeshen could be free, saved by their god. Or it would mark the end.

There had been no hope the vyeshen could have hidden the location of Phoenix's roost from Aitrox. She had perfected the art of scouring the vyeshen minds. Only Jantee had been able to keep anything hidden. It would have done no good for him to hide this secret from her. In fact, it would have clued her in to his ability to hide anything. So, he, too, had allowed her to know where Phoenix could be found.

At the heart of the Phoenix Montains, the tallest of the peaks towered far above the rest. Molten rock flowed down its slopes, the peak of the mountain constantly ablaze. A thrill of excitement raced through Jante's heart. He had never expected to see this sacred place again. Even under these terrible circumstances, he felt himself privileged.

As they neared, the mountain erupted into a shower of fire, rock and ash. Phoenix had answered Aitrox's challenge. Enormous shafts of fire arched through the sky, headed in their direction. Aitrox diverted the first assault with hardly a thought. It troubled Jante to sense how little effort it took her. Even this many of her tools should not have been that powerful, unless she had kept something secret from him. What other enhancements had she forced the vyeshen to make?

Flaming boulders hundreds of feet across hurled in their direction, and yet Aitrox's enhanced humans actually had the power to not only stop these enormous boulders, but to hurl them back from where they came. The first such boulder smashed into the very peak of the mountain in an explosion of fire, and rock. Jante could hardly believe what he saw. The boulder had been so large, it nearly destroyed the volcanic cinder cone at the peak. Aitrox had done that. How could she bring such power to bear?

Pheonix Answering The Challenge

The rumbling of the mountain quieted, and a nervous tension filled the entire mountain range. Was Phoenix retreating? Jante hoped so. Then, the magnificent fiery bird burst from the mountain top, shrilling a cry so deafening it filled Jante's mind with pain. Seeing Phoenix again, Jante remembered how feeble the vyeshen homage to his form truly was. Nothing they could do to their own threads could ever hope to emulate Phoenix. His feathery wingspan seemed to fill the sky, and his glowing talons made the sun appear dim. Jante saw his god and rejoiced. Aitrox was doomed.

The massive god dove from the heights of the peak and attacked. Jante couldn't possibly imagine how Aitrox could escape the wrath of his god. Sadly, he had forgotten the power her enhanced humans, created by his power, gave her. Even such a mighty, colossal being as Phoenix couldn't touch Aitrox, not when she knew his assaults before they came. To Jante's horror and dismay, an invisible force grabbed the fiery god's body and slammed it into the earth far below.

Phoenix's body plowed through the mountainside, setting pine forests ablaze in a wake of destruction. Before he could stand from the crash, boulders the size of mountains rained down on him. Phoenix shrieked in anger and pain, then went quiet, and his fires died. Jante could not believe it. Phoenix was dead.

No. Just as quickly as he went silent and his flames died, a new flame exploded in a massive growing shockwave. From the center of the holocaust, Phoenix emerged, renewed, invigorated and glorious. Jante should have known that a god could not have been killed so easily, if at all.

Aitrox had known to withdraw to a safe distance, warned by the foresight of her underlings. Even so, the heat from Phoenix's rebirth shocked even Jante. The entire mountainside erupted in flames, and black smoke choked the skies.

The battle between Aitrox and Phoenix raged long after the sun set. Phoenix's raging fires lit up the night skies, and cast spectral shadows through the billowing smoke. Jante lost track of the number of times Aitrox felled his god, only to see her foe emerge renewed and glorious from his ashes, yet Phoenix could not hurt Aitrox. The ceaseless battle had driven Jante to absolute exhaustion, a fact that gave him hope. Despite Aitrox's power, her tools could not last forever. Phoenix would eventually win. Every time Phoenix revived, Jante's heart grew warmer, more hopeful. His strength was fading. One way or another, he would be free soon.

As the first light of dawn struggled to illuminate the smoke-filled sky, Jante watched as Aitrox struck Phoenix down yet again in her futile attempt to dominate a god. To Jante's everlasting dismay and disbelief, no glorious eruption of fire and life followed. The silence hung in the air as the seconds, and minutes passed: still nothing. Phoenix was dead.

Despair unrivaled by any moment, except when he lost Ela, filled Jante's heart. Aitrox had defeated Phoenix. Why? What had she gained? Jante could not discern anything different about Aitrox, except the feeling of triumph, and her absolute confidence in her future. Jante knew that a being such as she would never feel that way without cause. Somehow she had done it. She had killed his god, and in turn become a goddess herself. In so doing, she had earned a new, terrible name: archos. It meant killer of gods.

CHAPTER 54

LIBERATION

I wanted to stay at that lake forever. In my wishful imagination, the serenity, peace and relaxation that makes a moment unique seems like it could be preserved forever. I knew, of course, that couldn't happen, but that didn't make it any easier when the time came to return to the real world. I could deal with the fact that I was likely going to my death, but I struggled with the reality of endangering those I loved.

"Eru!" Oko called, an urgent note of panic in his voice. "Eru, what are you doing?"

"I am sorry, I should have let you know what is going on," Eru answered.

"Wait a second, you heard me with nobody seized," Oko said.

"Yeah, he talks with us that way all the time," Volo interjected.

"No, he talks to everyone *else* like that, but not with me," Oko replied pointedly.

"So, Shanje didn't just turn you back to an archos," Rose responded, the pitch of her voice rising with her excitement. "You get to keep your freedom!"

"He did more than that. He has made me strong enough that Aitrox cannot seize me," Eru replied. Mentioning Aitrox without Oko's protection made everyone nervous. Eru saw Rose's nervously avert her gaze, and Volo bite his lip. Even Oko had a tell, his hand reflexively moving for his favorite dagger, despite the fact he had none on him.

Eru felt Aitrox's awareness strike him, like a powerful storm surge against a rocky shore. He drew confidence and courage in the strength he felt. Let her batter and beat his mind, he knew he could stand firm. Experimentally, Eru pushed back, grasping after Aitrox to seize her. She easily rebuffed his attempt, but the surprise she felt to find an equal brought a smile to Eru's lips. Aitrox was scared, terrified even. *'I am coming for you,'* Eru said in his mind.

"Oko, I think it is time for us to be hidden again," Eru said with a calm confidence that reassured everyone. Moments later, Eru seized Oko before saying more. "I just gave Aitrox the surprise of her very long life. She tried to seize me, and could not."

"Why bother seizing Oko then?" Janis asked.

"Because he doesn't want her to know specifics. Of course, she knows we will attack her soon, but he don't want her to glean details," Eru answered, speaking through Oko, again letting it appear that he was unseized.

"What kind of specifics? What are we waiting for?" Volo said eagerly.

"Janis's gift is only as good as her vision, and will not serve us well in the dark. If we left now, it would be dark when we arrived at Deor. Aitrox would strike us out of the sky with ease," Eru explained.

"So, we wait a few hours and attack at dawn," Rose said.

"Attacking at dawn sounds dramatic, but we would have the sun in our eyes. It would hardly be any better than attacking in the night," Eru answered. "We want to time our arrival when we will have the sun at our backs. We will be harder to see. The sun's glare will be particularly intense for Aitrox's Hawkeyes, and her Prophets won't be as useful to her."

"Meaning?" Janis asked.

"We will leave two hours after sunrise," Eru answered. "That will bring us to Deor at the right time."

The hours crawled reluctantly on now. The fragile peace they had enjoyed could not hold up to the open acknowledgment of looming battle. Eru's new-found capacity to rebuff Aitrox's power gave Eru's friends confidence, and Eru did not have the heart to dispel their confidence. Eru knew better though. Aitrox still had uncounted legions of Aegendi compared to their tiny crew. Worst of all, Eru still had no idea how to defeat her, and his only way to find out required leaving everyone exposed.

Nobody slept well that night. Their ordeal in the mines had left them exhausted, but it had also thrown their normal patterns off. The weighty sense of anticipation refused to let anyone's minds escape its grasp, making any sleep fitful and shallow. As usual, Eru did not sleep, and he could not afford to release Oko now. It would be impossible for his friends not to reveal the timing of their attack were they left unprotected. When the time drew near, Eru broke the nervous silence.

"Can everyone hear me?" Eru felt the attention of each of his friends turn his way. "I want you to know how much your friendship has meant to me. Those who come with me now, must know that I do not like our chances, but I would not go if I did not believe we can win. I will not fault any of you who decide not to come."

"Aymis would want me to help you," Janis said. Eru did more than listen to the words, searching her heart for conviction. Of course, he felt fear, but Janis had never been the one he worried about. He knew she would do whatever he needed her to do.

"I will go," Rose said firmly. Again, Eru probed her heart, searching for the truth in her feelings. From the beginning, Rose had joined their cause because she believed it could make the world a better place. She remained committed to that goal, despite the impossibility of their task.

"Watching after you is a tough job, sis," Volo said with a wink. Eru could hardly believe the change he sensed in Volo's heart. Before the time in the mines, protecting Rose had been his only true conviction. Now, talk of protecting her was a façade. Even if Rose were to back down, Volo would come. Rose said nothing in reply, but she turned and nodded her support to Eru.

"I will follow you, Eru," Supe said. She knew the dark side of the archos world like nobody else could. She had every reason not to offer her help, but also every reason to fight. The coming battle posed particular perils for Supe, especially if they failed. Any help she could offer threatened to undo all the recovery she had fought so hard for. Eru wanted to forbid her, but he couldn't deny such a strong desire to help despite the terrible risk.

Eru didn't ask Oko, but he knew where Oko stood. Oko lived to kill archos. Oko shared a similar passion for that cause that Telu had once shared, and like Telu, Oko had much blood on his hands already. Destroying Aitrox might just bring about an end that justified his life of violence.

"I want you to understand something," Eru spoke again. "Aitrox will likely kill me, but she may not be so kind to you. Once I am dead, she could claim each of you to be hers. She will use you for terrible things. You are all willing to risk death, but this would be something far worse," Eru said in one last attempt to drive the gravity of the moment home. The thought of going on without any one of them pained him terribly, but the idea of any one of them forever enslaved by Aitrox broke his heart.

"Then we had better not fail," Janis said. Eru felt his warning sink in for each of them, and didn't know if he felt relieved or more afraid when each person's resolve held firm despite the dangers.

"Well, let's get going then."

The laden hours, full of fear and nervous tension, passed slowly as the landscape flew by far below. Eru had no idea what to expect, but at least Oko could ensure they would have some element of surprise. Eru timed their travel perfectly. The late afternoon sun cast long shadows pointing towards the city as the massive settlement came into view in the distance. Eru suspected that they would have been spotted already had it not been for the sun's glare at this time of day. He saw Aitrox's first defensive attack with plenty of time to avoid it thanks to Janis' gift.

Eru saw the virtual storm of projectiles, like a vertical downpour, with enough time take protective measures. Long before they drew near to Deor, Eru had freed up most of Volo's power by having Shanje and Kelwu carry Eru and Supe. He also flew them towards Deor in a single-file line, reducing the area he needed to defend. Those small preparatory acts, combined with Janis' foresight had been just enough. The maelstrom of stones, glass shards and blades flowed around them, the occasional projectile coming perilously close to Shanje and Eru at the front.

They still were far enough from the city for only Hawk Eyes to have been able to find them. Eru searched with the vyeshen's mental senses to find the Hawkeye that had spotted them. When he found the Aegendi, he directed the full force of both wyverns to sever Aitrox's hold. Eru's newly granted strength put tremendous power behind the wyvern's assault, and the blow nearly killed the Hawkeye, likely leaving his mind permanently useless. Having a feel for the combined force they could wield gave Eru a measure of confidence.

As they drew closer to the city, Eru turned his focus on finding Aitrox's Wizards. He burned through hundreds of Wizards as they approached but it hardly slowed the oncoming barrage of projectiles, everything from an unfortunate resident to the broken off head of one of the many statues of Aitrox. Janis and Volo's gifts were barely enough to keep them alive. Eru had to wonder, if these were the Aegendi she had guarding the city, what waited for them in her citadel? He had expected defeat, but he had hoped to at least make Aitrox squirm.

Janis's vision revealed an impending death blow. He could hardly believe her prophetic sight. As Janis he saw the cobblestone streets of an entire district ripping from the ground and converging on them. Hundreds of thousands of stones would pulverize an area so large they couldn't possibly get clear, and his single Wizard was nowhere nearly strong enough to deflect stones with so much momentum behind them. How could she bring so much force to bear? It defied everything Eru knew about the Aegendi. By the numbers, Wizards were rare enough that all of Deor couldn't possibly have given birth to the tens of thousands required for such a feat.

Eru responded with the only thing he could possibly do. He had dedicated his vyeshen to finding and suppressing individual Aegendi. They quickly found a Hider, and subsequently reduced the man to a comatose state. With the Hider gone, Aitrox's massive, powerful presence burst on the scene.

Eru felt fear, hatred, loathing, excitement and anticipation fill Shanje and Kelwu. Their lives as heretics among their kind culminated in this confrontation. Aitrox had killed their god, and now they would bring his death down on her shoulders.

Eru channeled the wyvern's evolved power, slamming Aitrox's awareness with all the force he could muster. The assault flooded Aitrox's brain with noise, like the clamor of a million thoughts. Every neuron in her body fired, sending spasms of pain and euphoria through her. Even Aitrox's incomprehensible mind hadn't expected such an assault, and it came just in time.

Deor's cobblestone streets had rolled up from the ground, like a wave rippling through a loose rope. The leading edge had already lifted high above the rooftops. The massive collection of stones, seemingly alive, suddenly went completely lifeless. The stones rained down on the streets and rooftops, leaving whole districts of the city looking like a warzone.

The wyvern's tactic had saved their lives, but it also ignited Aitrox's fury. Eru could sense her growing rage over the severity of the blow they had dealt, like a prize fighter who expected a rookie to go down without landing a single punch.

Their first hit caught her off guard, but a seasoned fighter would fight through a bloody nose, and with more fury at that. Already, Eru saw the indicators of another incomprehensibly massive attack beginning. Aitrox would not be caught off guard this time.

Frantically, Eru searched through Aitrox's massive citadel, touching as many minds as he could manage as quickly as possible. The towering complex erected to glorify her and end all doubt to her supremacy teemed with slaves and Aegendi, all under her domain. At least five thousand filled her citadel. Eru didn't know if he would have the time to sweep through all of them, nor if he would find the answer he needed. They only had a few seconds left now.

Eru felt a new type of Aegendi, another of her well-guarded secrets. Locating them proved difficult, because their threads had a different signature than any Shanje had encountered before. Eru understood their power, and why Aitrox had named her secret underlings Amplifiers. Aitrox had at least ten of them hidden throughout her citadel. Through one, she could make a single Wizard wield the strength of a hundred. To make things worse, she could stack the Aegendi's influence with exponential effect. With three of these Amplifiers she could make a single Wizard do incomprehensible things.

Eru hit the Amplifiers with the same overwhelming force he had brought to bear on Aitrox, burning out every neural pathway in their bodies. Streets, and buildings fell from the sky, filling the city with a terrifying, low rumble. Another of Aitrox's secrets exposed, but still she remained unassailable and invincible. Aitrox's citadel towered into the twilight sky.

Fortunately, the wyverns had discovered many unclaimed Aegendi as they soared over the city. Eru claimed them immediately, three Wizards, two Prophets and two Brutes. Having struck a severe blow to Aitrox's strength by killing her Amplifiers, and more than doubling his own with his new-found Aegendi, he knew the time to move in for the confrontation had arrived. Eru exploded the massive, gaudy stain glassed windows into her throne room, and brought his entire team in for the kill.

Aitrox's Wizards dispelled the raining glass as easily as a wind would move dry leaves. Amidst the showers of sparkling glass, Eru and his team streamed into her grand throne room and landed to make their final assault.

"I have to hand it to you. You do know how to make an entrance!" a dangerously intoxicating voice said, ringing through the clamor with an unnatural clarity. That voice could have been heard through a hurricane, filling every ear with the single-minded desire to please it. That voice had praised their entrance! Eru could die happy for such words. Were that voice to present him with Aymis resurrected from the dead, then command him to slice her into a thousand pieces, he would do it. The power of a Silvertongue wielded by Aitrox completely overwhelmed Eru's capacity to resist its allure.

"Now kill that vyeshen piece of filth before I do it for you," the powerful voice commanded. Eru could hardly wait to fulfill his command. He would kill a thousand vyeshen if it would bring another moment of praise.

Fortunately for Eru, the vyeshen communication had nothing to do with hearing, and Silvertongues had no power over Shanje and Kelwu. The vyeshen ability to maintain some mental autonomy under archos control foiled Aitrox's well laid plans yet again. Shanje and Kelwu assaulted the Silvertongue, filling him with pain and turning his seductive voice to sickening agpmozed shrieks.

The terrible cries filled Eru with revulsion. He had to make it stop, no matter what the cost. Snapping out of the Silvertongue's grip, he recognized the threat and obliterated the Silvertongue's mind like he had the Amplifiers.

The fear and anger coursing through Aitrox's soul ratcheted to new, unimaginable heights. Eru knew he had to strike now. Using his Wizards and wyverns in concert, he slammed Aitrox's mind while hurling the broken metal frames of her windows towards her like long spears. Numerous slaves leapt to intercept the projectiles. Several fell dead, but others simply pulled the massive beams from their chests nonchalantly. Eru, however, pushed with enough force to propel the metal rods through the human shields straight into Aitrox's ribs.

Eru thought he saw a smile on her cruel archos face as she pulled the beams from her chest. The bright feathered dress of crimson and orange hardly showed any blood on it. Eru thought he saw the feathers themselves right their shape, and seconds later it looked as if nothing had happened.

"No! That's impossible! How?" Eru shouted furiously.

Aitrox took advantage of his momentary shock and disorientation, sending a barrage of shards towards Eru. Eru's additional Wizards should have been strong enough to deflect all of the hurtling objects, but his reeling mind missed a few. One struck Supe through the skull, but she recovered immediately. Another struck Janis, blasting through her thigh in a crimson splash. She would have screamed in pain were the matter left to her. In Eru's unprepared state, he didn't shield her pain enough, and she felt the blow with dizzying effect.

Just at that moment, one of Aitrox's slaves who had escaped Eru's notice leapt forward, swinging another piece of debris. Eru brought Rose forward and she caught the beam with both hands. The sharp edges sliced her palms, but she held firm. Immediately, Rose thrust upwards and released the improvised club, sending the Brute soaring to the tops of the chamber and colliding with the upper wall before falling to his death. Aitrox hadn't even bothered to save him.

An army of twenty Brutes, assisted by five Prophets and five Immortals charged. Apparently every one of her closest slaves were Aegendi. How they had escaped Shanje's detection was a mystery Eru didn't expect to live to discover. The onslaught came too fast for Eru to stop it with his vyeshen. He fought with his Brutes, but Aitrox's Prophets and Immortals ensured that she had the advantage. In a quick moment of trickery, he diverted the forces of his Wizards, and the suspended projectiles shot off at a tangent, slicing through a few of the foes. Aitrox's Prophets had seen it coming, but not in time to save all her Brutes. The Immortals however shrugged it off and continued fighting.

As the fighting raged, Eru felt Aymis's loss with new intensity. He couldn't defeat her, not without seeing deeper into her mind. Without a reader of his own, he would have to return to the void to use the power Shanje had given him. Doing so would likely end the struggle instantly, but he had no other choice. Continuing the fight as they were would only keep them alive for a few minutes longer anyway.

Eru readied himself to release each of his friends, feeling his love for them more keenly as he knew his time with them had come to an end. Eru carefully positioned his friends so that Aitrox's next wave of projectiles would spare them. Being the desired target, Eru knew he would at least spare them an immediate death when he released them. Finding the void in the chaos and intensity of battle proved a struggle in its own right. Thoughts of abandoning his loved ones who had become so much more than teammates filled his mind, pushing him back into the fight. It felt like ages before he finally did find the void and released everyone.

"No!" Supe exclaimed. Eru had left her closest to him, and to his dismay she stepped in front of him as the wave of deadly projectiles came. She couldn't get there in time to stop the first few, but those that she did intercept hit her with devastating effect, killing her before Eru could seize her. Eru tried to seize her, but there was no life left. Supe was gone.

Kelwu had leapt into the air, having sensed Eru's plans. Another large portion of the objects that would have obliterated Eru like a meat grinder pierced Kelwu in hundreds of locations. Black feathers and crimson blood burst from his body, and Kelwu fell. Not even the vyeshen healing would be enough to spare him. Kelwu had moments to live.

Three shards still made it to Eru, piercing his abdomen, shoulder, and thigh. In the void, Eru only noticed it through the impact it had on his mental awareness, but the intensity of the moment overshadowed the blow. As soon as Eru found the void, his new senses rushed into Aitrox's mind, and he perceived the secrets of the miserable immortal goddess. In the blink of an eye, Eru knew her final, greatest secret.

Eru watched through thousands of eyes, Aitrox's underlings, as Phoenix plummeted from the sky yet again. Anticipation coursed through Aitrox's soul as she watched a god brought low by her power. Phoenix's flames died, and Aitrox sprung on the downed being like a hungry predator. In his full strength, not even Aitrox could hope to touch Phoenix's mind with any lasting effect. Countless times, Phoenix had rebuffed her attacks even as he died, but not this time. She wrestled control from the god, forbidding his glorious, fiery rebirth and bringing his will to her subjection. Compared to his power at full strength, it was a meager prize, yet so long as she held Phoenix in her grasp, death could not touch her. Eru knew what he had to do.

Yet, the discovery presented an opportunity only Eru could seize. Only Aitrox, and now Eru had the strength to subdue the downed Phoenix. Eru could claim Phoenix's power. With Phoenix's power, and access to the threads of life, Eru could become the lifeweaver the world so desperately needed. He could correct the wrongs of both the vyeshen and Human races. He could live forever. No. Eru could do it, but he would not. He would not betray the trust Shanje had shown in giving him such strength. Any who would do that, could not be trusted with the power Phoenix presented. Furthermore, immortality felt a tragic gift to claim. What would happen to Eru's heart and mind as he lived on while those he loved died? When it came down to it, Eru had no doubts. Whatever death held in store, he wanted to share with those he loved.

Eru returned to the void. His renewed purpose made it easy. He seized everyone he could, and flung them out the windows, as a preemptive evacuation. Shanje and Kelwu's senses found the traces of Phoenix's being and Eru set the god free.

A violent, flaming explosion erupted from Aitrox's feathery dress. In the flames, Eru heard the screech of a thousand tortured eagles, drowning out the cries of pain and terror Aitrox expressed through the slaves and Aegendi around her. Eru's preemptive evacuation of her throne room had barely been enough to spare them all a fiery death. All of Aitrox's slaves were consumed by the flames as Eru and his friends escaped. Following on their heels, like angry serpent tongues, came flames shooting into the darkening night.

Eru could hardly believe the sight as the entire throne chamber erupted into bright red light that filled the darkness like the sun at mid-day. Even as Volo carried them further and further away, the heat felt oppressive. Suddenly a massive flaming bird, more beautiful and glorious than anything Eru had imagined, burst through the top of Aitrox's citadel, showering more debris on the shocked and bewildered city of Deor. With a furious shriek, the enormous god, whose wings seemed to spread across the entire horizon, disappeared into the darkening sky, leaving Aitrox dead.

CHAPTER 55
THE UNKNOWN

Aitrox was dead! I may as well proclaim that a rock would fall up or fire burn cold. It felt contradictory to the natural order of the universe, yet it felt so right. We had done it. We had accomplished the impossible, ending her reign of death, fear and trauma. The feeling will forever elude description. For a short time, we would enjoy the victory, before contemplating the long, difficult road ahead.

E ru watched in amazement as Aitrox's citadel crumbled and burned. Phoenix's fires had practically melted the top third of the massive structure immediately. Even from a distance high in the sky, Eru felt the heat of the flames. All throughout Deor, people emerged from their homes, wandering into the streets with shocked, bewildered looks on their faces. The battle had taken a heavy toll on almost everyone in Deor. Aitrox had ripped apart entire districts of the city with her Amplifiers, and the spreading fires would surely destroy several districts as well. They all would feel the price paid for freedom. Eru too felt the pain and grief of loss, adding bitterness to his moment of triumph. Supe gave her life for the cause. Her sacrifice was what allowed Aitrox to be defeated. This made the wounds the others suffered seem inconsequential, though severe bleeding would soon threaten the lives of Janis and Rose.

Eru took his crew to the foothills outside of the city. Even from miles away, the burning citadel shone like a bright beacon of change. Eru released everyone, letting himself take in the amazing moment through all of their eyes. He felt the throbbing, relentless pain in Janis's thigh, and the sharp, deep stinging in Rose's hands. Amazingly, Volo had escaped without any wounds, as had Oko.

Shanje made it through the battle unscathed, but the outcome affected him powerfully. He was the last of the wyverns. True, he could now work his life threads back to his old form, but the vyeshen would never accept him back. He didn't know if he wanted to return. He felt that he didn't know anything anymore.

Phoenix's return wasn't the only revelation that threw Shanje's world into confusion and turmoil. Eru's choice to free Phoenix defied all of his expectations of an archos, even one whose emotional make up had been altered. The moment Shanje perceived the choice his puppet faced, he had despaired, expecting Eru to replace Aitrox. Perhaps Eru would have started well, but immortality combined with tremendous power would have darkened and corrupted Eru. At least that is what Shanje had thought. Now, he didn't know. Perhaps one such as Eru, one who could walk away from such an opportunity, could have wielded it to better the world. Perhaps the world would have been better off had Eru harnessed Phoenix's power, and worked to mend the world's errors. Shanje could hardly believe he would ever have considered such a notion. Despite himself, he was beginning to understand how Jante saw the humans. He almost considered Eru a friend.

Shanje's loyalties to Phoenix were much harder to discern. The same could be said for Phoenix's loyalties to the vyeshen. Shanje may have freed the vyeshen from the mines, but he wondered if they would be better off down there. Could anyone, even a god, emerge unscathed from the ordeal Phoenix went through? Uncounted centuries trapped in limbo, neither dead nor living, but constantly dominated and harrowed; what effect had that had on Phoenix? The world made sense to Shanje with Phoenix dead. Only time would tell if they had liberated a whole or broken and insane god.

Eru witnessed the turmoil of questions swirling in Shanje's heart. They both had envisioned victory not to feel so... uncertain. Eru had plenty of his own questions as well. Did Phoenix hate humanity? Would he be grateful to Eru for freeing him, or see him as a threat? Humanity and the vyeshen had both been nearly shattered by Aitrox. Could they rise from the ashes together, or did the future only hold more conflict and misunderstanding? For the moment, Eru did his best not to worry about all the unknowns. He had wounded friends to care for, and an impossible victory to relish.

Eru watched the citadel burn the rest of the way to the ground through hundreds of eyes throughout Deor. A heavy mood of uncertainty rested on the city. People couldn't imagine anyone escaping the fires alive, but the thought of Aitrox dying felt equally impossible. *Was Aitrox dead?* Eru felt that question repeated thousands of times, followed shortly by the realization that they hadn't been seized and punished for such blasphemous, dangerous thoughts. The realization spread, as each person reached his own mental conclusion. It took longer for any of them to muster the courage to put their thoughts or their jubilation into words. Generations of conditioning couldn't be easily overcome.

A murmur rolled through the city, but there were no exuberant proclamations, no shouts for joy, and no dancing through the streets. To many, the idea of Aitrox's death felt too impossible to be true. For others, her power had felt so inescapable that they feared her reach even from the grave. The reality of the situation filled others with doubt. For many, Aitrox's shadow had darkened their lives, but provided security and constancy as well. What would tomorrow bring with her gone?

None of Eru's friends felt the immediate press of reality. Cobblestones hadn't just rained down on their entire neighborhood, destroying homes and killing neighbors and friends. They had of course lost a friend in Supe, but none except Eru had really had time to know her. She had only returned to a semblance of normalcy in the last few days. Eru would forever regret the life she had been robbed of. It seemed a cruel twist of fate that the one among them whose life had been most darkened by Aitrox's evil would be the one who gave up the right to experience life outside her shadow.

"We did it," Volo said quietly to his sister, looking at her bleeding hand with concern. She sat on a log, wrapping her hand in her shirt to stanch the bleeding. She smiled back, obviously happy and relieved despite the pain. "Eru, please take care of her hand," Volo called. Eru worked through Volo's eyes, doing everything he could to help her. Eru seized Rose for a moment, using her strength to rend Volo's shirt into several strips. Even with one hand, some clever working combined with her strength made quick work of Volo's shirt. With those strips, Eru then managed to improvise a suitable bandage that would maintain enough pressure to stop the bleeding.

"I am sorry I can't do anything for the pain," Eru said.

"It's worth it. We actually did it," Rose said quietly. Eru felt her thoughts settling back on the day Eru had used her neighbor John to slip a letter under the door. "We found our life of freedom, Volo," she said quietly with a smile.

"Yeah, sis, you told me so, I know," Volo said teasingly. "To think it would end like this."

"I don't think it has ended," Oko said.

"It has for us," Volo said vigorously as he sat on the log next to Rose.

"There are a lot of archos out there still," Oko said.

"Is that the future you want now?" Rose asked. "Do you want to spend the rest of your days killing archos?"

"It's what I do," Oko replied.

"In the old world maybe," Janis said faintly. She sat on the ground leaning against the log Rose and Volo sat on. Her whole body quivered from the pain in her thigh and blood flowed freely from her injury. "This is a new world now. The world my daughter dreamed of."

Eru turned to Janis and began attending to her wounds. Janis kept her eyes fixed on the gaping hole in her thigh, giving Eru the ability to see his hands work. He felt clumsy, working without seizing others, but it felt amazing to do something with his own hands for once.

"What are you going to do, Eru?" Volo asked as Eru continued to apply pressure to Janis's leg.

"I hope never to seize another," Eru said.

"That will be a tall order," Oko said in response.

"So was destroying Aitrox," Eru said confidently.

"So, what exactly happened back there?" Volo asked. "What was that fiery eagle thing?"

"That was the vyeshen god Phoenix," Eru explained. "Aitrox defeated him thousands of years ago and seized him while he was vulnerable. That was how she gained immortality..." Eru paused. "That's how I could have gained immortality," Eru finished, not realizing he had said it loud enough for the others to hear.

"What do you mean?" Rose asked.

"When I freed Phoenix, there was a split second where I could have seized him myself."

"Well, why didn't you?" Oko asked. "I wouldn't pass up on immortality if I had the chance."

"I would be forever separated from those I love." Eru remembered Shanje's angry rebuttal to his hope for anything beyond death. The vyeshen cured aging and natural death in their kind rather than facing the unknown. Eru, however, couldn't help but see death in a different light. He may never know what awaited him in that instant when his life would end, but if it held a glimmer of hope to see Aymis, Ama and Supe again, he wanted it. Someday Rose, Volo, Janis and Oko would pass away as well. Could he willingly deny himself passage to follow them?

"Eru, are you sure about what you did?" Rose asked.

"Yeah, immortality sounds pretty nice to me," Volo agreed.

"No, I am not sure about it. I may never know for sure," Eru answered.

"Then why did you do it?" Volo asked.

"Because he welcomes the unknown," Oko said quietly.

"What do you mean?" Rose asked.

"Eru was willing to face the unknown about what the world would be like without Aitrox in the hope of something better. Thousands of people lived before him, willing to tolerate the known rather than take a risk in the hopes of something better," Oko said.

"But, the world is a better place without Aitrox," Janis rejoined. "We all knew it would be."

"No, we hope it will be. Deor's future is completely unknown, and we freed a god we know nothing about," Eru answered.

"But, life will be better without Aitrox," Rose said through the pain in her hand. "It may not be easier, especially at first, but it will be better."

"If you passed on immortality, does that mean you think there is something better waiting after you die?" Volo asked.

"I hope so. I hope to see Aymis, my mother and Supe again," Eru answered, feeling woefully inadequate at expressing the feelings in his heart. Perhaps he felt they would never understand his thoughts or his hopes. He had never dared confide to them his hope to see Aymis again, until now. He had never told them about his dreams when he saw those who loved him. They may have told him the same thing Shanje did, that those dreams were the product of his own mind. Eru would never know for sure who was right while he lived. He didn't doubt that he had many years ahead of him facing the unknowns of a world without Aitrox. He almost felt anticipation for that time when he believed he would see those he had lost again. Suddenly the unknown didn't feel so terrifying.

The End

Thank you for reading Lifeweaver, by Dan Staten. Dan has a new series, Elenya's Saga, that will be available in 2026.

The goddess Elenya has lost herself, sacrificing everything to fend off disaster for all her creations. Dedicated to the world she wrought, abandoned by the god she loved, and endangered by the god she spurned, Elenya's fate lies in the hands of her mortal children.

- Bondsword's War

- Summoner's Song

- Guardian's Peril

- Chosen's Ascension

- Fugitive's Flight

- Emissary's Return

- Queen's Craft

- Successor's Burden

- Protector's Mandate

Find out more at https://danstaten.com/

About the Author

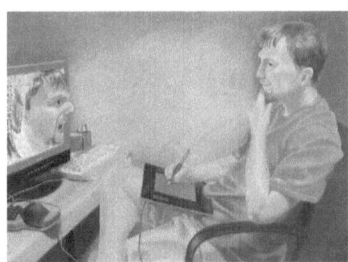

Software engineer during business hours, author and illustrator by night, dad and husband always. Dan grew up in the Salt Lake City area. He served a two-year proselyting mission for the Church of Jesus Christ of Latter-day Saints in Honduras and graduated from BYU with a degree in Computer Science. Along the way, he took many illustration classes and nearly changed majors to Illustration.

Dan lives a few blocks from his childhood home and works as a Software Engineer for the Church of Jesus Christ of Latter-day Saints. He is married with one son. In addition to writing and illustration, he loves the outdoors and staying active. He and his son mountain bike together in the summer and ski in the winter.

www.ingramcontent.com/pod-product-compliance
Lightning Source LLC
Chambersburg PA
CBHW032004110726
47901CB00004B/956